ANGEL OF
VENGEANCE

Also by Ron Cutler

ICE MAN

ANGEL OF VENGEANCE

RON CUTLER

PINNACLE BOOKS
Kensington Publishing Corp.
http://www.kensingtonbooks.com

To Elaine Markson, with appreciation.

PINNACLE BOOKS are published by

Kensington Publishing Corp.
850 Third Avenue
New York, NY 10022

All Kensington Titles, Imprints and Distributed Lines are available at special quantity discounts for bulk purchases for sales promotions, premiums, fund-raising, and educational or institutional use. Special book excerpts or customized printing can also be created to fit specific needs. For details, write or phone the office of the Kensington special sales manager: Kensington Publishing Corp., 850 Third Avenue, New York, NY 10022, attn: Special Sales Department. Phone: 1-800-221-2647.

Pinnacle and the P logo Reg. U.S. Pat. & TM Off.

First Pinnacle Books Printing: April 2005

10 9 8 7 6 5 4 3 2 1

Printed in the United States of America

One

The road wound along the river that shone like burnished metal in the fading light.

It was broken in places where the asphalt crumbled to dirt, compacted by tire tracks and the deep tread of tractors. The area was still rural, unblemished by the developers' tracts edging into the eastern side of the county. They still farmed here, the gently undulating fields separated by thick patches of wooded land.

It was late in October, yet the man still walked here every day at this hour. A figure in a black windbreaker moving with a purposeful stride along the edge of the road. He walked alone, taking the path that led away from the small stone farmhouse where he lived alone. The house was nestled secretively within a dark glade, where the river ran shallow over sharp rocks creating a rapids of swirling water. It was almost invisible from the road, providing a unique kind of seclusion. The man did not mix with his neighbors, other than to pick up groceries at one of the local stores. His bland features and quiet demeanor did nothing to mark him as out of the ordinary. His comings and goings were not remarked upon or discussed. And if anyone remarked that someone had moved into the old Caldwell place, it was usually greeted with an indifferent shrug.

The man was tall and lean. He was nearing fifty. His hair was close-cropped, framing a pale face and watery gray eyes protected by aviator glasses with wire rims and opaque lenses. He had the look of someone used to being in control, but he offered no clues to his occupation, spoke seldom, and rarely smiled. Other than his daily solitary walk, he seemed almost invisible.

Until he saw the boy.

He had first seen him through the window of the house as the boy stood in the stream casting his fly rod. Fishermen often came to fish the rapids that fronted the property, but except for an occasional glance the man was almost unaware of their presence. The boy was different. There was a special grace to his movements as he performed an intricate ballet with rod and line. The man watched with fascination as the fine filament caught the light and touched down on the surface without leaving a scar or ripple. The boy was beautiful to look at. His blond hair glinted like a helmet, setting off his deep-set blue eyes and classical features. He had the body of a dancer with long well-shaped limbs and wide shoulders. He lived on the neighboring farm and came to the stream almost every day through the end of September. When he failed to appear, the man felt an ache inside, a deeply resonant surge of desire that plunged through him like a foaming tide.

The intensity of the feeling would not abate. It tormented him throughout the day and disturbed his sleep. He tried to pray, kneeling on the cold wooden floorboards of the old house, fingers clenched around the rosary, trying to resist the temptation that seemed to be devouring his soul. He went to the closet and stared at the surplice that was now forbidden to him, but he did not put it on. The thought of wearing it was much too painful. At night, he stripped naked and lashed his back with his leather belt, raising painful welts and lacerating the skin until his back became a bloody washboard. But desire throbbed even through the pain, a desire he could no longer resist.

It had been his companion throughout his life, in spite of the shame and degradation it brought, and had led ultimately to his disgrace. But the thought of the boy's smooth thighs and quivering belly drove him to distraction. He could not help himself. The feeling was beyond his control. And when the boy next appeared, the man left the house by the back door, circling back into the woods until he emerged on the road farther down, heading back toward where the boy was positioned on the bank as if he happened on the scene by accident.

He stopped and waited, watching as the line went taut and the rod bent signaling a strike. The trout flew up out of the water and rose, twisting in the air acrobatically as it fought to break free. The boy was an expert, teasing the line, allowing it to play out, then reeling it in. It took almost twenty minutes until he gaffed the fish and put it into his basket. The effort exhausted the boy and he dropped onto the bank almost at the man's feet.

The man knelt and asked if he could see the fish. The boy turned, seeing him for the first time, and smiled. "Sure," he said, "go ahead." The man could see the glint of pride in the boy's eyes, the eagerness to show off his trophy. And so his courtship began. Exchanging bits of conversation. Locating where the boy lived and where he went to school, what he wanted to study and what his interests were. Useful bits of information, like the bait the boy used on his hook, unaware that what he provided might be used to hook him. They met, but not every day. The man had to be careful. Extremely careful. Someone might be watching. But over the next few weeks, things had progressed to the point where he felt safe enough to invite the boy inside ostensibly to see the old house, something the boy was curious to do.

The man had left his study door ajar when he went into

the kitchen to get them a drink. He had left certain books and pictures around for the boy to see. Images filled the internet screen. The boy's face flushed when he examined them. The man could see his eyes fill with excitement. He allowed the boy to sate himself before he stepped inside with the tray. The visit did not last long. He had offered the boy a nibble, a glimpse of pleasures to come. Now he had only to reel him in.

He had picked the moment with off-handed casualness. The boy had mentioned an old barn dating to the early Dutch settlement. The man expressed an eagerness to see it and the boy offered to act as his guide. It would be a perfect opportunity. He had rarely been disappointed.

The man continued along the road. The boy would be coming from his house taking the path that led into the wooded glen dividing their property from his. The man intended to encounter him there.

The road curved ahead. A path trailed off to the left, wriggled between several oaks, then pointed directly into the dark stand of trees beyond.

It was only four o'clock but the sky had already begun to darken.

The trees closed in quickly, forming a murky canopy over head. The man quickened his pace. His heart was already beginning to hammer. He felt daggers of excitement deep within his gut.

There was a quiver of movement ahead and the man thought he saw the boy approaching. But it was only a shadow.

The trunks grew thick on this stretch of the path. The light had almost disappeared. He continued between the thick stands of brush, then halted abruptly.

Someone was on the path ahead.

For a instant his heart rose with anticipation. But it was not the boy.

The figure remained motionless, silhouetted by the light filtering from above.

The man took a step toward the stranger, then another. He had only to pass him and continue. The thought that it might be the boy's father suddenly assailed him, but he quickly dismissed it. Even if it were, he had done nothing wrong. He was just spooking himself. It was probably just another fisherman or even a hunter out scouting the woods, since deer season was almost upon them.

He purposely broke a branch underfoot, stepping on the dead leaves so as to warn the stranger of his approach. But the stranger did not move.

He was only two or three feet away when the stranger turned.

His face was in darkness. The man saw only his eyes. They were dark and intense, glittering like a cat's.

"Nice to see you, Father Mckay."

The sound of his name came like a shock. No one knew him here. His heart began pounding.

"Out for a walk?"

They were the last words he remembered before he smelled the suffocating odor and the darkness closed around him like a shroud.

Father Mckay opened his eyes.

He felt as if he were emerging from a dream. At first he could see nothing in the gloom. Then gradually consciousness returned. It was dark and cold. He was crouched painfully in a narrow iron cage. His wrists and ankles were bound in heavy iron bracelets that chaffed his skin. He was dressed in some kind of robe beneath which he was naked. The air was cold on his flesh. The material had an almost paperlike consistency that did nothing to warm his body. He shivered with terror as his fingers gripped the metal bars. He felt a dizzying sense of fear that forced him to cry out with a bowel-wrenching moan. The sound came back to him, reedy and thin, like a dying bird.

His movements caused the chains to rattle. The cage was suspended over some kind of void. He sensed the emptiness below and was gripped by the dizzying sensation that he was about to plunge into darkness. He could feel his heart beat, pulsing like a trip hammer. He closed his eyes and forced himself to pray but lost the sense of the words. *Our Father, who art . . . Our Father . . .* He fought the surges of panic that rushed through him, trying to steady himself, to remain still. Slowly, his heart began to regulate. The effort exhausted him. His lids closed.

He lost all sense of time as he lapsed in and out of consciousness. There was only the darkness and the fear and the constant terror of falling into some abyss. Then somewhere in the void came the sharp creak of metal on wood.

The cage began to move.

He was being lowered into the darkness. He was overcome by a sense of vertigo.

A dim iridescence began filling the chamber.

He gripped the iron bars, staring through the murk at the stark stone walls surrounding him. He was in some kind of tower, a structure from another age, huge and imposing.

The cage came to rest on the stone floor. He tried to speak but no sound came from his lips. He felt dizzy. His fingers gripped the bars. He closed his eyes and when he opened them, the room was filled with light.

Two yellow tapers were set on metal stands, their flames flickering. They were set on either side of a towering podium that resembled a pulpit or a seat of judgment.

He felt a strange chill, an in-rushing sense of doom.

"Father Mckay." The voice echoed ominously.

He looked up. A dark figure sat at the podium. He wore a black robe. His face was shrouded beneath a hood like a medieval figure of death.

Startled, Mckay realized that the figure was dressed in the black robes of the Inquisition.

Mckay glanced down. He was wearing the scarlet robe of

the accused. His mind reeled. This was madness. Something out of an ancient nightmare.

The hooded figure leaned forward. His voice resonated like a hollow drum. "You are accused of violating your Holy Orders. Are you ready to confess your guilt?"

"What guilt?" Mckay responded.

"By using the cloak of sanctity you tortured the innocent."

"No. I never did that. I never tortured anyone!"

"You are accused of sodomizing over sixty innocent young men and boys over a period of years. Of forcing them to copulate with you orally and anally. Have you anything to say before this court passes judgment upon you?"

"No!" Mckay shouted, his voice a rasp. "You have no right to judge me. Who are you?"

"I have been given the power to avenge."

"That right belongs to God. The law released me."

"You are being judged by a different law."

Mckay's voice quavered. "The statute of limitations ran out on the charges against me."

"I am not bound by such statutes. I ask you again. Have you anything to say in your defense before sentence is passed upon you?"

"This is wrong. The law released me. I can only be judged by God."

"I am bound by the Cipher. My duty is to bring to judgment those who have evaded punishment."

Mckay stared at the dark figure above him. His knees were shaking. He gripped the bars as he searched for something that would save him. But his mind refused to function. There was nothing he could say. He had been stripped of his priesthood and sent into exile while his church sought to deal with the multitude of lawsuits that stemmed from his transgressions. He had been tried and convicted in a court of law. He had been sent to prison, then miraculously freed because the appellate court decreed that the statute of limitations had run out on his crimes. He had taken that as a sign that he was being forgiven.

"I ask only for forgiveness," he pleaded. "I have repented for my transgressions and done penance. I deserve a reprieve."

"You must answer for what you did. And what you were about to do. Which places you beyond repentance."

He began to utter something, but the words caught in his throat, almost choking him. He could no longer speak. *They knew what was in his heart.* He was doomed. There would be no reprieve.

He dropped to his knees. His body shook and he began to sob.

"Please, oh, Lord, save me," he whispered.

There was a rustle of parchment. Then the voice intoned, "As you did unto others, so shall it be done unto you. So it is written in the Cipher. May God have mercy on your soul."

Mckay rose. "Mercy!" he cried. "Please, God. Have mercy."

There was no one there. The figure had disappeared. The podium was empty. There was only silence and the hiss of the candles.

Mckay's mind was in turmoil. Was this real or had he been dreaming it? Was this some monstrous joke being played on him? He laughed aloud and shook his head, trying to clear his thoughts. There was a creak of wood on metal as the cage slowly turned. It made half a revolution when he saw it.

A thin rod of bronze stood in the center of the bare stone chamber, pointed and tipped, glowing white hot.

For an instant he did not understand; then the horror speared through him as the chains jerked taut and the cage rose high above the floor.

"Please, God, no!" he shouted. "Have mercy on me! "

He heard the creak of the wooden joist as it lifted the cage and swung him over the glowing shape. Then sound of gears as it lowered him, cog by cog. The bottom of the cage fell away. He was suspended over the glowing rod, hanging by the iron bracelets surrounding his hands and feet. The chains snapped taut, spreading his legs. He felt intense heat sear his skin as he was lowered. He fought against the chains, trying to rise, to twist his body away. But it was no use. He was caught like a fish on the end of a line.

The thin spear of flame entered his body, opening him like a steel drill bit eating through wood. He screamed as the worm of pain began to consume him, turning his bowels into smoking ash.

He heard his screams as if they were somewhere outside him, as if they came from someone else.

It was the birds that alerted the curate.

Ravens.

Black-winged, their beaks like tiny spears. Bound together in a kind of frenzy.

They rose in alarm as he made his way toward the thickly growing trees at the far end of the compound that housed the bishop's residence.

It was still dark when the curate was awakened by the racket. He hastily dressed and went to see what the problem was. As he exited the residence, he stepped into a layer of ground fog that reduced visibility to only a few feet. He carried a flashlight and wore a heavy jacket against the morning chill. He saw more clearly as he crossed the barren yard and approached the stand of trees that formed a kind of park at the far end of the walled acreage. The birds had gathered around something in the center of a small clearing within the trees. He could make it out now. A figure was standing motionless in the center of the clearing. He must have been feeding the birds for them to have been reacting that way. It might be one of the younger priests, of which there were several housed in the main residence.

The curate squinted, trying to make out the man's features

through the thick fog. It was no one he recognized. He was about to shout a greeting when the words caught in his throat.

Something was wrong. . . .

He halted at the edge of the clearing. His hand opened, dropping the flashlight as his eyes bulged in horror.

The figure was facing him. He was naked. His skin was bled of color, startling white, like the bleached bones of an animal. His body was suspended on some kind of metal frame like a grotesque scarecrow, the arms spread in a mockery of a crucifix. It took an instant for the curate to re-alize that the body had been hacked into four separate pieces, the flesh suspended from hooks like a slaughtered cow. And another moment to see that the figure's head was impaled on a spit that bisected the body. His face had been punctured by the sharp beaks. Blood ran from the empty sockets where the birds had been feasting. The features were bloated almost beyond recognition.

But it was a face he knew.

He was staring at the dismembered remains of Father Aubrey Mckay.

The curate shrank back, unable to detach his eyes from the grotesque image. He felt a wave of nausea, but he fought back the reflex to be sick and turned, running back through the trees the way he had come. Feet pounding the path as he cried out, trying to erase the terror that now filled his mind.

In a moment, the birds returned, cawing down from the trees until they covered the body with a cape of fluttering wings.

Two

The intake was not going well.

Holly Alexander put down her pen and looked up at the smiling inmate seated opposite her at the formica table. The table and the two stainless-steel chairs were the only pieces of furniture in the bare-walled interview room. There were no windows. Light came from the fluorescent strip in the ceiling, cold and stark.

The inmate's name was Martinez. He was an illegal immigrant from Central America and a serial rapist who preyed on maids and other hotel workers, many of whom were also illegals and afraid to report the assaults to the police, a situation he counted upon. He was a small man with swarthy, unattractive features, sallow skin, and black hair combed back from his pimply forehead. His expression was frozen in a contemptuous smirk that Holly found particularly annoying. She wanted to reach across the table and slap his face. But she controlled the impulse. She was used to inmate arrogance. It was the usual attitude they assumed upon arrival at the Brandywine Center. Holly recognized it as a defense for being sent to an institution for sexual deviates. But this inmate's contempt was particularly irritating, combined as it was with the usual brand of Latin macho.

His eyes had undressed her when he entered, appraising her as a sexual object he found to his liking and could have had if he had encountered her under a different set of circumstances. Holly understood his thinking and was generally immune to ogling glances. She had been their recipient since first coming to the center five years before. It wasn't what she read in his eyes that annoyed her; it was the sense of superiority he radiated, the sense of having beaten the system even as it imprisoned him. The knowledge that people like Holly were bound to follow a code of conduct that guaranteed his rights, which were nonexistent in the land of his birth.

Or was it something else, something she brought with her into the room that morning?

"Uno momento, por favor," she said as she shuffled her papers.

Martinez shifted in his seat. Her Spanish had surprised him. He had expected an interpreter, but Holly spoke well enough for them to proceed without one. She had learned the language when she was an assistant district attorney in Nueva York. It was not the Spanish of Berlitz, but the lingo spoken on the streets. Her beat was the barrio and her clients Dominicans, Cubans, and Puerto Ricans. That was before she received a PhD in abnormal psychology and began working in the Brandywine Center for Sexual Disorders in the Pennsylvania criminal justice system.

Holly hated doing intakes. It was a chore no one liked and one the staff was forced to divide among themselves. It required her to take down the inmate's history and background, then provide a preliminary analysis of his disorder according to the strict dictates of the DSM-IV, the manual of psychological disorders that was the bible of her profession. The intake would then be given to her supervisor, Ted, who decided which therapist he would dump the case on. Holly had an uncomfortable feeling he would dump this one on her.

She raised her eyes and glanced at Martinez, who responded by widening his smirk another degree and wetting his lips with the tip of his tongue.

Rape was about power. It was about giving back the abuse the rapist himself had received. It was seldom about sex.

Holly wondered which category of abuse Martinez fitted into. She had a feeling it was something gut-wrenching and ugly. But whatever it was, she would be the one forced to find out.

Norman Lutz was blocking the corridor when she exited the intake room.

He was a short, wiry inmate in his late forties. He was washing the floor, moving a mop back and forth, but Holly knew he was waiting for her.

"Hey, Doc," he said, his watery blue eyes staring at her. His skin was washed out from chemotherapy, and patches of his hair and eyebrows were missing.

"Norman," Holly responded curtly.

"Any word on my case?" he asked.

"Nothing yet. I'll let you know as soon as I hear."

Lutz was a serial rapist who had served his sentence but had been denied release. He had been undergoing treatment for stomach cancer.

"You got to do something for me, Doc. I don't want to die in here." His eyes were pleading like a dog begging for scraps.

"We're doing everything we can. Please, step aside."

Norman looked at her. His eyes went fierce and he held his ground for a moment. Then he moved aside and allowed her to pass.

Inmates like Lutz forced Holly into a confrontation with

herself. Lutz had served his sentence but was still being incarcerated because the state believed he was still a danger. It
was an issue still clouded in the law.

Holly was no bleeding heart. The men she administered
to were guilty of heinous crimes, often against women and
children weaker than themselves. For that they had to be
punished. But they had also been abused and were acting out
that abuse on others. The pattern had to be broken somewhere, which was why she had taken the job at Brandywine.
There was no more challenging or more frustrating work
imaginable than trying to straighten out a bent psyche. She
did not subscribe to the notion that once bent meant it was
bent forever. Many in her profession believed that sexual deviates could not be cured. Not Holly. She believed they were
on the threshold of new advances.

There was hope. It was something she had to believe.

"So, this Martinez. What do you think?"

Ted leaned back in his chair and glanced at the intake file
Holly had just placed on his desk. He had small shifty eyes
that never looked at anyone directly. He was a master of deceit and evasion.

"I don't want the case. I'm on overload as it is."

Ted raised his eye brows and grinned. "Who said I'm giving it to you?"

"You're not?" A note of hope rose in Holly's voice.

"I didn't say that. I'm thinking."

"Just don't think about me. "

Ted grinned, revealing startlingly white teeth. He prided
himself on the brightness of his smile and used a special
whitening film which he glued on every morning. "My problem is that you're the best I've got. I don't think anyone else
could handle it."

"They're all licensed. They're all competent."

"He's a serial rapist. That's your specialty."

"That's bullshit and you know it. We don't have specialists here."

"You speak Spanish. "

"Not his kind of Spanish."

"Then how did you do this intake?"

"I made it up."

Ted looked at her and smiled. "You're not refusing me, are you?"

"Of course not. I'm just not taking this case. Dump it on someone else. I'm on maximum-stress overload. I'm about to have a breakdown."

"Take a few days off."

"You mean months. I'm going on maternity leave."

"Are you pregnant?'

"Not yet. Give me Martinez and I'll begin working on it."

Ted's grin widened. "I don't know what I'd do without you, Holly."

"And while we're on the subject . . ." Holly leaned in closer; her eyes had become steely dots of purpose. "Someone should report this place to OSHA. This center was built to hold two hundred and fifty inmates. It's holding over five hundred. Almost a hundred have served their sentences but are being confined on indefinite hold."

"They're dangerous sex offenders, Holly. You're not suggesting we just release them back into the community, are you?"

"Someone like Lutz isn't dangerous. He's dying of stomach cancer."

"He's still a sex offender."

"He's had himself castrated, for God's sake. He's not a danger to anyone anymore."

"I don't make the rules."

"Keeping them locked up is not only illegal but probably unconstitutional. It's also extremely dangerous."

"Not to the people of Pennsylvania."

Holly stared at the supercilious look on his face and felt her anger rise.

"I mean, to us, in here. We're short on staff and short on correctional personnel."

"I'm handling it."

"No, Ted. We're handling it. You're either in your office or cozying up to someone on the prison board." As the words escaped her lips, she knew she had gone too far, but she couldn't stop herself. His expression changed. His smile faded. His mouth became a grim slit of spite.

"I'll expect your report on Martinez within two weeks."

He looked up and their eyes locked.

"I told you no," she said firmly.

"Either you'll take the case or I'll be forced to bring you up on disciplinary action."

He extended the file toward her. He was no longer smiling. Holly stared at him, then ripped it out of his hand. She turned on her heel and strode out of the office.

"Shut the door," Ted hissed.

Holly grabbed the knob and swung hard. The sound comforted her all the way down the hall.

Clara was putting a layer of red lacquer on her nails when Holly entered. The bottle was on her desk, which commanded the room. Clara was approaching sixty but looked ten years younger. She was a handsome woman who kept her figure and clothed it from an account at Saks. She was the general overseer of the therapy staff, its sole secretary and chief protector. Even Ted tiptoed around her. She was a woman with considerable political outreach. She was also Holly's chief ally and best friend.

She looked up, eyeing Holly with appreciation. "Nice outfit," she commented dryly as Holly crossed to her mailbox and hoisted the considerable stack of material stuffed inside it. "New?"

Holly shook her head as she sifted through the mass of posted material.

"I haven't seen it before," said Clara.

"I wore it three times last month."

"It's early ALZ."

"No. It's this fucking place."

"Biting my head off won't help."

Holly paused and looked up.

Clara met her eyes with a bemused expression. She knew Holly's moods.

"Ted?" Clara said knowingly.

"What else?" Holly responded.

"Let me guess. He gave you Martinez."

Holly nodded.

"Did you tell him you were going on maternity leave?"

"It didn't matter. Nothing I said mattered."

"You didn't think it would, did you?"

Holly sat down on the chair alongside Clara's desk. "I think I'm burned out."

"No. You just need some time away from this place. When was the last time you had a vacation?"

Holly's face went blank. She could not remember.

"See?"

"I used up my vacation time helping Beth get settled," Holly said. The reference was to her younger sister, who had moved into her own apartment.

"Great, and now that she's in college and about to graduate, you can ask for a leave of absence."

"I can't afford it."

"I'll lend you the money."

Holly shook her head.

"Not no. Say you'll think about it."

"Okay. I'll think about it."

Holly rose and started toward her office.

"By the way, Dan Shepard called."

Holly's face colored. "Oh, really."

Clara smiled disarmingly. "It's strictly business. But you are still dating him, aren't you?"

"Yes, I'm still dating him," Holly said with impatience. "Like you didn't know."

"How would I know? You don't tell me anything anymore. Especially when it comes to sex. *I'm* the one who tells *you*."

"What did he want?" Holly demanded.

"That priest you were treating. The one whose sentence was commuted because of the statue of limitations?"

"Father Mckay. Aubrey Mckay," Holly responded. "What about him?"

Clara's eyes rose to met hers. "Apparently somebody murdered him."

Three

A biting wind cut across the yard when Holly arrived at the diocese residence, forcing her to tighten her arms around her torso and lower her head as she walked beside the lean figure of Inspector Dan Shepard of the Pennsylvania State Police.

Aside from offering her a quick hello and an even quicker introduction to the priest standing beside him, he had said nothing as they left the parking area and began following the priest across the barren windswept yard. Dan's car was parked beside several state police cruisers, but there were no other official vehicles that she could see other than the shiny black ones that belonged to the diocese.

They approached the area in silence. Yellow police tape enclosed a kind of park. Several benches were angled at the foot of a stand of towering fir trees. The priest guided them along a path that meandered between the trees until they emerged into a small clearing. That was when she saw it.

The object stood planted in the bare earth. It was shaped like a stick figure a child might have drawn. A skeleton with straight lines for arms and legs and a sharp projection for the neck. Only it had no head and it was made of pieces of iron that had been crudely welded together. The closest thing Holly could imagine was a scarecrow.

"I wanted you to see it before we took it down," Dan said.

"What is it?"

"I don't know. I was hoping you could tell me. Mckay's body was hanging from it."

"What do you mean?" Holly asked.

"He was butchered. His head was up on that spit. What was left of it after the crows got to him."

Holly tried to understand.

"You mean, his body was in pieces?"

"Four of them. He was split down the middle. Arms there," Dan said, pointing to the upper extensions, "legs there."

"He was naked," the priest added.

Holly was silent, trying to visualize the horror that had just been described.

"Who found him?" Holly asked.

"I did," the priest answered.

"It must have been quite a shock."

The priest nodded. She could see the stain of darkness in his eyes.

"Okay," Dan said. "It's cold. We've seen enough."

The priest's remains were displayed on a cold aluminum table in a corner of the medical examiner's white-tiled examination room. The ME drew off the plastic sheet covering the body and Holly took a step back.

She had tried to prepare herself on the drive over, reminding herself how many times she had been through the process, but it was always the same. The sight of a dead human body always caused a shock to her system, especially one that had been traumatized by wounds. Her father had taken her to see her first murder victim when she was about to enter law school. But nothing she had ever seen before could have prepared her for this.

The body was in four separate pieces. Five if you counted the head.

She felt the eyes of the others in the room fix on her, some of them sadistically waiting for her horrified reaction. But she was about to disappoint them.

"What could have done this?" she said through thin lips.

The ME shook his head. He was a tall, narrow-shouldered man of fifty with a deeply graven face and the pinched expression of a skeptic. Deep lines marked the sides of his mouth and ran in furrows across his forehead. Dan had introduced Holly to him on the way down from his office.

"Can't exactly tell," he said. "That's the problem. An ax most likely, or something like it, but not any ax I've ever seen. The impact edges curve away, like a crescent moon. I'd have said a scimitar, an Islamic sword, but the cuts are not fine enough."

"Would it take strength to dismember a body like this?" Holly asked.

"Not especially. Not if you have the right leverage. But I'm still trying to figure it out."

"Are these entry wounds?" she asked, indicating several deep puckers in the dead flesh.

"Actually no. They're from the hooks used to hang the body from that frame he was suspended from."

"You've never seen that before either?" Dan asked.

"I've seen plenty of unusual displays, but this is a new one on me. They usually occur during a fetish killing or some kind of ceremony. The victim is usually suspended from a cross. But from a device like that, never."

"Was this done to him while he was still alive?" Holly asked.

"That's hard to say. He was impaled on something that burned up his insides. His bowels are gone. That could have been the cause of death and the body cut up afterwards."

"He's also been embalmed," Dan commented.

"Not embalmed exactly. But all the blood was drained

from his body. The killer knew where to make the most effective incision."

"He could be a doctor or someone in the medical field," Dan said.

"Or a hunter," Holly added.

"Yes." The ME nodded. "A hunter would know how to bleed his game." He stepped away from the table and turned to face her. "I suppose you want to see the head."

Holly felt her diaphragm draw taut. She felt like screaming no, but the ME lifted a plastic sheet on the adjoining counter, revealing Mckay's severed head.

Holly sucked in a breath. The face was almost unrecognizable. The crows had been both efficient and unusually vicious.

"Okay," Dan said. "Much obliged for the tour."

Holly and Dan were seated across from each other in the booth of a diner just a little down the road from the ME's squat white-brick two-story building. It was already dark. The sky beyond the window was a purple bruise. It was an in-between hour and the diner was only a quarter full. Dan had a cup of steaming black coffee. Holly had ordered tea.

"So what do you think?"

Holly looked up at him. His dark brown eyes were fixed on her.

"I don't know what to think. He wasn't my patient that long."

"How far did you get with him?"

"You know that's confidential."

Dan smiled. "Just asking."

Holly did not find it funny. Patient-therapist confidentiality was a basic commandment of her profession.

"Was there anything he told you that might have indicated anything like this? Someone who might have threatened him?"

"My God." Holly shook her head. "We're talking about someone who molested over sixty people. His case was all over the newspapers. I would have thought he had hundreds of death threats."

"He did. We're running them down. All of them," Dan said wearily. "So you may not be seeing my smiling face for a while." He paused, waiting for a reaction. But Holly only stirred her tea.

"Okay. Aside from the generic hate stuff, what I'm talking about is some kind of specific threat he might have disclosed to you. Something you could disclose to me now that he's dead."

Holly frowned. "I'll have to go back over my notes and think about it."

"Right now, the theory is that it's a revenge killing. One of his victims maybe. Or some outraged John Q who thinks he's doing society a public service. Frankly, I think his murder will make a lot of people pretty happy, don't you?"

She looked at him. "I suppose you're right."

"Me right? Is that possible?" he said with a grin.

She smiled in return. "Am I that critical?"

"No. Just kidding. How are things at the prison?"

Holly's expression changed. "Going from bad to worse. We've got a prison population that's reaching the boiling point and no one gives a damn. Especially not Ted."

"What about getting more correction officers transferred over from the main prison. Didn't Ted say he'd do that?" Dan was now very concerned and serious.

"He keeps promising, but nothing happens. No one wants to hire more guards because of the funding cutbacks. They already spend more on prisons than on schools and hospitals combined. I sound like I'm making a speech here."

"It's a dangerous situation. I wish you were the hell out of there and working somewhere else."

Holly shook her head. That was not a possibility.

"And Beth? How's she doing?"

Holly nodded. "Good. Very good. She's still getting all A's."

"She's still on track to graduate this semester?"

Holly nodded.

"That's great. She owes you a lot."

"No. She did it all by herself. Whatever help I gave her was secondary."

"You saved her life," Dan said.

Holly made a dismissive gesture and looked away. It was a subject she did not want either to remember or discuss.

Dan leaned forward. "I'm going to need your help in this Mckay thing, Holly. I mean it. You were his therapist. You were probably closer to him than anyone else. I know how overworked you are. But we've never seen anything like this."

"Dan—" she began, but he held up his hand to stop her.

"Do you know what's going to happen politically? The DA has already had the case assigned to his office. He's scheduled a press conference for tomorrow morning. You know how ambitious Art Pinero is. Once he announces the murder, it's going to go through the roof. We'll get national attention, which is what he wants. The pressure on us is going to be fantastic. Please, Holly, say you'll give us a hand."

"You've got plenty of experts."

"Sure, and each one has his own ax to grind. Listen to me. . . . You have the background, the smarts, and the fortitude. Besides, you don't think like they do. With them, I can predict, but not with you, and that's what I'm going to need. Someone who thinks outside the box. Because my gut tells me this is only the beginning. There are going to be others."

"You can't be sure of that until it happens."

"Let's try to make sure it doesn't."

Holly tightened. "I can't believe you're asking me. There are plenty of forensic specialists around. What about the FBI?"

"Sure. If Pinero lets them in. Which I don't believe he'll

do. Not unless he's forced to. He'll want to keep as much control over the case as possible. Say you'll help me."

"Tell me you'll look for someone else."

His eyes narrowed. "There is no one else."

Holly gripped the wheel as she drove home, trying to keep her mind from repeating the conversation with Dan. But his words kept circulating in her head. It wasn't fair to ask her to do any more. Her responsibility for Mckay ended the day he walked out of the prison. She had no further ties to him, as a therapist or as a human being. Contrary to what Dan said, she was not happy that he was dead. In spite of what he had done, and there was no way to condone or ameliorate his crimes, he did not deserve to be butchered. Not like that. Mckay had to answer for his crimes, both in this world and the next one he so vehemently believed in. He knew this and believed he was already damned. Only some divine forgiveness could save him.

She was conflicted over whether to help Dan or refuse him. Analyzing her relationship with the inspector didn't help. She was conflicted there as well. She liked being with him. He was intelligent and considerate. He could also be fun, an element that was always in short supply in her life. He had the ability to take her out of her usual state of concentration and move her to a place of air and light where she could loosen up and actually enjoy herself. He was also a good lover. She loved the feeling of being in his arms and had no problem reaching orgasm. That should have been enough. So why wasn't it?

Holly shook her head.

Her relationship with Dan would have made most women she knew very content. Then what was the matter with her? She could no longer use the excuse that she was still getting over the pain of her divorce. Time was erasing that scar. Perhaps he was too safe, too predictable. She had always been drawn to a point of danger, a place where she might slip and fall into some mysterious darkness. It was the sense of not knowing that had always galvanized her.

It had been there since her childhood, when her father had taken her hunting with him. They went after wild boar among rolling hills planted with millet that masked the animals' movements. It was extremely dangerous. The wild pigs traveled in packs led by enormous tusked males. Her father carried a rifle and she followed him on foot. Though the actual killing of the animals always repulsed her, she never refused his invitation. She hated it when anything had to be killed. But she loved the feeling of excitement, the tight knot that convulsed her gut and made her heart pump more quickly. She loved the keenness of being in the open where anything might happen and one of the monstrous four-hundred-pound beasts might charge them through the tall grasses, tusks thrust like razors, tiny red eyes filled with the lust for blood.

There was none of that with Dan. What he offered was a refuge, a place of safety and security. It was something she needed, and yet there was a reason she worked in a prison. She was drawn to danger the way a steel rigger is drawn to walk the skeleton of a skyscraper, fifty stories above the street. She shared with him the mysterious thrill of working without a net. Only someone who had been there really understood. Still, she cared for Dan, she could not deny that. But the answer to the question of where it was all going eluded her.

She tried to force these thoughts from her mind as she drove. But Dan's words haunted her.

There're going to be more.

What if he were right? Would she be able to refuse him then?

Four

The shift changed at seven.

Mary Donnelly checked her watch. It was almost midnight. That meant she had six more hours of her twelve-hour shift. She didn't mind working nights. It was quieter and there were no supervisors on duty. Of course, they each shared the role of team leader, but it was an informal arrangement and complications were always solved by mutual consent, not by some order that came from on high.

Working the crisis line could be exhausting, especially on nights when there were EPRP cases, which meant transferring a patient from an outside hospital to one within their medical group. That meant fielding a continuous stream of phone calls with doctors, nurses, and technicians until the patient was safely loaded on board an ambulance that would ferry him into the HMO system. She had been lucky. So far that night there hadn't been any to contend with.

Actually, it was a quiet night. That was fortunate because one of the therapists was out with the flu leaving Mary and her coworker Helen to carry the entire burden. Helen could be a problem. She usually allowed the phone to ring in the hope that someone else would pick up the call. There was a quota, of course; each of them was expected do an equal share of the caseload. But in Mary's experience, the night shift generally attracted those who wanted to do less. Normally, things fell off after midnight so that each of them got a second break besides the hour they were allotted by the union contract. They usually slipped into one of the psychiatrist's offices where they could nap on the leather couches.

Mary had been working the crisis hot line for almost four years. It was actually her second job. She was moonlighting from her usual duties as a psychiatric nurse in a Germantown hospital. Only psychiatric nurses and licensed therapists were permitted to work the crisis line. The overnight pay was exceptionally good, which was why Mary had requested the shift. Goodness knows she needed the money what with her mother in an expensive nursing home.

The thought caused her to open her purse and reach for her rosary. She was not ultrareligious, but she still attended Mass twice a month if she could, and she did go to confession at least once a year, usually just before Lent. She had never married, but her private life was her own. That had been established after a long silent tug of war with her parents. After her thirtieth birthday, she had moved into the converted apartment in the basement, which had its own entrance on the side of the house. She was free to invite whomever she wanted, male or female, no questions asked. She smiled to herself, wondering how the neighbors would react to a lesbian couple living in their midst.

Her fingers had just closed over the length of black beads when the phone on the desk in her cubicle rang. She dropped the beads back in her bag and reached out to pick it up.

"Livingston Emergency Crisis Line. This is Mary speaking. How may I help you?"

"I need to speak to a therapist."

"Certainly. I need your name and your Livingston Health Plan number."

"Jergen Schroeder," he said and rattled off the sixteen-digit number.

"One moment, please."

Mary began working the keyboard. In a moment the computer screen in front of her filled with data. The name and number checked.

"How can I help you, Mr. Schroeder?"

"Your name is Mary? Mary what?"

"I'm sorry. I can't tell you that."

"What I have to say is confidential."

"Everything you tell me is protected by our rules of confidentiality."

"So, you're like a priest?"

"In a way. In that way, yes."

"And you will keep what I say secret, as if I were talking to a priest?"

"Well. Yes. If you like to think of it in that way."

"You know that the seal of the confessional is inviolate."

"I understand." Her lips tightened. She had the feeling that this was going to be a tough one. He was either already delusional or on the verge of a psychotic episode.

"Are you a Catholic, Mary?"

Mary hesitated. "I'm sorry. That is not information I can share. Please tell me what you're calling about."

"All right, Mary, who is not a priest but who is bound by the seal of the confessional."

Mary leaned forward. There was something about his voice. Something compelling that elicited all of her attention.

"Are you listening, Mary of the seal?"

"I'm listening."

"I'm calling about the priest who was murdered."

"What priest is that?"

"You will know that very soon. I believe it will be in tomorrow's news. His name is Father Mckay."

"And what exactly is your involvement?"

There was a pause. Mary stiffened. She had almost stopped breathing. She did not want to break his concentration. She needed to keep him talking.

He began in an even tone, as if he were speaking to a child. "You have to understand. Those who betray the code must die. Which is why I had to order his death."

She took a deep breath. She had been here before with seriously disturbed delusional patients. But she had to tiptoe.

"I see. So you ordered his death. Why exactly did you do that?"

"I had to. It was my duty."

"Your duty?"

"Yes. You see, I am the anointed one. I am the Angel of Vengeance."

Five

The wind blew the remnants of fall foliage through the narrow valley like a tattered tapestry. The sharp-edged leaves rose in swirls and eddies in the violent air, forming momentary whirlpools that dissolved almost as quickly as they were formed.

Holly drove her four-door black Volvo through the shifting formations as she headed for the prison along the winding asphalt ribbon that bisected the valley. It always seemed to her a transgression to have located the penal institution in such a beautiful spot surrounded as it was by tree-covered mountains and long rolling vistas.

She had tuned her radio to the news station, which was, as Dan had predicted, full of the priest's murder. Art Pinero, the DA, held a press conference during which he promised to find the culprit or culprits and bring them to justice and he criticized the court for releasing the priest from prison in the first place, thereby playing both ends politically.

Holly wondered if Pinero had bitten off more than he could chew. The Mckay case was a hot potato. Vigilantism could not be tolerated, that was a given. Yet there were many who were appalled at what the priest had done and considered his murder an appropriate form of justice. There had been a serious discussion at Brandywine about what to do with the priest. Whether to keep him incarcerated in the unit or release him into the general prison population. The authorities were mindful of the murder of Father Gohegan in Massachusetts where an inmate had ordained his death. They did not want the same situation to occur in Pennsylvania, and on the verge of ordering Mckay permanently incarcerated at Brandywine when the appellate court had taken the responsibility away from them.

On the day Mckay had been released, he told Holly he had a premonition he would not live very long. Holly responded with as much reassurance as she could muster. But she knew in her heart that the priest might be right. He was a marked man from the moment he walked out of the gates. Yet the way he was killed was terrifying. Though she had put on a good front, the sight of his body had deeply disturbed her. She tried to put the images out of her mind, but they persisted deep into her dreams. Entering her condo, she felt a chill in the darkness and fumbled to find the light. She felt like a child again when she had been afraid of the dark, the fear of monsters lurking in the shrouded stillness.

Her sister's call returned her to reality.

Beth was a welcome antidote. She was Holly's opposite in so many ways, yet they had grown surprisingly close. Beth had been the rebel, while Holly had been the dutiful daughter, the striver and achiever. Dogged and determined. It was only later that she had rebelled and broken free of the iron restrictions set by her demanding father. He had given up on Beth. As a result she had done everything possible to hurt and humiliate him, only to hurt and humiliate herself. She had been in and out of rehab, finally breaking free of the addictions that plagued her. And now she was graduating from college, a triumphant achievement both for herself and Holly, who had never abandoned her.

Beth's voice was filled with excitement. "I called you at

work. Clara told me you'd left. She said Dan asked you in on the Mckay murder."

"Hold on. I'm not in on anything."

"You were Mckay's therpist, weren't you?"

"For a couple of months, that's all."

"So, you're not getting involved?"

Holly was silent.

"So you are involved?" Beth said, her voice rising enthusiastically.

"I didn't say that."

"You haven't made up your mind, is that it?"

"Something like that," Holly said.

"Why not? It sounds like quite a case. They said his body was cut into little pieces."

"Not little pieces. Discount half of what you hear on the news."

"But you saw it?"

Holly sighed. "Yes. I saw it."

"You wouldn't care to describe it, would you?" Beth asked, her voice rising eagerly.

"Not now," Holly answered with crisp firmness. "Tell me about your finals."

"Dull and boring. But I passed. Yippee!"

"That's great," Holly said, forcing herself to sound upbeat. "So what do you want for graduation?"

"A job."

"No. I'm getting you something special. You deserve it."

"Don't get me anything, please. We'll go out to dinner, and that's it."

"Whatever you say. Are you still seeing that guy, what was his name, Jamal?"

"That's over. I amused myself with his gorgeous body. End of story."

Holly knew better than to pry further. Beth had had a succession of young lovers ever since she moved into an apartment near the campus. All of them were fascinated by being with what they considered an older woman. None lasted more than a single quarter. Holly had met a few of them across a restaurant table now and then, but Beth never considered any of her relationships anything more than casual. They ended the conversation by setting a date for lunch.

"Hey. Listen. I'm immensely proud of you, sis," Holly said as they wrapped up.

"Thanks. Me too."

Beth clicked off. Holly waited an instant before putting down the phone. She felt a surge of emotion suddenly overwhelm her at the immensity of her sister's struggle. She had gone from outcast to graduate in the space of two years. Quite an achievement. It deserved more than acolades.

The prison loomed ahead.

Holly pulled into her spot and headed toward the series of gates that opened automatically when she approached. The gates were controlled by a guard in the tower above her. Holly waved at the figure of the correction officer silhouetted in the glass, and she waved back.

The Brandywine Center for Sexual Disorders was located in its own area within the prison complex. It had its own security system and a sprawling series of yards surrounding the modern structure. Holly had once seen it from the air when she had arrived by a helicopter provided for her exclusive use when she had made a special report to the Pennsylvania Supreme Court. It looked like something a child might have made out of Lego blocks. Four two-story wings branched out from a central structure. Each wing had two self-contained modules where inmates were housed and fed. Administrative, psychiatric, and medical functions were located in the central structure, which had its own small outlying wings and was separated from the main building by windowless corridors. That was where Holly did most of her work, doing individual and group sessions as well as all the clinical testing and evaluation that went along with it.

Once inside, Holly passed through a series of double-barred gates that opened noiselessly as she approached. The main corridor branched ahead. Uniformed correction officers sat behind bullet-proof glass windows monitoring the movement of inmates as they filed back and forth into Medical or Psychiatric. Holly turned into the pyschiatric branch, where her office was located. On the way she had to endure a gauntlet of hungry eyes from the benches where inmates sat waiting for their appointments, eyes that followed the movement of her legs under her skirt or fastened themselves to her breasts or rear end. Holly's eyes were fixed straight ahead as she strode with professional nonchalance. But she had never gotten used to the hunger imprinted on the faces of the men she passed. Whether it was a hunger for sex, or power, or some personal sadistic fantasy, she could only surmise.

Only now she sensed something else.

Was it anger? Or hatred? Or just the usual deep resentment?

Whatever it was, it was no longer just individual but part of the collective. A feeling of distrust and malice boiling just below the surface. In each set of eyes she saw a dagger and a warning.

Only when she was inside the staff offices did she breathe a sigh of relief and feel her diaphragm relax.

Clara swiveled around to greet her.

"I spoke to Beth last night. She called right after you left."

"I know. She called and told me."

"So?"

Clara leaned forward, her eyes fixed on Holly. "C'mon. Give. What did Dan want?"

"What he always wants."

"And which you won't give him," Clara said mischievously.

"How do you know I what I give him?"

"Sex I'm not talking about. I mean the real stuff. Emotion. With a capital E."

Holly was silent. She scanned the mass of paper in her mailbox. Each day there seemed to be more.

"Tell me about the Mckay case," said Clara. "It's all over the news. They say his body was in pieces. And that he was found on the grounds of the diocese residence. True or false?"

Holly shrugged. "The last part is true. The first is an exaggeration."

"A lot of people I know think finding him there was pretty appropriate. Laying the blame where it belongs. Right at the feet of the bishop and the rest of the power clergy. All those sanctimonious monsignors who knew what was going on but turned their back."

Holly nodded. "Maybe. I guess a lot of people are to blame."

"But the fact that Mckay was murdered doesn't exonerate them."

"No, I guess it doesn't."

"A lot of people wanted to get Mckay."

"Really?" Holly said, eyeing Clara.

"Hey! Don't look at me. I've got an alibi."

"Thank God for that."

"So, are you in?"

Holly smiled. "Is Ted in?"

"Don't try and change the subject. Are you or aren't you?"

"Aren't I what?"

"Going to work on the case."

"I'm not a cop, Clara."

"No, but you were Mckay's therapist. And you were an assistant DA, weren't you?"

"Yes. But that was a long time ago."

"It's like swimming or oral sex. You never forget how to do it. So. Tell me. He asked you, didn't he?"

"Yes, he asked me."

"And?"

Holly looked up at the older woman and their eyes met.

"Frankly. I haven't decided."

Clara smiled knowingly. "I think you have."

Six

Bishop Horan hurried out of the main banquet room of the downtown hotel and headed toward the entrance across the ornately decorated lobby. He was dressed in a black surplice and cape, his waist wrapped in a purple sash. He wore a purple skullcap on his head. His face was flushed from the excellent wine served at the banquet. A wonderful San Genoviese, one of his favorites. His ears still rang with the continuous rounds of applause that had greeted his speech. He felt content though many of the tables had not been filled. Still, the turnout had been considerable considering the times. Those who came formed the bulwark of his diocese. They were loyal and could be depended upon to dig deep into their pockets. His diocese was going to need a considerable war chest to combat the vicious pack of trial attorneys representing what was a continually growing army of those who claimed they were molested. The question was which of them were to be believed and which of them were faking.

Not that he was quibbling. He never publicly questioned the suffering of those who came forward. That had been a public relations coup. And an important one other bishops would have to emulate if they wanted to survive the scandal engulfing the Catholic Church in America. It required the greatest sense of tact and timing that he had ever been called upon to use. But of those skills, he was a master. They had not only gained him his present office but could one day secure him the rank of cardinal. He had only to bide his time and continue to play the press and the other bishops like pieces on a giant chessboard.

Faces turned toward him in the busy hotel lobby. Some were smiling, others turned away in disgust. A few leveled piercing glances of accusation. He considered the media to blame for that, especially the stories that played up the charges that he had not acted quickly enough to identify and segregate child molesters, that he had in fact instituted a secret program of having them transferred to other parishes where the parishioners were unaware of the vipers in their midst. Of course, he had denied every one of these accusations. The truth was far more complicated and subtle than the press would report.

Temptation was a terrible thing. All the saints were plagued by it. Understanding was called for. He himself had known the seductiveness of young boys when he had been at the seminary. He had not succumbed, but weaker wills had. Like alcoholism, it was a curse of his calling. Many lonely men had given in to it and paid the price of their despair. He had interviewed many who confessed their transgression. He had sent them for therapy and when they were pronounced fit, he had returned them to duty. What was wrong with that?

Those who called it dereliction of duty for not reporting it to the police were wrong. Why destroy a lifetime of vocation for a few slips? Besides, he was not entirely convinced that it did the kind of psychic harm many claimed. Oh, certainly, some victims were traumatized. No argument. But others just took it in stride the way they might any other early childhood sexual experience. He had done some unauthorized touching himself in the years leading up to his decision to take the vow of celibacy. Later, his own slips had been with women, of course, mature women who had been disappointed in their marriages. What they did together was a minor form of blessing for them, in spite of his breaking both his sacred duty and the commandments. But then, he was not the one on trial. He had long ago confessed and been forgiven.

Bishop Horan's lips formed a smile.

He had learned early on that the best defense is a good offense. Never let them see weakness, his college football coach had drilled into him. Even when you're losing. He had followed that advice ever since. There were those bishops who had already surrendered, opening up their coffers to any claimant no matter how long ago or how dubious their claim might be. He was not one of them. He and his attorneys had developed a program of rearguard actions calculated to plunge his adversaries into disarray by setting one set of plaintiffs against the other. It would be years before any of them saw a penny. In the meantime, by sounding alarms of distress as he had done tonight, he was sure of amassing a huge fund to hedge against the possibility of a settlement or a series of lawsuits whose verdicts might go against them. As an added bonus, there was no law against investing these proceeds and reaping the benefits while they waited for the final outcomes to be decided.

A group had collected near the entrance. Appreciative, respectful faces. Expressions he was used to. Hands were extended to him. Bishop Horan paused to shake each of them. He even gripped an elbow or two, his face breaking into an expression of humility as he exchanged a word or two with his well-wishers. Out of the corner of his eye he noticed a small group of young men approaching. What he read in their glowering eyes and aggressively hunched shoulders warned him to move on. He broke off quickly and while his arm was raised in blessing, moved to the exit door being opened for him by the grinning, obsequious doorman.

His limousine was at the curb, long, black, and gleaming.

The doorman hurried across the sidewalk and pulled open the rear door allowing the bishop to enter. The door was slammed shut, cutting off the advance of the young men who were shouting something he could not hear. He leaned forward and made the sign of the cross as the limousine pulled away and they blended with the busy weekend Philadelphia traffic.

Bishop Horan settled back against the plush cushions. The interior was luxurious and dimly lit. A small television screen was at his elbow together with a phone and fax. He leaned forward to the bar and lifted a square crystal bottle filled with the amber glow of an expensive single-malt scotch. He selected one of the etched Baccarat glasses, added ice, then poured himself a healthy amount. He took a sip, then put the glass down on the rest beside him, allowing the ice to melt.

He raised his eyes and glanced at the silhouette of the driver through the screen. The man was wearing his chauffeur's cap, a touch the bishop appreciated. He liked things that were old-fashioned and formal. That was why he enjoyed his stays in Rome. He loved the pagentry and the pomp of the Vatican, of the entire city for that matter. The Italians were a disorderly lot, but they appreciated the importance of ceremony. He loved the stately dress uniforms of the Roman police, and especially enjoyed the national devotion to the *bella figura,* something he himself was equally devoted to. He looked down for a minute at the heavy folds of his expensively tailored surplice, extending to the tips of his highly polished patent-leather shoes. He prided himself on still being the same weight he had been in his early twenties. He despised prelates who grew too fat. Presenting a perfect appearance was part of the influence he wielded. The idea of the new Archbishop of Boston wearing the simple cassock of a Dominican friar, though admittedly a good public relations concept, was well beyond the bounds of discretion and good taste. The very idea of a bishop in sandals drove him to distraction.

Bishop Horan brushed the disagreeable image from his mind. He lifted the glass and took a long sip of the pungent liquor. He sighed at the perfection of its smoothness. The dinner had been a good distraction. He enjoyed the adulation and displays of devotion. The food had been excellent, which was to be expected considering how expensive the hotel was. He had gone for a steam and a massage in the hotel's gym earlier, then had a lie-down in the suite provided for him. In spite of the traffic and potential danger, he always enjoyed his trips into the city.

He glanced at his watch. It would take them at least an hour to arrive at the residence. His stomach tightened for an instant as the thought of the Mckay matter entered his mind. The horror of it disgusted him. He had not been able to sleep well for several nights following the discovery of the priest's body. What kind of maniac would commit such a crime? The police were stumped, although he had been reassured by the DA that they would quickly bring him, or her, or it to justice. If only one could believe them.

Ambitious fellow, that Pinero. Horan liked ambition in politicians. It was extremely useful. Horan would need political help in the molestation cases down the road, of course. As the situation cooled and the public's attention drifted to other things, sympathetic judges would have to be appointed. Pinero might be one of them. They might even make changes in the statute of limitations that would extinguish certain claims and trim many of the awards. Their influence could be used as a club to force the more aggressive attorneys into more favorable settlements.

He glanced outside, but because the windows were tinted he was unable to make out their route. The highways all looked the same, just a collection of passing billboards and swerving headlights. The bishop leaned back into the cushions and lifted his feet onto the foot rest.

His eyes were growing heavy. He was not aware of exactly when his fingers opened and the glass he held dropped to the carpet. Nor was he aware of the limousine turning off the main route onto a side road some thirty miles or so outside the city, taking them down an unfamiliar road winding into darkness.

Seven

He came suddenly awake.

His head felt heavy. His limbs were leaden. He forced his eyelids open and stared around him, but there was only darkness.

The room was swaying. He could not get it to stop. He raised his hands feeling for the walls, but his fingers gripped cold bars of metal.

With horrific clarity, he realized that instead of the luxurious walnut interior of his bedroom, he was locked inside an iron cage, suspended within a bare stone tower. There were no windows. Light seeped down from somewhere above, but he could not make out from where. He looked down, but there was only darkness below. A bottomless pit.

His body ached. He reached down and realized that he was dressed in a flimsy gown of paperlike material. Beneath it, his feet were bare and he was naked.

Panic gripped him.

He felt as if he were being strangled. He tried to lift his arms and pull away the edge of the garment from his neck. What was this madness? Or had he gone insane?

He struggled to remember. Images of the previous evening

flashed through his mind. The banquet. The rising guests and the swell of applause. The students in the lobby and his quick exit to the limousine. He had taken his usual drink on the trip home. Only he had not arrived at home. Beyond the drive, he could not remember.

He tried to pray, but somehow the words would not come. His mouth felt dry. He needed a drink of water.

"Water!" he cried out. But the word only echoed back to him in the confined space.

At the diocese residence, his wishes would have been carried out immediately. Now he couldn't even get a glass of water. *God in heaven, what had he done to deserve this?*

He heard a groan that almost sounded human before he realized it was the creaking of metal against wood, the sound of a chain being unspooled.

The cage shook and began to descend.

He gripped the metal bars and held on as it jerked unsteadily. He felt dizzy, as if he were about to fall. To go flying earthward, crushed on impact like an insect seared against hot glass.

The cage continued down through the darkness, until the area began to suffuse with a golden light. He adjusted his eyes as the light grew brighter.

The cage struck the stone floor and threw him off his feet.

Bishop Horan pulled himself up and looked about him. The cage had come to rest within a windowless octagonal chamber. Light came from two huge tapers on iron stands on each side of a large wooden structure surmounted by a dias. The structure was decorated with unusual carvings of huge intertwining serpents.

A monk sat at the dais wearing a long black hooded cassock.

Joy rose in his heart. A monk! Then he was safe.

He could not see the monk's face within the folds of his hood.

"Where am I?" he asked.

The monk did not answer.

"Do you know who I am?"

The monk nodded.

"Can't you speak? Are you under a vow of silence? I can release you."

The monk said nothing.

Bishop Horan felt dizzy for a moment. "What are you doing?" he shouted. "This is preposterous. Release me at once! I am Bishop Horan. I order you to release me! Whatever this is, it has gone far enough!"

"Silence," the monk commanded. His words echoed ominously. "The moment of judgment is at hand. Do nothing to insult the dignity of this court."

The bishop closed his mouth. What court? He knew nothing of any ecclesiastical court being convened. He would have to have been notified and given time to prepare a defense.

"I protest—" he began, but the sound expired in his throat as the figure on the dais raised his hand.

The bishop was bewildered. This was something out of a medieval pageant. He felt as if he had been transported back to the twelfth century.

"Of what am I being accused?" Horan shouted.

"You have committed the sin of sloth. You have neglected your sacred duties."

"I?" Bishop Horan gurgled. "I neglect my duties? Impossible! I am the high prelate of this diocese."

"You have abetted evil, ignored evil, and propagated evil by your deceit."

"No. I protest! I demand to know the evidence against me."

"So you shall. Are you acquainted with a Father Aubrey Mckay?"

Something froze in Bishop Horan's throat.

"I know him," he gasped.

"You had knowledge of his transgressions, did you not? The molesting of innocent children."

"Yes." It was barely a whisper.

"And yet you did nothing to remove him from office. Instead, you transferred him repeatedly over a period of years, from one parish to another where he continued to commit injuries and do harm."

"I sent him for help. To a special clinic. Repeatedly. He was given clearances by the doctors to return to his duties."

"Yet instead of sending him to a place where he would not be in contact with children, you sent him to parishes filled with families who had no knowledge of his past transgressions."

"I . . . we had shortages of staff. The priesthood had shrunk. We had fewer and fewer candidates coming out of the seminaries."

"And that is your excuse for loosing a child molester on innocent unknowing children?"

"Others knew. Not only me."

"You were in charge, were you not?"

"Others condoned what I did."

"They shall not go unpunished."

Bishop Horan gripped the bars. He felt cold suddenly. Bereft of comfort.

The monk leaned forward.

"Your name is written in the Cipher. You have been weighed and found wanting. Your punishment will be in accordance with your sins."

"I demand the right to appeal."

"From this court there is no appeal."

"Wait!' Bishop Horan shouted. "You have no right to condemn me. I am a bishop. I demand a trial of my peers."

The monk rose and slipped back into the darkness.

The bishop heard the sound of the chain beginning to wind. The cage began to rise. Terror speared though him. He began to breathe more rapidly. His fingers tightened on the metal bars.

The winding stopped. The cage was suspended in darkness. He could no longer see the chamber below.

He heard gears clang and looked around wildly.

Out of the darkness on either side came two long rods of metal. At each end was a large pointed screw. They fitted into slots in either side of the cage. Bishop Horan had not noticed them before. He wondered what they were for.

Slowly, the rods began to turn.

Fascinated, he watched as the sides of the cage began to move. Coming toward him, inch by inch. Realization dawned with each turn of the screw.

He was going to be crushed to death. . . .

His mind reeled with the horror.

His fingers gripped the side of the incoming walls. But he had little strength. Not enough to prevent the metal walls from coming together like the jaws of a vise.

His mind rebelled. It was not possible. This could not be happening. But the screws continued relentlessly turning.

His shrieks echoed within the stone tower, filling his ears with the sound of his own terror. He was screaming for help. But there was no help.

The sound continued, accompanied by the high-pitched squeal of the metal screws and the piercing shrieks of the man in the cage. Screaming as they revved, the gears ground harshly as the walls met resistance, then crushed bone and gristle until the noise stopped.

The tower was silent except for the whisper of a monk's long robes on a stone floor, walking away.

Eight

Holly went to pick up the P-G herself.

She needed it to complete her report on Martinez. The Plethmysmograph was one of their most important tools. It worked like a lie detector registering an inmate's response to various kinds of sexual stimulation. Electrodes were attached to the inmate's genitals as various kinds of pictures were flashed in front of him. Theory dictated that the greater the inmate's response, the less effective he would be in controlling his impulses. It gave them a pretty good idea of the level of the inmate's sexual obsessions and allowed them to continually modify their treatment plans.

After spending a good half hour going over the P-G with the technician, Holly had a darkening sense of foreboding. Martinez was going to be a difficult if not impossible case. His level of stimulation was extremely high. Peeling away his layers of denial might be virtually impossible. She had dealt with inmates like him before. They were often incurable, although that was a word she never used. What they taught at Brandywine was impulse control. It was a lifetime illness, as with alcoholism and other addictive diseases. Sex offenders were also addicts. They were just as diseased.

It was something she hoped the public would one day understand.

She continued away from the P-G room along the transverse corridor back toward the pyschiatric offices. She was so preoccupied with concocting a treatment plan for Martinez, she failed to notice the two inmates who rose from the bench outside the dental office and fell into step with her.

She glanced up at the inmate beside her as she turned the corner toward her office. He was someone she didn't recognize. He was short and burly, with a full head of curly hair. The sleeves of his T-shirt were folded back revealing thick arms as loaded with tattoos as New York subway cars were once loaded with graffiti.

She had started down the transverse when the second inmate stepped in front of her. He was tall and blond and wore his hair in a ponytail.

"Whoa, Doc. Wrong way," he said, his lips curling into a smile.

She was about to speak when his hand rose and she saw the gleaming edge of a shank concealed in his palm.

"Just keep walking and nothing will happen to you. Fuck us, and I'll stick this shank up your spine."

The burly inmate moved in front of her as they started back up the main corridor leading to the housing units.

Holly started to speak. "Look."

"Shut the fuck up," the tall inmate hissed. " Don't say shit."

Holly felt her stomach clench. Fear clawed its way along her back. She gripped the report tight against her chest.

They were approaching the first checkpoint. A bored-looking CO sat inside his cubicle behind bullet-proof glass. The double set of steel-barred doors were open. Inmates had to pass through a metal detector that dominated the corridor just beyond the checkpoint monitored by the correction officer on duty.

Holly's lips tightened. She was not allowed beyond the checkpoint. The area was off limits to the medical staff.

"I can't go inside," she said.

"I told you to shut up, bitch," the tall inmate muttered. She felt something pointed prod her back. "Just keep walking."

They were almost at the checkpoint. Holly's legs felt like rubber. Her heart was pounding.

"Just a minute," the officer said, speaking into a mike. "I'll need a clearance to let you through, Doctor."

"You got it," the tall inmate said. He stepped to Holly's side and brought the shank up to her throat.

Holly watched as the officer's hand went to his console.

"Close those gates, and I'll cut her throat," the tall inmate said.

The guard hesitated. Anxiety flashed across his face.

The burly inmate stepped through the gates. He reached back to haul Holly along with him, as the tall inmate followed, his shank pressed against her windpipe.

An instant later they were through the metal detector.

An alarm went off. It began beeping incessantly.

The officer grabbed a phone and hit the release button.

The twin gates slammed shut. The double clang resonating along the hall behind them.

"Move it! Move!" the burly inmate shouted as he pulled Holly along. His grip felt like steel pincers on her arm.

The tall inmate was a step behind her; his hand was pressed against the small of her back, shoving her forward. She began to run, until they were sprinting down the corridor toward the barred gates that led to the South Module. Her eyes filled with a blur of motion. The officers inside would have heard the alarm. They would bar the way.

Incredibly, the gates were open ahead.

The tall inmate shoved her through.

Holly stumbled as she entered, grabbing the railing in

front of her. Her vision cleared. She was standing on the topmost tier. The module opened below her. A six-sided configuration lined with forty cells behind thick glass doors, and a large central area filled with bedlam.

The noise deafened her.

They were in the nucleus of a riot. Inmates were running in every direction. Some were tossing bedding over the rails. Others were dumping their belongings. Streams of toilet paper flew from the topmost tier like streamers over a parade.

The glass-enclosed control module that overlooked the area was empty. The COs who would normally have been manning it had disappeared.

The burly inmate stepped beside her and began banging on the railing.

"We got her, you assholes!" he shouted. "We got the bitch!"

Faces turned to look. From different parts of the tiers inmates halted and stared at her. Those filling the area below raised fists, screamed, and cheered.

Holly's insides turned to glass.

She stared straight ahead but her eyes refused to focus. Her mind reeled with a single dizzying thought. The South Unit imprisoned over a hundred of the worst sex offenders in the system. And she was now their hostage.

Nine

The call came in just after Mary's break.

They had been swamped since early in the shift, and Mary had been looking forward to her break, hoping that things would lighten up after it, but there had been no respite. The phones just kept ringing. She had taken two quick calls as soon as she resumed her seat in the cubicle. One was from a known crank who had to be disposed of quickly before he ate up any more time.

"You know the agreement, Mr. Luchese," she said in her best school principal's voice. "You've already had your morning call. You have to wait until after dinner to call again."

She felt sorry for the poor guy. He was an old man, virtually blind and bedridden, living alone with no one to talk to other than the woman who brought him his meals on wheels. But he would monopolize every minute of her shift if she allowed him to. The second call was to set up a referral to a psychiatrist, which took less time that she thought it would. She had just hung up when Millicent, an RN, who was seated in the next cubicle, called over to her.

"I've got a call. He's asking for you."

"A doctor?"

Millicent shook her head. "A client."

Mary made a face. That's all she needed, a fan. "Okay. Transfer it over on 9103."

Mary waited until Millicent transferred the call. Then she picked up the phone.

"This is Mary," she said, summoning her brightest response.

"Hello, Mary. Remember me?"

For an instant she blanked. The voice was low, almost metallic. Familiar, yet strange.

"I'm sorry. Who is this?"

"I'm disappointed. I thought I had made an impression."

The memory rocketed back into her mind. Her throat constricted as she sat bolt upright in her swivel chair. He had predicted the news of the priest's murder. And it had come true. Since then she had been waiting, anticipating his call, and dreading it as she dreaded the anticipation of a nightmare.

"Please let me have your name and medical number," she said through tight lips.

"Do we really have to go through that again, Mary?"

"Please."

She typed the numbers he dictated. The screen filled with data including her notes from their last conversation, words that stated, *I am the Angel of Vengeance. . . .*

"Have you been watching the newscasts lately, Mary? I'd advise you to. You might see a related story."

"What do you mean?" she said in a whisper.

"That will come clear very shortly. When a certain missing bishop is found."

Her throat constricted. Her pulse was racing.

"Which bishop?"

"Why spoil the surprise? You'll see. Actually, you're the first to know."

"I think I'm going to have to end this call."

"Oh, but you can't. You're my mother confessor."

She waited a moment, then said, "Any threat of potential violence to any person has to be reported."

"We're way past that, Mary. The violence has already happened."

"What do you mean?" Her heart was trip-hammering.

"Just watch your TV, Mary. It will become abundantly clear."

"Why are you doing this?"

"I told you. You wouldn't want me not to confess when I've committed a sin, would you, Mary? Thou shalt not kill. Although in this case it wasn't really murder. No more than any other execution is really murder."

"You can't take the law into your own hands. That's a criminal act."

"In my own hands? No. Mary. You misunderstand. Those who betray the law must be punished, isn't that so?"

She hesitated.

"Come now, Mary. Can't you answer a simple question?"

"Yes," she stammered.

"Very good. You see, whatever I am compelled to do is in the name of the law. The law of the Cipher."

"But we're bound by the law of this state."

"You perhaps. But I must follow the dictates of a higher law. A law that commands me to avenge its betrayers. Just as you must follow the law and maintain our bond of secrecy. Isn't that correct, Mary?"

She was silent.

"As long as we understand each other, Mary. And we understand our duty. I'll say good night now."

The phone went dead. Mary was shivering in spite of the temperature in the overheated office. She knew the difference between a real and a crank call.

The birds attracted the camper's attention.

Cawing and screeching, they clawed for position on the

swaying metal box that hung suspended by a chain from the old stone tower.

The tower was part of a mill constructed in the 1840's, then abandoned sometime in the depression of the 1930's. It had been used as a granary during the last part of the nineteenth century, then forgotten as the area fell into stagnation. The old stone houses were just shells by the time they were rediscovered and restored. There were few farms and many of these were no longer plowed, mainly used to feed dairy cattle who wandered through the neglected fields and patches of wooded land, overgrown with brambles.

Campers came up from the city or the universities. They set up sites along the streams and burrowed deep into the wooded hills. Most of the trails were unmarked. They fanned out into the woodlands and along the more picturesque of the ridges. A few of the old trails were used by off-roaders who plowed up the weeds with their studded tires and left deeply embedded gouges in the earth.

One of them made the discovery.

There were two vehicles, one following the other as they drove up along the ridge, then dropped down the steep side of the rise into the narrow valley between two hulking fir-covered mountains. The trail was narrow, but it had been used before. They were able to follow old tracks that cut along the bank of a swollen stream, then came up hard against a low-lying stone wall that marked the original property line. The drivers got out of their vehicles and urinated side by side. That was when they heard the birds.

One of them, a short thickset man in a black leather jacket, headed toward the uproar. He had only gone a short distance when he came through a stand of oaks and saw the tower. It was half-covered in ivy, which did nothing to ease its forlorn appearance.

Then he saw the birds.

They wheeled in a long black wave, rising and falling in a

continuous pattern from somewhere on the other side. Curious, the man followed the path around toward them.

. When he was in front of the old stone ruin, he stopped and looked up.

A black girder projected from the top of the tower. From it hung a metallic object about the size of a steamer trunk. Bands of metal formed a grid on all four sides. The birds gripped the metal bars of the grid, pecking at something inside.

The man in the leather jacket moved closer as the birds flew upward. Their beaks were running blood.

The report came in a little after four, announced by the blinking light on the phone on the desk beside him.

Detective Inspector Dan Shepard glanced at the light and as usual ignored it.

He had just finished checking the last name on the tenth pile of twenty-five separately stacked index cards lined up on his desk like Civil War regiments marching into battle. They listed the names of the three hundred-plus people who had threatened Father Mckay.

Most listed the names and numbers of those who had made telephone threats, and therefore were easier to trace than the threats that had come in by letter or that were dropped off anonymously at various churches throughout the territory of the diocese. All of them had to be checked back to their source. It was an impossibility at best. So far they had no real suspects.

Added to one murdered priest was one missing bishop.

The bishop had been gone for almost a week, but news of his disappearance had not yet been leaked to the media, which in itself was a minor miracle. The diocese had cancelled all of his engagements using the excuse that he was sick with the flu. The information on his disappearance had

come down through the highest channels and was strictly
hush-hush. Dan had been assigned the case by the DA personally, but there was almost nothing to go on. The bishop
had been last seen leaving the lobby of a downtown hotel
where he had delivered a speech at a fund-raiser. He had
been seen getting into his limousine, which had then driven
away. But his driver was still inside the hotel when it left. He
had been summoned by a bellman, who gave him a message
instructing him to escort the bishop from the ballroom back
to the car. There had been hostile threats made to the bishop
as well, and it was considered a wise precaution. But the
bishop never waited for the driver. Instead he went to the car
himself and was driven away. The bellman was questioned.
The message came through the concierge desk. The concierge
on duty had taken a call from a Father Nolan, who introduced
himself as the bishop's aide. Only, they later learned there
was no Father Nolan. Whoever had called was unknown.

Dan knew it was only a matter of time before the bishop's
disappearance was picked up by the media and the body was
found. Then all hell would break loose. There was no doubt
in his mind that the murder of the priest and the disappearance of the bishop were connected.

The blinking phone at his elbow would not desist.

He picked up the receiver. "Shepard," he barked.

The voice at the other end was terse and filled with annoyance at having been ignored for so long. But it delivered
the message he had been both anticipating and dreading.

A body had been found.

The preliminary ID indicated it was Bishop Horan's.

Ten

Dan Shepard stared at the metal cage with a look of bafflement.

The local cops had arrived on the scene and immediately summoned the local fire department, which was volunteer. They refused to go anywhere near the cage. So the locals did the intelligent thing, which for them was not usual, and called the CID. A team arrived and summoned forensics, who came along with several emergency vehicles. Forensics climbed fire ladders to reach the body, which was in a state of decomposition, making the ID difficult. But the general description fit the bishop. Same height, weight, age, facial and body characteristics. They would know better when they got the body to the medical examiner's. But Dan already knew with the certainty of someone who had been cursed with knowing. He had been sometimes wrong, true, but not very often. A cop is like a good poker player. Once he has a sense of who the players are, he can pretty well predict the outcome of the game.

But who the hell would put his victim up in a cage and suspend him from a tower?

Worse, it looked as if every bone in the bishop's body had

been broken. As if he had been crushed to death, then placed inside the metal container.

What the hell did it mean? What was the killer trying to signify? Was it punishment? Revenge? Or was there something else, some twisted logic of a diseased mind?

He signaled to the detective beside him.

"Forensics done? And photographers?"

The man nodded.

"Okay. Then let's get it down."

The detective drew down the corners of his mouth and started toward the emergency crew dressed in orange coveralls that congregated near the base of the tower. The corpse reeked even at this distance. It was going to be one hell of a job.

Dan turned and walked back to his car. He slid into the front seat and picked up his cell phone.

His lips were compressed as he dialed. He knew what Holly would say. But he wanted her counsel. She was an expert on deviates. And the individual who did this was a unique form of the species, of that he had no doubt. He knew she would balk and tell him she had no time. But he would have to wear her down. Besides, any amount of time he could spend with her was a plus. She was incredibly evasive. Trying to get a commitment from her was like trying to catch a trout in rapids with your bare hands.

The phone continued ringing.

Through the windshield he could see the emergency crews going into action as they maneuvered beneath the tower. One of the cranes was raised above the cage. From it dangled a chain and hook, which a two-man crew in the basket of a cherry picker was securing to the top of the cage. They were wearing masks but he did not envy them the task. One of them had ignited an acetylene torch, which he was using to cut through the chain securing the cage to the iron beam from which it was suspended.

Whoever had done this was incredibly devious. Just getting the cage up there must have been quite a job. And why here, in this locale, so remote and distant? Mckay's body had been left right there in the yard of the diocesan residence. The bishop was here in the wilderness. It didn't add up.

Shepard took the phone from his ear. It was still ringing. No one had picked up. That was strange. He had dialed the prison. There was always someone at reception.

He clicked off and dialed a different number. A moment later a male voice answered.

"Criminal Investigation Division."

"This is Inspector Shepard. Could you dial the Brandy-wine Unit at the prison. I can't seem to get through."

"Hold on, please."

Dan idled the receiver against his ear. The torch had cut through the chain. The guys in the cherry picker were man-handling the cage as the crane angled over them, trying to keep it from hitting the wall of the tower. He could see the body clearly now, huddled in the corner like a wounded ani-mal. The ravens rose shrieking from the top of the tower, angry at the disturbance of their prey. He did not like ravens. Death birds, he thought of them.

"Inspector," the voice at his ear said.

"Yeah."

"There's a situation at the prison."

"What kind of situation?"

"I don't know. But communications have been cut at Brandywine. And there's been an emergency call for addi-tional reinforcements."

The call would summon a state police emergency re-sponse team. That meant a riot or disturbance at the prison. Dan's chest tightened as he remembered his last conversa-tion with Holly and the fear she'd expressed.

"Thanks," he said, then tossed the phone onto the seat be-side him.

He turned the key starting the engine, jammed his foot on the pedal, and peeled out, headed back down the dirt road.

Startled by the sound, the birds rose in a single motion, wings spread, claws upraised, rising in a black wave against the sun.

Dan could see the media choppers as soon as he drove over the crest of the rise and entered the narrow valley where the prison was located. They rose in a swarm above the collection of buildings that housed the Brandywine Center like vultures over rotting meat.

He could see media vans parked one behind the other on the shoulder of the road as he approached, along with dozens of state police vehicles and a SWAT caravan. Police were trying to contain a slew of onlookers from the local area, forcing Dan to slalom between a line of brutal-looking SUV's that threatened to knock him off the road before he reached a series of checkpoints and could pull his car into the parking lot of the administration building. He pinned his badge to his coat as he got out and headed inside. He was directed to the command post by a heavyset trooper in a dark blue windbreaker. It had gotten colder. The wind was particularly vicious in this stretch of country, and he ducked his head into his jacket to protect his face against the up-swirl of sharp-edged leaves that flew around him.

His hat was almost blown off by the draft of hot air that blew down at him from a heater above the door—a service he particularly hated. The lobby inside was filled with reporters along with heavily armored SWAT cops and equally armed prison personnel, each with his mitt around a steaming cup of coffee. They were being served by several matrons in white uniforms stationed behind a series of long tables fortified with stacked boxes of pizza and doughnuts, a sight to gladden the heart of any peace officer.

Dan fought his way toward a set of double doors guarded by a phalanx of troopers who read his badge and stepped aside to allow him entrance to the chamber beyond. Big cardboard signs divided the area into sections. One for the corrections people. One for troopers. Another for SWAT, medical, and emergency personnel. And in the rear, a station for the DA.

Art Pinero's dome-shaped head towered over the other men surrounding him. The district attorney was over six-five. He was heavy-shouldered and built like a linebacker. The undistinguished features of his face were given intended emphasis by large horn-rimmed glasses. His head was shaved to the smoothness of glass. His small, almost piglike eyes missed nothing. Dan could feel them fixing on him as the DA raised his hand and gestured for him to enter the privileged circle of aides and sycophants bunched around him.

"You found a body?" Pinero said in a low voice as he drew Dan back away from the others, who eyed him with envy. The DA was on a politically upward trajectory and the men around him were jockeying for position for his next job, which might be as governor or U.S. senator. Dan had no desire to get caught in the crossfire.

He nodded in answer to the question.

"Any ID?" Pinero queried.

"Possibly."

"The bishop?"

"We're checking DNA now."

"You couldn't make a visual check?"

"No."

Pinero's lips drew taut. Dan knew that was the last thing he wanted.

"What's the situation here?" Dan ventured.

"Prisoners in South bloc have rioted. They've taken over the module."

"Hostages?"

"Five. Four correction officers and a staff psychologist. A woman."

"Holly Alexander?"

"You know her?"

Shepard nodded as his insides ground to gravel. "Any plan yet?"

"We're waiting for the negotiating team. We'll try talking to them first. Don't go anywhere. I want to know as soon as the lab confirms it's the bishop."

Pinero turned around and went back to his brain trust.

Dan was trying to keep his stomach from doing contortions. The idea of Holly being trapped inside with a hundred degenerates and serial rapists was taking him beyond nausea. He edged toward the rear of the room and went through a door marked Medical.

Grim-faced civilian personnel were grouped along the corridor outside their offices. One glanced at Dan's badge and asked if there were any news. He made a negative gesture, then continued along until he found Psychiatric and went inside.

Clara was on the phone. She looked up when he entered, said a few more words, then put down the receiver.

"They've got Holly," she said. Her face was tight with concern.

"I know. How did it happen?"

"We don't know. She was on her way back from the P-G room when they waylaid her and took her back inside with them. They got past the checkpoint by threatening to kill her if they weren't allowed through."

"Did they come for her specifically or was it just happenstance?"

"We don't know."

"Christ. Why her?" he exploded. His fists were clenched, his face was ashen.

"No one can figure that out, not yet anyway."

"What's the makeup of the unit?"

"The usual. A mix of rapists, child molesters, and other deviates. But a lot of the inmates have already served their time and are waiting for release. I can give you a breakdown. I've already run a couple of dozen sets."

"I'd appreciate it."

"What's going on out there?" Clara said as she hammered on the keys of the computer.

"We're waiting for a negotiating team."

"She could be dead by then."

Dan was silent. His eyes were distant. Then he turned toward her.

"I don't think so. I think they've got her for a reason."

"What reason?"

"We'll find out pretty soon."

The cell was dark.

Electricity had been turned off now for several hours.

Holly sat wedged in a corner of the bunk, her eyes fixed on the area outside.

She was alone in the second-tier cell. The glass door was closed. Two burly inmates stood guard outside, each holding a lead-weighted club they had stripped from the correction officers. She had seen no other weapons, other than clubs, sharp-edged shanks, and those improvised from tearing apart bedsteads and tables.

The rioting that had been going on when she entered had ceased. The inmates were quiet. Most had drawn back beneath the protection of the lower tier, their eyes focused on the angular domelike glass ceiling that covered the module. The glass was opaque, but through it they could hear the drone of circling helicopters ascending and descending in never-ending loops. The fear was that the choppers would begin firing, sending fusillades of bullets into the area below.

No one had said anything to her.

She had been hustled along the tier and shoved inside the cell. On the way she had glimpsed the correction officers grouped in a nearby cell, seated on the floor, their hands tied behind them, guarded by a group of muscular inmates.

She had lost track of time, though the light above was beginning to fade. Earlier, an inmate had entered with a pitcher of water. Other than that she had been left undisturbed, except by her own thoughts. She was a hostage. She knew the odds. Some survived, some didn't. Especially if they stormed the unit. She forced the concept from her mind.

The cell door was pulled open. The two inmates guarding her stepped inside.

"Outside," one said.

She rose and stepped toward the door. Fear gripped her intestines. She felt her legs shaking as she exited the cell. Faces stared up at her out of the darkness below. For an instant she was paralyzed with terror, conscious of the eyes fastened to her legs and breasts. A hand gripped her shoulder sending an icy shiver through her.

Both inmates closed in on either side and she started forward, walking between them toward the darkness at the end of the tier.

Eleven

The body found in the cage was all over the nightly news.

On some channels it was the lead story; on others it followed the disturbance at the Brandywine Center.

Mary kept clicking the remote, surfing from channel to channel to find out as much as she could, but the details were sketchy. Reporters speculated that it was the missing Bishop Horan, but they were waiting for DNA confirmation. The body was that mutilated. Several commentators and so-called experts made the connection to the gruesome murder of Father Mckay. All of them agreed that the Mckay scandal had torn through the diocese like a raging firestorm, splitting Catholics into armed camps, some calling for Bishop Horan's resignation, others supporting him. But none could fathom who might want the men murdered.

Only Mary knew the answer to that.

Mary stared at the screen, but she saw nothing. Her mind was in turmoil. The bishop was murdered by the man who had called her on the hot line. The same man who had killed Father Mckay.

She alone knew his name and where he lived and the rest of the pertinent data that should be on its way to the police, but for the regulations about confidentiality and her own promise of secrecy, a promise she had made to him and could not break.

Or could she?

He had confessed to her only after she had agreed that she was bound the same way as a priest. It was especially ironic since she had once been a nun. A novice actually. Still, she had given two years of her life to the convent, dropping out before taking vows. It was a pleasant conceit that she was still in some way attached to the Church, especially knowing that she shared the same confidentiality of the priesthood when it came to her clients' confessions.

What was she to do?

She had not informed her lover of the calls. She had not told anyone. Of course, she had recorded the conversations in her computer, and technically her supervisor had access to the files, as well as the upper-echelon staff at the HMO. But they never read her files. No one did. She made her notations and then referred the client to any number of services that were provided for the relief of their problems. Nothing like this had ever happened before. She was trapped by the ethics of her own profession.

But she had to do something.

What if he killed again?

The thought tortured her. He had already killed twice. There could be more. Who knows how many? Was she to just stand by silently while other innocent victims were slaughtered?

Agitated suddenly, she stood and threw the remote down on the couch.

There had to be a way to inform the police. Some way of letting them know.

She had to do something.

There were three inmates on the council.

Holly only recognized one of them. His name was Evans.

He was a serial rapist and had been one of her clients. She had worked with him individually and in group sessions, but because he was due for release, she had not seen him for over half a year. He was thinner than she remembered. His face was haggard. There was a desperation in his eyes, which were sunk deep in their sockets.

They brought her to the COs' off-duty room where the three inmates were waiting. She had to walk a gauntlet of piercing gazes from the inmates collected beneath the tiers. Even the faces she recognized, those who had been her patients, stared at her with alien glances. She felt the chill of hatred and became conscious of the sharp edge of separation between them. She was no longer the source of rehabilitation and the possibility of parole. Someone who could save them from themselves and the hopeless despair of their affliction. She was now their enemy.

The three inmates sat in semidarkness inside the room. Their faces were painted in stark tones of black and white by the sharp beams of the searchlights penetrating the glass dome.

"Sit down," Evans commanded.

A hand clamped over her shoulder forcing her into a chair set before the table behind which the three inmates were seated.

"Do you know why we brought you here?" he said.

Holly shook her head.

"Do you have any idea what this is about?"

"Conditions," Holly said. "The overcrowding."

He looked at her, his lips formed a sneer.

"Overcrowding, bullshit. There are a hundred and sixteen men in this unit. Forty-six of them have served their time but haven't been released. Does that tell you something?"

"I can't do anything about that," Holly said. "I don't set the policy."

"You're the only one in here who seems to give a shit about it."

Holly looked up at him, wondering how he knew. But then, the inmates seemed to know everything that went on in the prison, even before the staff.

"We brought you here because we want you to make the case for us."

Holly nodded. "I understand. And I'll try, but I don't think it will work. It's the political system you're fighting."

"That's why we thought we should make some noise; then maybe the politicians will sit up and take notice."

Holly waited a moment before she spoke. "It's a long shot. You realize that. The public isn't very sympathetic, especially not for . . ." Her voice trailed off.

"A bunch of rapists and child molesters," he said, completing her thought.

"You're not giving your lawsuit a chance," she said, referring to a suit taken on the inmates' behalf that had been making its way through the courts.

"That could take years."

"That's not what the lawyers say."

"All lawyers are liars and scumbags. We're tired of being in here, rotting to death."

Holly looked at him and nodded.

"Even if one of us gets released, where do we go? No one wants us near them. We've got to register wherever we go. Local people get wind of it and we get run out of the fucking area. Now, they won't let us out of prison even after we serve our time. Not even when you certify we graduated the program. So what the fuck do we do? Spend the rest of our lives in here?"

"Enough of this bullshit," the inmate beside him interjected. "Let's get on with it."

Evans shifted in his seat. "Okay, here's the deal. They got a negotiating team set up. They want to know what we want. You're gonna tell them. You're going to do the negotiating for us. These are our demands."

He pushed forward a piece of paper. Holly picked it up in both hands and briefly scanned the list. What they wanted was hopeless.

"What if they don't give in to your demands?" Holly asked.

The inmate beside Evans leaned in toward her. His hand closed over her wrist painfully. His eyes were dark points of menace.

"You better hope the fuck they do."

The report came in a little before midnight. It confirmed that the body was the bishop's. It was not very welcome news. But Pinero took it with a calm, almost stoic expression.

"And the cause of death?" he snapped.

Dan's lips tightened. They were standing in the small office belonging to the assistant Warden that the DA had appropriated for himself. It was just down the hall from the main command post where the negotiating team was stationed.

"He was crushed to death. Every bone in his body was broken. I mean, every single bone."

"How the hell does that happen? A steamroller roll over him?"

"It happens when you're placed in a metal vise and somebody starts turning the screws."

Pinero stared at him.

"What the fuck is this?" he spat. "First we get Mckay drawn and quartered and his head stuck on a pole, now the bishop gets crushed to death."

"And his body suspended in cage so the birds could have a picnic," Dan added.

"You think both crimes are connected," Pinero stated. It was not a question.

"You tell me."

Pinero stared into deep space. His eyes were smoldering. "I'm telling you they're not. Not unless we get a whole lot more to go on."

"What other conclusion would you draw?"

"Okay! Here's a conclusion. We've got a predatory priest who's responsible for sixty, maybe seventy separate criminal actions. He goes up and people are happy. Justice has been done. Only the appellate court says the statute of limitations has run out so he gets released on a technicality. People are angry. They want revenge. They want retribution. So someone or some group goes out and axes him. Cuts him up good. That's consistent with the anger in this community. Only the story doesn't end there. There's also a bishop who may have designed a cover-up, who may be responsible for sending Mckay out to do his dirty work. So someone one else gets angry. Got me?"

"Or the same individual or individuals," Dan added.

"Not until I say so. Then it's official. Right now we're looking for different strokes from different folks."

"It adds up to the same M.O. to me," Dan commented.

"Not to me," the DA snapped back.

"You can fool some of the people . . ." Dan's tone was dry.

Pinero glanced at him sharply, anger rising in his eyes.

"I want a task force set up. Now. No delays. Get me experts. Put them to work on this case and get me a result. I mean a result. Is that clear enough for you?"

"Clear," Dan said. "Whether you like the result may be a different matter."

"You let me worry about that. What are you waiting for?"

Dan nodded, turned on his heel, and left the office. He had started down the hall when Clara hurried out of the CP toward him. Her face wore a look of deep concern.

"What's going on?" Dan asked.

"They just got through to the unit. The inmates have picked a negotiator. It's Holly."

Dan looked at her. "Jesus."

"That puts her right in the middle of it," Clara said. Her voice was agitated. "Even if she wins, she loses."

"It won't get that far."

"What if it does and the negotiations break down and they go in?"

"They won't."

"They could. We could have another Attica on our hands."

"That's not possible."

Clara's expression changed. "Why not? The public has zero sympathy for cons in general. And we got us a group of predatory sex offenders. How many votes do you get if you send in a couple of SWAT teams and start slaughtering them? Just show me the body count. I'd say that would guarantee anybody's reelection."

Dan was silent. In his gut he knew she was right.

Twelve

Gunmen spread out on the roof.

Black-garbed, their silhouettes were visible through the glass dome, moving like the flitting shadows of ninjas across the shimmering surface. Everything now depended on the first few hours. They had to get their message out by then or everything they had done would fail. And the face that reported their message belonged to Holly Alexander.

Holly had no illusions. It was a message no one wanted to hear. A howling of the damned. She knew the prison authorities would have no qualms about storming the unit, quelling the riot, and killing the rioters. The question was, would they also kill the messenger?

These thoughts hammered in her skull as they hustled her out of the CO's ready room and into the glass-enclosed control booth overlooking the unit, sat her in a chair, and handed her the telephone.

"My name is Frank Jacobs. I'm going to do the negotiating. Have you been harmed in any way?"

She looked up. Evans stood opposite flanked by his two associates. He held another receiver to his ear. His face was grim. His eyes were almost invisible within their deep sockets. Other inmates were grouped on the tier outside; their eyes glared at her from the shadows. Though she could not see them, she was conscious of the other men below; all of them, she knew, were watching her.

"No. I have not been harmed."

"Who's speaking for the inmates?"

"I am."

The line went still.

"Are the other officers okay?"

"Yes. As far as I can tell. I haven't spoken to them but they seem all right."

"That's good. Are you able to speak without being overheard or is there someone else on the line?"

Evans made a negative gesture.

"No one else."

"Are there any guns in their possession?"

Again Evans shook his head.

"No."

"Explosives?"

This time, Evans nodded.

"I believe so."

"Can you be more specific?"

"These men are desperate. They will do anything to get released."

Evans nodded.

"All right," Jacobs said, "let's hear what they want."

"Before I talk to you, I want to talk to the television cameras. I want my own press conference."

Evans looked at her in surprise.

"What are you talking about?" Jacobs said.

"I want you to let a camera crew in here. They'll be perfectly safe. They can come down the corridor and we'll meet them halfway. No prison personnel. Is that understood? In exchange you get two of the correction officers."

Evans's expression clouded. He grabbed the phone out of her hand and slammed it down.

"What the fuck are you doing? Who told you to say that?"

"I thought you were doing this to get your message out. How do you expect to do that if you don't involve the press? You can't expect the prison authorities to speak for you."

Evans looked at the other two.

"Why did you promise them the hostages?"

"You've got to give them something. That's how it works. Besides, you'll look better if you release them."

"Fuck. If you're trying to pull a number on us . . ."

"What number could I possibly pull? You wanted to make your case, didn't you? Isn't that what this is all about? I'm giving it to you. Or you can just forget it."

She saw the confusion in Evans's eyes.

"We're supposed to go out there and speak to them, is that it?" Evans said.

"No. Just me."

The men flanking Evans shook their heads.

"No fucking way," Evans said.

"If you're there, it'll looked coerced. I'll look like the victim. And that's the last thing you can afford."

"What if you decide to take a walk?" one of the men said.

"You've got two more hostages that guarantee I won't."

Holly looked directly at him. Strangely, she felt no fear. The panic and trepidation she had felt earlier had gone. She felt calm inside. I must be crazy, she thought. But she had needed to take some measure of control. She could not tolerate being helpless. She might ultimately be their victim, but she did not have to go to her doom quietly.

Evans had withdrawn to the far end of the booth along with his two cohorts. She watched as the inmates shifted uneasily outside. She heard them muttering and realized how delicate the balance of control was. It could slip away from Evans at any moment. Then the organization he had imposed would dissolve like wet tissue. One misstep and she would be faced with a howling mob.

Evans came back toward the desk.

"Okay," he said. "Let's try it out and see what happens."

Dan stood in a corner of the crowded room filled with
state police and prison brass and watched as the negotiator
put down the phone and turned to face the others. Jacobs
was a sturdily built veteran with graying hair and the hardened eyes of someone who has seen much more than he ever
wanted to.

"They want a press conference," he said.

Voices broke out in disgust. Pinero raised his hands, si-
lencing them.

"What does that mean?"

"TV cameras. Talking directly to the media."

"Whose idea was that?" Pinero snapped.

"Hard to say. There's one voice on the line, but they're
probably monitoring her."

"And this is the hostage speaking? What's her name?"

"Alexander. Holly Alexander."

At the mention of Holly's name, Dan's brows knitted. He
knew Holly's feistiness. She wouldn't be anyone's mouthpiece. She knew these men. Some of them had been her patients. They had kidnapped her for a reason, which was quickly
becoming apparent.

"Where's her supervisor?" Pinero said looking around.

"Right here," a voice called out from the rear of the room.
Heads turned toward Ted, who took a few steps toward the
front. He did not look particularly happy at being the center
of attention.

"So what do you think? Is she being used by them or is
this her idea?" Pinero said. The question was hurled like a
jab.

Ted considered for a moment. "That's not easy to say."

"Without the bullshit. Is she on their side or ours?"

Ted hesitated. Dan could read the calculation in his eyes. To support Holly or dump her.

"Hold on a minute," Dan called out as the eyes in the room turned toward him. "She's on nobody's side."

"How do you know?" Pinero responded.

"Because I know Holly," Dan continued. "I've worked with her. The inmates kidnapped her because they thought she could help them. They want to put a sympathetic face before the public is my guess. They know she's fair. But she's nobody's fool. Especially not theirs. She knows who they are and what they're capable of."

"Is that right?" Pinero said as he turned to Ted.

"She made a case that keeping them beyond their term was unconstitutional," Ted said.

"She was worried about the potential that this place might blow. She never made a case for anyone," Dan said. His tone was harsh.

"This isn't getting us anywhere," Pinero said. "The question is, do we put her on the air?"

"They've offered to release two of the hostages," Jacobs said. "How's it gonna look if we turn that down and something happens to them later on? I say, let them have their news conference."

Pinero looked at the faces around him. He could read the consensus in their eyes.

"Okay," Pinero said. "Give it to them."

Dan let out a deep sigh of relief. Pinero was a ruthless bastard. But the one thing he was not was reckless. He knew they had to keep the situation low-key, short, and bloodless. Dan prayed that would be the case.

Holly was surprised.

The reporter they had chosen to let in was a woman.

Holly recognized her from the never-ending parade of

early evening news anchors. She had the polished anchor-woman look, a hard-boiled expression, highly styled hair, and overly done makeup. She came toward Holly down the long stretch of windowless corridor, past the control booth in the center manned by several correction officers in bullet-proof vests, military helmets, and gray one-piece jumpsuits. She was trailed by a beefy cameraman whose face was obscured by the viewfinder he was filming through.

Behind Holly were the two nervous-looking COs who were to be exchanged. When the reporter crossed the mid-point, Holly nodded and the two officers hurried down the hall passing the reporter and cameraman who came toward her.

Farther down was a group of correction officers armed with automatic weapons. Holly's stomach tightened. She did not want to get caught in the middle of a shoot-out. She glanced back over her shoulder. Evans and a group of inmates were lined up against the wall. Like the others, Evans's face was covered with a pillowcase cut with two eyeholes. They concealed sharp-edged shivs in their hands. Holly worried that the officers had orders to rush the inmates. Please, God, she prayed, don't let that happen. The presence of the reporter seemed to guarantee against it. But Holly had little faith in the logic of the Department. She had seen too many decisions made by prison officials go the wrong way.

"We've got ten minutes," the reporter said when she stood across from Holly. "I'll introduce you, then ask a few questions, if that's okay?"

Holly could see the nervous strain on the reporter's face though she was doing a good job of masking it.

"Shoot," Holly said.

"Let's hope not." The reporter glanced back over her shoulder at the phalanx of armed officers behind her.

"Okay, Len?" she asked the cameraman.

"We're rolling," he answered.

"Good. He'll shoot over my shoulder. So just look into the camera."

Holly nodded.

"This is Evelyn Brooks. WKYN news. We're inside the Brandywine correctional facility. With us is Dr. Holly Alexander. She is a psychologist at the prison. She is also a hostage. She has been given permission by the inmates to represent them. Okay, Dr. Alexander. We're listening."

Holly shifted the paper in her hands containing the outline of the inmates demands. She looked up at the camera and began to speak.

"So, what do you think?" Pinero asked turning to the men gathered in front of the TV with a questioning glance as he snapped off the remote.

The image had just switched from the hallway, where Holly had just finished speaking, to the anchor desk, where two clueless talking heads attempted to interpret what they had just seen to the viewing public.

"She laid out their case, but she didn't do a bleeding-heart routine," Jacobs said. "I give that to her. She's got guts, going back in there. She could have bolted."

"Granted," Pinero said. "So where do we go from here?"

"I'll get back on the phone and see what I can do," Jacobs said.

"How long are they prepared to wait it out?" a voice called out.

"I don't see this going more than seventy-two more hours," one of the prison administrators said. "Not without food, water, or electricity."

"We don't know how much food and water they got stored away," another voice added.

"We'll give them twenty-four hours," Pinero said.

"Then what?" Jacobs asked.

"We'll storm the unit."

The room grew silent.

"You're prepared to lose the hostages?" Jacobs asked.

"I'm not going to be dictated to by the lowest form of slime in this society," Pinero said.

That was going to be the sound bite, Dan realized. He had miscalculated. Pinero had made his decision as soon as the riot was announced. He had balanced out the possibilities. Long and bloodless against quick and gory. He'd opted for blood. It would make excellent headlines. *DA puts down prison revolt. X number of sex offenders killed in prison takeover.* It made perfect sense. The public wanted their blood anyway. What the hell, even he wanted their blood. It was only Holly's involvement that made him balk.

"That makes no sense," Dan called out as heads snapped around.

"And why not, pray tell?" the DA said, his pig's eyes narrowing to slits. He was not a man you contradicted, especially not in front of a room full of cops.

"Because, number one, they're not going anywhere. Number two, they're not a menace to anyone except the three hostages, who they'd be pretty stupid to harm. And three, not after they just had their little protest pretty effectively aired before forty or fifty million people."

"Finished?" Pinero said. His eyes were glaring.

Dan nodded. He stared back hard at the DA.

"Any other comments?" Pinero said. No one spoke. He glanced at his watch. "Seven-thirty tomorrow, this is history. Get on it."

The room burst into activity as the various department heads went into the chief administrator's office to work out the details. Dan took a step toward the door, passing Ted, who glanced at him with a chilling look just as his beeper went off.

Dan checked the number. It was detective Sergeant Frank Palumbo, his second in command. He took out his cell phone and dialed.

The call was answered after two rings.

"I think we may have something," Palumbo said.

"Like what?"

"A lady who works a psycho crisis line who says someone confessed to the murders of both Mckay and the bishop."

"Come on, Frank," he said impatiently, "those are the usual nuts. They always come out of the woodwork as soon as they hear the news."

"Maybe. Only this guy called before anything was reported. She's got it recorded."

Holly put down the phone and paused before she looked up at Evans and the other inmates who had crowded into the command module. She had just listened to the call from Jacobs.

"They've given you twenty-four hours to surrender," she said in a quiet tone.

Instead of the anger she expected, the men around her were silent.

"And if we refuse, what?" Evans asked.

Holly realized the question was aimed at her.

She waited a moment, then shook her head. "I don't think you have a choice."

"You think they'll risk a bloodbath coming in here? You think Pinero has the balls?"

"I think that's exactly what he wants," Holly stated.

"And why is that?" someone asked.

"Politics. He's calculating that the public will give him brownie points for squashing a few of your heads, removing you from the taxpayers' responsibility. Think about it."

"You think he's willing to risk you and the other hostages?" Evans asked.

"I don't mean anything. Not to someone like Pinero. He wants to climb into the governor's mansion and you just handed him a stepladder."

"So, what do we do?" Evans said.

"Pull the carpet from under him. Tell them you're ready to surrender now."

"Now?" Evans said.

Angry voices broke around him, shouting, "Fuck that!"

Holly forced herself to remain calm, to ignore her hammering heartbeat. Evans raised his arms and the voices quieted.

"What the hell do we get out of it?" Evans asked.

"Ask for two conditions. First, that they guarantee no retaliation. And you get it in writing."

"What's the second?"

"A guarantee that your case is moved up to the appellate court for immediate consideration."

"You think they'd do that?" Evans asked.

"It's worth a try. It's what you want, isn't it?"

Faces turned to one another. Holly could see her argument was making sense.

"Look, you got your plea out to the public." She raised her voice slightly. "What more do you want? Holding out in here, without food, water, or electricity, makes no sense. You won't get any public sympathy. You're only punishing yourselves. You're not free. You just don't have any guards watching you. Releasing us will add to the impression that all you want is a fair hearing. Think it over."

"Only one problem," Evans said.

"What's that?" Holly asked.

"There are only forty of us. The other sixty-plus guys in this unit are still doing time. They're not getting shit out of this. If they want to keep this thing going, it's gonna keep on going. Do I have to tell you what that means? You done good. But if they want to keep on rioting, how many of the guys in here are going to risk their necks looking out for you?"

Holly looked into his eyes.

What she saw in them sent a tremor of fear along her spine.

Thirteen

Their objective was a small frame house located on a back road in what had once been a deeply wooded area but was now bisected by two four-lane expressways. The house and the others nearby were the last remnants before the developers' bulldozers swept them aside.

"Jergen Schroeder." Palumbo said under his breath. "Come on. Give us something."

The suspect was forty-seven. Had a wife and two children, a boy and a girl. He had lived in the same house for thirteen years and worked as a manager of a small factory that made plastic tablecloths. It didn't get much more average than that. If he had decided to blend in with the background, his was a masterful disguise.

"Nothing," Palumbo muttered from his place in the passenger seat beside Dan Shepard.

"Nothing?" Dan echoed.

"Two years in the Air Force. Ten years in the reserves. Honorable discharge. No arrests. No rap sheet. Nothing criminal, either civilian or military. The guy maybe gets a speeding ticket every ten years or so. That's it."

"Let's go talk to him," Dan said.

They got out of their car and headed toward the house. Dan glanced around. His unit was spread out around the place, covering the driveway, the woods, and both ends of the road.

A boy of twelve or so answered Dan's ring.

"Who are you?" he said. He was holding a computer manual in one hand and squinting at them through the thick lenses of his glasses.

"Your father in?" Palumbo asked.

"Who wants to know?" the boy responded.

"Would you tell him we'd like to see him?"

"Sure. Who are you?"

"We're from work."

The boy looked at them doubtfully. "You don't look like you're from work."

"Do me a favor," Palumbo said, trying to mask the irritation in his voice, "go get your old man."

"He's not an old man." The boy turned and walked away. He left the door open. Dan glimpsed a barca lounger in front of a plasma TV screen. A shelf on the wall behind the TV held a grouping of soccer trophies and a framed portrait of a round-faced man in an Air Force uniform, his eyes circled by metal-rimmed glasses. A moment later the photograph materialized.

"Help you?" the man said.

"Jergen Schroeder?" Palumbo asked.

"That's right. My son said you were from the factory. Is everything all right?"

"We're not from the factory, Mr. Schroeder," Dan said holding up his ID. "We're investigators with the state police. We'd like to come in and talk to you."

Dan met the man's gaze. His watery blue eyes were filled with a strange expression. Whether surprise or terror, Dan could not yet say.

* * *

The cell was cold.

The damp cheerless chill of cold concrete.

The module had a dank smell, not of death exactly, more as if nothing had ever lived inside it. It was the smell of mausoleums and the dark cellars of old houses.

Holly remembered it from her childhood.

She sat on the bunk wrapped in a blanket that provided little warmth. She had lost track of the hours since she had been led out of the module to the cheers and whistles that came out of the darkness around her. Some inmates cursed her. Others called out words of desire or expressed graphically what they would do to her if they ever got her alone. She was no stranger to this kind of language; it was the language that filled her days, the dreamscape of her clients. Only now she had to fight to keep the words from terrifying her. At any moment they might become real.

It was Evans who ordered her removal to a cell when the voices inside became too raucous as the inmates began debating their next step. Holly had made her arguments. Then she had shut up. Years of conducting intensive group therapy had taught her when to stop talking and when to start. But there was a always a buzzer she could push for a guard if the arguments got out of control. She had nothing now but her fear.

In spite of the almost total darkness, the unit roiled as if it were an angry sea. Groups of men moved through the darkness. Voices exploded. Men argued and there was an occasional scuffle. But these were broken up quickly. So far there had not been a major incident. No one had been knifed. Not yet. But Holly knew it would only be a matter of time before that happened. The darkness would provide cover for some to settle old scores or revenge themselves for some wrong or perform some act of blood out of some mysterious dark need. Lack of impulse control was the reason most of them were in here. To expect them to act rationally was idiotic.

The longer it went on, the more the opportunity for violence would present itself. She had no illusions about that. The only question was whether it would erupt inside the module or come from the outside.

The calm she had felt earlier had dissipated, replaced by a stomach-clenching sense of anxiety. She was more than a target. She was an object of desire. A craving, so far unfulfilled. She was still being guarded by two of the inmates, but she wondered how long that would last. Or when her guards would become her attackers.

She bit her lip and tried not to think. Just listen to the terrifying movement around her and wait.

Jergen Schroeder sat in his chair and stared at them from across the table in the dimly lit interrogation room.

Dan felt as if he were asking questions in a foreign language.

"So you're saying you never made a call to the crisis line."

"Never," Schroeder said.

"You never spoke to a Mary Donnelly?"

"Never."

"Your health care ID is 906908. Is that right?" Palumbo said.

"That's right. That's my number."

"You never gave it to Ms. Donnelly on any of the nights we mentioned?"

"Never."

Schroeder had gone voluntarily when they asked if he would mind coming with them to the precinct. He had never even asked about what. His wife, son, and daughter stood docilely in the doorway watching as he was loaded into their car and driven away. He eyed his surroundings with a casual glance. "This is a little like TV," he'd said when they brought him into the room.

Was the man innocent or guilty? Dan had not yet made up his mind.

Usually he had a premonition. He had learned to rely more and more upon his instinct as he got older. Experience was a funny thing. It both taught and deceived. But he was not getting the usual signal from his gut. In fact, he was getting nothing other than indigestion.

"Did you know a Father Aubrey Mckay?" Palumbo asked impatiently. His face was turning red.

Palumbo was pudgy and inclined to overeat. His skin was pasty and moist. The line of work he was in was unhealthy. He should have gone into something else, Dan thought.

"Not personally. Only from the newspapers."

"Do you know a Bishop Horan?"

"I read about him too."

Dan leaned forward. "Can you tell us where you were on the nights we mentioned?"

Schroeder bent over the list of dates circled in red on the calendar page that lay on the table in front of him. "Bowling. On this night."

"You're sure?"

"It's Tuesday. I always go on Tuesday unless one of the kids are sick. We have a league. We're pretty good. Five and one," he said. His face lit with a smile, as if he expected congratulations.

"And on this date?"

Schroeder's brow creased. "Frankly, I can't remember. Do you have a *TV Guide*? Maybe I could figure it out from that."

Palumbo looked over. Dan saw the look of helplessness in his eyes.

"Maybe you could find one," Dan said.

"A *TV Guide*?"

"Just for the week in question."

Palumbo rose wearily and started out. The door closed quietly behind him. It sounded like a sigh.

"So you never called the hot line? We are checking your phone records, you know."

Schroeder looked at him, bafflement spreading across his placid features. "I never called a shrink in my life."

. For Mary Donnelly, each night had turned into a little hell.

The tension produced by each incoming call had become intolerable. With each ring the same message sounded somewhere in her brain.

It might be him.

Her instructions from the police were clear. If he did call, she was to make sure it was on the recorded line and she was to inform them the moment she hung up. But he had not called and that was even more agonizing than if he had.

Her mind was torn between the possibility of his calling and the guilt she felt for having betrayed his confidence. She knew she'd had to. Murder was involved. It was her duty. Still, what she had done violated one of her mostly deeply held precepts. Perhaps this was her punishment.

Razor edges of guilt sliced through her thoughts, making it difficult to sleep. Her lover, Georgina, had tried to comfort her, trying to ease her mind with comments about doing the right thing. But Georgina was not a Catholic. She had not been raised by parents who had wanted her to become a nun and offer her life to the Church. She did not understand what a promise like the one Mary had made actually meant. Mary felt as if nails had been driven into her skin. Her dreams had become strange tortured landscapes, inhabited by horrific-looking demons. Once she awoke in a frenzy believing her hands had been pierced with nails. She stared at them as if they were decorated with Christ's stigmata. She actually felt the syrupy thickness of blood on her skin. But of course, it was only an illusion.

She had lain awake for hours afterward, her nightgown

soaked with sweat. In the morning she had said nothing to Georgina, but after her lover went to work, she had dressed and driven past the old gray limestone church on Washington Avenue. She intended to stop and make her own confession. But somehow she had been unable to. It had been years since the last time. The burden of her intervening sins seemed too great. Besides, it seemed like an equally sinful betrayal of the life she now led and shared with her lover.

She drove around the block, unable to bring herself to park and enter the gloomy interior that smelled of incense and wormwood. She recalled the sourness of old Father Lenihan's breath and the bulk of his stomach beneath his shiny well-worn cassock. That had been so many years ago. Of course, he wouldn't be there now. Still, the shame of having to confess what she had become stung her cheeks as she drove beneath the shadow of the old edifice. In the end, she had driven home without even getting out of the car.

Mary glanced at the clock. It was just past one.

The section was strangely quiet. There hadn't been a call for at lease twenty minutes. There were three of them on duty tonight. One was away from her desk. She was an obese RN who clothed herself in shapeless flowered dresses. She was in the bathroom, Mary supposed, or off somewhere scouring the building's vending machines for something to fill her endless cravings. The other woman was slumped in her chair before the keyboard, her eyes closed.

Mary felt her tension ease. He had never called this late. She checked her watch. It was less than thirty minutes to her break. In half an hour she could lock herself inside one of the shrinks' offices and try to sleep. She was bone-tired. She prayed that this time she would not dream.

The phone was ringing.

Mary glanced over at the sleeping woman in the next cubicle. By rights this was her call. Irritated, Mary reached for the receiver, omitting the usual lead-in. People who called this late knew who they were calling.

"Help line. This is Mary. How can I help you?"

"How does it feel? Violating the sanctity of the confessional?"

It was him.

Mary sat bolt upright, her heart pounding. She almost allowed the receiver to slip from her fingers.

"Not going to answer me, Mary?"

"I . . . I don't know what you're talking about."

"Don't play games with me, Mary. You know very well what I'm talking about."

His voice frightened her. The almost syrupy cordiality he had expressed before was gone, replaced by a steely accusation.

"Please . . ."

"Have they instructed you to keep me on the line so they can trace the call? They'll discover that it's not possible."

"I'm sorry. I can't continue this conversation."

"You can and you will. You betrayed me, Mary. Worse, you betrayed yourself. There is a price to be paid for betrayal, Mary. I think you know that."

"You killed someone. I couldn't keep that secret."

"You surprise me, Mary. I placed my confidence in you and you betrayed that confidence. Those who betray must be punished. You know that, Mary. You of all people. You were once a nun. A nun now living in sin with another woman."

His words startled her. He knew all about her. She was frozen. Terrified.

"It is beyond me, Mary. It is the sacred law and I am bound to avenge those who betray it. Farewell, Mary of the Carmelites."

The phone clicked off.

She sat still. She was not breathing.

Her pulse hammered in her ears. She knew she had to call the police as she had been instructed, but that no longer mattered. Nothing mattered anymore. She felt the crushing vise of guilt enclosing her as his words echoed and reechoed in her mind.

It is the law and I am bound to avenge those who betray it. . . .

Georgina had made her swear to call her if he made contact with her again. But neither Georgina nor anyone else could help her. No one could help her. She had transgressed and her transgression must be punished. It was as if she had been waiting for this ever since she refused her veil and quit the convent. She could do nothing now but wait for her fate to find her.

Fourteen

They came for her just before dawn.

Holly opened her eyes.

She was on the upper tier. She had two blankets wrapped around her and she was still freezing. It was terribly cold. There was no heat, no water or electricity. The unit was already beginning to smell with the rank odor of urine.

She had been unable to sleep, only dozing off for an hour or so at a time. But her sleep was shallow. She did not dream. She slept listening with one ear, with the alertness of a trapped animal. The unit had quieted down sometime after midnight. Until then it had resonated with shouts and cat-calls.

During the night, what she had been most afraid of had begun to happen. The group of inmates controlled by Evans, those who had served their time, began to lose control. Different groups had formed in the pitlike darkness. Some wanted to quit. Others wanted to keep the disturbance going. While others wanted to create as much destruction as they could before the inevitable end. This was the group she feared the most.

Evans had promised to keep her safe. But as the hours

passed, she doubted his ability to keep his promise. And now, she had no faith left.

She heard the sounds again.

She sat bolt upright on the cot with her legs beneath her. She leaned forward and craned her neck.

The door was ajar. But there was no one guarding it. The two inmates Evans had stationed there had disappeared.

She swung her legs over the edge of the cot and rose.

The sounds were louder now. They sounded like fingers scraping on metal, growing louder as they approached. She realized someone was coming up the stairs.

They had to believe the guards were still there or they wouldn't have been so quiet.

She threw off the blanket and went to the door.

Above, the glass dome glowed with solemn predawn grayness. But it offered no illumination. The tier beyond was as inky as the mouth of an underwater cave.

She pressed her body against the door frame and fought for calm.

The stairs were to her left. She heard the scrape of leather on the metal rungs. The damp shuffle of a body against the railings.

She had to move. And move now.

She ducked through the doorway and started down the tier to her right.

She kept back against the wall, moving cautiously in her stockinged feet. Heading for what, she had no idea. What was in front of her promised no safety. She was among predatory sex offenders. The touch of her body could set off them off. Even her smell was dangerous. Raping her under cover of darkness was one of their dream fantasies. She had heard enough of them during daylight therapy sessions. Now she was among them and they were protected by the very darkness they dreamt about.

Her heart was trip-hammering. She fought to keep her breathing quiet. Her fingers slid along the wall and touched the doorway of the next cell. She slipped past the open glass door and kept going. The tier was circular. If she went too far, it would take her back around to where she had started. There was another staircase halfway around. It led down to the tier below. But most of the inmates had congregated on the lower tiers to be away from the dome. That was where they expected the attack would begin. With choppers firing heavy-caliber rounds through the glass. Just as the troopers had done in Attica. She knew this from listening to the inmates' voices in the darkness. She knew that was what they were most afraid of. They knew the longer the standoff continued, the surer they were marked for death.

She moved past another cell. Then another. None of them seemed occupied. The thought of hiding inside one of them crossed her mind, but she realized that if they found her she would be cornered with no chance of escape. Her best chance, she reasoned, lay on the tier outside the cells.

She took another step as hands suddenly stabbed through the darkness.

They seized her by the shoulders and threw her down to the hard metal floor.

"I've got her. I've got the bitch," a voice hissed.

She doubled her leg and drove it upward as hard as she could. Her knee found its mark. She felt the soft under-flesh of his groin.

He cried out, howling in pain.

The hands released her. She reached out, found the railing, grabbed it, and scrambled to her feet. She dodged forward as movement erupted behind her.

Several bodies collided behind her. They were as blind as she was. She heard curses, then the thud of feet against the floor plates. Panicked, she realized there was no place to hide. They would be on top of her in an instant. She started to run.

"Evans!" she shouted.

"Shut the bitch up!" someone behind her whispered.

"Where the fuck is she?"

"There. Ahead. I can see her. Stop her before she gets to the stairs."

Holly became aware of the light. The whole dome glowed as day broke. She could see the doorways of the tier ahead and realized that she was visible. Her stomach convulsed with fear.

A dark shape came up from the stairway ahead, cutting her off.

It was Martinez. Her serial rapist. Ted's revenge on her.

His mouth widened in an obscene grin.

She turned, but there was nowhere to run. In an instant, they would be on her.

She halted and turned to face the men behind her. She could make out their shapes but not their faces. Terror welled up in her like a giant wave.

In that instant, as the wave swept down to engulf her, she saw their mouths tearing at her like ravenous hyenas. Their bodies thrashing as they penetrated her, then the knife that swept toward her like a sliver of glass, descending to slit her throat.

She heard her own scream.

But the sound seemed to come from a distance, not from her open mouth. Then it wasn't coming from anywhere but from everywhere. A deafening shriek that erased all sound, followed by a searing explosion of light that burnt her retina, wiping out all the details of her vision and leaving her blinded by the whiteness of an arctic winter.

The assault on the unit was completed in less than twenty minutes.

Stun grenades were followed by a phalanx of COs in riot gear, carrying shields and batons, along with members of the State Police SWAT team with automatic weapons. Electricity was supplied to the gates, which rolled open as the officers went in.

The inmates' barricade of piled tables and chairs did not withstand the charge. Blinded inmates sat or wandered in dazed confusion. There was no organized defense and except for one or two belligerent inmates who were quickly subdued, no one offered any real resistance. The officers seized control of the command platform and rescued the hostages. None of them had been harmed. Evans and the other ringleaders were seized and hustled off to solitary. There was no bloodshed, to the disappointment of the DA and his staff as well as the mob of media waiting outside.

Dan went in on the heels of the first wave along with a squad of state troopers dressed in protective gear. He raced through the tier, shining a powerful searchlight into each cell, then went up the stairs to the second tier, where he found Holly crouched against the railings. With the help of two of the troopers, he was able to get her back to the administrative area, where she was checked by one of the doctors in the medical team that had been standing by. Other than being in shock and suffering the temporary blindness from the stun grenades, she was physically in good shape. All they had to worry about was her mental condition.

Clara was waiting when she was released from Medical and led Holly back into the office. The area was empty. Clara had coffee brewing and placed a streaming cup in Holly's hands. Holly sipped it gingerly.

"What happened to the hostages?" Holly asked.

"They're all okay," Dan replied, accepting another steaming cup from Clara. "Looks like no one was hurt."

"Any inmates injured?" Holly asked.

"Nothing serious. No body counts, this time."

Holly nodded to herself. The medics had put a bandage over her eyes that she was to wear for the next few hours.

"So, how's our girl?"

Dan looked up as Ted stepped inside. Dan's lips tightened with distaste.

"Holly. It's Ted. How are you doing?"

"I'm okay," Holly said.

Ted perched on the edge of the desk opposite.

"You did great," Ted said. "Everyone's glad you made it."

"Including Mr. Pinero?" Holly said, her voice tinged with sarcasm. "I'll bet he wasn't happy with the box score."

Ted forced a smile. "Same old Holly. Now I know you're all right."

Dan glanced at Clara and by the chilling look she gave Ted, he realized there was no love lost between them either.

"Here's the deal," Ted said. "You're on medical leave until further notice. Full pay and benefits. So, you got yourself a nice little vacation."

"Suppose I don't want a vacation," Holly said.

Ted's grin widened. Dan could see the effort he was putting into it.

"Hell, Holly. After what you've been through. You deserve it."

"That's very decent of you, Ted. But I want to be sure I understand this sudden concern for my welfare."

Ted's smile faded. Ice formed in his eyes. "What does that mean?"

"Cut the bullshit, Ted. I'm being put on leave because I was the mouthpiece for the inmates and that doesn't sit well with the powers that be. True or false?"

"Not exactly."

"Then what exactly?"

Ted rose. "Enjoy your leave."

"And when do I come back?"

"You'll be informed in due course."

Ted nodded in Dan's direction, then crossed to the door and exited without a backward glance.

"Fuck!" Holly exclaimed. "Fuck, fuck, fuck. That son of a bitch! There goes my job. Five years down the drain."

Clara knelt in front of her. "It's not as bad as that. Things will cool down. You're a tenured employee. They can't just fire you. You'll be back."

"Meantime, you can collect your pay and come work for me," Dan said.

"Doing what exactly?"

"I need a profiler. I've got to put a task force together and I want you on it."

"Working for Art Pinero? Not a chance."

"You're not working for Art Pinero. You're working for me. There's a serial killer out there and he's just begun."

"I don't think so. But it's nice of you to offer."

"I'm not offering it to be nice. You're the logical choice. I think this guy's some kind of deviate and when it comes to deviates, you're the best."

"That's some compliment."

"Just say yes."

Clara took her hands. "He's right. You're perfect. Do it." Clara was smiling at Dan and nodding at him encouragingly. "It's just what you need to take your mind off this place."

Holly was silent. Her lips tightened. "I'll have to think about it."

Dan nodded his agreement. But he knew how stubborn Holly could be once she made up her mind. He wondered if time would make a difference. And time was something he was quickly running out of.

Fifteen

Mary rose to her knees. The stone floor was cold against her skin.

Her knees were chaffed and bleeding.

She had prayed for a long time, then lapsed into a fitful sleep. But the cold woke her, chilling her to her bones. She was naked under the thin full-length garment, which was too thin to provide any warmth. In spite of the way it clung to her body, she felt totally exposed. Her head was still woozy. From what she could not even imagine. Some kind of drug probably. She remembered only walking back to her car from the rear door of the supermarket. It was dark and there were only a few other cars in the lot. She had been careful to scan the area for anything suspicious. But there was nothing out of the ordinary other than the big black Suburban parked in the spot next to hers. She had wheeled her shopping cart across the tarmac, unlocked her trunk, and started loading her groceries when she felt a wave of darkness overcome her like a soft thick cloud. She felt dizzy and for an instant she couldn't breathe; then she lost her balance and began to fall. But she never struck the ground. She was falling for a long time until she woke up in the stark stone cell, stripped of her clothing and her underwear and dressed in a surplice the color of dried blood.

Strangely, she was not afraid. Whatever happened had been ordained. She believed that deeply in her soul. She was prepared for whatever was to come.

There was no light in the room, only a kind of shimmering luminescence off the smoothly polished stones. She had found water in a metal pitcher beside the door that was made of ancient planks studded with huge nails and framed with rusting iron brackets. She had traced their outline with her fingernails. The room reminded her of the cloister where she had gone to become a nun. It had thick stone walls and dark recessed arches where the sisters walked in silent prayer. Yet there were certain sweet memories she treasured. Her first taste of another woman's lips and the tensile feel of a tongue exploring her mouth. There were other intimacies too she would have to atone for. That was why she was here. To be judged and to receive her punishment. Still, she prayed, if not for deliverance, then for forgiveness. She had sinned and now she must pay.

She halted suddenly, her hands clasped, her lips still forming the words of the prayer.

The door was being unlocked.

She heard the scraping of the key. Then the squeal of the heavy iron hinges as the door swung back.

She was blinded for an instant until she could adjust to the light streaming in from the outside.

She got off her knees and went to the door, facing the long corridor dimly lit by burning tapers held by brackets fixed into the stone walls.

A voice echoed, "Come."

She shook the garment free from her legs and walked out of the cell and down the cold stone corridor toward the dark archway beyond.

* * *

Graduation.

Why did it always come with a sense of pain?

Was it for a past that could never be recovered or the unrealistic expectations that had not been met? Whatever it was, a needle of anguish was present in the pit of her stomach. A needle that would not go away.

Holly had driven over to the campus with her sister Beth, who looked lovely in a pretty black dress and smart leather coat. She had given her a corsage, which Beth had accepted with a smile. She had half-expected Beth to make some sardonic remark and pin the flowers behind her ear. But that had not happened. Something had changed in her sister since she decided to complete the course work for her degree.

As they drove, Holly realized that the pain she felt was not for her sister, but for herself. She was now compiling the list of regrets. Everything from her failed marriage to her inability to form a commited relationship with Dan Shepard. So instead of sharing in her sister's joy, her stomach was tight, soured with vinegar from the past. She tried to shake herself free of the emotion, but it wrapped itself around her like a cassock.

It had been almost a week since she had been given the leave of absence. The wound was still deep. She felt betrayed as much by her coworkers as by the system. Few of them had called to express their support. Clara kept telling her that everyone felt bad about it, but Holly was not inclined to believe her.

"What's the matter, sis?" Beth asked as they approached the campus. "Got the graduation blues?"

Holly smiled. "Oh, just feeling that Mom and Dad would have liked to have been here."

"Oh, come on," Beth retorted sharply. "Mom and Dad? Dad couldn't stand being around me."

"They would have liked this."

"I didn't do this for them. I did it for myself." Beth paused and looked away. "And maybe for you."

Holly was silent. "Thanks for saying that," she said.

"Forget it. When it comes to family, you've been it. End of story."

Holly could not blame Beth for feeling the way she did. As much as she tried, she could not make the past come out right for her sister.

They turned into the campus following the directions of the student parking guides.

It was very cold. The trees were bare and stiff, standing gritty and barbed with clawlike branches. The lawns were brown and dotted with icy puddles. Holly and Beth put their heads down and walked side by side along the path toward the hall where the ceremony was being held.

"See you later," Beth said as she headed toward the rear clutching the box that held her cap and gown.

The hall was already filled, but Holly managed to find a seat along the side aisle where there were still several empty chairs. She perused the program and found Beth's name. There was an asterisk beside it indicating that she was graduating with honors. Holly was surprised. But it was just like Beth not to tell her anything about it. Holly felt a surge of pride and could not help smiling.

"Something I should know about?" a voice beside her said.

She turned in surprise to find Dan seated beside her.

"That smile," he said. "It's been some time since I've seen it."

Holly flushed and showed him the program pointing to where Beth's name was asterisked.

"Nice going. You must be very proud of her."

"I am," Holly said. "What are you doing here?"

"I was invited," he said, holding up his invitation. "Is that a problem?"

She shook her head. She felt a twinge of embarrassment. He had left several messages and she had not yet called him back.

"I owe you a call," she said.

"You certainly do. Been busy?"

"I've been trying to catch up on my files. I had some reports to do."

"Still no word on your reinstatement?"

Holly shook her head.

"Give it more time. Just don't let it drive you crazy." He looked at her. "Or has it already done that?"

Holly shrugged.

"So come work for me."

She was silent. Music filled the hall. The familiar sounds of Elgar's processional march. There was a murmur of excitement and they all stood as the graduates began filing into the hall.

The floor was cold beneath her feet.

She struggled forward but the corridor seemed interminable. She had lost her strength. She stumbled ahead and each time she faltered, the same deep voice intoned, *"Come."*

She could not fathom where it came from. It filled the space like a kettledrum. Her own heart beat wildly inside her chest. She thought she was ready but she was not. All the calm she had felt, the calm feeling of resignation, had evaporated, leaving only terror in its wake.

"I'm afraid," she whispered. "Please, Lord. Protect me."

But even as she said it, she knew there would be no protection. No divine intervention. No one would save her. She was beyond saving. She was on the threshold of the eternal.

"Come."

She hadn't realized that she had halted. She took a breath. The icy air singed her lips. Her limbs felt leaden. Her skin felt covered in permafrost. Perhaps she was already dead. But she knew she was still alive. The throbbing of her pulse in her temple informed her of that fact. It felt as if a nail were being driven into her brain.

She staggered forward, pressing her hands together in front of her in the position of prayer. Her lips formed the words of her catechism. She beseeched Mary to intervene in her behalf. But the sound was a rasp. She had lost the ability to speak.

Ahead was another archway. It grew brighter suddenly as she approached. She saw two huge tapers on iron stands. Light from both candles licked the slick stone walls. She was in some kind of tower. Darkness rose beyond her ability to see.

Facing her was a wooden platform. Steps rose to the top. A curtain surrounded it.

The voice rang out.

"You have been judged and found wanting."

She struggled to speak but the cry was strangled in her throat.

She heard the rustle of the curtain and looked up. The cloth was being drawn back.

At the sight of the device, she felt the blood rush away from her head and she dropped to her knees, terror twisting in her bowels.

The diagonal blade glinted in the candlelight. The sense of its sharpness traveled like a shiver down the length of her spine. She lost control of her bladder and felt warm piss on the inside of her thighs. She began to shake her head.

"No!" she cried again and again, "no, no, no!" as if the words could prevent what was to come. Tears, like streaming acid, bit into the skin of her cheeks. The sound of her cries echoed back to her in the darkness.

"Come."

It was the word her lover used when she held her in her arms. Now it commanded her to climb the platform and face the gleaming blade that was her death.

*   *   *

The restaurant was noisy.

It was filled with celebrants, families mostly, proud of their graduates, many of whom still wore their wine-red gowns. Dan had reserved a booth and ordered champagne, and insisted on refilling their glasses. Holly was glad he was there. So was Beth, who smiled shyly when he made a big deal of looking at her diploma. She had introduced them to several of her classmates and professors, many of whom came over to congratulate her. Holly was surprised at how many people Beth knew. She smiled to herself when she remembered Beth's many incarnations. But she could not help liking this one. Perhaps because this time Beth seemed to embrace her future. In all the others, the future was something she seemed to despise.

"So what now?" Dan asked once they finished dessert.

"I don't know," Beth said. "Everyone keeps pushing me toward graduate school. But I think I want a job."

"What are your prospects?"

"Zilch. Art history isn't exactly going to open any doors. Not unless I get something in a museum."

"Would you like that?" Holly asked.

"Are you kidding? I'd kill for it," Beth answered. "But you have to have the connections. Most of the people who do curator work have independent incomes."

"But not all of them," Dan said.

"Maybe not. I'll have to start looking and see what I can come up with."

"And if nothing materializes?" Holly asked.

"There's always advertising," Beth said with a grimace. "I might get something there. I wouldn't mind working for a cool magazine."

"Neither would I," Holly stated.

"You've already got a career," Beth said.

Holly was silent. She wondered if that were still true.

"You two won't mind if I leave you, will you?" Beth asked.

"There are parties to go to and people to see. I'm like the auntie around here, so they sort of expect me to show up."

"Of course not," Dan said.

"Sis?"

Holly shook her head. "Go and have a great time."

"Don't wait up for me."

"When have I ever done that?" Holly laughed. Beth had planned to spend the night at Holly's. Why exactly was not clear. But Holly agreed as soon as Beth proposed it. It was to be a celebration of sorts, a way of acknowledging her debt to her older sister. As usual, Beth could always be counted upon to change her plans, leaving Holly to deal with the disappointment.

Beth leaned over and kissed her, then gathered her things and rose. "Thanks for this," she said, looking at Dan. "And all the champers."

"My pleasure," he responded.

She started out of the restaurant, waving to several of her classmates.

"She's going to be all right," Holly said.

"Yeah. But will you?"

Holly looked at him. She reached for her glass and brought it to her lips. "I'm allowed to get drunk, aren't I? All things considered."

"Absolutely," he said with a grin. "I might even join you."

"I thought you were on duty."

"I'm always on duty. Didn't you know that?"

He moved closer to her. "You know, I've missed you." His eyes were fixed on her.

Holly was silent.

"Any possibility of us getting together for dinner, or a drink, or a little sex? I'll take any of the above."

Holly smiled. "Keep your fingers crossed. It may just happen."

"Which?"

"Be patient. Maybe you'll get lucky."

He raised his glass and they touched glasses. Right on cue, his beeper went off.

"Shit."

He reached inside his jacket and took it out. "My office. Three alarms. I've got to make this call."

"Go right ahead. I've got this to keep me company." She tilted her glass.

He made a face, then drew out his cell phone and hit a button.

"Shepard. Go ahead."

Holly tuned out the conversation, which consisted of one-syllable words. She bit into a breadstick and was chewing absently when he put the phone away and turned to her. His expression had changed. He was all cop.

"Something wrong?" she questioned.

"I think we've got another victim."

"Who is it?"

"A priest. Ex-priest. Father, or no longer Father, William Cole. One of the priests released along with Father Mckay by the appellate court because the statute of limitations had run out."

"I didn't know there were any others beside Mckay."

"There weren't. Not immediately. It was purely political. They were released from different institutions at different times. The governor's office didn't want it to appear as if the gates were opening and all the child molesters in the state were being let out onto the streets at the same time."

"What happened to this Father Cole?"

"He disappeared about two weeks ago from a halfway house run by the Dominican Order. They didn't report it at first. Their people go missing all the time and usually turn up after a binge. They reported it to the diocese and we were notified. It's been kept from the press. "

"And now?"

"We think we may have a body. That's what the call was about."

"So you have to go?"

"I want you to come with me."

Holly paused. "Isn't the DA running your task force?"

"The only one running it is me. I put on who I want. That's the deal."

"You think he'd let me work with you?"

"He doesn't have a choice."

She looked at him and her expression changed. "You know, that's a concept I think I could get to like."

Sixteen

They could hear the dogs as they approached, their howls high-pitched and excited.

The kennel was located on a back road, set among the trees amid a collection of trailers and sheds.

A large wooden cutout of a dog was set in front, indicating that they specialized in pit bulls. A sign beside it read: ANIMALS TRAINED FOR SECURITY AND HOME PROTECTION. The darkness was pierced by yellow spots strategically placed around the area. From the road they could see two rows of kennels facing each other with a large enclosure at one end surrounded by wire-mesh fencing. That was where they had discovered the body.

Yellow tape had been stretched across the long curving drive, which now contained an assortment of police vehicles, their lights flashing brightly against the sodden sky. Dan drove in and pulled up alongside a police cruiser. He rolled down the window allowing a trooper to lean in. The trooper glanced at Holly, then whispered something in Dan's ear.

Dan's lips drew to a grim line as he turned to face Holly.

"Look. This is going to be rough."

Holly returned his look. "I'll handle it."

Dan nodded, then opened his door and got out as Holly stepped out of the car. They followed the trooper along the driveway as he filled them in.

"People were out for the evening. They came home and found the dogs had been let out. Then they found the body."

"They never saw him before?" Shepard questioned.

"Nope. Though the husband said he recognized him later from the papers. It's around this way."

They followed the trooper around the back of the kennel heading toward the large enclosure at the other end. A forensic van was drawn up in front of the open gates. Several white-suited figures moved back and forth hauling out equipment. The dogs had been herded into a side enclosure. They leaped and snapped at them as they went by.

"Watch yourselves," the trooper warned as they approached. "They're trained to tear people apart."

Holly drew back as the slathering jaws tore at the metal fencing. The dogs were large and powerful with muscular chests, thick necks, and the frightening ugliness of the breed. Holly had always been wary of them. She eyed their wide dripping mouths with distrust as she rounded the enclosure and approached the open gates.

"Where's the body?" Dan asked.

"He's hanging over there." The trooper gestured as they stepped through.

They halted in their tracks as they looked up.

"Jesus Christ," Dan said through clenched teeth.

Holly's chest tightened in a vise of horror.

In the center of the enclosure was the naked body of a man suspended in midair.

The body was lit by a small yellow spot fixed in a nearby trailer. He was hanging from a chain attached to a girder protruding from a metal shed. The other end of the chain was affixed to a gleaming metal hook embedded in the base of his skull. His head was enclosed in a metal helmet.

Painted on the front was a grotesque distortion of a human face.

For an instant, Holly was unsure of his sex. His genitals were no longer there. Neither was his belly. Only a single dripping cavity. Her eyes dropped. Below him on the ground was a shredded mass, something indescribable.

Holly felt nausea rising in her gorge. Her legs felt rubbery and her vision clouded.

"Steady," Dan whispered as his fingers gripped her arm. "Take a deep breath."

Holly tightened, sucking the chilled air into her lungs. Her vision cleared.

"Okay?" he asked.

She nodded. "Okay."

One of the forensic technicians came toward them, a young Asian with the muscular body of a gymnast.

"Inspector."

"Hey, Norman. What's the deal?"

"Too early to tell. But it looks like he was hung up there first, then somebody cut him open and let the dogs do the rest."

"His genitals?"

"Cut. By a razor or some kind of surgical knife. Looks like the dogs got that too. Could have been the appetizer."

"Was he killed first?"

"Can't tell yet. Have to wait for the autopsy."

"What's your best guess?"

"I think he was still alive. Maybe that was the whole point of the procedure."

Dan nodded. His mouth formed a tight line.

"Dig the mask," Norman said. "Something out of the movies, huh? This guy's got some sense of humor."

"Not any movie I'd want to see," Dan said. Norman nodded and headed back to his van.

"Number three," he said in a low tone.

"You think they're all connected?" Holly said.

"You tell me. That's why I'm bringing you on board."

* * *

Her sleep was dark and fitful. Filled with disconnected images and dangerous precipices on which she struggled to keep from falling. She woke several times. The room was cold. She went down to check the thermostat. On the way back she opened the door to Beth's room. It was two-thirty and Beth was still not home. The house felt alien, as if it were not her home but some stranger's house. It felt that way even when she put on a light. She went into the kitchen and made herself a cup of tea, struggling to rid herself of the image of the man in the kennel and the horror of what had been done to him. Her mind was divided. He had been a molester of young women, and deserved to be punished for it. But not like this.

The tea was cool enough to drink just as Beth came through the door.

"Still up?" Beth said with surprise.

"I couldn't sleep. How was the party?"

Beth slumped down at the table opposite Holly. "Parties, plural. There must have been a dozen. I think I wound up at all of them. But I didn't get laid, in case you were wondering."

"It never crossed my mind."

"It should."

"You're impossible. Do you want some tea?"

Beth nodded. "I must have had ten martinis."

Holly looked at her as Beth smiled. "All nonalcoholic. Can you even imagine a nonalcoholic martini? It's like a Shirley Temple but without the little umbrella. I used to love that little umbrella. I hate being nonalcoholic. But I was the designated driver. So you can pin a medal on me. No wonder I didn't get laid."

"Can we change the subject?" Holly said as she prepared the tea, regretting the words almost as she said them.

"Aha. Now we're getting somewhere. When was the last time you got laid?"

"None of your business."

"Is it still Shepard's business?" Beth said with a sly look.

Holly put down the cup in front of her sister.

"The witness is pleading the fifth," Holly said as she resumed her seat.

"What's the matter. I thought you and he were a couple."

"Not exactly."

"What does that mean?"

"We see each other from time to time, when we can."

'Which means you haven't had it in how long?"

"Oh, come on."

"No. You come on. I thought you liked him."

"I do."

"But?"

"But nothing. It's just been hard, what with our different schedules."

"Do you like the guy or don't you? And if you do, why aren't you sleeping with him?"

"I *have* been sleeping with him. But it's more complicated than that."

"If it is, you're with the wrong guy."

"I'm going to be working with him from now on."

"Ah! The plot thickens. Doing what?"

"Profiling."

"Good. Profile yourself while you're at it. You might find out something interesting."

"Like what?"

"Like why you can't commit to a relationship with a guy you've been dating for almost two years."

"I think I'm going to bed," Holly said as she rose.

"Nighty night."

Beth was smiling like a Cheshire cat. Holly shook her head and continued upstairs. She got into bed and pulled up the comforter. The room was warm now. Her eyes closed and she slept. She dreamed she was alone on a raft beneath dim gray skies in the middle of a silent heaving sea, drifting to nowhere.

The task force was located in the back wing of an old red-brick two-story building that once housed the administrative functions of the state police but was used now primarily as a records storage center. Dan had two adjoining suites on the second floor. One was set up as an analysis center containing several large green bulletin boards on wheels containing information on each of the victims. Adjoining it were an informal office and lounge area where the members of his task force could make calls, eat, and consume endless cups of coffee from three glass percolators that were constantly brewing. The offices were in need of paint and airing out. They reeked with the musty aroma of disuse. It was an orphan operation, connected to the DA's office only by a tenuous umbilical through which it received its finances and authority. One that could be easily snipped if it in any way proved embarrassing.

Holly arrived early and was introduced to several of the detectives working on the analysis team. There were three besides Shepard and Palumbo. Two of them were women. The other was a veteran in his early seventies who was fighting his own war against retirement. His name was Betts. Nicola and Dawson, the two women, were in their late forties but looked older. They wore unsmiling expressions and greeted Holly coldly. Dan seemed oblivious and gave them a brief rundown on Holly's background indicating that she would be handling the profiling. Hearing that news, Nicola, the older of the two women, shoved a thick brown manila folder toward Holly.

"This is what we've got so far," she said brusquely. "Enjoy."

"Thanks," Holly responded. "I'll try."

Father Cole's photograph was taped to the green board together with his arrest record and indictment. Beneath it was a map of the various parishes where he had served. It resembled the other two green boards except for the index cards indicating the different leads. The small force of field operatives consisted of three two-person teams. Exactly six in number.

"Not a very big commitment for a task force," Holly commented.

"When do we let her in on it?" Dawson said. She was a short blonde with a crew cut and a generous figure restrained by her bullet-proof vest. She wore braces and her fair skin looked raw, as if it had been sand-papered.

"Let me in on what?" Holly asked.

Nicola edged back onto the desk, fixing Holly in her gaze. "Hang around long enough. You'll find out." She was taller than Dawson, flat-chested and wide-hipped.

"Why don't you just tell me," Holly said.

"You were part of that prison thing," Dawson said, her eyes narrowing with distrust.

"That's right," Holly responded. "Is that a problem?"

"Not for me. People around here wouldn't have minded if they blew the place up instead of giving those scumbags therapy."

"I'm one of the therapists who treat them. Have you got a problem with that?"

"We don't have any problems," Dawson said with a icy smile.

She turned her back and walked away. Nicola swiveled around on the desk and picked up the phone. Holly nodded to herself, lifted the file, and walked toward where Dan was conversing with Betts. He motioned with his hand, halting the conversation as he turned to Holly. "You okay?"

"Sure. Where do I work?"

"Use that desk over there." He pointed to an empty desk in the corner opposite the green boards.

"We'll be doing a briefing as soon as the autopsy report on Cole comes in."

"Thanks." Holly crossed the room and took a seat at the desk, opening the folder and spreading the materials across the surface. She glanced up and caught Dawson staring at her, her forehead knotted in a frown. Holly ignored the look and began to read. She had dealt with bitchy females all her life. She could handle this.

An hour and a half later the briefing began.

Holly and the others formed a half circle around the green board as Dan faced them. "The autopsy report concludes that Cole was alive when he was hung up in the kennel. He was disemboweled while he was still breathing. He was also castrated. There's no way to tell if that was done before or after his guts were sliced open and fed to the dogs."

None of the faces showed any reaction.

"Forensics is still working on the area, but so far there's nothing that would give us a lead."

"No tire tracks, nothing?" Betts commented.

Dan shook his head.

"So it's like the others. Nothing to go on," Betts said.

"Exactly. Whoever's been doing this is adept at covering his tracks. He or she is also good with a knife. No wasted strokes. No hacking. Everything is clean and sharp."

"Medical training?" Betts asked.

"Possibly," Dan responded.

"What about the mask?" Nicola questioned.

"Good question. Anybody got an idea?"

No one spoke.

Dan turned to Holly. "What do you think?"

Holly paused. "It looks like something out of the Dark Ages, which would tie it to the other two murders. It could be a signature. Or it could be some kind of joke. The first victim was impaled, then drawn and quartered. The second was crushed and hung out to dry. This one was castrated and disemboweled."

"What's your best guess?"

Holly shrugged. "Too early to tell. But I think whoever is

doing this is trying to send some kind of message. What, I don't know. But it seems as if it's all been preordained. As if there's some kind of logic behind it."

"What kind of logic?" someone said.

"I don't know exactly. These all seem like a series of ancient punishments. Where they come from, I don't have a clue. This is just a guess. But I am assuming we're considering them all connected? I mean, officially."

Their faces turned toward her appraisingly.

Dan was quiet for a moment before he spoke. "Officially, there is no connection. Not without absolute corroborative proof. Which, of course, we do not have."

Holly stared at him. "Then we might as well quit."

"Then we'd have nothing. The investigation would go back to homicide and be distributed on an individual basis. Case by case. By keeping them here, we can at least explore different possibilities. Look for links. Just as long as none of them are official. Do you understand what I'm saying?"

Holly nodded. "I think so."

Betts raised his hand. "So where do we start?"

"At the beginning. At every place he ever worked. Parish by parish. He had a forty-seven count indictment. We'll investigate every one of them. One of his victims may have opted for revenge or there may be a citizen out there with the same idea. Any comments?" He looked around. There were none, only expressions of futility.

"Okay. Let's go to work."

"Why didn't you tell me about the constraints?" Holly said fifteen minutes later when she managed to corner Dan in the glass cubicle he used as a private office.

"There are no constraints," he answered.

"What you said out there, about officially—"

"Forget it. You do whatever you need to."

"I don't understand."

Dan sighed looking up at her from behind his desk. "It's very simple. Pinero only authorized this so-called task force as a public relations gimmick. He doesn't want us to establish any connections between these crimes, not officially. That would mean there's a serial killer or killers out there and that's the last thing he wants the public to know."

"But that's what it looks like this adds up to."

"Maybe yes, maybe no. We're giving him plausible deniability. No matter who accuses him of what, he can always say he's got a police task force on the job. Experts who have come up with no evidence of any kind of serial killing."

"But what if we do?"

"Then we might just go public first. Look, the fact is he trusts me as much as I trust him. Which is zero. He's using us and we're using him. And in the meantime we do what we're supposed to. We find this killer and put him away. Clear?"

Holly looked at him and smiled. "Clear. I'm sorry I doubted you."

"You should be sorry about a lot of things when it comes to me."

He was smiling. Holly looked away. She felt a twinge of embarrassment. He was probably right, but she would fight like a demon before she would ever admit it.

Seventeen

He didn't see the bees, not at first.

Only the mysterious flutter that seemed to vibrate the air and suddenly made him tense.

He had been walking along the path that led past the ball fields, then crossed behind the old farm that had once belonged to the convent but was no longer being farmed. The orchard still bore fruit but no one seemed to be tending it, or so it seemed to the boy. He was fifteen, though he looked a little older. His upper lip was covered with a dark growth of down. Acne was beginning to percolate on his forehead.

He turned up his collar against the biting wind and continued following the serpentine path of muddy earth as it switched back and forth along the border of the fields.

He had already walked several miles, but he was not tired and was determined to cover at least another mile or two before he turned back. He had decided to go out for track in the spring and was in the process of building up his legs for the effort. The cold weather made it more difficult, but he would not change his routine. When it got boring, he just went off in a different direction.

He could see the convent wall clearly now. The red brick

buildings were largely deserted, but several old sisters still lived in the place. Most of them were impossible to recognize as nuns now that they no longer wore any kind of habit. But once in a while he spotted one or two of them shopping in one of the local malls. You could always tell who they were by the plain clothes they wore, their simple unstructured haircuts, and often a black crucifix dangling from a chain around their necks. They had a look of serenity on their faces that reminded him of his own grandparents, whom he saw less often than the nuns since they lived almost halfway across the country.

He followed the path around the wall where it switched back again to avoid several old free-standing sheds tucked in a corner of the orchard.

That's when he discovered the bees.

It was strange, because he knew that when the weather got cold, bees sort of hibernated. He wasn't clear on the details, but he knew they no longer swarmed the countryside as they did in summer. Yet there they were. Flying back and forth over the half-dozen or so small green painted boxes that normally held their hives.

The boy was nervous about approaching. He did not want to get stung. But the bees seemed not to notice him as they continued their circular movements around the boxes. Most of the old hives were dilapidated. Backs had fallen off. Tops had caved in. It looked like deliberate vandalism, but it could have been neglect. But the bees did not seem to mind. He could see the exposed grids inside where the insects built their colonies. The buzzing grew louder as he neared them.

There was a lot of activity, especially around the last one. He quickened his pace, not wanting to linger. It could be dangerous. He had never had much trouble with bee stings, but he had heard of people who did and someone had once told him a severe sting could be fatal. In spite of these warnings he kept to the path, fascinated by the danger and being so close to the hovering creatures. He had forgotten about the dreariness of the landscape and the tiredness in his legs. His adrenaline was kicking in and he felt a surge of exhilaration as he approached the final hive.

Something was not quite right.

Bees were all over it. Masses of them. Buzzing and whirring in an intense kind of frenzy. There was something inside. Something yellow and waxen. But it was not structured like the others. This was rounded. The shape familiar.

He bent and picked up a small round stone and flung it hard at the side of the box.

At the impact, the swarm rose like a covering of hair blown back by the wind.

He saw what was beneath and froze in horror.

Covered by the thick ooze of amber honey was a human head.

Beneath the waxen gel he could make out the features of a woman. Her mouth was open, filled with furry crawling bodies.

Her empty sockets were filled with the movement of a hundred tiny wings.

Eighteen

The Forester Institute stood on the crest of a wooded ridge like some medieval fortress prepared to repel an invader.

It was an imposing collection of buildings in the neo-Renaissance style, made of brick and marble with colonnades supporting rows of intersecting arches. The buildings wrapped themselves around atriums open to the sky. Luxurious gardens were enclosed within shadowed cloisters. It had once been a Benedictine monastery, but that was long ago in the 19th century. Newer wings had been added, but in conformity with the original style. Besides extensive collections of religious art and carvings of the Middle Ages, it had one of the best medieval libraries in the country, containing the most comprehensive archive of church documents outside the Vatican.

It was there that Holly went to hear a lecture on the fine art of revenge.

The lecture was given by Victor Pascal, an expert in medieval history and one of the curators of the institute. All of that was printed in the colorful folder that accompanied her ticket of admission. She had never been to the institute before. But she knew that it had been endowed by the Forester family, one of the wealthiest in the state. They had made their money in coal and steel in the long-ago days of the robber barons along with men like Frick and Carnegie. Like them, the Foresters were known for their many endowments and charities. But they never carried the stigma of ruthless exploitation like the other two.

Holly was immediately impressed by her surroundings. The grounds were enormous and sprawling. Even the parking area had been constructed to seem as though it were a part of the medieval surroundings. The lecture hall was located just off one of the marble-lined galleries that exhibited various works of religious art. Holly was fascinated by several of the reliquaries. Fashioned out of ivory, they were meant to serve as portable altars during pilgrimages and contained carvings of tiny figures of saints as well as Mary and the infant Jesus.

The lecture hall was wood-paneled with a high arched ceiling that reminded her of a chapel she had once seen in a cathedral in Brittany. Holly was surprised at the large turnout. The room was filled with scholarly types, retirees, and others who had purchased tickets to the series of lectures on life in Renaissance Italy given by Pascal. But then, she shouldn't have been. Entrance to the institute was only granted to scholars and visiting academics. The public was not admitted. So, for many this was a chance to enter the inner sanctum and savor the pungent atmosphere, as the man seated next to her explained with a smile of satisfaction as if he were about to be served a sumptuous meal. He also reminded her to turn her cell phone and beeper off.

When Pascal entered, the room immediately hushed.

Holly was again surprised. The man behind the lectern was only in his middle forties. He was tall and slender with graying hair and well-defined, almost graven features. He had a deeply resonant voice and an imposing but not overwhelming manner that made what he said seem authentic without being pedantic or boring. There were no practiced jokes or pleasantries to charm his audience. Rather, he seemed like someone deeply steeped in a subject he immensely enjoyed and wanted to share with others. He was warm and charismatic, and Holly observed many of the women in the audience as they drank in what he said with glowing eyes. And a few of the men as well.

But it was what he said that really fascinated her.

Illustrated with slides from a hidden projector he operated with a remote, Pascal unraveled a tapestry of revenge, vendetta, and political murder committed in the name of the Medici, the Este, and the Borgias, as well as other powerful families of the period. Blood seemed to seep through the threads of the tapestries around them as he continued his tale of poisonings and assassinations. Holly was mesmerized. The room grew warm as the audience sat enraptured by the way the story unfolded, their eyes absorbed by the images that flashed on the screen.

At one point, Holly felt a claw of terror grip her flesh as the screen showed a man suspended in a cage, left to rot to death. Others showed men being flayed alive or disemboweled. In another, a man was drawn and quartered, his body hacked to pieces. Another showed a man being garroted as he sat in a chair, his eyes bulging like onions as the pressure forced them to burst out of his head.

She turned away as images of the murdered priests flooded her mind.

The lights went up as the room burst into applause. Holly glanced at her watch and realized that she had been there for over two hours, yet it seemed as if she had just sat down.

Pascal was surrounded by an admiring group of questioners, so Holly waited until they dispersed and he began to move out of the hall. She followed quickly as he headed toward a gate at the end of the gallery.

He sensed her presence and half-turned, a fixed smile on his face. "I'm sorry. The public isn't permitted past this point," he said.

"I'm not the public," Holly stated. "I'm with the police."

He paused and turned to face her. "What can I do for you?"

"My name is Holly Alexander. I'm working with the CID task force investigating the murders of Father Mckay and Bishop Horan."

She presented the temporary ID Shepard had obtained for her.

Pascal took it from her hand and scrutinized it as she examined his face. His eyes were a startling shade of blue. His jaw was covered with a steely black stubble. Not a beard exactly, more like several days' growth of hair. It contrasted with the neat blue button-down oxford and knit tie he wore beneath a tweed jacket with classic leather elbow patches.

"All right," he said, handing the ID back to her. "My office is this way."

A uniformed guard opened the gate passing them through. They entered a long wood-paneled corridor faced with imposing sets of double doors. They continued to the end where Pascal opened one of the doors and gestured for Holly to enter.

She stepped into a large anteroom lined with shelves containing hundreds of leather embossed volumes. Bronze sculptures rested on elegant antique marble tables.

"My office is inside." He crossed the room to a door in the opposite wall.

"Very impressive layout you've got here," Holly said.

Pascal smiled as he opened the door admitting Holly to the inner office, no less sumptuously decorated. A series of enormous windows opened on views of rolling hills and deeply forested glades.

"Part of the estate?" Holly said as she looked out.

"Yes. We have quite a bit of property. Please sit down."

Instead of going to his desk, he indicated a sitting area furnished with two facing leather couches and a glass-topped coffee table.

"Can I get you anything? Coffee or something stronger?"

"Just water."

He poured her a glass from a silver carafe and placed it in front of her as he took a seat on the couch opposite. Their eyes met for an instant, then each looked away.

"I was at your lecture," she began after taking a quick sip of the chilled liquid. She wondered if the bathroom taps ran champagne.

"Really? Is revenge an interest of yours?"

"Isn't it everyone's?" she said with a smile. "But that's not the reason I came."

"Oh?"

"There are certain details of these cases that have not appeared in the press as yet. I would have to have your word not to disclose them."

"What would I be signing?"

"Nothing. I would have to rely on your discretion."

"All right. I think I can manage that."

Holly looked up and caught the cool glint of his eyes measuring her. "Each of the victims was killed in a particularly gruesome way," she said.

"I'm not squeamish."

"I didn't think you were. Not from the lecture you gave."

"How were they killed?"

"One was impaled, then beheaded and cut into four separate pieces. His body was displayed on a metal device."

"What kind of device?"

Holly reached into the thin leather binder she had brought with her and produced a photograph, which she placed on the table in front of him. His eyes narrowed as he surveyed the image of the metal cross.

"And the other?"

"Bishop Horan was placed in an iron cage and crushed to death. Every bone in his body was broken. The cage was suspended from an old tower on some land owned by the diocese."

"Do you have a picture?"

Holly slipped a photograph out of her case and placed it alongside the first.

Pascal reached down and picked it up. His eyes grew intense, but she could not read his expression.

"There was a third victim. A priest named Father Cole. He was found hanging in a kennel. Dogs tore out his stomach. This was covering his head."

She placed a picture of the mask on the table.

"An iron mask," he said almost under his breath.

"I'm sorry?"

"It's been made to look like an iron mask. Do you remember the Dumas story *The Man in the Iron Mask*?"

"I thought that was fiction. Hollywood-style."

"It isn't. It existed. As did the man who was forced to wear it. No one ever discovered his identity. But the mask actually predates that."

"What do you think?" she asked when he placed the photo beside the others.

"That you're dealing with someone who would have enjoyed my lecture. Perhaps he was in the audience."

Holly forced a smile. "Can you make anything out of it?"

"First of all. What is your part in the investigation?"

"Why are you asking?"

"Because you don't seem like a typical detective." His eyes again fixed on her.

"I'm a psychologist. I work at the Brandywine Center for Sexual Disorders. I've been asked to develop a profile of the killer."

"I see."

"I need help. Lots of help. I'm not embarrassed to ask for it."

"That's unusual. Most of my colleagues would rather die first."

"How much of an imposition would it be?"

He shrugged. "The institute prides itself on public service. Since I'm chief curator, I suppose I should say none at all and that we'd love to be of service."

"What are you really saying? Because if that's a brush-off, I need to know now, so I can go elsewhere."

He looked at her and smiled. "I like your manner, Ms. . . . Alexander? Are you a PhD? I should call you Doctor."

"Please don't. Just call me Holly," she said. " But I'd like to know."

"I'm not brushing you off. I'll have to study these before I give you an analysis. If that's okay?"

"Of course," Holly said, relieved. "When can I expect it?"

"Just give me a few days."

He rose and Holly rose with him. He went to his desk and took out a small card.

"My number is on this. Fax and e-mail. Where can I reach you?"

"Oh, sorry." She fumbled inside her bag, then took out a card and handed it to him. "Ignore the number at the prison. I'm on temporary leave."

"I knew you looked familiar," he said. "You were involved in the recent disturbance, weren't you? You spoke up for the inmates."

"Sort of. It wasn't exactly voluntary."

"Maybe not. But you made some important points. It's something we as a society have to deal with."

Holly tried to smile. She was finding it difficult to meet his gaze. She felt her face redden every time she tried.

"Well, thank you for your time. I'll just leave the photographs."

"Fine. And don't worry. No one but me will ever see them."

He extended his hand. She took it. His skin was dry, smooth, and hard. Even slightly callused. Which was unusual for an academic, unless he sailed or golfed.

Ten minutes later she was back in the parking area. She drove away with a warm feeling in the pit of her stomach.

Exactly why, she refused to question. She didn't need any more complications in her already overburdened existence. She reached into her bag and changed her beeper from silent to sound, and instantly the interior of the car was filled with the ringing of gongs.

Nineteen

The nun was covered in honey.

Her head was a hive. Her body housed their queen. From her flesh the colony rose, a tormented, buzzing twister dazed by the plume of gas shot from a spray gun wielded by a man in a biohazard suit, looking like some medieval specter as he came through the gray cloud of dust.

Holly and Dan stood at a distance along with the rest of their task force and a brigade of fire and emergency units. A police chopper circled overhead making useless sweeps of the area as a fine misting rain came down, creating halos in the reflected lights of the police cruisers.

The DA remained secure within the phalanx of his public-relations people. The press was not yet in evidence, which in itself was a minor miracle.

After the first report had come in, police had gone out to investigate, retreating quickly as the bees began a defensive operation to evict the intruders. This was explained to Holly as she waited beneath the sheltering umbrella that Dan had secured from his trunk. A young long-distance runner had discovered the body. He stood nearby protected by a blanket, his hair a wet mat across his forehead. A beekeeper who had been called in, who gingerly made his way toward the hive, where he authenticated the boy's discovery and made a discovery of his own. The rest of the woman's body was cut in separate pieces inside the other hives, each segment of her flesh cocooned in a solid coating of beeswax.

"This is one diabolical son of a bitch," Palumbo muttered.

"Or bitches," Betts added.

"Or bastards," Nicola said, a grin spreading across her tired features.

"So who's right?" Dan asked.

"I don't know," Holly answered. "But why a therapist? What the hell had she done?"

"She was a nun. Maybe there's some connection."

"But so long ago and she never took final vows."

"She was a lesbian," Dan said hopefully. "If there's priest-on-boy abuse, there could be nun-on-novice."

"There could be a lot of things," Holly responded. "Right now I need to hear the tapes."

"What tapes?"

"She worked a crisis hot line, didn't she?"

"Go on."

"Every call is taped. That's how they work. She would have made tapes of her conversation with the person she said confessed to her. The tapes will be on file."

"We'll need a subpoena. That means getting Pinero involved. And that could take who knows how long, especially if he decides to stall. He'll fight like hell to keep this listed as a separate crime, unconnected to the others."

"Maybe we can get it without one," said Holly. "But I'll need you to back me up."

He looked at her. Holly was staring straight ahead, but her eyes had that look of fierceness that both frightened and attracted him. He nodded to himself. If there was any doubt in his mind before, it was now erased. She had finally locked in and come on board.

* * *

The crisis hot line was located in a medical complex in a crumbling older suburb north of Philadelphia. The complex was sited there a few years ago because the land was cheap. The local township board was hungry for any kind of development in the area; that and a few well-placed donations did the trick, never mind that most of the HMO's patients had to travel great distances to visit their doctors. When it came to the medical care system, Dan was a longtime cynic.

The supervisor they went to see was a hardened veteran, a blond-haired psychiatric RN named Lacey, with long years of service in the state's mental hospitals, now working happily in the private sector, which made lavish pension contributions on her behalf. She admitted them to her office, offered them a chair, and left almost immediately on an emergency.

"I think we're in trouble," Shepard murmured. "She looks like a Mafia hit man in drag."

"Easy on the similes," Holly shot back. "They may be recording."

Dan stared at her as Holly smiled. "Joke."

The RN returned, making no excuses for her absence.

"So, what can I do for you?" she said curtly.

"Mary Donnelly was a therapist here."

'That's right. She's missing."

"Not anymore," Dan said. "We just found her. She's been murdered."

The RN stared at them with widening eyes. "My God! When? I didn't see anything on the news."

"You will," Holly said. "That's why we're here. We need copies of her tapes."

"Her tapes, why?"

"Not all of them. Just several conversations she reported to the police."

The RN's eyes narrowed. "She reported conversations to the police?"

"We believe the man who made them may have been her murderer."

"They're confidential. They're protected by law."

"We can request a subpoena, but that would be a public record and could expose you to accusations of breaching confidentiality. People insured by your system wouldn't like that very much. It would also call into question your internal systems, the way you protect patients' records and lead to all sorts of other unpleasant accusations. I really don't think you want that."

The RN leaned forward. "What's my guarantee that none of that will happen anyway?"

"We don't give guarantees," Holly said. "But we have to find Mary's killer."

The RN looked at her and Holly could see the calculation in her eyes. "So long as they don't leave the building."

The tapes were indexed and dated, which made it less of a chore to go through them and find the applicable conversations. Since the caller had used the name Jergen Schroeder and provided a system ID number, it was not difficult to locate them. The RN provided Holly with an empty office located on a distant floor. It contained a gray desk, a swivel chair, and an empty filing cabinet. There was a phone on the desk, but it was not connected. Holly was provided with a tape recorder and several long metal boxes containing copies of the tapes. Before she left, the RN reminded Holly that she was not to listen to any of the other tapes. As if she wanted to! Holly felt like swinging a bat at her.

Hearing the voice of Mary's probable murderer was a shock. Holly had to keep reminding herself that nothing was proven. The call might be from someone who was seriously deranged. Dan did not have to remind her that the woods were full of the species. The police dealt with them every time there was a spate of crimes. The more bizarre the crime, the more the nuts came out to claim it.

The first time she heard the man's voice she was uneasy. The voice sounded unnatural. The tone was artificial. Almost mechanical. "This doesn't sound real," she commented.

Dan listened, then slipped one of the tapes into his pocket. "We'll run it through the lab and see what happens," he said.

"They're not supposed to leave the building," Holly said.

"Who said they were leaving the building?" he remarked innocently.

While she waited for him to return, Holly transcribed what she heard on a large yellow pad. She wrote down each phrase, playing it back for accuracy. She made no judgment as to what she heard until she was finished. There were only three conversations in all. Each lasted for only a few minutes. But what she heard was frightening.

Dan returned an hour after she finished.

"You were right," he said, seating himself on the edge of the desk. "We ran it through a vocal synthesizer. He spoke through some kind of device that would make the caller unidentifiable by a voice print."

"What about the sex?"

"Impossible to tell. Could be either a man or a woman. What have you got?"

"There were only three conversations," Holly began, "each lasting for only a few minutes. First he set the ground rules. He likened their conversation to a confessional and made her the priest."

"How do you mean?"

She turned the page so he could see. "He says, 'and you will keep what I say secret, as if I were talking to a priest.'"

"What did she say?"

"She said, 'Yes, if you like to think of it that way.' Then he said, 'The seal of the confessional is inviolate.' He even asked her if she were a Catholic."

"What did she say?"

"She refused to answer."

"Then what?"

"Then he repeats that she is bound by the seal of the confessional and goes on to talk about the priest who was murdered."

"Did he say how he heard about it?"

"No. He said it would be in tomorrow's news. I checked the date. Mckay's death hadn't been reported yet."

"Jesus," Dan exclaimed. His eyes narrowed with intensity. "This really could be the guy. Go on."

"When she asked him his involvement he said, 'You see, Mary. Those who betray the Cipher must die. I am the avenging angel. Which is why I had to order his death.'"

They both looked at each other.

"The Cipher?" Dan said. "What the hell is that?"

"I think the second conversation will tell us. He talks about the bishop being missing. He tells her it's a related story. When she asks which bishop, he says 'Why spoil the surprise?' He says she's the first person to know."

"What does she say?"

"That she's going to end the call. She tells him any potential violence has to be reported. But he tells her the violence has already happened. It's not potential. He tells her to watch her TV. She warns him not to take the law into his own hands. But he says, 'In my own hands? No, Mary. You misunderstand. Those who betray the law must be punished, isn't that so, Mary? What I am compelled to do is in the name of the Cipher.' She says, 'You mean the law of this state?' But he says. 'I must follow the dictates of a higher law. A law that commands me to avenge its betrayers. Just as you must follow the law and maintain our bond of secrecy.'"

"Which she obviously didn't do," Dan stated. "And he may have murdered her for it."

Holly nodded. She placed her fist on the pad. They sat silently for a moment, feeling the excitement of a major breakthrough, but weighed with the knowledge that they could not rerun the tape or make its reality reverse itself.

"This Cipher," Dan said. "What do you think? Real or imagined?"

"I don't know. Real in what sense? That it's something he's written down? Or are voices dictating it to him? Or is he making it up as he goes along?"

"Son of Sam listened to a dog," Dan said. "Is that what we're dealing with? Judging by the way he's killed his victims, he very well could be hearing voices."

But Holly shook her head. "No. I don't think so. There's a method here. I can sense it. I don't know what it is yet, or what this Cipher is. He may very well be insane, but I don't think he's psychotic. Meaning, he's not listening to voices or existing in another reality. His conversation is logical and precise. He sounds perfectly rational. Look how he split hairs about 'potential' violence!"

"Then how can he be insane?"

"Only in the way that his logic differs from the rest of ours. The way a man may be perfectly normal in every other respect, only he believes all Eskimos should be killed. And decides to actually kill them for reasons only he understands."

"Hitler?"

"Exactly," she said.

"So where do we go from here? I've got a voice no one will be able to identify. And a Cipher that may or may not exist."

Holly nodded to herself. What he said was true. But there was a single outside possibility that they might be able to find out. She was praying it might come through.

Twenty

They had lunch in a spacious walnut-paneled room with a huge bow window looking out over the institute's vast wooded grounds stretching away to a horizon of verdant evergreens. They were served by a waiter in a white jacket, black bow tie, and white gloves. The food was delicious and extremely well prepared, the table set with old silver and antique crystal.

"Do you eat this way every day?" Holly asked Pascal, who was seated opposite her at the huge polished table, which she estimated could seat at least twenty people.

A smile lit up his handsome features. "Actually no. This is usually for special guests. I generally take a tray in my office when I'm here."

"I'm honored," Holly said, trying to match his expression. "You don't sound as if you're here very often."

"My job comes with a certain amount of traveling. Often to Rome for consultations with the Vatican libraries. Others as well."

"Interesting work."

"It can be. But it doesn't sound as interesting or exciting as yours."

"It's overrated."

"I don't think so. Not after what I saw on television."

Holly felt her face redden. "That wasn't entirely my doing."

"So I understand. Still, you were in the middle of it. Were you ever frightened?"

"All the time."

He shook his head. "Somehow I don't quite believe that. You don't look like the kind of person who scares easily."

She smiled and lowered her gaze. "You'd be surprised."

The waiter cleared away the dishes and brought them coffee in an ornate silver service.

"Another treat," she said.

"Just coffee and some cake."

Holly stared at the array of confections on the tray being presented to her. "Madam would like to select?" the waiter said.

"How about all of them," Holly said with a laugh.

"We can wrap them for you to take home. They'll only go to waste."

"Somehow I doubt that."

Holly made her selection, a gorgeous-looking slice of chocolate mousse cake. As it was placed in front of her, she looked up at Pascal. "This is going to sound very pushy, but I have a sister who just graduated from college. She took a degree in art history and wants to be a curator eventually. Is there any chance you might have heard of something entry-level?"

"Possibly."

"Really? Where?"

"Here actually. I've been looking, or rather not looking, for an assistant. My last one left on maternity leave. Your sister isn't married, is she?"

"Not married, nor is she even seeing anyone."

"Well, that I can't prevent. I've just been traveling a lot

and haven't had the will to start interviewing. I've been putting it off. It's a process I hate."

"Can I have her send you a resume?"

"Why don't we just make an appointment? Who knows what will happen?"

He looked at her and smiled. She returned the smile and forced her eyes away. She felt her glance returning to his each time she raised her eyes from the plate. His gaze was compelling and magnetic, through she had trouble reading exactly what was in his look. He wasn't flirting with her. She realized that. He didn't seem the type who did. More like studying her or even analyzing her. But somehow she didn't mind.

When she called him and asked him about the Cipher, he had paused before he answered. She sensed he was the kind of man who thought before he spoke, a rarity. "I'll see what I can do," was all he said. He made no other promise, which was why Holly was surprised when the phone rang the next day and she heard his deeply resonant voice on the other end of the line. She liked the way he sounded. There was something about the way he spoke that intrigued her, something familiar yet foreign.

"I may have something for you," he said. Her spirits immediately rose. They were at a dead end since the discovery of Mary Donnelly's body, so anything, no matter how slight, was considered good news. When she informed Dan of the call, he raised his eyebrows, but she could see he was not impressed. "Sure. Go. Maybe he can help us with something. We need something. Anything," was all the enthusiasm he could muster. His attitude annoyed her, but what did he really expect from an academic like Pascal?

She had gone over Mary's tapes again and again, in the hope of gaining a deeper insight. But nothing revealed itself except for a series of half-baked theories, none of which sounded remotely convincing. In the meantime, Dan's outside teams brought in records of more interviews with an endless horde, people who were in any way touched by the murders of the two priests, the bishop, or the nun. They formed a huge interlacing web that still refused to yield a clue. Further frustrating her was the lack of news about her job. She was still on leave and no one seemed to know when it would be over and when she could return to work. Added to that, none of the promises she had been made on the inmates' behalf had been carried out. There was nothing she could do and no one she could complain to. Perhaps that was the method behind the madness of why she was being kept away from her job. Clara had suggested that, and when it came to the inner workings of the system, Clara was usually correct.

So she had gone to her meeting with Pascal with a sense of defeat, but when she saw him her entire attitude changed. He had a quiet charm that took her over. He asked if she had ever been through the institute and when she said no, he gave her a guided tour through many of the fascinating galleries. Besides the medieval manuscripts, the institute possessed extensive collections of medieval and Renaissance art and objects of every kind and description. From suits of elaborately embossed armor and weapons, to an array of magnificently jeweled stained glass, intricately carved ivory, and extraordinary pieces of ancient jewelry. She was astounded. It was like visiting one of the great museums of the world. After an hour, he paused apologetically. "I hope I'm not tiring you out."

"Oh, no. It's incredible. I had no idea."

"Not many people do. The Foresters were very secretive about their collecting. Why don't we stop for lunch. We can discuss what I found afterward."

She could barely contain her curiosity, but she nodded and said she'd love to.

Now, the waiter made another pass with the dessert tray,

but Holly fended him off and Pascal waved him away. His eyes fastened on her and his face returned to seriousness.

"When you finish, I'd like to show you what I've found."

Holly placed her cup back on its saucer. "I'm ready."

He rose, and she followed after the waiter drew away her chair.

Pascal escorted her out of the room and back along the elaborately paneled corridor. He opened a door and they entered a small anteroom where an elevator was waiting. He pressed a button and they descended to another level.

"We keep certain manuscripts in a private area," he explained as they stepped off the elevator into a long vaulted corridor. Unlike the upstairs galleries, the walls were plain. The area was dimly lit and cooler than the other rooms.

"Sorry it's so dark. The lighting helps preserve the materials, many of which are quite ancient. We also regulate the temperature."

"I understand."

"Here we are."

He stopped before a closed door, took a key card from his pocket, and slid it into the slot. The tiny light on the lock turned green and he turned the handle, admitting them to a large windowless chamber whose walls were a soothing shade of green. A large wooden table was positioned in the center. On it were several reading lights and magnifying lenses on stands. In the center was a large leather-covered folio embossed in gold with the initials FI, for the Forester Institute. A carafe of water and two glasses had been set out on a tray beside a phone console.

"Please have a seat." Holly settled herself in the armchair he indicated facing the folio. He took the seat alongside her.

"When you first approached me about the situation, I didn't think I could be of much help. The instruments you described were generally typical of the late medieval period. They were usually used for punishment of serious crimes.

But there was something about the way each of the victims was killed that puzzled me. Each was given a unique twist that somehow didn't quite fit the pattern. The first victim, for instance."

"Father Mckay," Holly added.

"Yes. Father Mckay. He was beheaded and quartered. Normally, it was either one or the other. Usually beheading was punishment for treason or an attempt against the life of the ruler. As was being drawn and quartered. But he was also impaled."

"Which seems to have been done first," Holly interjected.

"Yes. With a white-hot iron, as the autopsy seemed to indicate. And then he was quartered while he was still alive. Why both?"

"And Bishop Horan?"

"The same thing. He was crushed to death. Then hung up for display. Also curious in that it combines two punishments that were unusual for the time."

"I don't understand."

Pascal paused and clasped his hand together. They were long and well shaped. Pianist's hands, Holly thought.

"Well, a prisoner was usually condemned to be put on public display and was sometimes placed in a small cramped cage in which he couldn't stand or sit. The cage was usually hung from a tower until he died of exposure or starvation. Crushing a prisoner in the same kind of cage wasn't common at all. In fact, I couldn't find any reference to it anywhere. So that also piqued my curiosity. "

"How?"

"It's obvious that whoever is committing these crimes has an unusual familiarity with medieval implements. But more than that, especially when we examine the implements themselves. They're not only elaborate copies, but they indicate that the killer might be following an almost ritualistic method of killing his victims."

"Being disemboweled by dogs?"

"Oddly enough, yes. It was used to punish especially egregious sex crimes. Pigs were also employed. It was common practice to feed them the victim's intestines and sex organs while he was still alive."

"My God." Holly shuddered.

"Human history is not pretty," he said grimly.

"What about placing his victims in a hive?"

"I'm not certain how that fits," he admitted. "But honey is a lure. If the woman had in some way lured him to do something or give him her trust and then betrayed that trust." He ended, his glance fixed on her.

"That is plausible," she responded.

"But too far-fetched?" he said with a smile.

"A little perhaps. But what kind of ritual are we talking about?"

"I'm not quite sure. But it occurred to me that the perpetrator might be doing each act as a punishment for a specific crime he considered his victims to have committed. Am I making myself clear?"

Holly nodded. "Perfectly. It's consistent with the motives we've been considering. Both revenge and retribution."

"Exactly. So when you called and told me about the Cipher, it suddenly fit. I remembered reading something about a manuscript years ago when I was a student in Rome. It was called the Demon Cipher."

"The Demon Cipher?" Holly said. "It sounds pretty ominous."

"I had forgotten all about it until now. I don't know if this will have any bearing on the case. But I thought you should have a look for yourself. Please feel free to use the phone. If you get hungry, dial nine and our concierge will see to it, as well as anything else you need. We like to make our visiting scholars as comfortable as possible."

"I won't have a problem," Holly responded.

When he left her alone in the room, she opened the leather folio and began to read. The phrases she read wove a tapestry of another time and place, filling her mind and imagination until the words became pictures and were restored to a life of their own . . .

Twenty-one

Fra Alfieri hurried through the darkened streets of the ancient city. The stones of Rome were beneath his feet. Dark stones that ran with blood.

Alfieri was huddled in his robes, his face shadowed within his cowl. His was the narrow face of an ascetic. His deep-set eyes glittered with the fervor of his belief. His beard was as coarse as the long brown garment tied around his waist with a thickly knotted rope. He wore sandals though it was winter, and his feet were red and chapped. Beneath the coarse material of the robe he was naked. Naked and cold. He welcomed the knifelike chill as he welcomed the chaffing of the rough wool against his skin. Pain kept him vigilant. All around him was sin and lasciviousness. The city reeked of it. Evil permeated the walls and crept out of the sewers. Sin, blood, and the vitriol of minds poisoned by lust and greed.

Many of these wore the cloth of the Church.

The rich silken robes of cardinals and bishops.

The highest ranks of the Holy Church had been corrupted by sin.

The monk had witnessed much. He was, after all, secretary to Cardinal Volpe, who was the cardinal responsible for car-

rying out the most secret missions of the Vatican. Tucked inside his robe was the message he had been entrusted with. It
carried a heavy waxen seal impressed with the crossed keys
of ultimate power.

Its delivery promised death.

In the beginning there was the word.

And it was his facility with words that caused Alfieri to
leave the monastery and be summoned to Rome. He had entered the thick masonry walls of the Benedictine fortress
when he was only seventeen. But already he had shown a vocation. He had been selected for religious training by his village priest whom he had attended as an altar boy. His father
was an ignorant peasant who had sired a dozen children. Fra
Alfieri came along somewhere in the middle. Slightly built
and not strong enough to handle the heavy wooden plow that
sliced through the rocky thin-layered soil, little Paolo was
disregarded by his wine-guzzling father, who made little objection when the priest selected his son for special duties at
the church. When it was mentioned, his father would wink
and make a screwing motion with his middle finger, indicating what he thought was going on in the name of religious
studies. But he was wrong. The priest was pious and celi-
bate, a rarity in that part of the Abruzzi, the rugged moun-
tainous area southeast of Rome. He was also literate, which
was also a rarity, especially in a small village like theirs, which
was no more than a jumble of red-tiled roofs and white-
washed houses leaning along narrow twisting lanes clinging
to the edge of a precipice overlooking a narrow valley.

The priest recognized the boy's innate intelligence and
thirst for learning and strove to satisfy it. By the time he was
nine, Paolo spent almost all his time in the church, assisting
the priest with Mass and a dozen other functions while ac-
quiring as much knowledge as the priest had to offer. He
could write like an angel and was so adept in literature that

he had virtually memorized the few books possessed by the priest. By the time Paolo was in his early teens, the priest recognized that he had little more to offer the boy and decided to find a better place for him. The monastery in nearby Arrezzo seemed a logical place. After conferring with the abbot and the boy's father, it was decided that he should enter the monastery. His bothers and sisters would miss him. He was a loving, affectionate boy. His mother wept but was secretly pleased that one of her children should attain such a lofty social position.

Life in the monastery seemed to suit the boy. He was obedient, devout, and innocent, and quickly earned the abbot's trust. The protection of his innocence was of special interest to the abbot, and his quarters offered the boy a sanctuary from the lasciviousness of many of the other monks. It was common practice for an older monk to take one of the novices into his care and then into his bed. The abbot saw to it that his young charge was protected from these sodomites. He recognized a special talent in the boy for scholarship and encouraged him in every way he could. He saw to it that the monastery's extensive library was open to the boy, who seemed to devour everything on the shelves.

The boy was considered something of a pet by the other monks, who regarded him with resentment. He was often waylaid and pummeled mercilessly. But he never complained of his treatment to the abbot, who was aware of these torments but did nothing to intercede. How the young monk bore his travails was a matter of intense interest to the old man. The boy's trials were reported to him regularly by his little coterie of spies. There were times the abbot himself suggested ways the other monks might torment his young protégé as a method of testing him. Beatings, even ostracism, were employed. How he bore his sufferings revealed the steel-like determination of the young man's character and his ability to withstand suffering. By his nineteenth birthday, Fra Alfieri was a prodigiously accomplished scholar and the abbot considered where he would be most useful to the Church.

The abbot himself was a member of the Arbori family, one of the most prominent in Italy. He sent a letter to his cousin, Cardinal Volpe, who was part of the pope's inner circle. In the letter, he recommended the young monk to the cardinal in specific and glowing terms. The cardinal was intrigued, especially since the young monk was a peasant. Cardinal Volpe was a master of diplomacy and intrigue. Italy was divided into dozens of independent states each ruled by a separate dynasty. The Church controlled much of central Italy. Its armies were constantly at war with the other princes. Cardinal Volpe was at the center of dozens of intrigues, plots, and counterplots as each party and faction struggled for advantage over the other. The cardinal could always use a young man of intelligence and discretion. It was decided to send the young monk to Rome.

On a hot Sunday in May, Fra Alfieri arrived in the Eternal City on the back of a donkey, as part of a caravan of Tuscan traders.

The city was teeming with life. It was a time of enormous change and exuberance. The Renaissance was in its infancy. Rome was the center of the continent. The pope was the most powerful spiritual and temporal ruler in Europe. Artists streamed into the city to perform work for the Holy See. Rome's chief rivals were Venice, Florence, and Milan. War was the chief occupation of its rulers. Trade was transforming the continent. And all trade flowed from the Ottoman East through the Mediterranean and up the Italian peninsula controlled by families like the Este and the Medici, hungry for power and prestige.

Fra Alfieri was overwhelmed. He had never seen such opulence. The cardinal's palace seemed like something out of a fairy tale, filled with marble and statuary that shocked the still-innocent young monk. Naked young women were revealed in every kind of pose, along with naked young men. The anterooms and chambers were filled with young men in skintight hose stretched taut over their firm buttocks. They wore multicolored codpieces that protruded from between their legs like enormous battering rams. Young women in low-cut gowns paraded like harlots, their eyes dark with kohl, their full curling hair filled with paganlike wreaths of flowers that seemed to mock Christ's crown of thorns.

It amused the cardinal that his new young secretary was so modest, so innocent. Who reddened whenever a young woman was present. Who insisted on wearing his coarse monk's robe though the cardinal had offered to outfit him with an entire new wardrobe. But the young man's capacity for work was prodigious, even in the most stifling weather when Rome lay under an unlifting cloud of humidity.

Each night he retired to his small, plainly furnished room, where he studied his Bible while the courtyard below was filled with musicians, dancers, and merriment. There seemed to be a lavish fete each evening attended by the highest dignitaries of the Church. Besides being an astute diplomat, the cardinal was a voluptuary who loved food, fine wine, and beautiful boys. He dressed in an astonishing array of silks and jewels. It shocked the young monk that his employer would sometimes forsake his red robes for the elaborate dress of a courtier, including a codpiece and a sword with a jeweled hilt.

In the cardinal's vast chamber were couches on which young men lolled, idly tasting the assortment of sweets and condiments put out for them by a small army of servants. Fra Alfieri was ignorant of who they were and why they were there. But his ignorance did not last long. Sent to deliver a message to the apartment of a bishop, he was told to use a special back passage to gain entry to the bishop's apartment on the other side of the palace. Breathlessly, the monk hurried along the dark windowless passage that traversed the interior and came to a small wooden door. He knocked but there was no answer. He opened the door and stepped inside.

A young man was stretched out facedown on the bed, his eyes closed. The bishop lay over him, his purple robes parted. His thick engorged organ was pistoning between the young man's plump white buttocks. The bishop looked up and saw the young monk. He stretched out his hand.

The monk was unmoving. His eyes were as blank as a statue's, his breath frozen in his lungs.

"Come. The letter!" the bishop shouted impatiently.

Fra Alfieri stepped forward and handed him the letter he had been sent to deliver. The bishop tore open the missive, then made a gesture of dismissal. He never stopped moving against the boy.

Fra Alfieri turned and left the chamber, hurrying back the way he came. His head was pounding. His breath choked in his throat. What he'd seen disgusted him. He felt that he was in the house of hell, serving a minister of the devil. He wrote a letter to the abbot requesting that he be allowed to return to the monastery. His request was refused. There was no longer a place for him there. His duty was to serve the cardinal.

And serve him he must.

For the next five years, in the darkness of the Roman nights and the bright sun of its days, he wrote the instructions that sent men into exile, or torture, or death. By the knife, the garrote, or by poison. It delighted the cardinal to specify which. The cardinal kept no secrets from his young secretary. No important ones anyway. He enjoyed discussing his political moves, indicating the strategies by which he removed his enemies and evened scores, or satisfied the demands of a vendetta. All of it, he claimed, in the service of the Church, to advance the power of its prelates and of the pope himself.

Fra Alfieri served the cardinal, standing by as the pope's bastard children came and went in the palace making demands, which the cardinal and his staff bowed and scraped to fulfill. Prelates openly escorted their mistresses, who sauntered past with swaying hips. The cardinal enjoyed holding lotteries in which he auctioned off the prettiest boy. Other prelates sent young men as gifts, passing the handsomest among them. Christ seemed to look down from his position on the cross, his eyes filled with pain for the crimes being committed in his name. The young monk accepted it as his own private martyrdom. He felt nails piercing his own hands, though they were invisible.

What he was forced to do took its toll. His eyes sunk deeper in their sockets. His cheeks were thin and hollow. His slender body seemed ravaged by some invisible, unknown disease. His back was interlaced with scars from the self-flagellation he performed each night, lying facedown on the stone floor of his chamber, bringing his arm up again and again as he struck himself with the strands of a lead-tipped scourge.

None of this escaped the cardinal. His spies were everywhere. Especially within the walls of his own palace. Fra Alfieri was unaware that a peephole had been bored into the ceiling of his chamber and that strange eyes peered down at him at night, eyes that reported his every action to his master. The vein of sadism in the cardinal came into full bloom when it came to his secretary. He forced him to witness torture. To watch as the poison administered by one of the cardinal's assassins slowly worked its way through his victim, who died in agonizing convulsions. The cardinal required that his secretary report on the progress of the poison by sending him full reports in which the symptoms were recorded in every detail. He was sometimes required to bring back proof of an assassination by transporting back to Rome the head of the victim in a metal box.

In the dark cavernous catacombs beneath the cardinal's palace were chambers where these heads and other body parts were stored, clearly visible as they floated within a resinous liquid in rows of glass containers. Among them were hearts, livers, and sex organs, all perfectly preserved. One of the monk's duties was to catalog these curiosities, as the cardinal called them, for the pleasure and entertainment of his guests. On certain evenings, the young monk was summoned from his chamber to escort one or more of these guests on a tour of the catacombs. The dripping walls would echo with laughter and surprise as each guest viewed the horrors. Some were chilled, others pretended to be amused. But all were deeply impressed by what they saw.

Fra Alfieri was forced to witness the slow and horrific deaths of the cardinal's enemies. No matter what the hour, he would be admitted to the cardinal's bedchamber to give his report. "No. No. You are too hasty. Tell me exactly how he died!" the Cardinal would say sprawled out on the bed with a naked young man beside him. The monk was forced to recite the details. How the victim's eyes bulged under the pressure of the garrote. How his tongue stuck out. How the blood bubbled from his lips. Or how the points of the iron maiden pierced the victim's skin. How he or she shouted out in agony as they were wracked. The snap of their backbones as they broke, causing the cardinal to laugh in delight along with his catamite, who often paraded nude in front of the young monk at the cardinal's request.

"So, what do you think? Is he too thin? Should I fatten him up a little?" he would whisper to the young monk whose eyes were riveted to the floor in shame and revulsion. He would be sent away with their laughter following him.

He went directly to the chapel afterwards, dropping to his knees and praying for forgiveness for what he had been forced to do. He sometimes thought of taking his own life, but quickly dismissed the idea as an even greater sin. He felt trapped, unable to consider what to do. He had no friends. No patron other than the cardinal. There was nothing he could do. He was a servant of the Church. A soldier bound to serve for life.

On his thirtieth birthday, the young monk received a summons from the Holy Inquisition, a summons that could not be ignored or delayed.

The cardinal was at his summer palace outside the city. There was no time to appeal to him to intercede. The young monk racked his brain trying to understand what he had done to warrant being called by the Holy Inquisition. In Rome, a man could be denounced by simply placing his name on a piece of paper and placing it in a metal box located outside one of the city's many churches. He had seen wretches paraded in an *auto da fe*. They wore red paper gowns and carried crosses on their way to their executions. Heretics were burnt alive. Their screams filled his ears and shivered through his dreams.

He left the palace and hurried to the appointment, which was for seven that evening. The Inquisition was located within the walls of the Vatican. Navigating the dark twisting streets of the *campo fiori* in the oldest part of the city took skill, filled as they were with every kind of peddler, merchant, and thief. Not that he had anything to steal. Whatever the cardinal gave him in the way of money he gave away to charity. He kept nothing for himself.

He hurriedly crossed the Tiber and entered the gates of the Vatican. Painted harlots prowled the dark passages between the buildings. He saw a door open and one of these women slip inside admitted by a grinning priest. He entered one of the palaces and was escorted to the office of the Inquisition by two Swiss Guards carrying halberds. As they walked, he could almost feel the sharp steel of the ax blade against the skin of his neck.

He was escorted along a long marble-walled corridor to another set of doors. Inside was a huge anteroom filled with tables inlaid with multicolored stones. Everywhere he looked he saw the double crossed keys of the papacy. Instead of comforting him, they only induced fear.

A door at the other end of the room opened and a priest beckoned him to follow. Inside the adjoining chamber, three figures in black robes sat peering down from a huge wooden seat of judgment. In front of the seat was a wooden prie-dieu, a kneeling bench.

"Approach," one of them intoned.

Fra Alfieri came forward. His stomach was knotted. Fear ran through him like molten lava.

"Kneel."

He dropped to his knees, clutching the bar of the bench.

"You are the monk known as Fra Alfieri?"

"Yes," he gasped.

"Due to the kindness and generosity of your patron, Cardinal Volpe, you have been appointed a member of this body. Henceforward, you shall be known as an officer of the Holy Inquisition."

Fra Alffieri stared at them in stunned silence. It took another moment for the words to make any sense. An officer of the Inquisition? *Why?*

So began his journey into madness.

As he returned to the palace, he was dumbfounded. He staggered through the streets like a drunk. The aim of the Inquisition was to purge the Church of moral offenders. But the greatest of these was the man who had appointed him. He could not act against his own superior, the man to whom he was bound to serve. But there was a greater service, the one owed to the Church itself. It superceded his duty to the cardinal and anyone else. A great weight was suddenly lifted from him. He had been allowed a way out of his quandary. A path had been found. He would take up his office and purge the Church of its violators. It was as if a ray of heavenly light had suddenly shone down on him. He fell onto his face, prostrating himself in thankful prayer.

In the weeks that followed the young monk worked with fanatical fervor. With his intimate knowledge of the cardinal's affairs and his access to the cardinal's secret archives, he began amassing documents and preparing indictments. He worked in secret, afraid that knowledge of what he was doing might be discovered. He found a hiding place beneath the floorboards of an unused chamber, one the cardinal's spies would not discover. There he placed his evidence.

His brain was in a fever. Yet he had to remain outwardly calm, lest he arouse any suspicions. He had to work quickly before the cardinal returned. It would be much more difficult then, especially when the weather cooled. Rome was sweltering. The papal court had removed to Castel Gondolfo outside the city. In spite of the heat, Fra Alfieri worked demonically, remaining awake through the night, his coarse woolen robe soaked with sweat. Sometimes it became so hot he had to remove the robe and work naked at his desk, candles burning all around him, the shutters sealed so that no one would see the light.

When the weather cooled and the cardinal finally returned, almost two dozen indictments were ready for presentation, hidden beneath the oak floor of the unused antechamber. The cardinal summoned him as soon as he returned to his apartments.

"So, you are an officer of the Holy Inquisition?" he said mockingly. "Have you burnt any heretics since I've been gone?"

There was laughter from the assembled court.

"No, Your Eminence."

"Pity. And I had hoped to light up your summer."

More laughter erupted.

"One day you will probably want to burn me," the cardinal said, his lips pursing in amusement.

The monk reddened, but was used to being the butt of the cardinal's abuse.

"Master Danielo is to be my new acolyte," the Cardinal said, lifting his hand toward a beautiful young man standing nearby. He wore a cap with a long purple plume. His shapely legs were sheathed in skintight red-and-white stripped leggings, the colors of the cardinal. An enormous purple codpiece stood erect between his legs. The young man bowed and kissed the cardinal's hand. Their eyes met and the boy smiled rougishly. "See that he is furnished appropriate quarters. The apartment below mine is vacant, I believe."

Fra Alfieri blanched. That was where he had hidden his parchments.

The monk was forced to install the cardinal's newest concubine in the apartment directly below the cardinal's. It was connected to the one above by a secret staircase. The boy was installed that very day giving the monk no time in which to retrieve his indictments. What if they were found? He had to do something, but his desk was now piled with papers from the cardinal, more orders and secret directives. Papal forces were preparing to move against the Milanese. The cardinal was planning alliances with Florence and Genoa in the campaign. The Milanese were lining up the French on their side, a move that had to be prevented at all costs. The court was in a ferment of activity. Fra Alfieri was in the center of the fury. All the cardinal's directives passed through him. He lived in a torment of anxiety, fearing that at any moment his secret trove would be discovered. He knew he had to act before that happened. But the only way he could would expose him to the greatest danger. The antechamber was locked. The only way in was through the cardinal's chamber. But he had to act. God was directing him.

One night, when he knew the young acolyte was inside with the cardinal, Fra Alfieri opened the connecting door between the cardinal's office and his private apartments and slipped inside. To reach the secret stairs he had to cross the cardinal's dressing room. The dressing room was dark, but the door was open to the bedchamber beyond. Through it he could see the cardinal. He was lying on his back, moaning with pleasure. The young acolyte was kneeling between his legs, his lips surrounding the cardinal's engorged flesh.

The monk was as silent as a shadow. He crossed the room to the open door of the staircase, went through it and down the tight spiral. The room below was now filled with furniture. The hiding place was hidden under an armoire. The monk had to move it. With all his strength he managed to ease it aside. Then he removed the planks and took out the rolls of parchment. He was soaked in sweat. His breathing was tight as he edged the heavy armoire back into place. Spots of perspiration were spotting the floor. He wiped them up with the edge of his robe, then started back upstairs.

He heard laughter as he reached the top. He glanced out. There was movement in the room beyond. He waited, trying not to breathe. He knew that if he were discovered it would mean his death. He heard running footsteps and his heart froze. But it was only a game. The cardinal was chasing the young man around the bedroom. Then he heard the young man cry out in pain. The monk edged around the door. The cardinal's hairy white body was on top of the boy, thrusting forcefully as the boy cried out in agony. Fra Alfieri recrossed the darkened dressing chamber. When he was halfway through it, the Cardinal lifted his head and brayed aloud in pleasure.

Fra Alfieri slipped back outside. He went through the anteroom into the office and exited quickly, carrying his burden. No one who saw him thought anything of it. The cardinal's secretary was always carrying an armload of scrolls.

The young monk kneeled on the wooden prie-dieu. Above him were the three robed figures of the tribunal of the Inquisition staring down at him from their positions on the seat of judgment. The chamber was dark and silent. Light from thick yellow tapers illuminated the room, leaving deep pools of black shadow. The judges' faces were dark. Their features were hidden. Only their eyes were visible, luminous in the candlelight.

The young monk lowered his head. His fingers were pressed together prayerfully. His heart was pounding, suppressing a feeling of joy. This would be his moment. His instant of vindication against the evil he had so long witnessed.

He had presented his parchments to the tribunal and waited for the summons he knew would come. Days passed in a suspension of reality. He went abut his chores methodically. His thoughts were focused on only one thing. The message that would summon him. When it finally came, he practically flew to the Vatican as if his heels were winged like the pagan god Mercury.

The senior judge spoke from his position in the middle of the other two. His voice was a rasp, the sound deep and grating.

"Fra Alfieri, what was your purpose in delivering these indictments to this tribunal? Was it to defame the Mother Church? To hold it up to ridicule and shame before the entire world?"

The monk felt a chill grip his heart. "No, Father. My purpose was to see justice done."

"Justice? What kind of justice? To denounce the highest prelates of the Church? To see them dragged down and punished? To defame the names of the greatest families in Christendom? Is this their payment for raising you from the dung heap of your beginnings and bringing you to the glory of your present position? Is this the way you repay their trust and kindness?"

"I have only thought to see those punished who are guilty of moral wrongs."

"You have accused a prince of the Church."

"The evidence is clear."

"We see no evidence. Only the product of a deranged sensibility. For you there is only prayer and contrition. Renounce these charges immediately or face retribution from this panel. Those are you choices."

The monk knew he had lost. All his hopes had collapsed. He bent his head.

"I renounce these charges," he whispered through a constricted throat.

"They were made in envy and the desire to punish your betters, is that not so?"

Through his constricted lips he whispered, "Yes. It is so."

"So it shall be noted. Observe."

The monk turned. Two robed figures entered the chamber. Their arms were filled with parchments. They approached the fire burning in a grating at the other end of the chamber. Into the fire they deposited their burdens.

Fra Alfieri stared at them in anguish. They were burning his scrolls.

"Bare your body. And prepare to do pennance for your sin of pride."

He looked up. A robed figure stood beside him. In his hand was a heavy leather whip tipped with lead.

The monk removed his robe. He bent as the robed figure raised the whip and brought it down across his naked back.

He was unaware of the eyes staring down through a special peephole cut into the stone wall high above. They were the eyes of Cardinal Volpe. His lips formed a smile of pleasure as the whip cut into the young man's naked flesh.

To lie in darkness wrapped in coils of despair.

A darkness deeper than he had ever known. His body felt licked by the tongue of demons. He was in the cocoon of his personal hell. Several times he rose to grasp the hilt of a dagger he had secreted in his chamber. He held it in his hand as he lay outstretched on the cold stone floor. His eyes stared at the sheen of light on the razor-keen edge. What prevented him from sliding it along the front of his throat, he did not know. Somehow he found the will to go on.

On the third day of his abnegation he heard the voice.

It whispered to him, words he could not hear at first. Then the sound grew louder. It seemed to come from somewhere inside his head. He wondered, am I going mad? But the voice persisted, directing him, offering him a way, a path to his redemption.

He appeared in the cardinal's chambers looking like a

ghost. His eyes were hollows. His skin was gray. Others, hearing whispers of his disgrace, shied away from him. He waited in the rear of the chamber each day as people came and went petitioning the cardinal for favors. The cardinal did not deign to notice him. But he did not have him expelled. So he waited, humbled and denied, waiting to do what he was conditioned to do, like a dog preparing to serve his master.

Then the magic moment happened. The cardinal raised his hand. The room observed and parted. Fra Alfieri came forward through the throng. He knelt and kissed the ring on the short fingers extended to him. The cardinal began speaking as if nothing had happened. By evening, the monk had resumed his duties. The cardinal eyed him with supreme satisfaction. It amused him that the victory he had won over his secretary's rebellious spirit had come with such special delight. It was almost a shame that he felt no sexual desire for him, especially not in the monk's ravaged state. Had he felt any, his satisfaction would have been topped with the monk's seduction. But that day might not be far off. The cardinal's appetite was large and the ways of fulfilling it were varied.

That night, alone in his solitary chamber, the monk knelt before the small altar in the corner while the rest of the palazzo slept. His eyes were filled with a new resolve. Something had to be done or the Church would be lost forever. Just as the Angel Gabriel had appeared to Isaac, the voice had chosen Fra Alfieri to bring justice. He would work in secret to purge the church of its violators.

He would become the avenger . . . the sacred Angel of Vengeance.

He rose and went to his desk. On it was a folio made of velum bound between twin leather covers and held together with a leather thong. On the cover was a cross. A red cross dyed in the monk's own blood. He opened it and began to write.

He wrote the name of each of the men he had accused. These were the names in the scrolls he had seen burned in the fires of the Inquisition.

Beside each name he listed the nature of the accused's transgression.

Alongside that he wrote the method to be used to punish each of their crimes.

Then he added what the voice had commanded. After each act of vengeance, the one who avenged must purify his soul. He must confess his act and do penance. He must never act out of personal motives. His soul must always be kept pure.

He took the dagger and with a single movement sliced it across his palm. He opened the folio to the first page. In his own blood, he wrote the title.

THE DEMON CIPHER.

He had his mission. But how to carry it out?

He had no power. Only the nobles had power. Again the voice instructed him.

The cardinal had power. And he was the cardinal's secretary. The cardinal acted through him. He was the cardinal's implement. He would turn that implement to his own use.

The cardinal had given him access to two things.

Gold and assassins.

In his sadistic desire to corrupt the young monk, he had unwittingly provided him with the tools of his own destruction. The cardinal was a nobleman. He never soiled his hands. He left it to others to do his work for him. So it was the young monk who had to arrange each assassination and act of duplicity. It was he who paid the assassin and provided the plan. Now he put this knowledge to his own purposes.

He made an arrangement with the Brazzi, a family of assassins from Lucca, a family he often engaged on difficult missions. They had seldom failed him. They asked no questions and cared nothing about the intrigues of the nobles and the Church. They cared only for the gold the young monk placed in their hands. They were brazen and fearless and would have assassinated the pope himself had they been paid enough for the job.

So it began.

Cardinal Rossi, abductor of children, was abducted in a children's brothel. He was spirited to the cellars of the cardinal's palace where he was brought before an inquisitor whose face he could not see. His crimes were read out to him and judgment passed in spite of his shouts of outrage. He was impaled on an iron spit and roasted alive in the bakery ovens beneath the palace. His body was found the next morning, displayed in the Piazza Navonna. In his mouth was an apple. Inside the apple was a tiny scroll listing the nature of his crimes.

Rome was aghast. Who would dare touch someone as exalted as Rossi? He stood on the right hand of the pope himself. But it was just the beginning.

His Eminence Archbishop Naponte, a pederast and lecher, was found hanging beneath a tree on one of the tiny islands in the Tiber. His insides had been scooped out and fed to the wild dogs that roamed the island.

The bloodthirsty Cardinal Sonoto was discovered in the Forum. His severed head had been colonized by bees.

Cardinal Bonserra was slaughtered like a hog. His body parts were hung on hooks in butcher shops along the Corso.

A child rapist was discovered hanging in a cage suspended from an abandoned tower, eaten alive by ravens.

A torturer of innocents had been dried and cured like a joint of beef.

The heads of five prelates, each a notorious sodomite, were displayed in the Piazza Popollo. Each sucking on his own severed penis.

The prelates were all members of the same cabal. Suspicion immediately fell on Cardinal Volpe, who led the opposing faction. The cardinal was terrified, fearful of revenge. The palace was sealed off. Armed retainers patrolled the corridors and guarded each entrance. The cardinal locked himself in his apartments with only a few trusted aides, one of whom was Fra Alfieri. The cardinal's sleep was fitful, even though he was unaware that he had locked the demon in with him. He ordered opiates to help him sleep. He had a vivid dream in which he awoke to find himself facing a hooded figure staring down from the seat of judgment.

It was not a dream.

The cardinal realized he had been drugged. His wrists were in manacles. He recognized his surroundings. He was in the deepest catacomb beneath his own palace. A place used for questioning his victims. In the shadows, he could see the dreaded implements of torture. On shelves all around him were his trophies, the hearts and vital organs of his enemies. Sometimes just showing them to his victims produced the result he wanted, forcing them to comply with his demands. Of course, there were other times when, no matter what they agreed to, nothing could overcome the compelling desire he had to witness their agonies.

The hooded figure intoned a litany of his crimes. The names of the men and women he had ordered to be killed or tortured. For each, he was condemned to suffer a different punishment. He was to be the victim of his own tortures. He screamed and protested, but there was no one to hear him just as no one had been able to hear his victims. Burly men in leather hoods seized him on either side and hauled him away.

"I demand to see who accuses me!" he shouted.

The figure rose and stripped away the hood covering his face.

The cardinal shrank back in shock as he recognized the face of the young monk. He babbled incoherently as they dragged him away to the pit where a viscous oil was being heated and in which he would soon be boiled alive, but not before he had a taste of the devices ranged along the walls, their keen edges sharpened and gleaming like razors.

* * *

The young monk was filled with satisfaction. Each of the names contained in his original indictments had been punished. He knew he must now confess. But to whom? He trusted none of the prelates he had come in contact with. Each of them had been corrupted. There was only one man he knew he could trust. The abbot of the monastery where he had been trained.

The young monk slipped out of the palace before the disappearance of the cardinal could be announced. He had prepared his own alibi. He was carrying messages and instructions signed by the cardinal ordering him on a special mission. No one would suspect anything, since the young monk was constantly being sent away on such affairs. When the cardinal's boiled remains were finally discovered hanging within the frame of an iron maiden deep in the cellars of his own palace, the monk was already nearing the crumbling walls of the ancient monastery. Rome assumed that it was an act of revenge perpetrated by the cardinal's enemies in retaliation for their recent losses at his hands.

The old abbot was overjoyed to see his young protégé.

He embraced him and regarded him with pride.

Then the young priest knelt and asked for the abbot to hear his confession.

What he told him chilled the abbot's heart with dread. His face went pale and his hands began to tremble. When he was finished, the young monk fell prostrate. His body shook with sobs, so great was his release. But when he asked for absolution, the abbot failed to answer. He asked several questions, which the monk answered.

The young monk was escorted to his old cell. The abbot ordered him locked inside. Then he returned to his chambers and to the conflict now raging inside of him. In the morning, he went to the stables and had his horse saddled. Two days later he was in Rome. He went directly to the offices of the Inquisition. Though he had not been in the city for some time and his position was far from important, he was still a member of the Arbori family and their influence was significant. His name commanded respect and his presence was deferred to when he demanded an audience with the Chief Inquisitor, Archbishop Romano.

He was admitted to the archbishop's presence, where he presented his case. In order to do so he needed permission to violate the seal of confession. This was granted him. He then told his story, revealing everything that Fra Alfieri had told him. The archbishop was at first disbelieving. But the age and revered status of his guest caused him to probe further. Agents were sent for. They arrested several members of the Brazzi family, who quickly confessed their part in the affairs. They protested their innocence, saying they were merely servants of the cardinal's secretary.

An armed guard was dispatched to the monastery. Fra Alfieri was transported back to Rome and taken to the palace of the Inquisition with utmost secrecy. He was brought before the archbishop and questioned. He confessed to what he had done. There was no shame in his manner. He expressed no contrition. His was a divine mission.

Facing the exalted expression on the monk's face, the archbishop was perplexed. He had condemned heretics who wore the same expression, as if they were bathed in some divine cosmic radiance. He was awed by its appearance and fearful of the danger of it spreading. Such heresies had to be contained or the Church would splinter into a thousand pieces.

"Are you aware that what you have done is a heresy of the most profound order?" the archbishop asked.

"I have been instructed by the messenger of God," the monk answered. "Those who transgress must be stricken. They have broken the sacred laws and committed sins of the vilest kind and manner. Their victims must be avenged. So it is written in the Cipher."

"Those you accuse are princes of the Church."

"They are servants of the devil and damned to eternal

hell. They have been judged and found wanting. So wrote the hand of the Lord. So I have written."

The archbishop turned to look at the abbot, who was seated behind a screen. The abbot was clearly struck by what he had just heard. His lips trembled. His hand rose to his throat. "Perhaps I have committed the greatest sin," he whispered.

The archbishop sent the abbot back to his monastery. The prisoner was submitted to judgment under the archbishop's special seal. He was excommunicated, then taken to the cellars of the Inquisition. There the monk was hung on a rack. His anus was forced open with huge iron pincers and a hungry ferret was introduced into his bowels. The pain as the animal's razor-sharp teeth and claws burrowed his way inside was beyond excruciating. His screams echoed through the dark cavernous catacombs that crawled and twisted beneath the palazzo. The animal was finally removed and the prisoner was slowly and painfully flayed alive. The skin was removed from his body in narrow strips using razorlike implements. Still, the monk refused to die. He exhibited the intensity and devotion of a martyr. When the skin had been removed from his torso, and he hung quivering in agony, his body a bloody pulp of exposed muscle and sinew, the blood seeping in a pool at his feet, he still refused to recant. His eyes remained fixed somewhere distant as his lips repeated the same phrase again and again.

I am the avenger of God . . . I am the Angel of Vengeance. . . .

The archbishop gestured. The headsman raised his ax. The monk's head was severed from his body in a single downward stroke.

Twenty-two

Holly closed the book.

She sat back. Her eyes stared straight ahead as she tried to digest what she had just read. She took a sip of water from the glass beside her, then lifted the phone receiver. When someone answered, she asked for the concierge and informed him that she had finished. Several moments later the door opened and a uniformed guard entered. She rose and followed him along the corridor, then to a set of double doors. He knocked and opened them, ushering her into Pascal's spacious office.

It was dark outside. Lights illuminated the roadway behind the institute, but the woods beyond were a mass of interlocking shadows, mysterious and threatening like the images now floating through her mind.

Pascal was seated behind his desk. He rose when Holly entered and ushered her over to the sitting area. She took a seat on one of the facing brown leather couches.

"Would you like a drink?" he asked with smile. "I think you've earned it."

"Scotch. On ice, if you have it."

"I think we can manage that."

He went to a cabinet and took out a decanter. He poured them both a drink. The crystal glasses were large and heavy. Holly took a sip of the smooth amber liquid. She was no expert, but she could tell it was very old and very expensive.

"How is it?" he said, slipping into the couch opposite and crossing his legs. The lights had been turned low giving the room the mellow atmosphere of a lounge.

"Excellent. I needed it."

"You survived your ordeal," he said.

"How do you mean?"

"Some people might find it pretty gruesome going."

"It was. I don't suppose you have a copy of the Cipher?"

He shook his head. "It was never found."

"Really?"

"You sound disbelieving."

She made a face. "I wondered, that's all."

"Some people think it might be hidden away in the Vatican archives. But I've never seen a reference to it."

"Then how did people find out about it?"

"Somehow knowledge of Fra Alfieri's existence and what he did was kept alive. It's not clear exactly by whom. The Arbori family perhaps. The old abbot could also be a culprit. He may have rationalized that what the monk did was justified. It may have been kept alive by monks in his monastery after his death. A kind of cult formed over the centuries."

"A cult?"

"In some respects, yes. Alfieri's teachings seem to pop up every so often. They revived again during the period just before the Reformation when the Pope Julian was selling indulgences all over Europe to fund the construction of St. Peter's. Julian was quite a character, if you remember. He was responsible for commissioning the Sistine Ceiling. He even wore armor and went into battle. That was not the only time. Whenever there was a period of scandal within the Church, there seemed to be a revival of the cult."

"You think that's what we might be dealing with?"

He shrugged. "I don't know. But the similarities in the method of killing is hard to ignore."

"This will be a hard one for the police to swallow. An ancient cult of avengers." She took another sip. The scotch was warming its way through her.

"Yes. I suppose it will. Sorry for complicating your life."

"No. Actually, you may have simplified it. You've supplied me with motive and method. Now, all I have to do is convince myself."

"That won't be easy?"

"No. The other killings fit, but why kill a therapist? And why that way?"

He looked at her and their eyes met. Like the scotch, his look had an equal power to warm her. She glanced away.

"Well," he began. "If the avenger is barred from confessing to a priest, then who better to confess to than a therapist. Aren't you all in the confessing business? And if the therapist betrayed him, then she would have to be punished in the same manner Alfieri decreed in the Cipher."

"Exactly like Mary Donnelly was punished."

"Yes. Exactly."

There was a silence between them. Holly felt a strange sense of terror envelop her, a chilling premonition of danger. It could have been caused by the darkness outside combined with the eerie interior lighting. But it was there nevertheless. Yet, she knew she was not in danger. Her connection to the killings was only peripheral. She was only a consultant. A profiler. She was not in charge of running down the killer and seeing him caught. But the effect of what she had read was both frightening and compelling. The way the victims had been killed drove a spike of fear into her soul. It foretold of a mind so dark and twisted it would stop at nothing to reach its aim in the fanatical belief in its own righteousness and justification for the act of murder.

"It's getting late," she said finally, placing her glass down on the coffee table between them.

"I could order dinner," he said.

"Thank you. Perhaps another time."

"Why not now?"

Holly searched for an excuse, obsessed by the need to be alone with the thoughts now tormenting her.

"You really don't have a reason to refuse, do you?" he said with a smile.

"No. Actually, I don't."

Half an hour later they were seated in a private dining room surrounded by the luxurious glow of expensive hardwoods and the expressive light of burning candles. The table was set with linen, china, and flowers. Through the large wraparound windows spotlights illuminated the institute's formal gardens surrounding a shimmering pool and a display of fountains.

She had freshened up in a marble-walled dressing room complete with a steam shower, sauna, and an assortment of expensive body lotions. There was a vanity faced with mirrors and a bidet. What more could a girl ask? Clara would be in wonderland.

The dinner was served by a waiter in a white jacket and black tie. The food was delicious and the wine incredible.

"This is the second extraordinary meal I've had here," she said as they began dessert. "What are my chances of moving in?"

"Very good, actually," he replied. "We'd just have to appoint you a visiting scholar."

"How do I apply?"

"I'll give you an application before you go."

They exchanged smiles, as she twisted the stem of her wine glass between her fingers. He plies you with scotch, then wine, she thought Who knows how the evening might end up?

"How did you get your job here?" she asked.

"It's quite a long story."

"I have nowhere to go."

"All right. But if I begin boring you, just raise your glass and I'll stop."

"I don't think you'll bore me," she said as their eyes met.

"I was born in Montreal. My parents died when I was very young. I was brought up in an orphanage run by the Dominicans. They helped me get a scholarship for college. The Forester family subsidized it. Somehow they took an interest in me. Especially Dr. Forester. He guided me in my choice of a career and continued financial aid through graduate school."

"Where was that?"

"The Sorbonne. Oxford. Then McGill."

"I'm impressed."

"You needn't be. They're just schools."

"Very good schools. And then?"

"Then, I came to work here under Dr. Forester, helping to catalog new acquisitions and helping him continue to build his collection of medieval manuscripts."

"And now you're the curator?"

"Yes. Dr. Forester named me as his successor."

"So, in effect you run this institute."

"Not really. There's a board of trustees I have to answer to."

"Do you?"

"They're usually very agreeable," he said with a grin.

Regarding him, she had no doubt why. He was elegant, handsome, and extremely charming. He would have been anyone's choice to represent the institute.

"What do you do besides collecting manuscripts?"

He smiled. "I have several other interests. We also collect primitive art. We aid in preserving the ecology. And in helping to keep endangered ethnic cultures alive in remote parts of the world."

"So you travel a lot."

"Let's say, I get around."

It was Holly's turn to smile. "Sorry for all the questions. But I meant your personal interests."

"Well, I like to ski. I scuba dive. I like doing photo safaris. Sometimes I climb when I have the time. But that's getting harder to do."

"Mountains?"

"Sometimes. Rock faces mostly. I like the challenge. Now tell me about you."

Holly made a face. "Nothing as exciting or interesting."

"I'd have thought working in a prison would be both exciting and interesting."

"It has its moments."

"You seemed troubled by it."

"I think I'm experiencing a little burnout."

"Anyone would, after what you've just been through. You sound like someone who puts a lot of pressure on themselves."

"That's me all right."

"It's not healthy."

"Tell me about it."

She looked at him over the rim of her glass and his eyes locked with hers. The message she read in them was unreadable. Neither flirtatious nor questioning, but neither of them looked away. Attractive as he was, she felt herself tighten. It was too soon. She was not yet ready. She lowered her eyes.

"I love this wine." She said.

"It's from our cellars."

"I'd love to see them."

"I'll take you through one day. They're in one of the older wings."

"The part that used to be a monastery?"

"That's right."

She put down her glass. An inner voice warned that she had to stop drinking or who knows what might happen.

"I think I'd better go. I have an early day tomorrow."

"That's too bad. One of our driver's could take you."

"I'll manage."

"I think it might be a good idea."

She realized she did not want to argue. He walked her down to the entrance. They stood in the vestibule as the concierge helped her with her coat.

"Thank you for a lovely evening."

"Then let's repeat it one day soon," he said with a playful grin.

"I think I'd like that."

A black town car pulled up. He opened the door for her.

"How will I get my car tomorrow?"

"Don't worry about that. Just leave me the keys and we'll have it delivered."

She opened her bag and handed him her keys. She stepped into the car and the driver shut the door. Vincent waved as they drove away. She returned the gesture, watching him as they made the turn and headed back down the long tree-lined drive toward the huge iron gates. She glanced back through the rear window as the towers of the old section came into view. They were striking, silhouetted dark against the sky. They returned her mind to what she had read that afternoon.

The strange sensation she had felt earlier now returned, bringing with it a feeling of dread. Images of stone walls, the screams of dying men, and the dank smell of fear. She felt as if something preordained were about to happen, something culled from the primordial darkness of the human soul.

Twenty-three

She had barely gotten inside the door pausing to watch the town car pull away when the phone rang.

It was Dan.

They had another body.

It was tentatively ID'd as Brian Berman, an ex-priest who had been serving ten consecutive sentences for child molestation. He had pled guilty to all the counts of all the indictments and was freed because the statue of limitations had run out.

She had barely begun to explain why she didn't have her car when Dan cut her off. "Just stay there. We'll come and get you."

They sent a police cruiser for her. She sat alone in back behind an officer who said nothing as they drove. Her mind was warped with confusion. She'd felt a jab of guilt when she picked up the phone and heard Dan's voice. Guilt for feeling something for a virtual stranger that she had prevented herself from feeling for Dan. Her stomach was still twisted with desire. She felt a throbbing between her legs. Scotch followed by wine was a potent cocktail that had weakened her natural defenses. The walls had been breached and emotion had poured in. It was a hard thing to pull back from. Even as her head began to clear, what she was feeling showed no desire to lessen. She was cold sober now, but her emotions were still in a state of intoxication.

Holly was barely aware of the route they were taking. She had not even asked the officer where they were going. She sat in a deep velvety silence, still visualizing herself at the table in the institute, candles infusing Vincent's image with dancing light. Still caught in the rapture of his smile.

Holly became aware that they'd left the series of four-lane highway traversing the commercial hub of the county and were traveling on a web of back roads taking them deeper into the mountains. It was late when they arrived. Almost midnight.

The crime scene had all the allure of an after-Christmas sale, lit by the throbbing roof lights from the assortment of official vehicles parked in a haphazard formation surrounding a crumbling old stone manse. It was a house that had witnessed all the history of the sprawling county, from the early Dutch settlements through to the present. It had been an important tavern once, sitting astride a trail used by the early settlers. Now it sat in decay, part of a stagnant rural backwater, a place of rusting farm machinery and fields overgrown with brush.

Dan was waiting for her. He was wearing a huge fur hat, the kind the Russians had popularized. His team was scattered over the area searching for evidence. Holly got out of the cruiser and approached him, avoiding his eyes. It was bitterly cold, but somehow she was not affected by the temperature. Her body was still warmed by the alcohol.

"Sorry to get you out here so late. What was wrong with your car?"

"I had to drop it off at the shop," she lied.

"Anything serious?"

'No. I'll pick it up tomorrow.'

"No loaner?"

"They were all out. Like your hat."

"I got it in St. Petersburg. I was there for a police conference a couple of years ago."

"It's very becoming," she said, still unable to meet his glance. "Where is he?"

"Inside. Come and have a look. But be prepared. It's not pretty."

He escorted her toward the house. A door faced them bleeding yellow light. They stepped inside.

"It was used as an ice house," Dan commented, as Holly held up her hand to shield her eyes from the twin standing lamps set up by the police. They were aimed at a large block of crystal, shimmering in the center of the room.

Inside it was a naked man. He was short and middle-aged. His hair was thin, standing away from his large domed skull. His flesh was pink. Bloated unnaturally as if he were made of inflated rubber. His eyes were open and staring. His tiny penis was no longer than Holly's little finger. His testicles hung immaturely, like those of a ten-year-old boy.

"Let me introduce Father Berman. He was boiled, then frozen and ready to serve."

Holly stared at the victim and all the images from the reading she had just done flooded her consciousness, each murder locking into place.

If she believed it. IF.

She would have her killer's method and his motive. All she had to do was believe it. A myth locked in time that had suddenly sprung to life.

The phone was incessant.

Holly tried to ignore it. She plunged deeper into sleep, curling in a tight ball beneath two quilts. In spite of the heater running continually all night, the house was still cold. The wind struck the northeastern corner of the town house where her bedroom was located. Having an end unit was considered desirable, except when the winds blew down from the arctic.

The phone would not stop. She reached out and grabbed the receiver, drawing it down into her whirlpool of blankets and bringing its unpleasantly cool plastic surface to her ear.

"Yes?"

She half-expected to hear Dan's voice. She had remained at the ice house for another hour until he shipped her back home in the same cruiser that brought her.

"Holly. It's me, Beth."

She sat up. Half-expecting the worst. Her sister's bad news usually came at this hour. She was exaggerating. Any hour really.

"All right. What happened?"

"What happened is I got a job," Beth said excitedly.

"Really? Where?"

"Your friend offered it to me."

"What friend?"

"Mr. Pascal. At the Forester Institute. The Forester Institute, for God's sake. Do you have any idea of how hard is it to get in there? Just for a visit, never mind working there. "

"He offered you a job?" Holly said incredulously.

"He called me personally. He said he liked my resume and why don't I come for an interview."

"But that's impossible. It's too early."

"Honey. It's noon."

"Noon?" Holly gasped in surprise. She had slept all morning.

"I had the interview at eleven. He offered me the job as his personal assistant and took me on the grand tour. I just left. You're the first person I've called. Isn't it fantastic? I got a job!"

"Yes. It's wonderful. I'm very happy for you."

"I have to thank you, sis. You really came through for me. Like always. Now, I've got to run. I have a million things to get out of the way now that I'm a working woman."

"When do you start?"

"Now. Today."

"My God."

"Bye. I love you. I love you."

"I love you too."

The phone went silent. Holly blinked. A job. Starting today. Her sister had a job. Truly amazing. She realized that she was smiling.

It was a smile that faded a few minutes later when she sat in her kitchen over breakfast, one eye idly on a TV news show, and saw the DA's pugnacious expression invade the screen over the words BREAKING NEWS. He stood in the corridor outside his office in the county court building surrounded by a crowd of media.

In a ringing voice, Pinero said,"I'm here to announce the arrest of a suspect for the murder of Bishop Horan."

All of Holly's mental systems went on immediate alert.

The screen went into a digital omelet then reformed itself with the features of someone Holly had never seen before. Nondescript features, mid-twenties, short hair, puffy eyes marked with the watery indirect gaze of an addict.

"The suspect's name is Edward Bogner. He has served two terms for felonious assault and attempted murder. Mr. Bogner is in police custody and will be arraigned in due course. A statement will be released later today giving further details."

Questions were shouted, but Pinero turned and went back inside his office.

Holly watched as the anchor hastened to rehash the DA's live announcement. It was obvious that nothing else was known and after a meaningless ad-lib, they quickly cut to a commercial.

Not possible . . .

Pinero was vamping. Throwing the public a knuckleball.

Making them swing at a sucker pitch to avoid the stigma of impotence. She layered the dishes in the washer, then hurried upstairs to finish dressing.

It was time to put up or shut up.

Twenty-four

The office was empty.

Only Dan was inside his glass cubicle. All the other officers were elsewhere.

Holly cut straight toward him.

He raised his eyes, saw her coming, and winced. He knew that look. Her jaw was set like a hunting hound's.

She threw open the door and burst inside.

"Okay. So who is that guy and why didn't you tell me?"

"Why didn't I tell you?" Dan said, leaning back in his prized leather-backed swivel chair, purloined from one of the empty offices in their wing that had once belonged to some now-defunct commission. "Because I heard it on the box like everyone else."

"And the perp?"

"First of all, sit down. You're accelerating my adrenaline."

Holly tossed her coat on the couch and threw herself down beside it, one leg tucked beneath the other.

"There's coffee. I like your boots."

She was wearing knee-high close-fitting brown leather boots that accented her shapely legs, together with a brown tweed skirt and a red turtleneck sweater.

"Thanks. I don't want coffee. I just want to know who this guy is."

"From what I can gather, which isn't much, he's a two-time loser who was molested by a priest when he was a kid."

"Pinero didn't even tell you?"

Dan shook his head. "Does that tell you something about our relationship?"

"You're supposed to be running his special task force," Holly said.

"That and two bucks will get you on the subway. If it's still two bucks."

"What evidence does he have that this guy did it?"

"From what I can tell, there is none. Other than some kind of confession. I haven't seen it. All I know is that he's a juice-head, brought in for possession of a significant amount of meth. Why or how he confessed, I haven't a clue."

"Pinero didn't let you question him first."

"First? How about never? I told you, he'll use us when it's convenient. We're just a backup to bolster his credibility. And right now he's got a sacrifice."

"It won't hold up," Holly said confidentially.

"Why not?"

"Because he didn't do it. We both know that."

"I'd like to believe that. But so far I have no proof either way. Are you about to tell me something?"

Holly looked at him. Her stomach was churning. "I think I am. But I don't think you're going to want to believe it."

"Try me."

Holly rose and faced him. "This is going to sound pretty wacky. But you've got to go with me."

"Go ahead."

"I went to the Forester Institute. They're the experts on medieval manuscripts."

"I know who they are."

"I wanted some insight into the implements the killer's been using."

"And did you get it?"

"I got a lot more than that."

"I'm listening."

"I know."

"So why are you hesitating."

"Because this is going to sound completely off the wall."

"That's why I brought you in."

"That's very flattering."

He made a face. Then pointed to his watch. Holly took a breath.

"Okay. Here goes. Over five hundred years ago a monk named Alfieri was executed for killing high Church officials in Rome. Cardinals, bishops, prelates he believed were morally corrupt."

"Five hundred years ago?"

"Stay with me."

"Go on."

"Alfieri wrote a book. He called it The Demon Cipher. In it, he listed every kind of moral sin and next to it the punishment he prescribed."

"What has this got to do with what's going on now?"

"Every one of our victims has been murdered in the same exact way."

"The same exact way? Come on."

The look on his face was pure skepticism.

"Listen to me, Dan. I read the witness accounts. Everything he prescribed was done to our victims. In exactly the same way. Impaling. Quartering. Hanging them in cages. Boiling them alive. Everything. I could go down the list. It's a perfect match."

"Even Mary Donnelly?"

"Even her. Using his victim's skulls as a hive. It's all there. Like our killer copied everything he did."

Dan's expression had changed. He looked at her with wary eyes.

"Okay. I hear you. Tell me how it connects."

"I'm not a-hundred-percent sure. But I think Alfieri's book became the basis for a kind of cult."

"A cult. Oh, fuck. We got Manson now?"

"I know what you're going to say. But hear me out. What Alfieri did was repeated in various times in history. It slowed down after the Counter-Reformation when the Church took steps to reform itself. But its always been present. And . . ."

"And," Dan said warily.

"Alfieri called himself the avenger. Just like our guy did on Mary Donnelly's tapes."

"There's more, isn't there? I can see it in your face."

Holly was vibrant. Her face was flushed. Her eyes were lit like beacons.

"Alfieri decreed that the avenger had to confess after each of his acts in order to keep his soul pure. That's why he called the hot line."

"Why not use a priest? Isn't that what they're for?"

"Alfieri confessed to a priest. The abbot of his monastery. The one man in the world he trusted. And the very man who betrayed him."

"So no priest."

"No. Those who came after him rejected the idea of going to a priest. They had to confess to someone else. I don't know who they used in the past. But in our age, it's a therapist."

His eyes were still narrowed. But some of the skepticism was gone.

"So, you're saying this killer is part of a cult?"

"No. I said he could be. I don't know how they recruit. But I would say he was someone who had a background in theology. Or was drawn to it. I believe he is extremely intelligent. A true believer who thinks he's on a mission. Part of a historical mission to root out evil in the Church and avenge the wronged."

"So we're looking for a man?"

"Historically, the way the Church was set up. Yes. I don't

think it's a woman. And it was a man's voice on the tapes, though he used a synthesizer to disguise it."

"And you think he's not acting alone?"

"I'm not entirely sure of that."

"So, he's a cult of one."

"That's possible."

"My God, Holly. This is some story."

"I know. But why else would he kill this way? Using such elaborate devices? Why the same extraordinary historical matchup? It's way beyond coincidence."

"How come there's never been any record of this cult?"

"I don't know. I'm calling it a cult because of the ritualistic method of killing and the almost religious mission to avenge. I don't know what it is. Is there a historical link or did the killer somehow find out about all this and decided to replicate it?"

"You mean a copycat killer?"

"Yes. Only the people he's copying lived a long time ago."

"Where is this book, this Demon Cipher?"

"No one knows if it still exists or not. It hasn't been seen since the day the monk was arrested."

"You said he was executed?"

"He was tortured, then flayed alive and beheaded. It was done secretly. There's no official record of any of this. The Church tried to erase all evidence of his existence and the existence of the Cipher."

"Then how did any of it get known?"

"The evidence points to the abbot he confessed to. He must have come to believe that what the monk did was right after all. He may have hidden the book as an act of contrition. It's possible the cult began in his monastery. And continued down through the centuries."

"Why now?"

"I don't think there was a reason until now. There hasn't been this large a scandal involving clerical abuse. Not ever.

There were always cases, but they were always quickly hushed up. Clerical abuse has been mostly kept secret until now. But we know it's incredibly widespread. In this country and others."

Dan was silent. He turned away from her. His eyes were hard, fixed somewhere in the distance. Holly took her place on the couch. The explanation had exhausted her. Now she waited for its effect.

Shepard swiveled back suddenly, his eyes riveted on her.

"Okay. Let's see if it'll fly."

Her presentation to the DA took an hour and sixteen minutes.

Pinero sat rigidly in his chair at the center of a large conference table in an impressive walnut-paneled chamber of the county court building. Dan sat directly across from him. The rest of the high-backed leather chairs were empty. Pinero asked no questions. His face was impassive. His eyes followed Holly as she stood in the front of the room using several charts she had made to illustrate her thesis.

They listed the current victims and showed the similarities in the way they were killed to those of Alfieri's.

She illustrated the similarity in the killer's need to confess.

She tied that need to Mary Donelly.

She paraphrased Mary's tapes. Emphasizing the killer's description of himself as an avenger and connecting that to Alfieri's description of himself as the avenger.

Through it all Pinero's expression never changed.

When she was done there was a long silence.

"Are you finished?" he asked.

Holly nodded.

"Thank you. I appreciate your time and the effort you've put into this. Lieutenant, can I see you alone, please."

Pinero rose and walked to the double doors at the other

end of the room. Dan pushed away his chair and followed, giving Holly a glance and a shrug. Then they both went out the door, which closed behind them.

She took a seat in one of the chairs and waited, wondering how many fates had been determined in this room. How many judgments made. How many individuals sent into incarceration or death. The door closing on them forever.

And the killer?

What doors was he hiding behind?

As she thought it, the door opened returning Dan to the room. His jaw was set, his expression grim. Holly reacted, almost knowing, as she rose to face him.

"He didn't buy it, did he?"

Dan was silent. His eyes were fixed on hers.

"Worse. He wants you out of the unit. And off the case."

"Off the case? Why?"

"You want it straight?"

"Of course."

"He thought your theory was cockeyed, completely nuts. He lambasted me for bringing you in and wasting his time. He totally rejects the notion of a serial killer. He believes he has already apprehended one of the perpetrators and will apprehend the others. He thinks each case is individual."

"In spite of the ritual killing of each victim. How does he explain that?"

"He doesn't and he won't."

"He can't ignore it. It's going to have to be explained."

Dan stepped back, positioning himself on the edge of the table. His face was drained of expression. "I'm tired of this bullshit. As tired as you are. But I have to put up with it. You don't, thankfully. Like to change places?"

"So I just go home and forget this ever happened?"

Holly was feeling rage inside. A painful twisting surge of anger.

"No. I told him that his decision was unacceptable. That I need you on the team."

"Well, fuck him. I'm not quitting whether I'm on the team or not."

"What do you mean?" Dan asked. "What do you think you're going to do?"

"I don't know. But I'm not giving this up. "

"Holly, please. I know you're angry. Anyone would be. The man's an asshole. Don't do something you'll regret just because of him."

"It has nothing to do with him. This is about me."

Holly turned and carefully gathered up her charts. She was seething. Murder was in her heart. Instead, she put her charts in her carrying case, picked up her bag, and walked out of the room.

Twenty-five

She was at a dead end.

What she had said to Dan was spoken out of anger and frustration. She had no desire to hurt him or his task force. Though she knew he would fight to retain her, it was a battle she did not think he would win. The wisest thing for her to do was to back away. What she would do afterward was shrouded in uncertainty. She no longer had any pretense to authority or any real power. All of that was now gone. All she had was a theory, one that she herself was not totally certain of. She had only the documents Pascal had let her see. But it was more than just a surmise. What she needed was evidence. And there was precious little of that to go around. The killer or killers had concealed their tracks with incredible skill. Forensics had discovered nothing that led anywhere. It didn't seem possible, but after five killings there were no prints. No car tracks. No fibers. No DNA. Nada. Nothing.

If that wasn't frustrating enough, there was her job. Or lack of it.

Clara delivered the bad news over coffee in her kitchen after work.

"Ted won't speak to me about it anymore. All he says is, when the board tells him, he'll tell me and then I can tell you."

"I don't get it. How long to they expect me to stay out? I was a hostage, for God's sake. I didn't plan the damn thing."

"Face it, Holly. You may have been a hostage, but you created a lot of problems for them by the way you represented the inmates. You put them in the bull's-eye. They don't exactly love you for it."

"I just told the truth."

"How many times have I told you, be careful with the truth. Truth is dangerous. It hurts. Not many people can take hearing it. Especially not the prison board."

Holly said nothing. She sipped her coffee and edged her fingers toward one of Clara's homemade chocolate chip cookies.

"Go ahead. Eat the damn thing," Clara said.

Holly shrugged, placed it in her plate, and broke off a section.

"What about the task force?" Clara asked. "How's that going?"

"I'm not on it anymore. I got kicked off."

"Why? Don't tell me you socked Pinero in the nuts."

"Something like that."

"Funny. I didn't think he had any."

"I presented a theory he didn't like. So he decided I was a menace to society."

"What kind of theory?"

"Without giving you all the details, I think the crimes are connected. He doesn't see it that way."

"I can understand why. So what now?"

"I haven't a clue," Holly said breaking off another section. "Probably sit here every day, consume all your cookies, and gain two hundred pounds."

"Sounds like a plan. As long as you just let go."

* * *

But she couldn't let go.

Somehow the case had become an obsession. It devoured her thoughts, forcing her to go over each file again and again, trying to piece together a connection, something they had missed.

Whenever Dan called, which was frequently, she pretended that she was occupied with other things. She lied and said that her return to the work at the prison was imminent. But he knew her too well.

"Come on, Holly. Stop the bullshit. You're as involved in this as I am. Come back to the office."

"I can't. Not yet."

"When?"

"When I have something to show you."

"How are you going to do that sitting at home?"

"I don't know yet. But you don't need me. I've told you what I think."

"I need your persistence and your ability to punch holes in whatever I come up with."

"When I have something, I'll come in," she said wearily.

"All right. I'll keep you posted."

Her guilt over her relationship with Dan still plagued her. Feelings she had blocked with him were now surging in another direction. Thoughts about Pascal were becoming more and more persistent. She wanted to hear his voice again. Her hand reached for the phone repeatedly. But she never made the call. With Beth working as his personal assistant she had all the excuse she needed, but she couldn't bring herself to do it.

Beth wasn't very forthcoming. The few phone calls they had exchanged were general and not very detailed. It had only been a couple of days. She was enjoying the work; in fact she was thrilled by it. Pascal was easygoing and laid back. But he was often gone from the office. That suited her sister fine.

"I like it when he's away. It gives me a lot of freedom plus I get to make decisions. He's like that. When something comes up he asks me what I would do, then he actually listens, even though I'm just learning what goes on here."

"Which is?"

"God. So much. Preparing bids for auctions of new materials. Which, by the way, is pretty exciting. He let me listen in on one. It's done by phone from Sotheby's. It's like being at a horse race. Only you have all the money in the world to bet with. Then there's the planning for all these seminars and conferences, which bring people from all over the world. Plus there's constant contact with the Vatican, because we have so much material on Church affairs."

"What else?"

"Well, the institute funds so many programs and endowments, it's unbelievable."

"So you like the job."

"Not like. Love. I can't thank you enough."

"When will you have some time so we can dinner together?"

"I thought you were all tied up with that task force."

"Not anymore."

"What do you mean?"

"I got fired. The DA didn't buy my theory. Which, incidentally, your boss was instrumental in configuring."

"And Dan just let it happen?"

"No. He backed me up. He refused to fire me. But I can't let him take that kind of heat. So I'm backing off. But he still keeps me involved. Unofficially."

Beth was silent.

"Maybe there's something we can do? I could ask Victor."

Holly felt a flutter of panic. "No. He's done enough. Please, don't involve him. It's my problem."

"Okay. If that's what you want."

* * *

Only it wasn't what she wanted. Far from it.

She wanted something very different, something so childishly dreamlike she wouldn't readily admit it to herself. So when the phone rang two days after her conversation with Beth, she felt a sharp pang of apprehension when she recognized Pascal's voice.

"Holly. It's Vincent Pascal."

"Yes. Hello."

"How are you?"

"Very well. I understand you've been traveling?"

"My usual occupation. Nothing earth-shattering. Just Rome again."

He paused. Her pulse was trip-hammering. She felt like a high school senior about to be asked to the prom.

"I'm calling for a reason," he said, as his tone changed.

"Yes?"

"I know what's been going on. Your sister informed me. Unfortunately, I have very little influence with the district attorney's office. But I think there is a way around this. And perhaps a way of breaking some new ground."

"Anything would be appreciated. We're pretty much at a dead end."

"So I understand. This may help. As you know, I have pretty good connections with the Vatican. They're very disturbed not only by the scandal in general, but especially over the murder of these priests. They've assigned a psychologist to the diocese. A specialist in deviant behavior. His name is Father William Terrance. I took the liberty of contacting him and told him about you. He's eager to meet you and offer any cooperation he can. He has total access to all the records of the diocese. Even those that were kept secret. So it may lead somewhere. "

"That's terrific. I don't know what to say."

"Say you'll have dinner with me one evening very soon."

'Of course. I'd love to."

"I'll be looking forward to it. Let me know what happens

with Father Terrance as soon as possible. I'll be awaiting your call. This is his number, and you should also have my private number."

Holly wrote them down.

"So, very soon then," he said in an intimate tone.

"Yes. And thank you again."

He rang off. She turned and stared at herself in the mirror. Her face was flushed.

"What are you, fifteen?" she said aloud. But she could not control the mounting feeling of excitement that felt like a drum beating in her chest. Both at the thought of seeing him and the knowledge that she would soon be tunneling into the deepest secrets of the past. She had been at a dead end and suddenly a door had opened, an opening that might lead to the identity of a serial killer.

Twenty-six

The diocese chancery was a huge red-brick Victorian pile sporting turrets, ornate chimneys, and a massive slate roof. A police cruiser blocked access and two uniformed cops stood guard at the entrance. The terrorism they sought to prevent came not from some overseas menace, but from the community itself. The chancery was besieged by the parishioners it had been created to serve.

Just outside the spiked iron gates, a thin line of picketers moved sluggishly in a rough circle watched by several bored-looking cops slumped in their nearby car. A chilling wind was blowing and the pickets had a tight grip on their signs, which bent and twisted as the gusts tore at them with clawlike talons.

From what Holly could make out, they were protesting the diocese's refusal of the plaintiff's latest offer in one of the multitude of molestation suits presently afflicting the Church.

She pulled up to the side gate and showed her pass to the guard seated inside a white wooden-framed kiosk, his face hidden within the fur trim of his massive hood. Her pass disappeared within his pawlike mittens long enough for him to mark the number on a clipboard. He handed it back to her and waved her to a spot on the far end of the lot.

Holly parked and walked toward the entrance as the pickets took up their chant. The wind swept the words down the long tree-lined avenue making them impossible to comprehend.

She presented her pass to the two cops outside, who glanced at it with watery eyes and passed her through, stamping their feet against the chill. Inside, she was assaulted by a blast of hot air that rippled through her hair as she stepped into a large marble-walled entry.

The reception clerk seated behind a wooden barrier fixed his eye on her credentials, made a note in his logbook, and gave her a visitor's pass with a gummed back, which she pressed to the lapel of her leather coat.

She was directed to an elevator, which took her to the floor below. Two priests hurried past dressed in black floor-length cassocks. One offered a quick nod. The other averted his eyes. She felt like a pariah. This was not a place where women were accustomed to enter. She was an alien presence. She wondered what their reaction would be if they knew she had come to uncover something dark and malignant.

Thankfully, she rode the elevator alone. The doors opened on a floor tiled in a pattern of back-and-white diamonds that led her along a dimly lit windowless corridor between solid walnut doorways with numbers in large enamel squares. In the place of gas lamps there were ornate electric fixtures enclosed in frosted glass. The high heels of her suede boots echoed on the tiles. She felt as if she had entered a time warp. One of the doors would open and out would step Dr. Watson and Sherlock Holmes. Or more appropriately, Dr. Jeckel and Mr. Hyde. But none of the doors opened. The place felt abandoned.

The corridor continued on. She was one level beneath the

ancient building. It was cold. The hallway was unheated and she felt a chill. The area smelled of mold and disinfectant. And something more familiar, the dry rot of yellowed paper moldering in ancient cardboard boxes. She felt a slight tremor of anxiety. Had she made a wrong turn? But the numbers continued on. One after the other. Then she made another turning into another corridor, even less lit. Even chillier. She felt a distinct draft now as if she were heading for an open window. Hell, she thought, I'll never get back. I should have scattered breadcrumbs.

"Hello." She called in a soft tone. "Come on, number Seventy-two. Where are you?"

The door she sought finally appeared.

She tapped on the wooden panel. Then knocked harder.

There was a long dead silence, then the door finally opened.

She faced a middle-aged man in his fifties with square shoulders and an athletic build. He was bald and was dressed in a black suit and a Roman collar.

"Father Terrance?"

"Dr. Alexander?"

"Please call me Holly."

"Absolutely. Come on in. You can call me Bill."

He stepped back admitting her to a huge white-tiled chamber with a high arching ceiling. Globes hung down on metal fixtures filling the chamber with light. Long rows of shelving were neatly filled with uniform rows of cardboard boxes. Several electric space heaters glowed along the floor, filling the room with warmth.

"This way," he said, leading her between rows of shelving rising over their heads.

An office had been carved out of the maze made of glass-walled partitions that reminded her of Dan's office in the CID building.

He stepped inside and held the door open for her.

There were a desk and several chairs along with piles of open boxes, and two additional space heaters, which glowed with orange intensity.

Holly entered and stood alongside the desk as the priest closed the door behind him. The heaters filled the room with a surprising warmth.

"Nice and cozy," she said.

"Yes. It can get pretty cold down here. Even in nice weather. I usually wear a parka. But today I'm in uniform."

"How long have you been working down here?"

"Oh, about six weeks now. I'm sort of a pariah around here, as you'll soon discover."

"Why is that?"

"Well, I'm here to uncover the past and find evidence of moral turpitude. No one likes that idea, especially no one in the diocese. Everyone looks at me sideways, expecting the ax to fall."

"I thought the policy these days was full disclosure."

"What do they call it now? Transparency? Well, that may be the policy, but it's not exactly making me popular. Remember Diogenes? He went around looking for an honest man. You can imagine how the Greeks must have treated him."

Holly laughed. "I understand."

Father Terrance was smiling. He had thin lips and sharp blue eyes like the ice in a glacier's core.

"I understand we're in the same line of work," Holly commented.

"So I understand. You work at a prison, don't you? For sex offenders."

Holly nodded. "I used to anyway," she went on. "I seem to be on indefinite leave."

"Why is that?"

"Let's just say the powers that be think I presented them in a bad light. So now I'm paying the price."

"Vincent told me. He said you were a hostage who became the spokesperson for a prison takeover. Sounds like an interesting bit of work."

"Take my advice. If it ever comes your way, turn it down."

Father Terrance laughed. The blue of his eyes lit up like tiny Christmas lights.

"I'll remember that."

"How is this going?" she asked.

"Why are we standing?" he said, as he sat on the edge of his desk, gesturing for Holly to take the chair opposite. She sat down and opened her coat. She felt warmer now. She was wearing a blue turtleneck sweater and a black woolen skirt that came to mid-calf.

"Sorry I can't offer you anything except some cocoa I brought with me in a thermos."

"I'm fine."

"How is this going, you asked," he said in a serious tone. "I'm not sure. It's a little bit like breaking an enemy code during a war. There's a lot of deciphering. What I've got are records of priests who were sent away for specific counseling. Or relieved of their duties for various reasons. None of them are stamped, 'this priest exhibited deviate behavior or was a child molester.' I don't want to use the word cover-up. But there are layers of misdirection that amount to disinformation and outright deception."

"I understand."

"Now from what Vincent told me, you're looking for the heirs of Fra Alfieri. Is that correct?"

"You know about him?"

"Not many do. But yes, I'm one of the privileged."

"Do you actually believe such a thing is possible?"

"A cult of avenging angels existing down through the ages?" He smiled wryly. "It's always possible. Alfieri lived. We know that. But his Cipher was never found. And yet, down through the centuries certain prelates have met with gruesome deaths that were identical to the kind of murders he committed. So you tell me."

"I'm not sure about the 'down through the ages' part. But someone is obviously copying his methods in the here and now."

"Yes. I agree."

"Do you think I'll find anything here?"

"It's always a possibility. Besides, I don't think there is anywhere else you can look, is there?"

Holly glanced at him. His icy blue eyes were fixed on her with steel-eyed precision.

He was right. There was nowhere else.

They took no pleasure in the work.

Each file they selected was a little labrynth, a twisting maze of bureaucratic ingenuity devoted to the art of the cover-up. They dug out of them hundreds of moldering pages secreted within boxes within boxes within boxes, like those little Russian dolls.

Each day, Holly made the trek to the chancery, descending to the record chamber on the lower floor. No matter how early she arrived, she found Father Terrence already hard at work.

To prevent any interference or pilfering, he had the door bolted with a special lock to which only he had the key. They worked in different parts of the chamber, each of them alone as they sifted through the enormous mass of material. Holly wore two sweaters and a pair of gloves to keep out the chill. But the walls seemed to leak the cold.

The task was seemingly impossible, but there were certain key words that the priest had given her. They were the red flags that signaled she was on to something hot.

Terrance had oriented her on the first morning they began working together. He was waiting for her in the marble-lined vestibule and quickly guided her back out the way she came in. She almost didn't recognize him. He had exchanged his black suit and Roman collar for baggy cords, a red flannel shirt, and a well-worn leather bomber jacket. His head was protected by a tweed slouch cap pulled low over his eyes, which were shielded by dark glasses. He looked like an out-of-work actor.

"Where are we going?" she asked as they headed toward the parking lot.

"Somewhere quiet where we can talk."

"Quieter than that tomb we've been working in?"

"You never know who's listening."

"Down there? The walls must be ten feet thick."

He smiled. "To quote the poet, even the thickest walls have ears."

They got into his car, a battered maroon hatchback, and he drove them to a chrome-sided diner alongside the old rail-road tracks. The diner was almost empty at that hour and he guided her to a booth in the back.

"They make a great breakfast here," he said as he perused the plastic-coated menu.

"Just coffee, thanks. I've already had something."

In truth, she had gulped down a small glass of orange juice before she hurried out into the cold. Now that she was a woman of leisure, she barely had time for breakfast. Ordinarily she made time for toast or an English muffin, even oatmeal, and at least one cup of coffee, which she took into the car with her in a plastic cup.

He looked at her over the top of the menu.

"You look like you could use something," he said.

She returned the stare, as the waitress sauntered by, pausing to ask if they were ready.

He ordered eggs, ham, and coffee. She ordered pancakes.

"That's more like it."

"I won't be able to finish them."

"Don't worry. I'll help you out."

A young Mexican busboy brought them steaming mugs of coffee.

"So. How long have you known Vincent Pascal?"

She was discomfited by the question. She felt her cheeks flame.

"Not long. I went to hear him lecture. I thought he could help me."

"Did he?"

"That depends where you sit. I was on the police task force as a consultant, for the purpose of providing them with a profile of the killer. What Pascal provided gave me an insight into something quite unexpected."

"Fra Alfieri?"

"Do you believe he existed?"

"More important. Do you?"

"Why more important?"

"You deal in facts. Don't let the jacket fool you. I'm a man of faith, remember."

She smiled. "Yes. I believe he existed. "

"And that a cult of Alfierites is operating to this day?"

"That was my conclusion."

"Which I understand you paid for with your job."

Holly nodded.

The food arrived, steaming on the thick white porcelain plates. He picked up his utensils and tucked in with a nod for her to begin. She doused her pancakes in maple syrup and cut a small triangle. They were surprisingly delicious.

"Good?" he asked.

"Very."

"I told you."

She cut another triangle out of the short stack, then another, realizing how hungry she actually was. She had been eating very little since Ted had relieved her of her duty.

"How long have you known, Vincent?" she asked.

He looked up from his plate. "Vincent? Oh, hell. Quite a while, I suppose. His foundation funds the Chapter of Life."

"I'm sorry."

"Ah. I should have realized. I suppose it's not generally

known, even in our profession. I suppose it was meant to be kept that way."

She took a quick sip of her coffee. "What exactly are we talking about?"

"The Chapter of Life is a kind of retreat. A sanitarium, you could say. Though that word has gone out of fashion. We don't have many of them anymore."

"Where is it located?"

"In Michigan."

"And its purpose?"

"To rehabilitate wayward clergy. It was founded back in the early fifties by a psychiatrist named Richard Stark. Have you ever heard of him?"

Holly frowned. "The name is vaguely familiar."

"Well, Stark was very well connected. He had been a top physician. He was on the faculty of several prominent universities and had treated several important political and military figures. He was concerned with the amount of mental illness he saw in society and tried to put together a combination of religion and psychiatry to try and get a handle on it. He was one of the first to convince the nation's religious leaders to get rid of their antagonism toward Dr. Freud and use psychiatry as a tool in treating the clergy as well as parishioners. He got some financial backing from people like the Foresters and set up shop. He called it the Chapter of Life."

"I'm beginning to remember some of this," Holly said. "I think I remember reading about it."

"Probably. It was a pretty successful operation. At first, it only received wealthy patients. But by the end of the sixties, it was one of the places where diocese sent priests they wanted cured of various disorders. Alcoholism and drug abuse being the major ones. Which were often used to hide the most important one of all."

"The abuse of minors."

"Yes. Women too, but the best-kept secret was the molestation of children. Especially young boys."

"Secret from whom?"

"The public. You see, the Church thought it was fulfilling its duty by sending these priests to seek psychiatric care, without reporting them to the police for breaking the law. That's what's at the bottom of this scandal. Not that no one knew, but that the crimes were known and covered up."

"How exactly?"

"In the past, whenever it was reported that certain bishops had knowingly allowed priests who had been accused of multiple acts of abuse to continue practicing, the charge was always refuted by the bishop in question. He'd say, 'But I sent the offender to a psychiatric institution as soon as I knew.'"

"And he was lying?"

Father Terrance shook his head. "To the contrary. He was telling the truth. When the priest was returned to his ministry, the bishop thought he was off the hook. They believed the priest was merely having a lapse. That his condition could be cured by more counseling. They used psychiatry as a cover-up. What they really believed was that once a priest confessed, he should be immediately absolved of all blame. No matter what the crime. Or how serious the offense. Once absolved, he could return to his parish."

"Where he could continue to abuse children."

He looked at her, his ice-blue eyes narrowing. "That's right. In actuality, the Church had lost control of these cases. When the higher clergy was confronted with the truth, they ducked. They believed these men were ill and could be cured by systematically returning them to places like the Chapter of Life. Once the priest returned from treatment, then the real healing could begin. See, they didn't see this as a psychiatric problem, but as a religious one. If an abusing priest found it too shameful to confess to another priest, then he could always confess to a lay psychiatrist. The psychiatrist wouldn't judge him on moral grounds and was unable to report his actions to the authorities under the ethics of his profession. But by telling the truth and showing contrition, the abusing priest could receive absolution."

"And forgiveness," Holly said.

"That's right. Which is how these bishops justified covering it up."

Holly took another sip of her coffee.

"So they used psychiatry to ease their consciences."

"More than that," he said. "They used it as a tool to maintain the status quo and keep the evil alive. They used it to lull the legal system into a state of complacency. See, it wasn't until the mid-sixties that most states required sexual abuse to be reported. Then it was made a federal crime. Since psychiatrists and clergy were exempt from mandatory reporting in many jurisdictions, those who knew reported to each other. Which was the case with the Chapter of Life."

"In what way?'

"They specialized in the treatment of sexual misconduct. They used all the latest techniques. Behavior modification. Medication to control sex drives. Everything short of castration."

"Sounds like my shop."

"More than likely."

"And the priests they treated?"

"They were sent back to their parishes after six months with the usual stipulations that they not minister to minors without supervision, blah, blah. But in none of the cases were the police or the authorities ever involved or even notified. Which of course flies in the face of everything we know about effectively curtailing abuse. The only way to make such treatment effective is to add the component of legal punishment. Without it the offender is doomed to repeat and repeat and each time he lapses the lives of more and more innocents are destroyed."

Holly was silent as she contemplated what he said. She lifted the cup and stared into its oily surface.

"They can't get away with it, not anymore," Holly said quietly.

"No. Now they've been forced to deal with these crimes."

"And their punishment."

Each glanced at the other. The meaning was clearly scribed within their eyes.

Twenty-seven

They now had their Rosetta stone, the key which they could use to open the files.

Like the ancient Egyptian stone that unlocked the understanding of hieroglyphics, the words Chapter of Life imprinted within each file gave them a way to access its deepest secrets.

It took the better part of a day and hours of patient labor before they uncovered their first major find. Holly was working through a series of overly stuffed boxes piled against a pillar in the rear of the room when she found it.

"I think I've got something," Holly said.

Father Terrance dropped the file he was examining and hurried across the dimly lit chamber.

"What have you got?" he said eagerly.

"It's a discharge summary from the Chapter. His name is Father Jeffrey Bonner. He was admitted on three separate allegations of abuse."

"What do they say?"

"Not much. They describe his stay as uneventful."

"And?" the priest said impatiently.

"It goes on to say that during certain stressful periods of

his ministry the patient became obsessed with certain immature sexual objects."

"Objects?" Terrance spat. "We're talking about children here! Live flesh and blood!"

"His psychiatrist goes on to say that Bonner did not exhibit a classic case of pedophilia, in that the abuse was fragmentary and sporadic. That it did stop and had a playful, childlike quality to it. Not sadistic or without remorse. And not eroticized or sexually stimulating."

"My God. Did you ever hear such bullshit. No wonder the Church used them. They're totally complicit. How many times did he see this shrink?"

"Five times a week for solo sessions. The usual fifty-minute hour. Plus he went to group four times a week. A clergy group. A human development program and an assertiveness training group where he confessed he had oral copulation with prepubescent boys over a five-year period."

"My God."

"It goes on to say that the patient has reassured us that these impulsive episodes of pedophilia were now under complete control because of his involvement with therapy. And that his life has taken a positive turn."

"Well, isn't that wonderful."

"Listen to his discharge diagnosis. Atypical pedophilia in remission." Holly stared at him. "We consider cases like this incurable."

"But not the Chapter. They believe that because of celibacy and the Church's idea that desire for women is evil, it focuses interest on young boys. And that you can reprogram an offender by giving him therapy and teaching him how to manage his leisure time."

Holly could see the fury building in the priest's eyes. "Imagine. Managing your leisure time. Teach him golf instead of sodomy and you cure the problem. Does it say how many boys he molested after being discharged?"

"He was admitted three successive times after that."

"I rest my case."

Dan was waiting for her just inside the entrance as she came out.

She introduced him to Father Terrance, who shook his hand and smiled at each of them before heading toward his car.

"How did you know where to find me?" she asked Dan.

"Clara told me. How about a cup of coffee?"

"I'm beat. Not tonight, if you don't mind."

His lips tightened. "What exactly do you think you're doing?"

Holly glanced around. The receptionist was eyeing them with more than casual interest. Priests and laity moved through the cavernous marble-lined vestibule, some heading through the doors, others conversing in small knots.

"Not here," she said.

She started out through the door with Dan a step behind. She led him to her car, opened the door, and got inside. He went around and got in beside her.

She turned on the ignition allowing the interior to warm up.

"Are you going to answer my question?" he snapped.

"Why are you so angry?"

"Because you disappear without a trace. No calls. You don't even answer mine. Then I find you here. What the hell is going on?"

"Nothing's going on. I'm doing some research, that's all."

"Research into what?"

Holly was silent.

"I have no claim on you, Holly. I know that. But I do care what happens to you. And I still want you back on my team."

"I can't come back. Not after what Pinero said."

'Fuck Pinero. I told you that. I'm running the task force, not him."

"I would only be a detriment. There's enough shit in my life right now without becoming the cause of a battle you don't have to fight."

"Why don't you let me deal with that?"

"I'm sorry. I just can't."

"So, what the hell are you intending to accomplish here?"

She remained silent for a moment staring at the layer of frost covering her windshield.

"I don't know yet."

"Don't you think I have a right to know what it is you're doing?"

Holly knew he was right. She probably should have informed him. "I'm trying to find other priests who committed sexual offenses. They could be our next series of victims."

"And Father Terrance is helping you?"

"No. I'm helping him. He was there before I was. He's on a special assignment from the Vatican to uncover the truth."

"Do you realize the risk you're running?"

"What risk?"

"If there is a cult of avengers or even just one. Why would they stop with priests?"

"I'm not a target. Only those who offend."

He looked at her with an incredulous expression. "You're trying to stop them, aren't you? Isn't that what this is all about?"

Holly had never considered that possibility. She was unable to contradict him. "I understand."

"Does that mean you're actually listening to me?" he said.

"What do you want me to do?"

"For starters, I want you to turn whatever you find over to us."

"I don't know if I can do that."

"Then what's the point?"

"I owe something to the people who allowed me to do this work. I have to consider them."

"Holly. You won't be able to protect them or yourself. Not without us."

"I know."

"But you won't allow me to protect you?"

"Please try to understand."

He stared at her, then his eyes narrowed as he reached for the door handle. "Have it your own way."

The sound of her door closing had the unforgiving sound of finality.

Luck was running with them.

The following morning they found a second file.

It belonged to a Father Harold Shea, the director of a Catholic elementary school for boys. He was a thirty-four-year-old priest with a record of seven relapses. All of them accompanied by statements from the Chapter psychiatrists that he was considered clinically safe to resume his pastoral duties after evaluation and treatment that lasted a mere three months.

The report contradicted everything Holly knew and had learned.

Her work at the prison was primarily intended to prevent relapses, not effect cures. The most effective treatments were aimed at restraining an offender's access to children, along with libido-inhibiting drugs and behavior-modification techniques, monitored with diagnostic devices like the penile Plethysmograph, or peter-meter as it was called by her colleagues.

Added to this were mandatory twelve-step programs like those offered to alcoholics and drug abusers. But first and most important, for any of it to work, each offender had to know that his actions were being monitored by a legal authority that could send him back to prison if he offended again. Did any of it work? Maybe? Sometimes. It was the cause of many of Holly's sleepless nights, knowing she

might be sending men back into the outside world who were
not in any sense of the word cured.

The words she read in the Shea file were particularly discouraging. No one treating him seemed to be having any
nights without sleep. They indicated that it was all right to
return him to his educational duties. That he would not present a risk for the children of his parish, in spite of the fact
that he was a multiple recidivist.

Holly was dismayed by what she read. Her eyes became
black pits of disgust as she read witnesses' statements revealing how Father Shea had molested a young boy inside a
gym locker room and repeatedly seduced others inside his
office. Others in which a mother reported that he had abused
both of her sons and she'd recorded the obscene phone calls
he made to them over a period of years. She was ignored by
the diocese after her repeated pleas to have Shea removed.
The diocese finally took out a restraining order against her.

Each relapse was followed by a return to the Chapter.
After each release they conducted a follow-up in which the
Chapter concluded that Father Shea felt he was continuing to
do well. They concluded that he remained psychologically
fit for work, including important duties as an educator, in
which he excelled. *He monitors himself well and has his sexual drives under firm and complete control.*

Father Terrance read the papers after Holly offered them
to him. She watched the lines of strain form around his eyes.
He looked up at her. His face seemed to collapse, his expression reflecting an inner despair.

"They returned him to his victims, again and again," he
said.

"Why?" she asked.

He shook his head. His eyes glistened with agony.

"Fear, I suppose. Why do bureaucrats do anything? I say
bureaucrats. Not real priests. That had gone from them long
ago. Automatons. Robots. Afraid to expose the truth no matter that they were destroying the very thing they had been

consecrated to uphold." He broke off. His eyes were wet.
Holly looked away. She was beyond tears.

The call from Beth came just before they were about to
quit. Holly had not turned off her cell, and the sound of its
ringing filled the tile-walled chamber with a reverberating
echo. The priest looked up from the boxes he was sorting
through. The amused look he gave her made Holly feel embarrassed as she flicked open the cover of her phone.

"Hi, sis," Beth began. "How is it going down there?"

Holly was surprised to hear her sister's voice.

"Okay. How are you?"

"Terrific. But this is not about me. Vincent wants to know
if you're free for dinner."

Holly hesitated. She had been so absorbed in her task she
had almost forgotten everything else. Now his image filled
her mind accompanied with the unsteadying sensation she
had felt before.

"Yes. I'm free."

"Don't sound so glum. He's really pretty nice."

"I'm glad you feel that way."

"So, say seven. All right?"

"All right."

Beth hung up leaving Holly slightly unbalanced. Wondering
why Vincent had had Beth call her and what exactly it was
he wanted.

Twenty-eight

The institute was illuminated by amber lights.

Holly felt apprehension as she drove up the now-familiar drive. There was something about the place that felt off-putting. Perhaps it was the enormous wealth it radiated or the formal nature of its geometric gardens and walkways. Or was it the grandiose façade with its medieval towers and crenellations from which imaginary archers seemed to be firing their arrows down at her?

She was being foolish and smiled to herself at the image, trying to relax. She wanted to appear calm and collected, contrary to the turmoil she felt just below her belly. She had made a quick pit stop home. A shower had washed away the grit on her body. Not real grit, but the feeling of it that seemed to coat her skin. The pollution that seeped out of all the rancid files she had been going through with all their sordid attestations of abuse made her feel dirty. It was a feeling she had sometimes at the prison. She tried to deny it existed. But it was there. Clinging to her. It was as if the acid hatreds inside the souls of the men she treated had found a way out through their pores and somehow infected her with their poisons. She shuddered at the thought and eased her car toward the reserved parking area after the guard at the gate checked her license plate, placed a sticker on her windshield, and waved her through.

An attendant greeted her and escorted her along a softly lit corridor filled with paintings in ornate golden frames, each lit by a separate spot hidden high in the coffered ceiling. They took the elevator up. The door opened on the second story, and she stepped out as the door closed with the attendant still inside. Beth was waiting for her.

"I thought you'd be gone by now," Holly exclaimed.

"I had some work to finish."

They quickly embraced. The sight of her sister wearing a smart navy blue suit, earrings, and a new haircut that set off her pretty face sent a shiver of satisfaction through Holly.

"God. You look terrific," she said as she walked beside Beth, who led her back into the now-familiar chambers.

"Thank you. You look pretty good yourself."

"Do you know why he asked me here?"

"Not really. But anytime you want to trade places . . ."

Holly glanced at her.

"I'd kill for an evening alone with him."

Beth wiggled her hips suggestively. They both laughed. But Holly felt her throat tighten.

Beth halted. "Okay. This is where I get off. He's waiting inside. See you soon, I hope."

"Beth." Holly halted her. "You do like it here?"

"Like it here? I love it here. And I love you for getting it for me."

She smiled warmly, waved, and headed for an adjacent corridor Holly assumed led back to Pascal's suite of offices. Holly waited a moment before turning toward the doors facing her. She had started toward them when they opened and Pascal stood facing her.

"Hello," he said. "Sorry this was such short notice."

"That's all right."

The sight of him drew her up short. His lean figure was backlit leaving his face in shadow. He extended his hand and she took it, feeling the smoothness of his palm.

"I hope you like lamb. We're having a crown roast."

"One of my favorites."

"Wonderful."

He led her inside and escorted her to the table, which had been set for two. Again she was overwhelmed by the beauty of crystal and china. The soft linen and the Chinese oxblood vases filled with flowers.

He poured the wine himself. A deep Burgundy.

He took the chair adjacent to hers so that they sat at an angle to each other.

"What do you think?" he asked after she had taken a sip of the rich red liquid.

"About the wine?"

"And about the work you've been doing."

"It's been pretty interesting."

"Father Terrance said you'd come up with something. But he didn't specify."

"I don't know if I'd be breaking a confidence."

Pascal smiled. "We're not bound by his rules."

"Why exactly did you want me there?"

"I thought it would help your investigation."

"Was that the only reason?"

He paused and his expression changed.

"We—by that I mean the institute—have made significant endowments to the Chapter of Life."

"And you want to know if your money was well spent?"

"Money we continue to spend. But money is not the point. We have to know if what we're doing is preventing abuse or enabling it."

"I understand."

"Both you and Father Terrance are experts in your fields. That's why I asked you."

"And the diocese? Do they know?"

"No. They were forced to accept Father Terrance. The order came from Rome."

"Did you engineer his appointment?" Holly asked.

He glanced at her. His eyes lit with amusement.

"Do you think I did?"

"Actually. Yes. Did you?"

His smile widened.

"That's something I can't answer. I have to plead the fifth."

"But you did engineer my appointment."

"I merely asked Father Terrance if he could use an assistant and he said yes."

A waiter appeared and served the appetizer. A delicious artichoke salad. Holly drank some more wine and the waiter filled her glass.

"I get the feeling your interest goes beyond the endowment, doesn't it?" she asked when the waiter stepped outside the room.

"The affairs of the Church have always been of concern to the institute," he said, his eyes clouding with seriousness. "I won't lie about that. We have perhaps the largest collection of Church documents outside the Vatican. The Forester family has always been a major contributor to Church charities and associated activities. We are deeply concerned over this current scandal. It is of major importance that the Church be cleansed of wrongdoers. No matter who they are and where they are found. Otherwise we will lose the confidence of those who still believe."

"Do you?"

He was silent.

"I believe in many things. But I have a position here that requires me to act in a positive way toward the entire institution. An obligation to preserve and support it."

"Even if you don't actually believe in it?"

He did not answer. The question hung in the air as the waiter entered with the main course. It was a magnificent crown roast of lamb; each rib circled like an upraised sword.

They ate in silence as the waiter served them.

When he stepped outside, Holly leaned back, holding her wine glass in one hand, and looked at him.

"Inspector Shepard asked me to turn over whatever I find to his investigation."

"What did you say?"

"That I couldn't do that without checking with the people who put me there. I never mentioned your name."

"I see. Was that all?"

"He thought I needed protection."

"From who?"

"Whoever is killing these clergymen."

"Why should they target you?"

"He thought it's possible they might target anyone trying to stop them."

Pascal nodded. "Just what have you found?"

Holly hesitated. There was no reason not to tell him. No rule of ethics or confidentiality she would be breaking.

"So far. We discovered two priests who were sex offenders. Both were returned to work repeatedly on the positive recommendations of the Chapter psychiatrists. Each time they offended again."

"But the Chapter still cleared them," he said grimly.

Holly nodded.

"What were their names?"

"I don't think I can tell you that. Not without checking with Father Terrance."

"That's all right. I understand. I had no right to ask."

"Can I ask you a question?"

"Of course."

"How is my sister working out?"

He looked surprised. "Beth? She's terrific. Eager to learn

and very competent. She'll make a very good curator. If that's what she really wants. I've already trusted her with some pretty important stuff."

Holly smiled. "Thank you for taking her on."

"I should thank you."

Their eyes met. This time she did not pull away. His look made her feel slightly off balance. But she felt none of the conflict that her relationship with Dan provoked.

"I'm glad you came tonight, Holly. I've been wanting to call you."

"Why?"

"Do I have to have a reason?"

She took another sip of wine, then stood and went to the window still carrying her glass. She looked out over the grounds. They were spotlit in places throwing deep shadows across the manicured lawns, strange shapes, like the play of fingers against a strong lamp.

She looked up. He was standing beside her. Their eyes met. He took the glass from her hand and placed it on the sill.

She took a step toward him and his arms came around her.

His apartment was on the other side of the dining room, reached through a long walnut-paneled corridor. The rooms were large and dimly lit. She expected sumptuous furnishings like the rest of the museum, but she was surprised to find that they were decorated simply, almost starkly modern.

They walked through the rooms slowly, their fingers linked. Each of them was holding a wineglass they had taken with them from the dining room along with the half-filled bottle. He led her into his bedroom lit with a small amber lamp. The window opened on the same view of the grounds. He made no move to draw the drapes. They stood apart for a moment, their eyes fixed on each other. He put his glass down and she came to him with a little gasp as his arms folded around her. She closed her eyes as his mouth took hers.

His lips caressed her shoulders, then slipped across her breasts. His fingers opened her and found her wet. He entered her while she was still half-dressed, still in her camisole and bra. She cried out as he thrust, tightening her grip on his arms. She came almost immediately, so hard she had to turn her head into the pillows to keep from screaming. He continued to move inside her and she became lost in the continuous sensation. She rose against him in long climbing breakers, allowing the luxurious waves to crash over her again and again and again. . . .

She drove home in darkness, in the freezing chill of midnight.

Her body still resonated. She felt a kind of numbness, as if she were enclosed in a prolonged sensation. She could still feel the pressure of his hands on her, the taste of his lips. The weight of his long lean body as it moved on hers. She had wanted him again, but she had resisted and gotten dressed as he lay in the darkness and watched her. He had not said a word, nor had he tried to stop her. She went to him and touched his lips with her fingers; then she slipped out of the room and found her way back to the elevator, and returned downstairs, then outside to her car. There was a different attendant on duty. He merely looked up from his desk, then returned to the book he was reading.

The icy air attacked her as soon as she stepped outside, but she still felt the warmth of her body within her coat. She did not want to think. Nor did she want to rationalize the experience. Only to repeat it. When and if it happened again. Casually, and without premeditation.

The road was a long ribbon almost empty of cars and she guided the wheel almost without thinking. No thoughts. No regrets. No guilt. Only home and her bed and sleep.

That was when she saw the car.

Its dark shape was parked beneath the trees, hidden by their shadows. Someone was behind the wheel. A dark huddled figure.

She drew close to the house, drawn there as if in a dream. Dan's words reechoed in her mind.

They would stop anyone who tried to stop them. . . .

She turned the wheel making a sharp U-turn.

She had to pass the other car. As she accelerated, the car door opened. The dark figure stepped out, his face clearly delineated beneath the streetlight.

It was Father Terrance.

She turned the wheel back over and pulled up beside him. Her fingers touched the button and the window slid open, the icy air a slap against her skin.

"I'm sorry." She said, "I thought you were. . . ."

He made a dismissive gesture. His ice-blue eyes were intense, glistening.

"Sorry, I should have called but it couldn't wait. I think I found Fra Alfieri and located his cult."

Twenty-nine

It was a long gray drive under overcast skies.

Holly sat behind the wheel. Father Terrance sat beside her sunk into the seat, his blue eyes fixed on the road ahead. There was nothing to identify his calling. He wore his leather bomber jacket and red plaid shirt, his tweed slouch cap pulled down over his forehead. He looked more like a teamster than a priest. And that was how he liked it.

They had left early.

The night before had been spent in the dining room of Holly's townhouse going over what he had found. He took a file out of an envelope and spread the contents across her dining room table. The rancid smell of old paper filled the room as they scanned the yellowing sheets. It dated from thirty years before. From the earliest days of the relationship between the Chapter and the diocese.

The file belonged to a monk named Brother Dominicus. That was the name he had chosen. His given name was Bernard Coombs. He was a member of a reclusive order whose membership had shrunk to almost nothing and had been disbanded. The grounds had been sold to a developer years before, and now housed suburban families who were unaware that the plots they occupied had once contained a monastery.

Dominicus was one of the first patients sent to the Chapter. He had physically abused another monk when he discovered that the monk had been having sexual relations with the son of a local farmer. The abuse had been violent. He had beaten the monk so badly he had to be hospitalized. Dominicus spent two months at the Chapter undergoing various forms of counseling. After that he was sent to a retreat, then returned to the monastery. No other complaints were ever made. The record indicated that he had confessed that his behavior was a transgression and had seemed genuinely contrite. He participated in all the group sessions and was considered an extremely apt patient. However, the behavior was repeated less than a year later when he almost killed two monks he found having sexual relations with each other. He stabbed one with a knife, rupturing his gall bladder. The other was almost blinded. This time he was asked to leave the order.

"There's no record of him since then?" Holly had asked as they face each other across the table.

"That seemed to be it," Father Terrance said, taking a sip of the coffee Holly had hurriedly brewed. He had been sitting in the cold for almost two hours waiting for her. His hands and face were chapped. But he seemed not be bothered by it.

"I thought we'd hit a dead end," he said. "Then I went upstairs to the record office. And there, under the D's, was another file. It listed several complaints all from upstate communities. All about a Brother Dominicus."

"He used that name?"

"Apparently. Most of the complaints were from parents who claimed he had brainwashed their children and had absorbed them into some kind of cult."

"Were the police notified?"

"I don't know. Of course, the diocese could do nothing

since he was no longer affiliated with the Church. But he apparently let people know he had been, and that was the reason for the complaints."

"Did they say what kind of cult?"

"No. But the complaints run in spurts and cover a period of years. There's some kind of pattern here. He establishes his little cult. Then there's a gap. Maybe four or five years go by. Then we get another batch of complaints. That's the way it goes. Geographically, he seems to have wandered in a kind of circle. What do you think?"

"It's the closest thing we have."

"We could check with the police."

Holly pursed her lips. "There's no reason they would investigate. My theory of the case has been dismissed. They're not looking for a cult or anything else. Besides, they already have a man in custody."

"Someone you don't think committed any of the crimes?"

"Who I know didn't."

"What about the task force?"

Holly shook her head. "I'm not with them any longer. Besides, they're shorthanded."

"What do you suggest?"

Holly raised her eyes and met his.

"That we go and have a look for ourselves."

They bedded down for the night. Father Terrance slept in the guest room. By seven, they had wolfed down a quick breakfast and were on the road. The phone rang just as they left the house. Holly let it ring. She wanted no additional complications, no more than she already had.

The house was set back from the road.

It was a neat colonial with dormer windows and a wide front porch festooned with fall decorations. The house had a welcoming look and they drove up and pulled into the driveway behind a new Land Rover.

Father Terrance had called the people on Holly's cell phone as they drove. There had been some confusion at first; then the woman who answered had handed the phone over to her husband and after hearing what the priest had to say, he'd invited them over.

The door was opened before they got there by a middle-aged man wearing bifocals. His thin lips were compressed in a narrow line as he stood back to admit them. They stepped into the hallway and were ushered into the living room, where a thin nervous-looking woman stood waiting for them.

"I'm Father Terrance," the priest said. "This is Dr. Alexander."

"Don Lynn and my wife, Mary Ann." the man said as they shook hands. "Please sit down."

Holly took a seat on the couch beside the priest. The couple took chairs opposite.

"You said this was about Lorrie," the woman said, addressing Father Terrance.

"You filed a complaint with the diocese a couple of years ago," he responded. "Could you tell us about that?"

"What exactly is your involvement?" the man asked. His eyes were wary.

"I'm a special investigator with the diocese," the priest said, reaching into his jacket pocket and producing an ID in a leather-bound case, which he handed over.

The man studied it, then handed it to his wife.

"Dr. Alexander is with the state."

"I see," the man said, "Well, we haven't heard from Lorrie in over four years. Not since she went to live with that . . . person."

He seemed reluctant to say the name.

"Brother Dominicus?" the priest asked.

The man nodded, but his eyes shifted away.

"Why did she go there?" Holly asked.

"We don't know," the woman answered. "Lorrie was always searching for something. I think she was influenced by someone she met at one of those gatherings she would go to."

"What kind of gatherings."

"God. It was always something different. Hypnosis. Yoga. Meditation. Vegan groups. Animal rights. Eastern religions. Buddha. All of that."

"What was so different about Brother Dominicus?" Holly asked.

"He's been controlling her mind," the man said. "She thought he was God."

"Why? What did he make her do?" Holly questioned.

"We don't know exactly. But we can't ever visit her. She won't even see us."

Holly looked at them. "What did she say her reasons for joining him were?"

"To rid the world of evil," the woman said. "To end wrongdoing. Things like that."

"No matter what they had to do," the man interjected. "Even if it was committing murder. It was okay as long as it was in the name of some final good. That's all she would ever say."

"Was she a religious person?" Father Terrance asked.

The couple looked at each other.

"More when she was little," the man answered. "Later, she tried a couple of churches. She was even a Mormon for a while. She wanted to be a missionary, but it never worked out. Then she went Buddhist."

"Do you know for a fact that she's still with him?" the priest asked.

The man nodded. "We believe she is. Occasionally, people see her with him and the others."

"Do you know where exactly?"

The woman sighed. "We have an address. But it may not be current. They tend to move around. They rent old farms and stay on them for a while. Then they don't pay the rent and get evicted. I'll get it for you."

The woman rose and left the room.

"Is there anything else you can tell us about him?" Holly asked.

"He likes women. That's for sure. Most of the people up there are women. Some of 'em pretty young too. Better be careful, if you're thinking of going over there."

"Why?" the priest asked.

"He's pretty suspicious. Dangerous too. Especially when he knows people are coming to mess with his disciples."

"What do you mean by dangerous?"

The man's expression changed. "People have been known to disappear around there. And that's no rumor. Just ask the police."

Which is what was being done three hours and two hundred miles away.

It was Dan Shepard who got the call just as he was leaving his office. He hesitated for a moment, then stepped back inside and grabbed the phone on his desk.

"Yeah. Shepard here."

"Brace yourself." It was Palumbo on the other end of the line. His drawl usually signified something disastrous.

Dan leaned across the table. "Go ahead."

"Pennicott Manor. Every hear of it?"

"Can't say."

"Upscale halfway house over in Middletown. They dry out alkies, druggies, and who knows what else. Apparently they also warehouse clergy who are off the wagon."

"Come on," Dan said impatiently. "Get to the fucking punch line."

"Two of them are missing."

"Two of who? Alkies, druggies, what elsies?"

"Priests."

Shepard stood erect.

"Priests? What do you mean, priests?"

"Two of them were boarding there. I guess they'd been relieved of their duties. I asked, but the director said he didn't know why. They were in there for stress reduction. They didn't show for lunch or dinner. It's two days now."

"Did they check with the diocese?"

"Uh-huh. No record of them checking in. As far as the diocese is concerned, they belong in the manor."

"What if they're on a trip?"

"No trips. Not allowed. They're supposed to be under treatment."

"So how did they get out?"

"It's not prison. They go out for walks."

"In this weather?"

"Hey. Don't ask me. I just took the report. They called the local troopers, who had it flagged and called us."

"They went out together?"

"Uh-uh. Separate. Apparently, they didn't mix."

"Who are they?"

"You want their names?"

"Of course, I want their names."

"A Father Jeffrey Bonner. B-O-N-N-E-R."

"And the other?"

"Father Harold Shea."

They parked on a windswept knoll above the farm in a small culvert protected by a stand of bare-limbed trees. Holly had purchased a pair of binoculars in a local hardware store and they took turns watching the place.

The farmhouse stood a little off the road flanked by several dilapidated outbuildings and a large red barn that had an off-center lean. Two battered pickup trucks were parked outside next to a rusting antique yellow school bus. The house looked deserted and forlorn. The windows were shielded by dark curtains. Only the collection of dented garbage cans collected in a group just outside the back door attested to the

fact that it was inhabited. Occasionally the door opened and
a woman stepped outside and deposited something in the
trash. Each time it was a different woman, but none of them
was Lorrie, whose parents had given them a small photograph of a smiling blond teenager with an uncertain expression.

When Lorrie finally emerged, she had morphed into a
willowy blonde with sallow skin wearing cowboy boots and
a costume straight out of the sixties.

"There's our girl," Father Terrance said, handing the
glasses over to Holly.

Holly focused on the moving woman, who was headed
toward one of the pickups.

"Looks like she's going somewhere."

Holly started up. They were both relieved. They had been
watching for over two hours and their feet were beginning to
freeze.

Lorrie pulled out of the farm and onto the main road
heading back toward the nearby town as Holly followed her
at a distance. The pickup emitted a trail of dark smoke as it
went cruising at a slow, even speed.

"You're sure about this?" the priest said, eyeing Holly as
they drove.

"Tell me another way," she said.

"You think they'll buy it?"

"I don't know. But it's worth a try."

He shook his head. "I just hope you know what you're
doing. You heard what those people said—this guy is dangerous. And if it turns out that he's our suspect, he's triple
dangerous."

"I've got you as backup." she said with a mischievous
grin.

"Some backup. One old psychologist with prostate problems. Good luck."

The pickup rumbled along Main Street, then turned down

a side street. Holly made the same turn, following it into the parking lot of a market that advertised organic foods. Holly parked a short distance away, watching as Lorrie got out of the pickup and started into the store.

"Wish me luck," Holly said as she opened the door and got out, taking the duffel bag on the rear seat.

Father Terrance nodded, his face grim. He had not liked the idea in the first place, but Holly had gone ahead anyway. They had stopped at a thrift shop where she had purchased several items, then found a restaurant where she changed in the bathroom while he consumed a tuna sandwich. When she emerged she looked the part, he had to grant her that. She had wiped off her makeup and disguised her hair beneath an old baseball cap. She wore a dated denim skirt, a faded T-shirt, old track shoes, and a bulky sweater that had seen plenty of wear. To that she had added an old Army-surplus duffel bag stuffed with other pieces of clothing. He hoped it would do the trick.

Holly crossed the parking lot and went inside. She started down one of the narrow aisles. The store was small, its shelves packed with merchandise. There were organically grown fruits and vegetables and whole assortments of foods whose labels Holly had once known but had since forgotten. Her sister Beth had gone through several stages of counter-culture beliefs ranging from vegan diets to macrobiotics. Holly selected several items as she eyed Lorrie out of the corner of her eye. When the blond-haired young woman went to the vegetable area, Holly cut down the next aisle and came around to where Lorrie was engrossed in selecting produce.

"Hi," Holly said.

The young woman looked up and offered a pale smile.

"Excuse me. But I know who you are," Holly continued.

The young woman stared at her.

"You belong to Brother Dominicus' commune, right?"

Lorrie's eyes became wary.

"How'd you know?"

"I've seen you in town before. I wanted to come over and speak to you, but I was kind of nervous about it. My name is Holly."

"Lorrie," the young woman said.

They shook hands.

"I wanted to check it out. What you guys are into, I mean. I was in a commune over in Lancaster. But it broke up. I've been looking for something really spiritual. And I heard about Brother Dominicus and your group. Is there some way I could check it out? I don't have anywhere to live right now. But I'm not free-loading. I'm not a hippie. I've got money. And an ATM. I can work. I'd pay my share of everything."

Lorrie seemed hesitant.

"I don't know. I'd have to call."

"It would mean a lot to me," Holly said.

"I don't have any money for a call."

"I have some," Holly said as she dug into the knit bag slung over her shoulder.

"Watch my wagon, okay?"

"Sure."

The young woman went to the pay phone in the front of the store. She dialed and spoke into the phone. She waited, listening to the voice on the other end. Then she put the receiver back on the hook and came back to where Holly was waiting.

"Okay. You can come on up. You got some things?"

"Just this stuff," Holly said, nodding toward the duffel bag on the floor at her feet.

"I got to finish shopping first."

Father Terrance checked his watch.

Holly had been in the store for almost a half hour.

Anxiety twisted along his spine and shot arrows into his fingers as they drummed along the top of the dashboard. "Come on . . . come on," he said under his breath. He hated waiting. Patience was a hard-won virtue he had yet to attain. He glanced in the rearview mirror once again. Only this time he saw the door of the store open and both women exit. Holly was carrying her duffel bag as well as a large shopping bag. The other woman wheeled a cart loaded with paper bags.

He watched as they loaded their purchases in the back of the pickup and Holly slung her duffel inside. Then both women got in. The pickup started up in a roar of black exhaust and pulled out of the lot.

Father Terrance turned the key. He eased the Volvo out of the lot and followed as the pickup continued back the way it came emitting the smoke screen of a destroyer. He stayed well back, as they had planned. He drove by the entrance to the farm when the pickup made its turn into the driveway. He made a U-turn into the culvert and pulled up inside the protection of the trees. He grabbed the binoculars from the seat beside him and pressed them against his eyes.

The pickup pulled up to the back door. Several people came out of the house. Two women and a young man. They began unloading the truck, as Lorrie started into the house with Holly following a step behind. She stepped inside and the door closed behind her.

Father Terrance took a deep breath.

His stomach was vised in fear.

There was something narrow and oppressive about the house and its blackened windows. Something that made him want to retch. Some backup, he thought. What the hell was he supposed to do now? He couldn't see through the walls. The only weapon he had was a cell phone.

Holly was in there, completely on her own.

* * *

The house was dark, lit by cylindrical oil lamps that radiated a dismal wavering glow. The walls had been stripped to the lathing. There was something heavy and oppressive in the air. As if the atmosphere were weighted down with incense.

Holly followed her companion through the darkened kitchen lit only by a single lamp. Then down a narrow hallway and into a large central room with a low ceiling. It was filled with carpets, some Oriental, others patterned with Native American designs. Pillows were piled in clusters. Otherwise there was no other furniture except for a large low round table with brass legs. The room smelled close and airless. Several women rested on bolsters at the other end of the room. They had long hair and wore the same flower-child clothing as Lorrie. One of them was pregnant. They regarded Holly as if they had been expecting her. Their eyes were distant and unwelcoming.

"Wait here," Lorrie said.

She bent and whispered to the others, then rose and walked back outside.

Holly sat down, tossing her duffel bag down beside her.

A young man with long dark hair and a wispy beard stood in the doorway. His eyes fastened on her, cold and watchful.

Holly smiled at him, but received no response. She realized he was there to guard against her leaving. She settled back against the cushions, trying to appear relaxed. But inside she was a twisted bar of iron. The tension in her legs was causing them to tremble.

A teenage girl entered behind him. Her thinness caused Holly to wince. She had the scooped-out behind of an anorexic. She looked down at Holly with large hollowed eyes.

"So you're gonna be his new wife?"

Holly shrugged and smiled.

"He likes your type. He'll want you."

"Shut up!" the boy snapped. "Get the fuck back in the kitchen."

The girl gave Holly a pointed glance, then turned and went back inside.

Lorrie returned a few moments later.

"Come," she said to Holly.

Holly rose and bent to get her duffel bag.

"Leave it," Lorrie said. "He's waiting for you."

Holly nodded and followed her out of the room. The young man trailed behind them.

They returned down the corridor to the staircase at the end. Lorrie started up. They went up to the next level. The young man's boots sounded like drumbeats on the wooden stairs. Facing them was a long dark corridor with sets of identical doors facing each other, the way they did in a rooming house, Holly thought.

"Is he up here?" Holly asked,

Lorrie did not respond. She continued along the hall, which was lit by two oil lamps set on small tables at either end. Their light was feeble. How can light be dark? Holly thought. The young man was a step behind them.

Lorrie stopped at a door at the opposite end. She grasped the knob and opened the door. She turned and looked at Holly. "Inside."

Holly hesitated. The room was dark.

"Go ahead. He's waiting for you."

Holly felt a claw tearing at her insides. She tightened her lips and went past Lorrie stepping into the room.

It was pitch black inside. She could make out nothing except what looked like some kind of altar. It was cold inside. Waves of chill shuddered through her.

"Where is he?" she asked, turning toward the young woman in the doorway. "There's nobody in here."

"Who are you, bitch?" Lorrie said.

"I told you. I came from a commune in Lancaster."

"There is no commune in Lancaster," Lorrie said in a cold flat voice. "Now, who the fuck are you?"

"I want to see Brother Dominicus," Holly said.

"In your fucking dreams."

The door slammed shut. Holly heard the key turn in the lock. She was in total darkness.

Thirty

There were two of them in the containers.

It was night and they were naked beneath the flimsy paper-thin garments they had been forced to wear.

Each could sense the other's presence, but could not see where the other was because of the heavy metal helmets that covered each of their heads. Small holes had been bored in the metal, enough to allow in air but not large enough to permit seeing through.

They awoke inside a metal capsule that covered each from head to foot like an open mummy case. The harness was affixed to an iron bar that connected one to the other like identical salt and pepper shakers. They were deafened by the rough sound of an engine moving them across rough ground.

They could see just enough to realize that they were raised high above the earth, suspended from some kind of crane. Each could hear the other's muffled sounds but could not make out the words.

They were still dazed from the effect of the drugs they had been given when they had been abducted. Each had been taken off the street by a stranger who had pulled up in a white panel truck and asked for directions. What happened after that was mostly a blur in which reality went in and out of focus like a child twisting a kaleidoscope.

They found themselves on an icy stone floor, their wrists and ankles gripped by ancient iron manacles, facing a large wooden seat of judgment on which sat a hooded figure who read them a list of accusations, then pronounced judgement on them, citing some kind of Cipher. None of it made any sense. They were priests. Men of the Church. They protested their innocence and demanded their rights, a trial and lawyers, and that the diocese be notified. But their demands had been ignored.

After that, they were jostled into the back of a truck that went from the smooth surface of a highway to rough back roads, until they were hauled out of the truck and into the freezing night air and secured inside their metal prisons.

Now they waited as the icy air crawled along their skin. Each shouted a protest, but they were pleading with the wind.

There was a jolting vibration as the crane started forward. Then the suffocating odor of burning tar.

For an instant, they failed to comprehend what it was. But by bending their heads within the iron helmets they could see through the holes just enough to make out the twin pits of boiling pitch, seething just below their legs.

The impact of the horror slammed though them. *It was not possible . . .*

The crane whined and began lowering them toward the steaming pitch. They felt the incessant heat on their skins. Their bodies began to writhe within the narrow confinement of their prisons and in blatant contradiction of all they had said before, each began to scream out all the painful details of his guilt.

How many hours? Three? Five?
Holly had lost track.

She sat crouched in a corner of the room, her arms wrapped tightly around her knees. Shivering. Her teeth were chattering. The knuckles of her hands were stabbed by tiny icy needles. There were only darkness and the trembling sounds of the house, threatening and disorienting her. It was cold. A damp, seeping cold that penetrated to her bones. Colder than being out in the snow, or on ice, skating. The cold of a cave or a tunnel.

Or the grave.

Her mind churned, filling with the images of each of the victims.

Men spitted, then roasted alive.

Flesh torn by gleaming fangs.

Mary encased in beeswax, her body a living hive.

What punishment was reserved for her?

She did not believe she was going to die. Not here, not in this dismal chamber. But that was just denial. And she knew well all the twists and turns of that beast.

She had been stupid to put her trust in Father Terrance. He was out of his depth and so was she. Her entire idea was a classic of stupidity. She had pursued it because she was desperate to do something to change her fate. She was in limbo. She had no job. No life. Nothing. She had made a futile leap into the darkness. Hoping for what?

She heard herself sob. The sound made her jump, as if someone else was in the room with her. But she was alone. Totally alone.

She had to fight her despair.

But how?

She had to think. She had unwittingly placed herself in the hands of the killer of almost a dozen people. Soon she would be facing him. What weapons did she have? She could reveal her relationship to the task force. Her knowledge of Fra Alfieri and the motive for his killings. It was her only hope. She had nothing else.

But what would the result be?

Would he be able to allow her to go, knowing all that she did? If she were in his place, would she?

The idea chilled her.

Then what could she fight with?

She had gone over the room looking for some way out. But there was none. There was only the locked door and two boarded-up windows. She had nothing with which to pry them open. There was nothing in the room. No chair or table. It was completely bare. The floor was rough and she moved her hands across it hungry to find a nail or a piece of splintered wood she could use as a weapon. But there were no nails. No splintered shards. She had only her bare hands. And they were useless.

She heard a sound and froze.

Then another.

She edged around the room toward the door and pressed her ear against it.

The sounds were more distinct.

The tread of boots on the stairs.

He was coming for her.

She moved away, back into her corner. No. She would meet him there, in the center of the room. She would face him squarely when he opened the door. She edged toward the center, her hands spread out in front of her. Her eyes were wide open but she was blind. She felt dizzy for an instant as she sought to find her bearings in the darkness. Then she lowered her hands. She was sure this was the center and that she was facing the door.

The footsteps were louder. Approaching.

She stiffened, spread her feet, and dropped her hands to her sides, clenching her fists. Assuming a fighter's stance. Her final instinct of survival.

The footsteps stopped outside the door.

She heard the key turn in the lock.

She sucked in a breath and waited as the door swung open.

He was silhouetted in the doorway, his hulking figure dark and menacing in the gelatinous light of the oil lamps.

"Where are you, Holly?"

A small pulse of shock went through her. It was a voice she knew.

"Damn it, Holly. It's Dan Shepard."

There were no cruisers. No lights flashing red and white.

But there were police. People she knew. Palumbo. Bettis. Nicola, a magnum in a holster on her hip. Dawson, his eyes screwed with sarcasm.

They came down the stairs together. Holly first, with Dan a step behind.

Lorrie and the other members of the commune had been herded into different corners of the main room, separated from each other by members of the team.

Shepard guided her into the kitchen, where Father Terrance sat at one end of a wooden table, which was piled with file folders.

"Sit down," Dan commanded. His eyes were filled with reproach. "You look like hell."

"I feel like hell," she said, refusing to meet his gaze. She felt ashamed and embarrassed. Worse, stupid.

"You look like an angel to me," the priest said with a smile.

Holly took the chair opposite the priest as Dan sat at the other end. Father Terrance unscrewed the top off a large thermos and poured her a cup of steaming cocoa. Holly took it both hands allowing the heat to warm her before she took the first comforting sip.

"What have you got?" Dan asked.

Father Terrance pursed his lips and turned the folder he was reading around to face the inspector.

Shepard glanced at the material.

"What is this? Some kind of scrapbook?"

"More. Each folder contains a dossier of each of the victims. Newspaper clippings. Trial records. Dates of release from prison. Current addresses and telephone numbers. You name it."

They each glanced at each other.

"Do you think this is the guy?" Dan said.

"I don't know. But this is pretty incriminating," the priest answered.

"I may have to apologize," Dan said, looking at Holly with a different expression.

"Did you find him?" Holly asked.

"Not yet. We've questioned his people. All they'll say is that he hasn't been here for a couple of days. We ask where he might have gone and they say they don't know. It seems he took off whenever he wanted to and never told them anything. Around here, he was the great I am."

"What are you going to do?" the priest asked.

"First, we'll put this place under surveillance, then we'll try and track him down."

"And these people. Once they're free, they could warn him," the priest said.

"We have nothing to hold them on."

"They locked me up," Holly said. "That's kidnapping, isn't it?"

"Technically. We might hold them on that for a day or two. Possibly. But that's all. You invited yourself in here, remember? If you had come to me, we could have staked the place out and we might have got him."

Holly was silent. She still felt small in spite of the possibility that they might have found the man they were looking for.

"We didn't think you'd be able to," Father Terrance said. "What with Pinero breathing down your neck."

"You should have tried me."

"He's right," Holly said. "It's my responsibility. I screwed up and now he's gone."

"Do we at least have a description?"

Shepard shook his head. "No picture. Nothing. Other than he wears a beard. People in town hardly ever see the guy. He's a kind of recluse. Only his people ever go out. He stays inside except for his little trips here and there."

"He wouldn't have to go anywhere. They could have done the work for him," the priest said.

"Like Manson?" Dan said.

"Very possibly. They are a similar kind of cult, I believe. If it's anything like Manson's, they would have followed his orders to the letter."

Dan nodded. "Most of them are women. His wives, apparently. At least a dozen of them. One or two are pregnant. Only two men, so far."

"Women can do the job," Holly added.

Dan nodded. "No argument. We'll have to get forensics in. Try to find evidence that any of the victims may have been brought here. We'll put out a description when we have one. There has to be some kind of info on him."

"There is," Father Terrance said.

"Where?"

"In Rome."

Holly and Shepard looked at him.

"I couldn't find much about his past at the diocese. But there would have to be detailed information in the Vatican archives. I can be there by tomorrow night."

"Do you have to go?" Holly said. "Couldn't they send it to you?"

"You have to understand the politics," the priest said. "My appointment as an investigator was made over the objection of several important cardinals."

"But why? I thought they wanted to bring all this into the light," Dan said.

"That's the consensus over here. Over there it's different. There are those who want it buried as quickly as possible. There have always been scandals like these. The Church has always taken care of them. They don't understand that this time things are different. I'll have to go myself, otherwise I'll get nothing."

"So we cross our fingers and hope you find something," Dan said. "In the meantime, once he knows we're looking for him, he'll be ten thousand miles away."

"No," Terrance said. "He won't. He hasn't finished his business yet. There are other files."

"Even knowing we're looking for him?" Dan asked.

"He's on a mission," Holly said. "He can't stop. It's a form of compulsion. You have to think of him the way you would about a terrorist or any other kind of fanatic. His entire being is fixated on obtaining his goal. He won't stop until he reaches it, no matter what the danger is. As a matter of fact, often the greater the danger to him personally, the greater the exultation. He sees it as a sign from God."

"I think she's right," the priest said.

"How the hell are we gonna get our hands on him?" Dan asked.

"I think there's a way he'll come to us," Holly said.

They both turned to look at her.

"How?" Dan asked.

"He's already killed without a confession. He's overdue."

"Yeah, but to who? He killed Mary Donnelly."

"Yes, because she betrayed his confidence. In his mind she broke the seal of confession. He has to find someone else."

"But you said he won't go to a priest."

She nodded. "That's right. And he can't go to a regular therapist because that would have to be face-to-face and he'd have to reveal who he is. He would never chance that. He knows the therapist would be required to go to the police. He only has one other alternative."

"Which is?"

"The crisis line."

"After Mary Donnelly's murder they shut it down."

"Get them to reopen it."

"Who's going to operate it after what happened to her?"

"I will," Holly said.

Both men looked at her. Their eyes were filled with doubt.

"I can't let you do that," Dan said.

"You don't have a choice. Unless Father Terrance can get you what you need, or this guy makes some kind of mistake, which he hasn't done so far, it's the only possible way you're going to catch him."

Dan was silent. His eyes were calculating. "While you were up here, two more priests went missing."

Father Terrance glanced at Holly. 'What are their names?"

Dan took out his notebook. "Father Jeffrey Bonner. And a Father Harold Shea."

"Oh, no!" the priest said.

"What's wrong?" Dan asked.

"We discovered them in the files, " Holly stated. "They each had long histories of abuse."

Father Terrance's face was ashen. "I had their files stored in the file room. Someone must have broken in and taken them."

"How many people had access?" Dan asked.

"I was told only I had. But I never believed that. I always felt someone was watching us."

"Like who?"

"Someone from the hierarchy, most likely."

"And someone else," Dan said ominously.

Holly's face was pale. Her voice quavered. "We delivered both of them into the hands of the killer."

They were silent. It was a statement neither of them could contradict.

Thirty-one

Alone, Holly felt nothing but disgust for herself.

What she had done had led directly to the death of two men.

Or had it?

Sharp incisors of conflict bit deep. Why was she feeling guilty? She had not killed them. She did not even know if they were, in fact, dead. But the probability was evident. It was more than a probability, unless what she and Father Terrance had done by invading Brother Dominicus's commune had thrown him off balance and perhaps spared the two men's lives.

Spared . . .

The word reechoed in her head. She was concerned about sparing the lives of two men who had committed multiple wrongs against the innocent. Men who would have been in prison had it not been for a legal technicality. Men who had been denied redemption by their own church.

She was working to find their killer when at the same time, part of her felt they deserved the punishment the law was unable to mete out to them. How did she reconcile that? In truth, she was unable to. Only the idea of the law held out any comfort. Without it, there were only the brutal rituals of revenge and the quick degeneration into tribal warfare or gang slaughter.

It was the way the victims were killed that disgusted her.

Atrocities out of the dark sludge of time. Or was it any worse than the dark horrors of her own era, when she considered all the terrors of the past century? The death camps and nuclear holocausts, the firebombing of cities and the untold civilian slaughter. Still, the genocides continued. Cambodia. Rwanda. Africa was rampant with them. The children recruited to fight its wars committed the worst atrocities.

While one part of her sought retribution for the crimes that had been committed, the other claimed an enlightenment she did not feel. In trying to find the killer she was struggling for civilization, for the dominance of law over vengeance. She wondered if the struggle was worth winning. Should she not instead be searching out the killer to offer him thanks for doing what the state was incapable of?

Was not Fra Alfieri's way the way of justice?

Was he not the true righter of wrongs no matter how he went about it?

These question tortured her and prevented her from sleeping.

In the morning, there was Clara to contend with.

"Where have you been?" Clara began as soon as Holly picked up the phone. "You haven't answered any of my messages."

"I'm sorry. I didn't check."

"Holly. Really," she said with annoyance.

"What can I do to make it up to you?"

"You can keep in touch, that's what you can do."

"I'm sorry."

"Forget it. I have news. Big news."

Holly knew Clara would not just come out with it. It required fanfare.

"Okay!" Holly said, bringing her voice to the proper pitch of enthusiasm. "What is it?"

"I spoke to one of my contacts. No names. But he made a call to the prison board on your behalf demanding to know why, after all the personal risks you took, you haven't been reinstated."

"And?"

"Well, the usual bullshit. They hemmed and hawed and said it was for your own good and that you needed time to recuperate. All that crap. But in the end, he got them to promise to give you a date when you can come back."

"When?"

"Okay, when. Good question. That's what I asked. But you know these bureaucrats, they'll stall their own mothers. But Ted has been appropriately informed. The word is, soon. Very soon."

Holly felt a crumbling slide of depression. More dirt caving in on her personal tunnel of despair. But she fought to resist it. Clara was only trying to help.

"How can I thank you, Clara. You're wonderful."

"Thank me when I'm looking at your gorgeous face. So when?"

"Soon, very soon."

"Holly!"

"No. I mean it. There's just a lot going on."

"With that guy from the institute, I hope. I heard a very vicious rumor."

"From who?"

"Guess."

"Beth."

"I'm not saying a word, except she sounded very bitchy and more than a little jealous. So I'm taking it for granted that you scored. Tell me, I'm right?"

"Come on, Clara."

"Okay. I got the answer I wanted." Her voice dropped to a

whisper. "Ted just walked in. Got to go. Talk to you soon. Bye."

Holly felt worn out by the call. She poured herself another cup of coffee and hesitantly played back her messages, knowing the one she wanted most would not be there. She had two calls from Beth, both demanding details of the night she'd had dinner at the institute. And one from Vincent. So she had been wrong.

"Hello," he began in his deep, well-modulated voice. "I tried you several times. But no luck. I've been thinking about you. Call me when you get a chance."

She sat quietly, then played it back two more times.

Images of the evening they had spent together flowed back into her mind with astonishing vividness. His hands touching her. His lips against hers. The way he undressed her. The pleasure she had taken.

"No regrets," she said aloud as all the usual clouds began to rise up just beyond the sunshine of the memory.

Without waiting, she dialed his private number. She prayed Beth would not answer. If she heard her sister's voice, she would have to hang up.

Miraculously, he picked up on the second ring.

"Hello."

"Hello," she said. "It's Holly."

"Well. You're a hard person to reach."

"Sorry. I had to go out of town."

"Anything interesting?"

"I'd rather not speak about it over the phone."

"Then, how about dinner later?"

"I'd like to. But somewhere else, if that's not a problem.'

"Of course not. Say at seven. I'll pick you up."

"No. Let's meet."

"Fine. There's a very good restaurant in the Hotel Sussex. That's downtown. Do you know it? Unless you rather not go downtown."

"No. it sounds lovely. I'll meet you there at seven."

She hung up, keeping her hand on the receiver for several seconds as if wanting to retain his presence longer. But she would see him later. She would have to content herself with that.

The last call was from Dan. In his no-nonsense voice he said, "You're not answering your cell. I need to see you. And I mean now."

She arrived at the task force just before noon and went directly to his office.

Dan was seated inside his glass-enclosed cubicle. The room outside was deserted.

"Where is everyone?" she said as she came through the door.

"Out looking for Bro Domincus."

Holly perched on the edge of his desk as he leaned back in his large leather swivel chair.

"What about the two missing priests?" she asked.

"Still missing."

She glanced at the large white chalkboard against the far wall. It listed the murder victims, each name surmounted by a photograph. There were five of them. Below each picture were the details of how they were killed. Beyond that there was almost nothing.

"Not much new is there?" she asked.

He shook his head. "Typical for serial killers. You don't get anything for a while. Then you get more than you ever wanted to know."

"You said you wanted to see me?"

He looked at her and his forehead splintered into notches.

"I made arrangements with the hot line. They're back in business, starting tomorrow night. You got the late shift. Ten to six in the morning."

"How many people will be working it?"

"Just you and you alone. Isn't that what you wanted?"

"Actually, it's better that way."

"What if he calls and it's busy?"

"He'll call back. He has to."

"You don't think he'll think it's a trap?"

"He may. But he still has to make contact. I'm the only game in town."

"Unless he's already found someone else."

Holly nodded. That possibility was always there. But her instincts all shrieked a different message and like a gambler she was unable to resist their compulsion.

"You're gong to be pretty much on your own up there," Dan continued. "As you can see, we're stretched to the limit. Pinero won't give me any more personnel. Not when he thinks he's got the killer in custody."

"He will when you find those two missing priests."

The notches deepened. "You think we will?"

Holly's lips tightened. She nodded. "We led him right to them."

"It wasn't your fault. You didn't know the killer would get them."

Holly was silent. "Maybe we should have known."

"You think you were set up?" he asked as his eyebrows rose skeptically.

"No. Not exactly. I think we did what we had to. Father Terrence was on a mission from the Vatican. He had to dig into those files. It was his duty to know who the culprits were, to get beyond the cover-up. But the murderer knew someone was doing his work for him. He waited for us to find what we did and the rest fell right into his hands."

"Do you realize what the implications of that are?" Shepard said. "It points the finger right at the diocese. Do you really believe someone inside the Church is killing these people?"

For an instant, Holly could not answer him. "I'm not sure. I don't know what to believe. But Fra Alfieri was a member of the clergy. That's the whole idea. The clergy policing itself. Punishing those who break its codes. That hasn't happened since the Inquisition. Which, by the way, was its real purpose. Not what it became. Its real mission was corrupted."

"Very interesting," Dan said, pursing his lips. "Will there be an exam?" he added sarcastically.

Holly realized he wasn't really listening. "You don't think what I'm saying is relevant, do you?"

He raised his eyes to hers.

"Historically, maybe. But what relevance does it have now? It's an interesting theory and I stuck my neck out for you on it. But it's not helping us find who did this. Not that I can see. And digging into the Church is not exactly politically correct. It's political suicide. Unless and until we have a smoking gun. Show me the money, Holly."

Her eyes blazed. "Two priests are missing. The only people who knew we were digging were inside the Church. They had to be."

"What about your friend over at the institute? Didn't he set the whole thing up?"

Holly stared at him. She felt as if she had been slapped.

"Vincent Pascal has done everything possible to help me and to aid in this investigation."

Dan raised his hands defensively. "Whoa, Holly. I didn't mean that he was a suspect. I only meant that there are other possibilities. So far, Brother Dominicus is numero uno. And he is or was inside the Church. He may still have contacts there. They may have slipped him the names of those priests. So ultimately you may be right. But like I just said, I need something concrete before I go blasting my way into the diocese. If you think Pinero wants my scalp now, imagine what he would do if he got a call from them indicating that I was on a fishing expedition. He'd have my scrotum."

Holly's ire subsided. She knew he was right. Her theory was still only a theory. She had nothing to back it up. Nothing. Not a shred of real evidence. Only a legend, a myth, a whisper down through the dark tunnels of time. Tomorrow night, she would begin her vigil. And when he called, then and only then she would have something real.

The downtown hotel dated from the twenties and had been recently redone.

It had a spacious welcoming lobby decorated in the smooth dark woods and light marble that characterized the modern luxury hotel. Lights were soft and indirect. The staff wore dark suits and ties and affected a sleek European demeanor. Everything was elegant and understated. It was just the kind of place Vincent would choose.

Holly was guided to the entrance of the restaurant by a young concierge, who left her in the hands of a pretty hostess, who in turn glided her smoothly to a table in the corner with an envious view of the spot lit garden.

"Mr. Pascal asked that you be seated. He'll be joining you momentarily," the hostess said as she aligned the menus. She smiled and walked off. An instant later a waiter appeared to ask her if she wanted a drink. She did, desperately.

"A martini, please. Straight up. Two olives."

The room spread itself before her gaze, partially filled with diners. The array of silver and flowers made a pretty tapestry. The garden outside was a greenhouse filled with plants beneath a curved glass covering.

Her drink appeared in a blue-tinted glass. The waiter hovered as she tasted it. She smiled and nodded. It was perfect. When she looked up again, Vincent was standing in front of her.

"Good?"

"Yes. Very."

The sight of him made her stomach tighten. She lowered her gaze as he took the chair opposite and a waiter placed a huge Baccarat crystal glass in front of him filled with an amber liquid she assumed was scotch.

"It's very good seeing you," he said as his lips curved in a smile. Somehow he looked even more handsome in the subdued light of the room.

"I could say the same."

"I hope you will. And often."

It was her turn to smile.

"Are you hungry? I'm famished. Why don't we order?"

She opened her menu and glanced over as he perused his. His eyes were bright, intent. She liked the way he was. How he didn't disguise his appetites both at the table and in bed.

When they had given their orders and the waiter had stepped away, he raised his glass. She brought hers to his. They touched with a slight tinkle of sound.

"Your sister is spoiling me."

"Really?"

"She's very good, very dependable and very creative. She anticipates. Sometimes I think she can read my mind."

"She used to read mine," Holly said. "It can be a little disconcerting."

He smiled. "I think she'll go far in this field. She just needs a little sponsorship. It's not easy. It's a field that attracts some very well-connected types. I was lucky, the Foresters took an interest in me."

"You must have been quite a prodigy."

"Nothing like that," he said dismissively. "Just a willingness to work hard. Your sister has the same trait."

"I'm glad."

His expression changed suddenly. His eyes were startingly intense. "I spoke to Father Terrence before he left. He brought me up to date on your exploits. You took quite a chance going up there and doing what you did. I'm not sure I like it."

"There was no other way," Holly said, bringing her eyes to his.

"Anything could have happened to you. Father Terrance wouldn't have been able to prevent it."

"He's pretty resourceful. I knew I could trust him."

He shook his head. "You took a dangerous risk. You're taking one now. Just by being involved with this case."

"You want me to quit?"

"I know better than to ask you that. I just want you to take precautions. This killer is extremely dangerous. He was able to find out what you were doing, then steal the names of the men you found. If he thinks you're getting too close, he could try and prevent it by attacking you. Have you stopped to realize that?"

"It's a chance I have to take. I work with dangerous men every day. You learn how to deal with the risk."

"I'm sorry. I didn't mean to underestimate you. I'm just worried about you, that's all."

"I appreciate it."

Holly had intended to tell him about the hot line. Now, she decided against it. It would also have meant breaking her promise to Dan. She did not want to do that. She had already broken enough understandings between them.

"Father Terrance thinks he can get us information on Brother Dominicus that might prove his connection to the Alfieri cult. What do you think?"

His jaw tightened. His eyes held hers. "If anyone can, he can. He has enormous resources and some very powerful friends in Rome. He could unlock doors that have remained closed for centuries. Who knows what he'll find."

"Let's hope."

"This is very important to you, isn't it?" he asked.

"I don't know. I've been thinking about it. Wondering if I'm on the wrong side."

"What do you mean?"

"The victims have all been sexual predators who have never been punished for what they did."

"Don't you think being exposed like that is a form of punishment? The shame. The inability to continue your life's calling."

"Yes. But is that sufficiently proportionate to the harm they've done? I don't think it is. And I don't think most of the laity think so. Never mind the rest of us who are not in the Church. What they did was a serious crime. A crime against the innocent and the powerless. They deserve prison, only they didn't get it because of a legal technicality or because the Church covered up their crimes."

"But no one has the right to kill them because of that. Only the law has that right," he said emphatically.

Holly nodded. "Yes. I've been telling myself that. Then why aren't I convinced?"

"It's an age-old conflict between those who believe in punishment and those who believe in mercy."

"You think they should receive mercy?"

"I think they should receive the judgment they deserve. And I'm doing what I can to see that they get it."

"That could come with a price," she said.

"What do you mean?"

"You said before you thought I might be in danger. But so might you."

The thought suddenly struck her with implacable force. The man she had now transferred her affections to could be in serious danger of losing his life.

Thirty-two

Rome was colder than he remembered at that time of the year. Cool days were often followed by periods of balmy weather when the entire population seemed to pour out onto the sidewalks and fill the open plazas with bright-eyed exuberance like tourists coming off a cruise liner. It was typical. The city was a treacherous and unfaithful lover and Father Terrance had had a long and troubled relationship with it. Unlike most of his colleagues, he preferred his own apartment, which he kept in Trastevere, once a working-class *borgo,* but now an increasingly gentrified quarter on the other side of the Tiber, as its name implied—across the Tiber. Actually, it was on the same side as the Vatican, so it made for an easy commute. But he still preferred life on the other bank. The pungent throbbing capital of the ancient world with its intriguing ruins and mysterious by ways.

Also, unlike his clerical brethren, he preferred to dress in civilian clothing.

His own contacts in the Vatican archives were old and secure. But each archive was not only a storehouse of information and a record of Church history going back almost two thousand years, it was also a fortress. A vast, far-flung empire of information controlled by warring factions and feudal lords dressed in skullcaps and crimson silks. Conquering one did not mean conquering all. And what he was looking for was both a secret and a scandal, though it happened five hundred years before. In the Vatican, five hundred years was yesterday.

So, how to begin, without setting off the usual alarms?

Father Terrance was not by nature a devious man. He had been entrusted with many delicate missions in many parts of the world, usually attending to powerful clerics who had strayed and were in danger of disrupting their often wealthy and influential congregations. Over this time, he had secured a reputation for tact and discretion. It had won him many allies, especially for a lowly priest of no particular rank. What he had actually secured was a web of contacts that could be depended upon, a circuit of power that permitted him to be plugged into it. He did not fool himself that his position was an entitlement. He had to be very careful not to overload its circuits or he would be quickly disconnected.

So he worked carefully, almost molelike, nibbling and scratching until he could squeeze beneath the walls without arousing any interest. Arriving each morning at a particular archive, dressed appropriately in a freshly pressed black cassock though he would have preferred a motorcycle jacket, he seated himself at one of the ancient wooden library tables and began his search through the ancient volumes.

He never varied his routine. Three hours of research in the morning, then lunch at one of the small trattorias lining the narrow cobbled street of the *borgo* directly adjacent to the Vatican walls where he feasted on *abbaccio* and *tortellini in brodo.* He permitted himself a single glass of wine before taking a half-hour walk circling the rounded pile of the Castel San Angelo, site of the Emperor Hadrian's tomb. He returned to his labors until four o'clock, when he slipped out of the dark halls of the archival chambers and walked past the Swiss guards standing on duty dressed in their yellow-

and-red-striped uniforms and pointed helmets, their sharp-ened halberds supplemented with holstered 9mm Barettas, and took the bus home.

Evenings he spent ruminating over what he had amassed, seated at a table in one of the many restaurants that crowded the streets of his area. Afterward, he strolled the winding lanes, deep in thought, then returned to his tiny apartment and the shouts of children playing in the courtyard mingled with the decibel fury of televised soccer. Exhausted, he fell into a deep and profound sleep. His dreams mixed choirs of singing cardinals with the images of a farmhouse in rural Pennsylvania where he struggled to put a face on a dark fig-ure in a monk's cassock who constantly eluded him.

After his first week in the city, a singular pattern began to emerge. Just as all roads once led to Rome, the threads of his research all led to a single place.

The monastery where Fra Alfieri had begun and where his mutilated corpse found its final resting place.

Holly's orientation took almost a week.

The mentor she was assigned, in the person of a psychi-atric nurse named Bev Fowler, managed to guide her through it.

Bev was a twenty-eight-year-old brunette with attractive features and a slim, well-toned body. She worked days on the hot line after laboring almost five years in a locked facil-ity tending incurable schizophrenics. She was quick and yet patient, and Holly felt comfortable working with her. Nothing was mentioned abut the real purpose of her working the line. Bev was blissfully ignorant of what her superiors and Dan had arranged. She merely wondered why Holly liked work-ing the graveyard shift.

"I like the money," Holly said with a smile.

"So do I. But you've got to leave a little time for a social life."

Holly nodded. She had not told Bev about her background or her job at the Brandywine Special Treatment Center. So when Bev got around to asking where she had worked before, Holly had to do a bit of fudging.

"You are aware of what happened here to one of our staff?" Bev said in a lowered voice on the second day of Holly's training.

"I heard something about it."

"She was murdered. The police still haven't said exactly how. They keep stalling. No one can figure out why."

"Well, sometimes there are details they don't want to release; otherwise they might tip off the killer."

"Maybe," Bev said. But she didn't look convinced.

Holly was silent and Bev did not pursue the subject.

Dan made sure that the media was notified about the resumption of the hot line, which the local stations carried as a public service. Holly herself heard it broadcast on her way home one night. The news anchor mentioned it at the end of one segment just before they went to a commercial. He commented that the HMO was reestablishing its psychiatric hot line after a hiatus of several weeks due to the murder of Mary Donnelly, one of its specialists. The anchor mentioned that the police still had not released the details of the killing.

The report sent a jagged edge of fear along her spine.

Holly gripped the wheel.

Did she really know what she was doing?

Mary had knowingly betrayed the killer and she had paid the extreme price.

Now Holly was following directly in her footsteps. What made her actually believe he would call? All she had were her instincts and a gambler's certainty about a hunch.

A horn blared. She was veering into another lane.

She righted the car and slowed down as the light turned red. When traffic started forward again, Holly allowed herself to be comforted by the various strip malls and gas stations she passed, many of them already decorated for Christmas.

She knew he would call. She felt it in her gut. What she had said was true. She was the only game in town. There was nowhere else for him to go without exposing who he was. The hot line was open, available, and totally anonymous. What could be better for someone whose credo forced him into confession?

A small dark cloud swept over her reasoning. What if her theory was incorrect? What if this entire Alfieri thing was a myth, a fantasy? What then?

Her mind shook free of the doubt. As far-fetched as it sounded, there had to be a connection. The methods of killing totally matched. Then there was Mary's betrayal and the price he was forced to exact for it. Her death only confirmed Holly's theory. Otherwise it made no sense. Whoever was behind it had pledged himself to the Cipher. The tapes she heard proved it beyond a shadow of a doubt. It was only the DA who was fooling himself. And his denial was based purely on political grounds. His case would fall apart as soon as he presented it. Whatever evidence he had cooked up would be proven false.

She took a deep breath and felt a surge of renewed confidence. She was on the right track, she knew it. He would call and they would bait the trap.

The feeling lasted only an instant, dispelled by a single chilling thought.

She was the bait in the trap.

Thirty-three

The construction site was windswept and barren.

The boys squeezed through the opening in the steel-mesh fence, then plunged down a narrow culvert gouged in the earth by a bulldozer. Its jagged tracks resembled the teeth marks of some giant dinosaur.

There were three of them, twelve, thirteen, and fifteen. They had come up from the tract houses below where the land dipped forming a large open bowl between distant hills. The construction site had leveled the crest of one of the hills, which would become part of the new turnpike. Now it was a desolate wound in the earth, gouged by the jaws of mammoth earthmoving machines that stood waiting for the weekend to end so they could grind back into life.

The boys had brought their tagging gear. It filled their pockets and clinked when they walked. They were careful not to move too quickly lest one of the paint jars break and the paint fill their pockets instead of the sides of the machines they had come to score. They had watched from afar, squatting just outside the fence as the big machines had been unloaded from their carriers and begun the business of tearing up the trees and brush that formed the last line of forest in the area. They had played among the trunks when they were younger. It had been their first real place of adventure. They had watched as the scrub pine and diseased elms were uprooted by the massive blades. Tagging them would be as much an act of revenge as it was an act of rebellion, a first jab at the impenetrable covering of the world.

The boy in front was the tallest. He wore a grunge knit cap pulled low over his ears. His pants were huge and baggy, reaching only to mid-calf. He wore a green Army field jacket with bulging pockets. He moved in a straight line, heading for the big yellow crane perched high atop the rise. The other two followed, their heads down against the chilling wind.

The day was gray and cheerless. The light was already fading. Lower down in the distance were the trailers where the construction crew had set up their HQ. A security guard was posted there, but he had driven off somewhere to get his dinner. They had clocked his movements and were taking advantage of his routine. He wouldn't be back for at least an hour and a half. By that time they would have tagged several of the machines. If all went well, they might even do the sides of the trailers. That was their plan anyway. They had worked it out carefully, making preliminary drawings of the tags on sheets of paper, carefully folded and filling the bulging pockets of their cargo pants.

The tall boy scaled the other side of the ditch and scrambled to the top.

He started toward the rear end of the crane, his head lowered as if trying to reduce his image to any onlooker. Not that there would be one. No one came up here anymore now that the construction had begun. Only an occasional dog walker. But it was a long walk from the last block of houses and the weather was against anyone out for a casual stroll.

The boy reached the crane within several strides and rounded toward the front where he intended to place his first tag right across the operator's window. A massive slash of purple.

He looked up and halted in his tracks.

What he saw hanging from the crane's clamped jaws was at first a mystery.

They gripped a long iron bar from whose ends hung two oblong objects that looked like identical salt-and-pepper shakers each the size of a man. Both were encased in molten asphalt, oozing from them like a bleeding bandage.

The smell was unmistakable. The air reeked of it. It was some kind of tar used in the construction of roadways.

Two pieces of concrete pipe stood on their ends beneath each of the metal objects, each as tall as a man's head. Each was large enough for them to crawl into, which they had done the first time they snuck into the site. Each was so large, they could even sit up in it. Tar oozed from the top of each of the pipes like overfilled bowls of soup.

The boy turned his head as his two buddies came up to join him, the three of them standing side by side, their mouths agape, staring at the metal objects. They looked like cocoons, each containing some enormous insect. But what they contained were clearly not insects.

The creatures inside them were human.

Holly had no trouble finding the site.

She took the off-ramp Dan had described, then followed the directions he had outlined. The floodlights made it easy to find.

The police had blocked off the streets leading up to the site. A chain-link fence protected the site and kept the curious at bay. As she drove past the first police checkpoint, her headlights swept across a group of onlookers clustered against the fence. What they could possibly see at that distance was problematic.

Two media trucks were parked just outside the checkpoint. Reporters regarded her with bitter expressions as she was waved through. Two of them actually started toward her, mikes extended, cameramen in tow. But she accelerated and they were left flatfooted on the other side of the barrier.

A trooper waved her through the open arms of the gate, pointing out where she had to go with the beam of his flashlight. She waved a thanks and continued along the rough dirt track that meandered inside the perimeter, passing several monstrous earthmoving machines standing like buttes against the overcast sky.

She steered toward the floodlights, swerving to miss a steep ditch. Passed a huge stack of concrete piping and wheeled into a makeshift parking area patrolled by two troopers with huge arc lights who pointed her to a spot between the usual assortment of emergency vehicles parked in haphazard formation.

Holly got out of the car, drawing her leather coat tight against the chill. The wind was an icy scythe and she was glad she had taken Dan's advice and dressed warmly. She wore gloves and a wool hat and high rubber boots, which she had fished out of her downstairs utility closet. Her task force ID was pinned to her lapel, since technically she was still a member of the team whether Pinero liked it or not.

She eyed the vehicles for a sign of the DA's town car, but nothing resembling it was in evidence. She exhaled in relief. Her stomach had been churning out butterflies in anticipation of seeing him again. She didn't want to cause a scene, especially when she was persona non grata as far as he was concerned.

Dan was standing alone, checking his watch as she came up. She saw Palumbo, who gave her a quick wave. No one else in the knot of men and women standing nearby looked familiar.

Dan turned to her as she approached.

"This is really pretty," he said. His eyes were dark, his expression grim.

He made a gesture and she followed his gaze.

A scaffold was being set up around a floodlit crane. Twin

black objects hung suspended from its jaws, but she couldn't make out what they were. Below each of them were two concrete pipes sitting upright on their ends.

"What am I supposed to be looking at?" she said.

"Your two priests."

She looked at him. "I don't understand."

"Neither do I. But it looks as though they've been boiled in oil. Not oil exactly. But just as effective. That's asphalt. Tar. For covering the road they're making. It came from that machine over there."

"Asphalt?" she asked. "How?"

"Hung them from the crane and dipped them into those concrete pipes which were filled with boiling asphalt. My guess is, while they were still alive."

"That's ghastly," she exclaimed, feeling a twisting screw of anguish.

"So we can add two more to the list. That makes seven so far."

Holly was mute. Unable to speak. Her eyes were riveted on the two blackened objects whose shapes were silhouetted by the flood lamps.

"There's no other possible explanation?" Holly said, regretting it as soon as she uttered the words.

"Of course, we've got to peel the tar off before we can make a positive ID. But all things considered, I think he's added to his Christmas list."

"No one saw anything?"

"Apparently not."

"Wasn't there a security guard?"

"He's being questioned. He says he saw nothing. He heard nothing. Even though the crane's engine was obviously turned on as well as the asphalt machine. They both make quite a racket."

"Was he drunk?"

"Or on drugs. We think maybe both. Judging by the guy's priors."

"Some security."

"Who else are they gonna get to sit out here all weekend for six bucks and change an hour."

Holly was gripped by cold pincers of guilt.

"I feel like I'm responsible," she said. "If Father Terrance and I hadn't discovered their files—"

"If you hadn't found them, someone else would have. Terrence was being set up. Not exactly set up. He had his job to do, but someone was waiting for him to do it, just so they could get their hands on them."

"No word about Brother Dominicus?"

Dan shook his head. "Totally cold. We alerted the FBI. But so far nothing."

"What about his people?"

"They've been released on bail. We're indicting them on abduction and kidnapping. We've still got them under surveillance hoping he'll make contact. Maybe something will develop in that direction. But I'm having one hell of a time keeping it together. What with Pinero on my back."

"Won't this change things?"

"Don't bet on it."

"How can he say he's got the killer after this?"

"He can and he will. Until we have some real evidence, he'll say this crime was totally unrelated to the others."

"The public isn't that dumb. All the victims have been priests. Child abusers."

"About the public, we wait and see. I'm more concerned about you. How is it going?"

"I'm scheduled for tonight."

He exhaled slowly. "Okay. We'll see if your theory holds water."

They were both silent. Breath escaped their lips and hung in the air like tiny spectral clouds. Her cheeks were freezing and her feet felt numb, but her eyes refused to leave the twin dark objects suspended from the crane.

* * *

Fortresses within fortresses.

He was encountering them all. Walls that could not be scaled. Towers that could not be taken.

His week of research ended in defeat and frustration. Perhaps all along he knew it would be this way, just as he knew there was no real hope. Not this way. No frontal assault would succeed. The barriers had stood for centuries. They would not yield in a week. Not even to a Jesuit with a doctorate in psychology.

Father Terrance took his leave of the library, shouldering past the rector on duty, a consumptive-looking priest in a well-worn cassock who ogled him each day with eyes that dripped with suspicion, as if he had come to burn or steal the manuscripts. The man jumped at each of his requests as if he were holding a live wire. At times he pretended not to understand Father Terrance, whose Italian was not only perfect but properly tinged with a Roman accent. Perhaps his accent was too good, causing resentment in the man who obviously came from Calabria or points south.

Father Terrance had endured snubs, resentment, and ridiculous delays. Still, he persisted. But time was not his ally. He knew that. The man they were seeking would not stop his killing spree to wait for Father Terrance to discover his identity. That is, if Brother Dominicus was indeed the right man.

His nights had been racked with a gnawing doubt. What if it were someone else they were looking for? Still, he knew he had to run out the string. Somewhere in these vaulted chambers, he knew, lay the key to his search.

When he returned to the small apartment in *trastevere,* there was a message on his answering machine. The message was from Holly. Her voice was low, tinged with regret.

"Hello, Father," she began. "I tried getting you in person, but the time difference is impossible. Please call me when you get in."

He unbuttoned his cassock and drew it from his shoulders. It was a garment he particularly detested and always had. A feminine robe complete with a flowing skirt. Not the kind of uniform for a Boston slum kid and former minor-league ballplayer who had served two hitches in the Marines before entering the seminary. Still, if that was price he had to pay for his calling, it was one he could afford.

He sighed and opened a cabinet, from which he removed a half-filled bottle of twelve-year-old single-malt scotch, and poured a double shot into a tumbler. He took a sip, allowing the warmth to flood his throat before he reached over and drew the phone over to him. It would be late afternoon where she was.

She picked up on the second ring.

"Hi, Holly. It's Bill."

"Hello."

Her tone sounded flat. He could detect the grief behind it.

"What's happened?"

"They found the two priests."

"I see." He exhaled slowly. "I'm assuming they were killed."

"Yes."

"How?"

"He immersed them in boiling asphalt."

"Were they still . . ."

"We believe so. We'll have to wait for the medical examiner's report."

The image sent a shiver of dread through him. "Any luck with Brother Dominicus?"

"No. He's still out there somewhere. What about you?"

"A lot of dead ends so far."

"You're not giving up, are you?" Her voice was filled with anxiety.

"No. I've still got a few cards left to play."

He hesitated abut asking the next question.

"Have you started yet?"

"Tonight. I just finished the orientation."

"Let's hope it works."

"If it doesn't, I think they'll offer me a job."

They both laughed. "I'll bet you'd take it."

"The way my life's been going, in a heartbeat."

They were both silent. He felt a surge of affection for her suddenly. A desire to protect her.

"Holly. Be careful. Don't do anything without Shepard knowing about it."

"Don't worry. I'll be okay."

"Keep me posted. I'll call you as soon as I have anything. And take care of yourself. I need you as a partner."

He hung up and picked up the tumbler, finishing off the rest of the drink. He tightened, his chest filling with quickening sense of determination.

He had things to do and people to see, and the sooner the better.

Thirty-four

If Holly thought she would ease into the hot line she was wrong.

The action began immediately.

The phones never seemed to stop ringing. She had begun while the evening shift was still functioning. They would go off at midnight and then she would be all alone. But in the meantime, the action was nonstop.

She had been installed in a glass-walled cubicle that held a desk on which were a computer and two phones. Huge phone-book-size manuals were crammed into a shelf on either side and detailed the HMO's medical services. The place had the feel of a boiler room where frenzied hustlers pitched phony schemes to the greedy and the gullible. Only this worked in the opposite way. The frenzied and the desperate were on the other end of the line.

Since it was a psychiatric hot line, she fielded calls from people who were primarily paranoid or depressed. And all the various shades in between. The most desperate were on the verge of suicide and demanded immediate attention. To those she offered emergency therapy, like a medic on a field of battle. She had two of these within the first half hour.

"'Tis the season to be balmy," one of her coworkers wise-cracked.

But she was not far off. The holidays were approaching and Holly knew the effect it had on people. And how desperate they could become. For far too many, in a society of fractured families and splintered marriages, it was a time of loneliness and despair.

There were other problems too. Alcoholism and drugs being the two most difficult. Holly's job was not to cure, but to calm and contain until she could refer the caller to the proper venue for help. The job went against all of her nurturing instincts, the essential part of her that had been drawn to the profession in the first place. Aside from it not being her function to provide any but the most cursory of psychic Band-Aids, there was no time for anything else. She had to complete the call and get on to the next.

Because the service had been off-line for the last few weeks since Mary Donnelly's death, the backlog of calls was immense. By ten, there was still no letup. She threw up her hands. "What am I going to do?" she asked helplessly as the supervisor passed on her way to the exit.

"The best you can, sweetheart," she said with sympathy.

The next few hours were unrelenting. Three and four calls at a time were backlogged. She forgot about her break and worked straight through until the day crew arrived just before six.

Holly was drenched in sweat. Her back felt as if she had been lying on a bed of nails. She got up, feeling the tension in her legs. She had been pressing them into the floor for hours as the stress mounted. She took her things and staggered out.

She almost forgot the reason for her being there.

The next night was the same.

"It'll take a couple of weeks to clear all this up and by

that time we'll be into the holidays. So forget it. It's even worse then."

The statement was uttered by one of the psychiatric nurses manning the phones and echoed by the others. Holly wondered if she had made a mistake. Even if the killer did call, she wouldn't have time to listen.

Dan was waiting for her when she appeared in the parking lot on the way to her car.

"Let's get breakfast," he said as he got out and opened the door for her to get in.

All she wanted was to go home and collapse, but she nodded her assent and slid in beside him.

She ordered coffee and pancakes, which she smothered in maple syrup. After two nights listening to tales of unrelenting agony, all she wanted was comfort food, comfort of any kind.

"So, what's been happening up there?" he asked, as he poured milk into his steaming cup of black coffee.

"It's a madhouse," she answered. "Nonstop from the minute I walk in."

His lips tightened. "You think it was a mistake?"

She lifted her eyes to his. "Honestly. I don't know."

"How much longer do you want to give it?"

She shook her head. "At least until the end of the week. Maybe there'll be some letup. We know from the tapes that if he calls, it'll be late. Two to four in the morning, when it's generally quiet."

"You going to last until then?" he asked with a wry smile.

"I'll try."

"You still believe it'll happen?"

"I know it will," she answered, but her voice was weak.

His eyes scrutinized her. "You don't seem all that sure anymore."

"I'm just tired."

"Have you heard anything from Our Father who art in Rome?"

"Not really. I spoke to him just before I went to work. My God. That was two days ago," she said blankly. "You lose track of time on this job."

"So what did he say?"

"That he was encountering obstacles but that he still had some cards left to play."

"Let's hope. We're at a dead end here. Pardon the pun." He reached into his jacket and drew out a folded piece of paper, which he placed on the table between them.

"It's the ME's report on the two priests. Thought you might want a look."

She looked up at him. "Were they alive?"

He nodded his head, as his eyes met hers. Between them was a sickening visualization of horror.

She put down her fork. Her appetite had vanished.

"I haven't seen anything in the papers about it," she said, as she picked up the folded paper and placed it in her handbag.

"You won't. Not unless the media gets wind of it. Pinero is doing everything he can to see they don't. The site was isolated. When the media vultures asked, he put out the word that it was just a construction accident. So far no one's contradicted him. Which is a surprise in itself."

"What about his suspect?"

"He's still a suspect."

"You're not going to anything about it? The man is innocent."

"No, not innocent. Just not guilty of what Pinero says he's guilty of."

Holly looked at him. She had been a prosecutor and she knew exactly what he was talking about. But it was not something she could concern herself with now. She had to take care of more essential matters. And the first of them was sleep.

* * *

She fell into a comalike sleep as soon as her head hit the pillow.

If she had one dream or a hundred, she remembered none of them. She awoke minutes before the alarm as if her own body clock was also on alarm. Her muscles were sore and her back ached. She felt as if she had not slept at all. It was late in the afternoon. The day was already waning, sloping toward darkness as winter approached. She hated this schedule. She had always been a day person and hated missing so many hours of daylight.

She showered, dressed, and made herself a bite to eat, moving in a kind of slow-motion lethargy. She felt drugged, unable to think clearly. Clara brought her up to speed.

She called just as Holly was collecting her things.

"Hey!" Clara said in her usual bright tone. "Am I getting you at a bad time?"

"Not really. I was just going out," Holly said.

"Good. Well, hold on. I have news. You ready?"

"Go ahead."

"You've been officially reinstated."

Holly took a deep breath. But the wave of elation she expected to feel failed to materialize.

"Great," she said, forcing her voice to express some jubilation.

"You don't sound very happy about it," Clara said.

"No. I do. I'm just exhausted."

"They wearing you out over there?"

"Something like that."

"Anything you want to tell me about?" Clara said, lowering her tone to a confidential whisper.

"No. Nothing I can divulge."

"Uh-huh. So we can expect to hear something soon?"

"Don't count on it. Tell me some more."

"Well, officially there isn't a date yet. But Ted wanted me to call you and put you on alert. It could be any day now."

"I see. But you believe it's coming?"

"Oh, it's coming. I called my source as soon as Ted told me. He called me back and confirmed it. He's keeping the pressure on."

"I am happy about it, Clara. And I appreciate you calling and telling me. You've always been a real friend. And that's very rare."

"Miss you, kid."

"Me too."

"Got to go. Take good care. I'll call as soon as I have a date."

She hung up, feeling a throb of satisfaction surge through her. And about time too, she said to herself. But as much as she wanted her job back, what she was doing now had absorbed her totally. She had no idea how she would balance the two. But if she knew the bureaucracy, it would be several weeks before they released a date for her to return. The sting of what she had done by representing the inmates in front of the cameras was still fresh in memory.

The supervisor gave her a curt nod as she entered the HMO. None of the women she worked with were really welcoming. They were tight-knit little group and seemed wary of newcomers. It was just as well. Holly was not there to win friends and influence people. After the shift changed, she would be alone on the line, alone in the office and on the floor, and except for a security guard, she would be alone in the entire cavernous three-story building.

Being there after midnight brought its own measure of fear. It was a feeling she could never get used to. After midnight, they lowered the heat as well as the lighting so that she had to put on a sweater. But her fingertips were always cold. She couldn't wear gloves because of the typing she had to do on the computer. One or two of the other women had commented that she was lucky to have the late shift. There were always fewer calls and she could always catnap at her work station. But that was the last thing Holly would do. And yet that was exactly what she did.

She was unaware of exactly when her eyelids closed or when she drifted into the sweetness of being somewhere at sea. She was at the rail of a liner feeling the gentleness of the sea breeze. The ocean was an incredible shimmering blue. The sky was almost pink. She felt warm, expansive, and expectant. She turned her head and watched the male figure coming toward her. He was smiling at her. She returned the smile. He was someone she was waiting for. He was incredibly familiar, but somehow she could not quite make out his face.

The phone rang, shattering her ocean into crystalline shimmers, like the breaking of a mirror.

The clock read four-thirty.

She reached for the phone.

"Livingston Emergency Crisis Line. How may I help you?"

"By giving me your name."

"My name is Norma." That was the name she had assumed during training. " I need your name and your plan number."

"William Norris."

"He gave her a number and she wrote it down.

"One moment, please."

She clicked the numbers into the computer. The screen gave up the data. The number was a match.

"Now. How can I help you?"

"I think I'm actually going to wind up helping you."

She knew the voice. The sound was unmistakable.

It was him.

The killer was on the line.

Thirty-five

The priest was led through a series of dimly lit passages by a robust middle-aged cleric who had not introduced himself, but merely said, "Follow me."

Father Terrence marked the man as a Tuscan, less by his accent than his dry manner and brisk demeanor. It had begun that morning with a phone call. He had answered and a strange voice said, "Bargetto Gate. 10:30 P.M. Do not fail to appear if you wish to find what you are seeking."

He knew he had been summoned.

Father Terrance spent the rest of the day going over the material he had accumulated, looking for something, anything that could be a clue to the monk's identity. But he found nothing. A blank. Days had been wasted in a fruitless search for a shadow. There was no record of any Brother Dominicus. Of course, he could have changed his name. Anything was possible. But to have records disappear like that was not natural. It indicated that someone wanted them to disappear. Someone important.

He had made the proper calls. He had indicated what he was doing so that the word would spread in the correct circles like a rock tossed into a pool. He wanted them to know

that he was searching. He was the irritant, the tiny grain of
sand inserting itself within the oyster shell. He knew the
danger and courted it. Only by exposing himself to that danger could he effect the result he wanted. Otherwise the enor-
mity of indifference and bureaucratic inertia would finish
him.

So he waited for the call. And when it finally came he was
ready.

He presented himself at the gate exactly at the hour specified. It was already dark. Rome was damp with falling rain.
Not a hard rain, just harsh enough to soak the shoulders and
seep under the cuffs. Furtive cats peeked out under the chassis of parked cars, seeking the old women who fed them
each night with bowls of leftover pasta. Rome was a city of
cats. It was as appropriate a symbol as the mythical wolf
whose teats fed the infants Romulus and Remus.

Cats were sly and predatory. So were the men who awaited
him.

No handsome young Swiss Guard was on duty when he
arrived. The gate was silent. Empty on both sides. Through
the ornate ironwork he could make out a series of cobblestone alleys branching off in several directions between high
windowless buildings roofed with faded red tiles. This was a
small side gate, not often used and too small for vehicular
traffic. An ancient entrance to the fortress of the Vatican.
One perhaps used by an assassin or a lover in some bygone
age. He imaged their huddled shapes, faces hidden by their
capes as they waited for those who had summoned them.

He heard footsteps and the robust Tuscan appeared
dressed in a black cassock and Roman collar. His head was
bare, indifferent to the rain splattering down from the gutters
above. He did not look at Father Terrance; rather, he looked
past him, as if the priest's identity was a matter of indifference or was an identity that he might one day have to deny
knowing.

The Tuscan used a large ancient ornate key with the papal

seal. The gate opened and Father Terrance slipped inside. He was dressed in cassock and collar like the Tuscan, but he also wore a black silk-lined cloak and round-brimmed hat. These he seldom used except when he had to attend some function or other. The cloak smelled of mothballs. The hat had proved ineffective in keeping the rain off his face.

He followed the brisk figure through one alley, then another, until they arrived at an oak door. His guide opened it with another key and led the way inside. They climbed narrow stairs. The walls were smooth and undecorated. Stucco over stone. They went up three flights and came to a long narrow passage, also plain and windowless. They continued along the passage to the archway at its end, made a turn into an equally narrow tunnel-like passage lit here and there by dim bulbs set into niches where he imaged lit tapers had once illuminated the way. The floors were well-worn oak planks, which resounded dimly as they walked, like someone beating a small hollow drum. His pulse was keeping time with their footsteps. His heartbeat was somewhat elevated, but he needed to control it. He wanted to appear calm. He would need all his wits and his strength.

They came to a door at the end of the passage. The Tuscan knocked.

The door opened. The Tuscan stepped aside, his eyes averted. Father Terrance entered a large chamber with a high coffered ceiling, whose walls were faced with elaborate frescoes of religious allegories. The room was dark except for three small green shaded lamps set on a long highly polished table in the center.

Three men sat behind each of the lamps. The shades made seeing their features difficult. Two of the men wore the black attire of bishops. The one in the center wore the red robes of a cardinal.

There was a single chair in front of the table.

"Please, Father. Have a seat."

"Thank you," Father Terrance said as he took the chair.

Behind the table at the far end of the room was an elaborately carved wooden screen. There was a light behind it making the filigree of carving glow with an amber radiance. It occurred to Father Terrance that someone might be sitting behind the screen, listening. Someone of importance. But that was something he could not know.

"Father. You are on some kind of a search, are you not?" the cardinal asked. Father Terrance was able to make out a narrow graven face, thin lips, and high arched nose. He was bald, his head covered with a crimson skullcap.

'Yes. I'm looking for a monk named Brother Dominicus who was excommunicated from the Church and has been leading a cult of the gullible."

"Exactly why are you looking for him?"

"We believe he may be responsible for the murder of several priests and a bishop. He believes himself to be an avenger who follows in the footsteps of Fra Alfieri."

At the mention of Alfieri's name, the two bishops turned sharply to face the cardinal. Their eyes were filled with alarm.

"I see," the cardinal said. "When you say we, who do you mean?"

"I have been working within a Pennsylvania diocese with the help of someone on the state police task force. We discovered two priests who were being protected from prosecution. Unfortunately, this avenger managed to discover what we had found and murdered the two priests. I came to Rome to see if I could discover his true identity."

"For what purpose?"

Father Terrance was momentarily nonplussed by the question.

"Why, to stop him from killing any others."

"By what authority?"

"The same authority that ordered me to investigate in the first place."

"You were ordered to check and see that no other members of the clergy were being protected. Not to prevent a murder. You have already exceeded your mandate. Coming here was in violation of your orders."

"I beg to disagree, Eminence. I believe what I am doing is in furtherance of my assignment."

"In what way?"

"The Church in America is in a crises of the deepest proportions. Only action from the Church itself can alleviate the crisis and restore the confidence of the people. Not an avenger acting outside the Church and the civil law. What that does is reveal the Church as impotent to punish and correct what has been done."

Father Terrance paused. The men facing him were listening intently.

"The ecclesiastical courts of the Middle Ages were set up to correct inequities both within the Church and without. As was the Inquisition itself. But since then the Church has had no effective arm to investigate and root out the misconduct of its own members. That is why such a massive cover-up occurred. Local bishops handled each situation within their dioceses. To avoid scandal and protect their own reputations, they covered up the crimes of their priests. They sent them for psychiatric counseling, which proved ineffective since they were not supervised by a legal authority. Instead, the priests confessed and were forgiven. And committed their crimes again and again. Now, we have an even worse situation. Because of the vagaries of the American legal system, many of these offending priests have been released from prison and are the targets of this avenger. Each time he kills, he further weakens the Church, pointing up how ineffective we were in policing our own. He must be stopped. If not on legal grounds, on moral ones. He is not an angel of the Lord. He has no right to take justice into his own hands. Only God has that right."

He sat back in his chair trying to read the faces behind the lamps. But that was impossible. They were as immobile as statues.

There was a rustle from behind the ornately carved screen. He heard sounds. A voice he thought he knew. An old man's hoarse whisper.

Was it possible?

A moment later a stately-looking bishop stepped out from behind the screen and walked to where the cardinal was seated. He bent and whispered something in his ear. The cardinal looked up at him with surprise. He said something, but the bishop held up his hand and silenced him. The bishop turned and walked back behind the screen.

The cardinal faced him.

"You will be given whatever you need. That is all."

"Thank you," he murmured.

A hand touched his shoulder.

Father Terrance looked up. The Tuscan was standing beside him. He nodded and Father Terrance rose.

The Tuscan led the way out of the room.

At the doorway, Father Terrance turned his head trying to see beyond the carved wooden filigree. But he could make out nothing behind it. The Tuscan gestured for him to step back into the passageway. He turned and the door closed behind him.

Thirty-six

His voice resonated in her ear.

The sound was unnatural, metallic. The same as on the tapes. He was speaking through some kind of electronic device.

It was imperative that her own voice remain natural.

"How can I help you?" she repeated.

"What I have to say is confidential," he said.

"Every conversation is protected and confidential."

"I spoke to one of your colleagues once before. She betrayed me."

"I assure you that you are mistaken. Nothing we say can be repeated without your written permission."

"I doubt that."

"Then why are you calling us again?"

He paused. "Good question. Norma, isn't it?"

"That's right."

"Is that your real name?"

"Is that important?"

"We're dealing truth, aren't we? We don't want to start out with a lie."

Holly's insides constricted. She hated lying in any form.

But he was a killer and she owed him nothing. Her entire purpose here was a lie to snare and entrap him. A charade she must continue. He had lied about his identity the last time and probably now as well, but Holly could not let on.

"Why would I lie about something like that?" she said.

"People lie about everything."

"Why exactly are you calling?"

"Don't be impatient, Norma. All in due time. First I have to know who I'm speaking to."

"I told you. My name is Norma. Now, how can I help you?"

"Patience."

"I'm sorry. This line is for people who need our help. If it's just conversation you want, then there are other places you can get it." Her lips tightened. She was skating dangerously close to the edge. He might hang up on her, but she had to sound authentic.

"Help is what you can give me, Norma."

"All right. Now please tell me why you're calling."

"I'm calling about the two priests who were killed."

"Do you mean the ones in the newspaper?"

"No. No one knows about them yet."

"I don't understand."

"You will very soon."

"Did you have something to do with their deaths?"

"How astute you are. Almost as if you were waiting for me. Have you been waiting for me, Norma? If that is your name?"

"I don't know what you mean."

"I think you do. I think you've been waiting for me to call."

"Why would I do that?"

"To trap me, of course."

"Then why are you calling?"

"You'll find out very soon."

The phone clicked off.

Holly bit her lip. She had played it all wrong. Why had she asked him if he'd had something to do with their deaths? What she had done was stupid. She had jeopardized her plan. It seemed as if he knew exactly what she was doing, as if he were playing with her.

His last words were ominous. What did it mean that she would find out very soon? She felt a twinge of apprehension. Then fear. Was he out there, watching her? Toying with her in some way? Still, her theory had proven itself. He had called. He would have to continue calling. His need to confess was still unassuaged, a need he still had to satisfy. She felt clear suddenly, as if she had tied a knot of certainty. He would call back and they would be waiting.

The tape recorder clicked off.

Dan looked up at her, his eyes narrowing with respect.

"So you were right. He did call. Just like you said."

Holly was silent, seated in an empty office in the HMO complex that had been set aside for her use. She had waited an hour on the possibility that he might call back. But when the hour had passed she'd made the call to Dan.

He was not thrilled at being awakened at four A.M. But he tumbled out of bed and drove out to the complex, arriving with two Styrofoam cups of coffee and a soiled bag filled with croissants.

Holly welcomed the coffee. But she had no appetite for the buttery confections.

"What do you think?" he asked.

"I think he'll call back."

"Why?"

"Because he has to."

"Knowing that it's a trap?"

"I believe he thinks he's much smarter than we are. I don't think he'll let himself be trapped. But his confession is more than personal. I think he wants us to know something."

"Like what?" Dan said, tearing off a corner of a croissant and tucking it between his lips.

"I'm not totally sure. But I've been thinking about it. This is more than just between him and some erring priests. This has to do with the future of the Church itself."

"How do you mean?"

Holly sat forward. Her muscles ached from sitting in front of the computer for so long with the phone at her shoulder. But she felt suddenly alert.

"I think he wants to bring what he's doing out of the shadows. If the Alfieri legend is true, and I believe it is, then everything that was done in the past was done in total secrecy. Those who were punished had no real idea of what their actions would bring upon them. Because of the Church covering up so many crimes and the law freeing so many who committed them, there has been no real punishment other than what he has done. It's the sheer magnitude of what's happened that's influencing him. He wants each of the perpetrators to know what the consequences of their actions will be."

"So he's on a mission?"

"I suppose you could put it like that."

"And you think he'll call again?"

"I know he will."

The call came at two-thirty the following night just as she had predicted.

"Hello Norma," he said. "Remember me?"

"Yes. How can I help you?"

"Just by listening."

"We have rules."

"So do I. But I think you're breaking all of them."

"What do mean?"

"I think you're letting someone else listen to us."

"You're wrong."

"If I bought that, would I be stupid, Norma?"

"No."

"So you're asking me to trust you?"

"No. I'm asking you to allow me to help you."

"Isn't that the same thing?"

"If you want it to be."

"Trust comes with risk, you know that, don't you, Norma?"

"What kind of risk?"

"If I trust you and you break that trust, then you have to pay the penalty. Are you prepared to do that?"

"I'm prepared to help you, if that's what you mean."

"Don't be evasive, Norma. You know what I mean. Are you prepared to take the risk?"

"If that's what will satisfy you, then yes. I'm prepared."

"You won't be able to go back on your word, Norma. There won't be a way for you to do that. I won't be able to help you. Once you break the Cipher."

"What is the Cipher?"

"You'll know that very soon."

The phone clicked off.

Holly leaned back in her chair. Her pulse was racing. Sweat limned her brow. Her hands were trembling. She had just placed herself in the center of the target, just as Mary Donnelly had done. And Mary Donnelly had paid the price with her life.

Moments later the phone rang.

She cautiously lifted it to her ear.

"Yes."

"Holly? Are you all right?"

It was Dan.

"Yes. I'm okay. Did you get it?"

"We got nothing. He's using a disposable mobile phone. You can buy them anywhere. The signal was moving and he didn't stay on long enough. We need you to keep him on longer."

"I don't know if I can."

"You've got to try. Otherwise this is worthless."

"All right. Let's see what happens tomorrow night. But understand, there is no guarantee that he'll call."

"You said there was."

"I know what I said. But he's setting the rules. Not me. That's my worry."

"My worry is that he knows exactly where you are."

His words struck her like a hammered nail. For the first time since she began work at the hot line, she felt completely vulnerable.

The drive home was made in predawn darkness.

The roads were empty. Mist filled the hollows and blew across the asphalt. She had to use her defroster and wipers to see through the windshield. Every pair of lights that swept across the road or that she saw in her rearview mirror felt like the hungry eyes of a hunting animal that was after her as its prey.

Dan's words echoed and reechoed in her mind.

My worry is that he knows exactly where you are. . . .

Fear now dispelled her fatigue. She gripped the wheel with clenched fists.

The rest of the trip was a blur as she followed the familiar roads like a robot. The cul-de-sac was silent. Just the usual array of familiar vehicles. Someone had left a bike outside. Other than that, nothing seemed out of the ordinary.

She hurried to her front door and bolted the lock. But she still felt afraid.

The phone was blinking like the single red eye of a cyclops.

She picked up the receiver and pressed the message button.

The voice was Beth's, but the message was from Vincent Pascal. He needed to see her as soon as possible.

Thirty-seven

Holly made the drive to the institute after she had showered and changed her clothes. She felt tiny ants of fatigue crawling up her back, but the thought of seeing Vincent created its own kind of adrenaline.

His image had never been far from her thoughts even in the frenzy of the last few days when she had applied herself to learning the methodology of the hot line. It acted like a beacon of warm light that cut through the swirling mist of arcane rules and regulations that she had crammed into her mind. Her body ached for him. Sleeping alone on her narrow bed, she felt the deprivation of a nun. She needed his strong body beside her. The single intimate experience they had shared acted like a taste of heroin to an addict. She craved more.

She accelerated as she was waved past the checkpoint and drove through the familiar gates along the long sweeping drive toward the towers and walls of the imposing structure. The day was sodden and gray, promising rain, but she felt uplifted as she pulled into the parking area in front and hurried toward the reception desk where a pass waited in her name.

Beth met her when she got out of the elevator.

Her sister looked pretty and was smartly dressed. They hugged for an instant.

"God, I've missed you so much," Holly said.

"Me too. But you've been a very busy lady, from what I hear."

"What did you hear?"

"Just that you're hot on the trail of this killer."

"Nothing else?"

Beth shook her head. "I've been pretty busy myself. My boss is a bit of a perfectionist and one hell of a slave driver."

Holly looked at her in surprise. But Beth broke into laughter. "Just kidding. He's actually a great boss." Her voice dropped. "Don't tell him. But I've been reorganizing his archives. They're quite a mess. But he doesn't know it yet. It's a surprise."

"When will you show it to him?"

"When he comes back from his trip."

"Where is he going?"

"Rome, as usual. He got a special call from the Vatican."

"Is that usual?"

"Pretty much so, especially now with the pope so ill. We get a dozen calls a day. We've been going a little nuts."

Holly stared at Beth. Speaking about Vincent brought a bright glitter to her sister's eyes. Holly felt her insides clench. Was it possible that Beth was becoming emotionally attached? Dear God, she prayed. Please don't let that happen. The last thing she wanted was a rivalry with her own sister.

Beth escorted her through the open door into Pascal's office.

He was on his feet, the phone pressed against his ear. Every surface in the office was piled with files. His briefcase was open on his desk, folders spilled over the edge.

Seeing him, Holly felt a jolt of electricity course through her.

He turned and his face broke into a smile. He raised his

hand, gesturing for her to have a seat, then quickly concluded his call.

"Holly. Great to see you. Thank you, Beth. Maybe you'd like to arrange lunch for the two of you."

"Will you be joining us?" Holly asked.

"Too much to do."

Beth smiled and went out of the room, closing the door behind her.

"Hello," he said, stepping toward her.

He halted and looked at her with a scrutinizing glance.

"You're working too hard," he said.

"Does it show?"

He nodded. "A little."

She had wanted to rush into his arms, but the moment had passed. She felt diminished as she took the seat on one of the facing leather couches. He took the place beside her and his hand closed over hers.

"I've missed you," he said.

"And I've missed you."

His eyes were warm as they fastened on hers. She wanted desperately to kiss him.

"Is that the reason you called?" she asked.

"No. I know that what you're doing is important. I thought I'd better back off for a while."

"Then why did you ask me to come?"

He leaned back and his expression changed.

"Father Terrance called. He's sent you something. It arrived this morning. He wanted you to have it as soon as possible. I could have sent it over to you or brought it myself, but he specifically wanted you to hear it in a secure setting. So, I volunteered our conference room."

"Where is it?"

"Waiting for you inside."

Holly's stomach tightened. They rose together, as he guided her to the door at the far end of the room.

The conference room was located along an elaborately

paneled hallway. A huge highly polished table filled the room's center. Life-size marble statues filled niches along the walls. The huge bay window opened on views of green meadows and the woods beyond.

He led her over to the end of the table. A Fed-Ex package lay facing her.

"I'll leave you to it. We can talk later."

His eyes met hers magnetically. Then he broke away and left the room, smiling at her as he closed the double doors behind him.

Holly took a deep breath and pulled out one of the elaborately carved chairs. She sighed as she sat and took the package in her hands. It was still sealed.

A letter opener lay on the table alongside it. She used it to pull open the flap.

Inside was a smaller envelope. She drew out something carefully protected by bubble wrap.

A cassette tape.

Holly looked around. A wheeled table at the far end of the room contained a display of electronics. Plasma TV, VCR, DVD, and stereo. Holly carried the tape over. She turned on the stereo and inserted the tape.

There was some static, then the gravelly voice of Father Terrance filled the room.

"Holly. This tape is for your ears only. I'm sending it to Vincent Pascal because that way I know it won't be intercepted by anyone on your end who might not want you to get it. If I sound excited, it's because I am. For some unexplainable reason I've been permitted to see the secret archive on the Alfieri matter. It's quite astounding. There's no coherent narration. I had to piece it together from various documents. Some were old, others are more modern. They come from a whole series of sources. But what it boils down to is this. After Fra Alfieri's execution, his body was secretly transported back to his original monastery, which is located about forty miles north of Rome near Spoletto. He was originally buried in unconsecrated ground since he was also excommunicated for his sins. But the abbott who had sponsored him had him exhumed and carried back to the monastery where he was reburied, but this time in consecrated ground. The abbot who had betrayed him spent the rest of his life doing penance for what he had done. He went from a Judas to a believer.

"Not only a believer, but a fervent zealot of Alfieri's cause. He was a member of a wealthy and powerful family known as the Arbori. He enlisted several members of the family to his cause and they continued the work Fra Alfieri had begun. They were as secretive as Fra Alfieri and just as dangerous. The names of many high Church officials were added to the Cipher. Men who met with terrible deaths.

"Soon the Church realized what it had to deal with. By this time Julian was pope. He wanted St. Peter's built. The amount of money required to fund it was enormous. Indulgences were being wholesaled all over Europe. As you know, these were papers sold to people to relieve them of sin. Corruption became rampant. This, of course, eventually led to the Reformation. But while that was occurring, there were even more abductions and executions of corrupt Church officials. Not only was the Church fighting to survive from without, but also from within. A secret office was established to find and root out the followers of the Cipher. The Arbori were forced to go even deeper underground. But their wealth and power always protected them and the cult of the Cipher continued.

"To maintain secrecy, the cult was led by a single Avenger who would keep and maintain the Cipher. He in turn would select his successor. That way the tradition would continue. And so it has, down through the centuries. The archive contains reports of hundreds of prelates the Vatican believes were murdered by the Avenger.

"All of this is background, of course. I couldn't go into all of these past cases. It would take months just to read through the files. The archive itself is housed in a catacomb beneath the Vatican Museums. Thousands of tourists a day pass over it without knowing that what lies under their feet is one of the greatest catalogs of murder the world has ever known.

"The power of the Arbori lasted well into the eighteenth century. Then their wealth dried up and their influence waned. It was easy then to ferret them out. In 1790, the cult was finally broken. Sixteen members of the family were tried in secret and executed by the garrote in a courtyard of the Vatican with the pope as witness. The Inquisition assured the pope that the Cipher had been destroyed and the cult destroyed. They were wrong. It was not.

"For almost two centuries there were no reports of any deaths that could be attributed to the cult. Then several decades ago, a young monk was assigned to work in the archives. He stumbled upon references to the Arbori and somehow managed to gain entrance to the secret archive. It wasn't that difficult. So much time had passed that the archive fell into neglect and was barely protected. The monk became obsessed with the archive and with what Alfieri preached. He had also seen corruption. Indeed, he may have been the victim of it. He discovered that the Cipher had not been destroyed. Merely placed under special seal. He found where it was and stole it.

"The Cipher obsessed him. Other monks he knew were also disturbed by the permissiveness of the Church in forgiving those who had committed crimes and the lack of any real punishment. He organized them into a secret society. He compiled a list of offenders, but before he and his brethren could act, one of them had a change of heart and betrayed him to the Church authorities.

"The monk was expelled from his order and excommunicated. Then he dropped out of sight. Strangely, none of his records are available. Someone took his files out of the archives. We don't know his name, his nationality, or his order. The information I've given you is from a two-page summary.

That's all that remains of the case. The priests who compiled the record are all dead. But I believe that this is the man we've been looking for. The man now calling himself Brother Dominicus.

"I know that what I've told you seems like a dead end. But there's one more aspect to the story. The identity of the Avenger was always kept secret. But when they died, each was buried, not in the Arbori family tomb, but in Fra Alfieri's monastery. According to the archive, on each of their tombs is their death mask, finally revealing who they were. They always left something of themselves for posterity. Maybe our man did too. I'm leaving for the monastery. It's just possible I may find something there that could possibly identify him. I'll contact you as soon as I know something."

The tape clicked off.

Holly took a breath and sat back in her chair. Her mind was reeling. What the priest had told her was fascinating but led nowhere. Not unless he was right and he found something in the monastery. But why should he? Why after all these years?

No, she thought. Their best bet was the hot line. They would trap him there.

She took the tape out of the machine and slipped it into her bag.

She opened the double doors and went back to Pascal's office.

He was still on the phone, slipping papers into a folder. He looked up, smiled and shrugged, put down the folder, and walked to where she was standing.

"Call you right back," he said into the phone, then placed it on the desk behind him.

"I want to see you when I get back," he said quietly, his eyes holding hers. "Unless you're too busy."

"You look like you are."

"Not too busy to see you."

"I'd like to believe that."

"You should. It's true."

She tried to smile. Wondering how much of what he said she should believe. The timing was all wrong. She was caught in the web of her obsessive unsolvable case and he had his work. Why was that always the case? She felt jinxed. But shook the thought free of her mind. She wanted to believe him. She had to. She had been too often betrayed by the curse of skepticism, turning away from what might have been the beginning of a workable relationship because she felt her lover's words were false or meant to conceal something else. She wouldn't let that happen again.

"I'll be here," she said.

He took her by the shoulders and bent to kiss her.

She felt his lips on hers and closed her eyes, allowing herself to come close against him. Her stomach went taut. She wanted him to lead her to one of the leather couches and take her right there.

"Sorry."

She heard Beth's voice behind her.

His fingers relaxed their pressure.

Vincent stepped away as she turned to face her sister, who was standing in the doorway with a sheaf of papers in her hand. The expression on Beth's face only confirmed what Holly had felt before, a look of hurt Beth was trying desperately to conceal. Vincent might have been fooled, but not Holly. She knew her sister too well.

"These just came," Beth said as she stepped forward and handed the papers to him.

"Thanks. Why don't you two go to lunch?"

Beth forced a smile as Holly nodded. Both of their faces wore the deceptive masks of siblings who now were rivals.

They sat facing each other across the table in the sumptuous spaciousness of the employees' lunchroom. Like everything else about the institute, the employees' cafeteria would have rivaled a five-star restaurant in any luxury hotel anywhere in the world. The tables were covered with white linen and real silver. Beyond the huge bay windows that filled one side of the enormous room, trees were whipped by an unceasing wind.

They each toyed with their salads, but neither had any appetite. Each time Holly lifted her eyes to look at her sister, Beth's gaze shifted away.

"I'm sorry," Holly said finally. "I didn't know you felt that way about him."

"What way?" Beth said. Her voice was a challenge.

"Oh, hell. Let's not do this."

"Do what?"

"What we did before, when I was the bad sister and you played the injured martyr."

"I always thought you were the injured martyr."

Holly looked up and met Beth's mocking gaze. They both began to laugh.

"We're some pair," Holly said. "Both falling for the same guy."

"I guess it sort of crept up on me."

"Me too. You have to admit he's something special."

"No argument."

"So what are we going to do?"

"Nothing. He's obviously interested in you and that's that."

Holly looked at her sister. Her first impulse was to say, no, you can have him. Instead she said nothing. She knew her sister too well. She would never accept such a sacrifice. Besides, it wasn't one she really wanted to make.

"What's this about, this thing you're working on?' Beth asked.

Holly hesitated. She knew she should say nothing. But she had to speak. She couldn't cut Beth off, not now. Especially because of the hurt she knew her sister must be feeling. So she launched into a general background of the case, offering specific details but keeping back her role and especially omitting the hot line.

"The Demon Cipher? That's what it's called?" Beth said, shaking her head in wonder. "It's unbelievable."

"I know. Especially when you consider how far back in history it goes."

"And you think this guy you're looking for is actually this avenger?"

"I don't know. It's possible. Everything he's done points to it."

"You mean the way the priests were killed?"

Holly nodded. "Exactly. There is no other explanation."

"But the DA still believes the cases are separate? It's stupid and ridiculous."

"I know," Holly said. "He's afraid of having to connect them and what that would mean politically."

Beth's features expressed disgust. "You've got one hell of a situation on your hands. And it isn't even your job."

Holly shrugged. "I know."

"What about your job?"

Holly sighed. "Supposedly I've been reinstated. I'm supposed to get a date when to return. But nothing so far."

Beth looked up. "I feel like a big piece of chocolate cake. How about it?"

Holly lifted her fork. But Beth shook her head. "Uh-uh. No sharing. I need all these calories for myself. Order your own."

Holly looked at her sister, then smiled and signaled to the waiter. An obscene hunk of chocolate cake was just what she needed.

Thirty-eight

The monastery clung to the edge of the escarpment with talons of stone.

The escarpment rose sharply from the plain like an upthrust bayonet. It was reached by ascending a series of switchbacks narrow enough for a donkey but widened in the previous century to accommodate a four-wheeled vehicle, which is what the priest had to take to reach the top.

He hired it the previous evening in the village below. The village itself was a cluster of white-stucco-walled houses and dusty tiled roofs set so close together they resembled a Southwestern pueblo. Like a pueblo, it nestled in a crevice one giant step up from the flat plain below and took almost two hours to reach by bus from the railway terminus in Spoleto.

He had called ahead and expected to sleep at the monastery, but it was already dusk when the bus pulled in and unloaded its cargo of drowsy passengers in the tiny village piazza facing the narrow front of the ancient church and its knifelike bell tower. No one would dare the trip up the mountain after dark, so he had to spend the night in a room above the village's only restaurant outfitted to service the occasional tourist or prelate who came to visit.

After breakfast, Father Terrance waited outside the restaurant dressed in brown cords and a green infantry combat jacket as his duffel bag was slung in the back of a blue jeep by the twenty-something driver who advised that he buckle up. Then the driver jumped in and hit the accelerator, gunning his way through the twisting village streets at breakneck speed, which was exactly how he navigated the switchbacks. It was a trip Father Terrance made with his fingers gripping the chassis, his Adam's apple stuck against the back of his throat, and his guts in a twisted coil close up against his spine.

The abbot was waiting to greet him when they arrived at the top.

He was younger than the priest expected, with a dark suntanned face and the hands of a laborer. He wore a coarse brown robe and workman's heavy-soled steel-toed boots. He ushered the priest through the ancient splintered oak gates and into the monastery itself.

There were only a dozen monks presently in residence, the abbot explained. Their work consisted mostly of repairing and restoring the ancient structure. They used some local labor but did most of the work themselves. Several of the monks were expert stonemasons, as was the abbot himself. Father Terrance was awed by the massive walls and buttresses towering above them as they traversed the narrow cobblestone alleyways snaking between the crumbling buildings, several of which were masked by rough wooden scaffolding.

He was led into the main cloister and shown to a small chamber outfitted as a guest bedroom. There was no indoor plumbing, only a chamber pot and a ewer filled with ice-cold water. He followed the abbot up a winding stone staircase to a large chamber on an upper lever. The room was filled with several tables covered with blueprints and diagrams. The abbot offered him a chair and took the seat on the other side of the long wooden table he used as his desk.

"What can we do for you, Father?' he asked.

"Are you aware of my authority?" Father Terrance began.

"Yes. I have been informed by the secretary of our order. He said I was to afford you every privilege."

"I want to see the death masks of the monks of the Order of the Cipher."

The abbot's coal-black irises were fixed on the priest like steel bearings.

"I cannot allow that."

"You can and you must," the priest said calmly.

"I would be betraying a sacred trust."

"No. You would be obeying the orders of your pontiff."

The abbot's glance wavered. "You're putting me in an impossible position."

"I know. And for that I am sorry. But you must obey."

The abbot stood. His face had become stone. The priest followed him out of the room and back down a different stairwell that clung to the inside of a tower whose walls were pierced with narrow slits permitting glimpses of the vast green mist-shrouded plain below.

They reached the bottom of the tower and hurried through a narrow passage, then through a series of heavy oak steel-bound doors, which the abbot opened with a ring of keys he produced from a pocket inside his cassock. The abbot led the way until they reached a cavernous room with a high-domed ceiling bisected with the arms of two gothic arches. A staircase led down. The walls were polished like a granite headstone. Father Terrance held onto the sides of the gleaming walls as he went down, feeling a sense of vertigo on the steep narrow stairs. Light came from stained-glass windows inset high above. They reached the bottom and the abbot turned to face him.

"All of the members of the order are here."

"All of them?" Father Terrance asked. "Even the present one?"

The abbot's lips tightened. He refused to answer.

"I will wait for you here. More I will not do."

The priest nodded.

Before him was a low stone archway.

He bent his head and went beneath it, emerging into a large open space whose walls tapered upward to a high vaulted ceiling. Light filtered through rose-tinted glass. He was inside a chapel. At one end was a large marble altar. On either side were black marble sarcophagi fitted into the walls and rising high above his head. Each held the body of a member of the order. Then he turned and saw them.

The masks.

Gleaming white against black marble. Each was set in a special niche on the wall opposite the sarcophagi. Father Terrance stepped closer. From one of the outside pockets of his jacket he took out a flashlight. The beam traveled from one niche to the other, tracing each set of features. His heart had speeded up. He could feel it beating. What he was seeing was a history of the Cipher. The secret forbidden history of the Church. Each of its avenging angels depicted in the moment of their death.

He had not traveled here for nothing, some instinct told him that. There had to be something. Some trace, some clue, something that would unravel the mystery of the man they were seeking. Whether Brother Dominicus or someone else. It had to be here.

And it was.

In front of him in a niche, high up on the wall was a single startling mask. Not yellowed by age like the others, but gleaming white. As white as a desiccated skeleton. Not a mask of death, as the others, but from life.

It was the face of a young man.

The same young monk who had resurrected the Cipher and left his own image to mark what he had done joined the others in a fraternity of blood.

* * *

Two nights and no calls.

Holly waited in anxious frustration, but the phone failed to ring.

There were other calls, of course. Scores of them. Potential suicides she had to carefully assess and calm down. Repeat callers who used the hot line out of loneliness and desperation. Even one or two cranks calls. But none was the one she wanted.

It was later than usual. Almost at the end of her shift. She was tired, drowsy, craving her pillow.

When the phone rang, Holly answered on the third ring.

"Did you think I wouldn't call?" he said in a whisper.

Recognition was immediate. Adrenaline surged, dispelling her fatigue. She was suddenly wide awake.

"Can I help you?" she answered, trying to appear as dispassionate as possible.

"You must keep what I say secret. Something only you and I will know."

"You know our rules. I've explained them to you. You are protected by the rules of confidentiality."

"Will you abide by them?"

"I have to."

"And you know the consequences if you violate those rules."

"Yes," she said hesitantly.

"Say you understand."

"I understand."

"Good. Then listen closely. Tomorrow night I will complete my triad of vengeance."

"By doing what?" Holly said tensely.

"Removing the bishop's pawn."

"I don't understand."

"You will, if you think about it."

The phone went dead.

Holly sat bolt upright. Her mind flooded with images of the murdered priests. There was to be one more. Instead of confessing to a murder he had already committed, he was telling her about one he was about to commit.

Who was the bishop's pawn?

Her mind was in turmoil. She tried to calm herself down. The phone was ringing. She reached out to answer it. Her hand was trembling knowing it might be him. But it was one of her persistent frequent callers with a diagnosed personality disorder. He was on manic overdrive and it took almost ten minutes just to calm him down and another ten to get him to take his meds. But by calming him she had calmed herself. She checked the clock. The day shift would be here any minute.

She logged out on the computer, then crossed the starkly lit corridor to the office she had been allocated, turned on the light, closed the door, and took out her cell phone.

The beeper sounded within the enclosed stone walls.

Father Terrance had almost forgotten he was carrying it. That was easy to do within the monastery's ancient precincts.

He checked the numbers in the window and realized who it was from. He calculated the time difference and realized that it was just six A.M. where she was calling from, while here it was noon.

He reached into one of the many pockets of his infantryman's field jacket and drew out his chrome-plated cell phone. Miraculous. Here he was in the courtyard of a thousand-year-old monastery about to receive a call from another century. Fortunately, he had taken the precaution of placing his cell on an international circuit.

"Holly? Is that you?" he said.

"Yes. It's me."

"Where are you?"

"At the HMO. In a private office they gave me."

"What's going on? You sound out of breath."

"He called again tonight. Just a few minutes ago."

"Again? Then he called before?"

"Twice."

"I see. Go on."

"Instead of confessing to something he'd already done, he told me about something he's going to do."

"Slow down, Holly. What is he going to do?"

"He said he's going to complete his triad of vengeance. That he's going after the bishop's pawn."

'That's all he told you?"

"Yes.

"Did he say when?"

"Yes. Tomorrow night. Who is the bishop's pawn?"

The priest paused, deep in concentration.

"Father, are you there?"

"Right here. I can't be sure, of course. But if you asked me to put money on it, I'd say the bishop's pawn was Paul Mastino."

"Paul Mastino. Who is he?"

"He's a lawyer. A fixer. He worked with the bishop for years helping squelch the prosecutions of offending priests. He was also the bishop's muscle when it came to pressuring people not to press charges or file complaints. He's been fronting for the diocese on the issue of claims from those seeking redress for abuse. So far he's done a terrific job of seeing that no one gets a penny."

"You don't think it's someone on the bishop's staff, or someone else in the diocese?"

"No. I don't think so. The bishop changed his aides continually. Only Mastino was his consistent right-hand man. You can double-check, but the description fits."

"He'd be the first victim who wasn't inside the Church," Holly said.

"You're forgetting Mary Donnelly."

Holly was silent. She took a deep breath. "You're right."

"What are you going to do?"

"I don't know. Try and prevent it."

"You realize he told it to you in confidence. If he discovers that you betrayed him, you could become his next victim."

"Yes. I know," she said almost in a whisper. 'But I can't allow him to kill someone else without trying to stop it."

"You'll talk to Shepard, of course?"

"Yes," she said hesitantly.

"Promise me you won't do anything on your own."

"I promise."

"I've just sent you something. It's a photo of a mask. It might be the face of the monk we're looking for. It was done a long time ago. But it could help you identify him."

"What kind of photos?"

"I sent you the whole roll. It's the best I could do. I can't remove the mask. It was high up and too difficult to examine up close. The abbot wouldn't permit it. And I didn't want to wait to have it developed."

"You mean, you're at the monastery now?"

"Yes. I'm going to stay for another day or two on the outside chance I'll find something else."

"Be careful, Father."

"You too." There was a crackling on the line. "You're beginning to break up."

A moment later the line went dead.

He stared at the useless implement in his hand, suddenly overcome with a feeling of dread. For Holly especially and strangely, also for himself.

Thirty-nine

The lawyer was not difficult to locate.

He had a floor of offices in a prestigious office high-rise in downtown Philly and made himself visible at a whole slew of social and political functions, as the computer in the newspaper's research department could attest. The morgue it was called. Holly felt a shiver at the mention of the word.

She had typed in his name and the screen filled with references. Pictures in a magazine profile done a year or two previously revealed a short, pugnacious, jaw-thrusting terrier who favored big cigars and expensive custom-tailored suits. He was nearing sixty, between marriages, and tooled around town in a stretch limo, usually accompanied by long-legged females of the trophy variety.

He was a busy man, and not easy to reach. She had to decide not only when to warn him, but how.

The other question was, why hadn't she yet informed Inspector Dan Shepard?

She was alone and unprotected and about to engage in the single act of betrayal that might lead to her abduction and death. And she still had not informed the police.

She was able to formulate the question, but she was as yet unable to discover the answer.

She had told Father Terrance that she had told Dan. But that was untrue. She had not yet made the call. Had working with inmates made her less afraid of what criminals might do? Was she now more interested in investigating their convoluted mental processes? Or was there something else, a self-destructive drive in her nature, a need to walk as close to the edge as she could?

To experience the vertigo, the sensation of danger.

Or was she merely afraid that if she called Dan, his first instinct would be to remove her from any risk, making it impossible for the killer to locate her and therefore defeat the entire reason for exposing herself in the first place.

Whatever it was, it was blocking the voice of reason that shouted to her to pick up the phone and make the call. Instead, she drove into the city seeking to track down the elusive Paul Mastino.

It was not easy.

Mastino seemed always to be one step ahead of her. His office responded politely to her calls. Each time she was shuttled to one of his assistants who had a new location to point her to, but when she arrived, he was already gone. She missed him at lunch and at his club. They would not give her his full schedule. Not even when she introduced herself as a member of the task force who needed to speak to the attorney as soon as possible as it was a matter of critical importance. They kept telling her that he was aware of her and would respond as soon as possible. But no call came. By four-thirty, it was becoming obvious that he was ducking her. His office staff became evasive when she asked for his evening schedule, and she realized that there would be no hope of her locating him.

Desperate now, Holly realized she had run out of resources.

She drove to his office building and parked in the underground lot.

Ten minutes later she stepped out of the elevator and into the reception area of his law firm furnished with leather couches, marble surfaces, and expensive Oriental carpets. The receptionist smiled but her eyes were steely.

"I need to see Mr. Mastino immediately."

"And you are?"

"Holly Alexander. I've been calling"

"Oh, yes. I'll inform Mr. Mastino's assistant."

She picked up the phone, her smile fixed firmly in place, and spoke into the receiver.

"Please have a seat. Ms. Prescott will be right out."

Holly was too agitated to sit. She stepped away from the reception desk and stood in the waiting area, which was otherwise deserted.

It took five minutes until the double glass doors opened and Ms. Prescott entered the area. She was an efficient-looking brunette in her late twenties dressed in a tight-fitting pinstripped suit that leveraged her skirt well above the knee.

"Ms. Alexander? I'm Shelly Prescott, Mr. Mastino's assistant."

Holly took the hand she offered.

"Are you aware that I've been trying to see him all day?"

"Yes. We know."

"This is a matter of some urgency. Has that been communicated to him?"

"It has. And we checked your identity with the DA's office. They informed us that you were no longer with the task force."

Holly stared at her. "Did you call the task force?"

"We didn't think that was necessary."

The realization that she had trapped herself in a dead end overcame Holly as if a wet cloak had been suddenly thrown over her.

"Ms. Prescott, you have to understand. I am with the task

force and what I have to tell Mr. Mastino is critically important. At least, let me speak to him on the phone."

"I'm sorry. That's impossible. There's nothing I can do."

"Isn't there any way I can contact him?"

"I don't think so."

Holly's jaw tightened. She saw the futility of trying to overcome the young woman's defenses. Holly thanked her and turned toward the elevators.

It was dark when she pulled out of the garage. The air was chill with rain. Red lights bled into the asphalt. Commuters flooded the streets.

Her mind was reeling. She had to find him. She had to prevent another murder.

But she was lost and alone in the exodus of outbound traffic.

Street signs blurred.

She cut the wheel suddenly, making a turn into the maze of narrow lanes leading to the river. Where was she going?

Her cell phone was ringing.

She picked it up and brought it to her ear.

"Yes."

His voice startled her.

"You betrayed me, Holly. I trusted you and you destroyed that trust. You know what I have to do. What the Cipher demands."

The call ended. Her mind was spinning.

How did he get her number?

Her vision was swimming. The wipers made soup on her windshield. She went through a stop sign as horns blared an irritated cacophony.

He called her Holly. He knew who she was.

The streets suddenly widened. She drew to a stop and found herself on the terrace overlooking the river below. Street lamps glowed and splintered in the darkness.

She had to think. But she was beyond thinking.

He could be there on the street behind her.

Her heart was pounding. Quickly, she touched the lock button sealing the doors as sharp talons of fear tore at her. She had to force herself to reason. She had to think.

She picked up the phone and dialed Dan's cell.

"Holly?" he answered. "Where the hell are you? I've been trying your number all day."

She realized she had turned the phone off after each call to save her battery and neglected to check her messages, so absorbed had she been in trying to warn the lawyer.

"I'm downtown," she responded.

"Father Terrance called me about Mastino. He said you were trying to warn him."

"I couldn't get through to him," she said.

"Mastino's missing. We've been trying to track his movements. He disappeared during lunch."

"Didn't he have a limo driver?"

"The driver was outside the restaurant. Mastino never came out. The people he had lunch with left and according to the maitre d' Mastino went to the bathroom. He went in but he never came out."

Holly waited a moment. Then she said, "Dan, listen. He called me. The voice on the phone."

"You mean last night?"

"No. I mean just now. Ten minutes ago. On my cell phone. He called me Holly. He said I'd betrayed him and that I knew what he had to do. That the Cipher demanded it."

"Hell. Tell me where you are. I'll be there as soon as I can."

"No. I don't want you to come."

"What do you mean?"

"If he knows who I am, he knows where I live. Where I go and what I do. This may be our chance."

"It's too dangerous."

"That's why I worked the crisis line, isn't it? So we could find a way to trap him. We know he's going to come. He has to."

"You're not going to become the bait," he said firmly.

"Listen to me, Dan. I always was. We both knew that when you agreed. It has to be this way."

"I only agreed to let you work the crisis line."

"Dan. We've come this far. We're so close. We can't stop now. We can't lose him again. It's the best lead we've ever gotten."

She was silent. Waiting.

"So what now?" he said. She could hear the resignation in his voice. She knew she had won.

"I'll go home. Then I'll go to the crisis line. Somewhere along the way, he'll be waiting. And you'll be there to ambush him."

"What if he gets to you first?"

"That's the chance we have to take."

She hung up before he could speak. She turned off the phone and placed it on the seat beside her. It had become her only weapon.

Morning brought a chill to the mountain.

Father Terrance awoke at first light. He had been unable to sleep, worried now about Holly and the risk she was running by warning the bishop's attorney. He had called Shepard as soon as the line was clear. The inspector grew agitated as they spoke. He was too personally involved, the priest realized that now. But there was nothing he could do about it, certainly not from this distance. At least, the warning had been delivered. The priest was concerned lest Holly do something foolish on her own. He had come to respect her as he had few others he had ever worked with. She was dogged and, he suspected, fearless. Both were positive attributes but they could result in rashness. That he wanted to prevent. The demon they were facing would allow for no mistakes.

As he got into his clothing, another worry furrowed his brow.

This was the matter of the film he had taken actually getting to Holly. He was not certain of the messenger. He was the same young maniac who had driven him up the mountain in a nonstop roller coaster of a drive, with their wheels careening on the edge of the narrow track, oblivious to the fall of thousands of feet to the bottom. Assuming he got down safely, could he be depended upon to drive to the nearest sizable town and send the tiny roll of film by the fastest and surest way possible? This was Italy. The mail was uncertain. Letters frequently got lost and sometimes sold. That was why he had specified one of the international carriers and paid the young man accordingly. Perhaps too munificently.

Basta! Enough.

He would pray it got through. That was as much as he could do.

What happened next was in the lap of the gods. A heretical pagan thought, but they needed all the help they could get. He smiled at his little joke as he tied his laces. Then he rose and went to the ewer on the stand opposite his bed and washed his hands and face. Washing facilities here were primitive. A throwback to the time of Fra Alfieri.

He shrugged as he dried his face. *What if?*

The thought crossed his mind with disturbing force. What if the monastery were still a nesting ground for the cult or the order or however they characterized it? What if the young monks he saw were being trained to carry out the commands of the Cipher?

No. Impossible. He would never have been given access to their burial place. Not unless . . .

He allowed the thought to hang in the air, not wanting to push it further without the basis of fact. He was allowing his imagination to run away with him. The young monk who had been seduced by the Cipher and whose identity they now sought had been unique. He left no followers, not unless they counted the pathetic cult they had encountered in the wilds of rural Pennsylvania. He shook the thought from his head. He had to pursue the possibility that the young monk had left further clues to his identity here in the monastery located high on the mountain.

The priest pushed open his door and went through the dark passage leading to the door outside. The monks would be awakening soon to the sounds of matins, which they rang from the bell tower. He would be joining them for breakfast. A simple meal of oatmeal and coarse black bread. But instead of heading down the passage to the room where they ate, he made a right turn and mounted several steps, which led him through an archway and out onto the battlements.

The air was cold and pure. He took a deep breath as he scanned the valley spread out before him. Here, the monks would have defended themselves from the depredations of the barbaric hordes. The battlements would have been unscalable. No invader could have mounted an attack up here. No, here they would have been safe.

For the first time since arriving from Rome, he allowed his anxiety to ease.

Up here, high above the world, even he might feel safe.

He never heard the movement behind him, nor saw the single blinding motion that slipped the garrote over his head and beneath the line of his jaw.

The powerful hands crossed behind the priest's neck, drawing the garrote taut as a bowstring across his throat.

The wrists uncrossed, releasing the leather noose.

The body was shoved through the crenellations where the ancient archers once stood, allowing the priest to fall like a weighed sack onto the jutting granite rocks a thousand feet below.

Forty

The drive home was a journey into nightmare.

She was completely alone now. The killer knew who she was. Perhaps had known all along. There was no way for her to know. Perhaps it had all been a kind of cat-and-mouse game. A way of testing her, of seeing when she would perform her final act of betrayal. A betrayal he himself had set in motion. A kind of self-fulfilling prophecy.

She shook herself free of these thoughts. None of that mattered. What mattered now was where she would be when he came for her. And the prayer that Dan and his team would be there when it happened.

She felt alike a high-wire artist throwing herself into space in the hope her partner would catch her.

And if he missed?

She would not permit the thought to enter her consciousness. Instead she steadied the wheel with both hands and focused on the traffic in front of her. With the same laserlike precision she brought to her work, she steeled her mind in the immediacy of the moment, the totality of the now. Forcing herself to concentrate solely on the lights, which flashed from orange to red to green, the mechanics of changing lanes and the series of right- and left-hand turns that would bring her to her development and finally to the cul-de-sac in front of her town house.

The area was quiet. Dark. Lit by two distant street lamps and her neighbors' windows. Several of the units were still unlit. Their inhabitants were single women like herself who worked late and kept irregular hours. Women who lived almost totally for their jobs and were not often home until after ten. She had lived here for almost six years, but she did not really know her neighbors other than to offer a casual wave. Her own life seemed suddenly shrunken. A series of processions from work to home. The futility that was her job at the prison. The few people she really knew or associated with. A life of frustration lived within an incubator.

She struggled with the key until the car finally locked. Then she turned away from the car to face the flagstone walk way leading to the front door.

There were no lights on inside.

Had she rushed home too quickly, before Dan and his team could get into place? She glanced around quickly and saw no evidence of their presence. No telltale black van or vehicle from the cable service or other utility. But that would have been the giveaway, she realized. Dan was more savvy in his methods than that. His presence would be subtle. Invisible. She had to have confidence in that. It was essential if she was to go through with this. If she was to manage the fear churning within her.

She took her key out of her bag and went toward the door, forcing herself to remain as confident and as casual as possible. Forcing herself to perform one action at time. The key slid into the lock. It turned. The door opened and she stepped inside.

Into darkness.

Into where he was waiting.

She flicked the switch and the lights came on.

She started as her vision blurred. Sensing a presence coming directly at her. But it was only an illusion.

There were only the hum of the fridge and the sudden heartbeat of the heater as it throbbed into action alerted by the draft from the open door.

She closed the door behind her.

Her home was suddenly alien. A place where her killer might be waiting.

She forced herself to continue inside. Through the dining room and into the kitchen turning on lights as she went. She held her keys in her fist, the longest key thrust through her fingers like the blade of a knife. Her own set of culinary knives rested in their wooden chest on the kitchen counter, all of them safe in their slots. Each a deadly weapon.

She came round and faced the stairs.

She refused to think and started up, touching the wall plate and flooding the upstairs with light. There were three bedrooms upstairs. All were as she had left them. The beds were neatly made. The one she used as her office was just as she had left it.

She had not locked the front door.

She would leave it as it was. Open.

She had two hours before she was due at the crisis line. She would shower and change just as she always did.

He would come or not come. If he did, the police would be there and they would take him. She had to believe that. It was all the belief she had left.

Beth glanced at the clock on her desk.

It was almost eight and she was not even remotely finished with the tasks she had allotted herself. She listed these each day on a pad on the corner of her desk and crossed them off as they were completed. Other tasks were often added to the list, but the core tasks, the ones that formed the bulk of her work, were the ones she sought to strike off first. It gave her an incredible feeling of satisfaction to begin the next day with the previous day's chores already done.

The extra chore she had added that day was the one giving her the most difficulty. A Fed-Ex had come on the overnight from Italy, which she at first mistook for a missive from her boss. But it was from Father Terrance and was addressed to her sister, the way the previous one had been. That first package had been specifically left unopened, though she generally went through all of Vincent's mail as soon as it arrived. However, the package had come with a note specifying that it not be opened by anyone other than her boss, and she had brought it in to him directly without opening it.

Vincent seemed to be expecting it. He offered no explanation, and only after she discovered that its contents were meant for her sister did the understanding dawn on her that something specific and secret was going on between the three of them.

The situation brought with it an annoying sense of jealousy.

That her sister was somehow emotionally involved with Vincent had shaken her fragile ego.

She and Vincent worked so well together that she had allowed her imagination to run wild. After all, it was her sister who had set up the job and recommended her. In spite of this, Beth had claimed him as her exclusive possession. Only when she had seen them together had reality pierced the bubble. Now, she was glad of Vincent's departure. It had given her time to think, time to reorder her already disordered thoughts and emotions and put them back where they belonged.

Not that she was entirely successful. Emotions were messy. Her whole life had been deranged because of them. She refused to allow them to run wild again, in spite of the pain she felt. Not that Vincent had given her cause for concern. He was always the perfect gentleman. But she had allowed herself to hope and that had been her undoing. Work forced her mind back on the track, that and the discipline that had guided her through school gave her the ability to endure the pain and continue on the path she had set for herself. But when the second package came, it tore open the newly healing scab.

This time there was no note specifying that it remain unopened.

She used her paper knife to open the seal and found a small roll of undeveloped film. Instructions from the priest indicated that the roll be developed as soon as possible and the pictures given to her sister. The word "urgent" had been underlined.

Beth had sent it in for developing in the institute's own lab and now awaited the results. She had called down once or twice to hurry the process along. The technician who normally developed their film was busy on another project and tried to stall her. But she used Vincent's name. The man made a growling sound but agreed to make it a priority.

Before he left, Vincent had asked her to inform him if any further missives arrived from Father Terrance, so when the package arrived she immediately called his apartment in Rome. The call was picked up by the answering machine. But she had said nothing. The truth was she wanted to speak to him in person, to hear his voice and his laughter. He was not due back until next week and she needed a fix.

She scolded herself for the thought. She hated junkie talk. She had been one for too many years, a past she had put behind her. But the truth was that for all of her so-called internal discipline, she was still crazy about him and intensely jealous of her sister.

She fought these thoughts as she went through the passage that separated her office from Vincent's. The lights were off, but light streamed in through the huge bay window behind his desk. She turned on a desk lamp and opened his large leather-bound appointment book. There had to be another number where she could reach him.

Working with Vincent, even for such a short time, had already taught her that his life was divided into compartments, each of them closed and inaccessible to the others. What these were exactly, she didn't have a clue as yet. Just as she had no idea of his involvement with her sister. But they only served to intrigue her.

After several frustrating moments, she realized there was nothing on the surface of his desk that would in any way aid her in discovering his whereabouts. She paused and weighed the possibility of his anger should she discover something he did not want her to know. Still, she thought, what if he is with someone else? Shouldn't I warn my sister?

But that was not what drove her. She recognized more than a little of her old self behind what she was doing. The willingness to risk her job even in the pursuit of something just a little bit illegal. She had never followed the straight and narrow as her sister had. There was more than a little deviltry in her motives, no matter how she rationalized them. In this case, it was an overwhelming desire to explore the forbidden. She craved Vincent as a lover and there were things she had to know.

She turned and crossed to the cabinet built into the wall.

It was generally open during the day when Vincent was in his office. He was always careful to lock it when he left. She opened the paneled wooden doors that concealed it and stared at the metal door fixed into the wall. It was fastened with a small brass lock. She touched the burnished surface with her the tips of her fingers and smiled to herself.

She knew exactly where he kept the keys.

The drive to the HMO took longer than normal.

Holly was trapped in a single lane by an accident ahead. Lights flashed and blinked cheerlessly as they crept toward the scene of the disaster. Traffic in the opposite lane rolled by quickly, mocking her, as the rubberneckers, their appetites satiated, hit their accelerators.

The night was cold and she had to put her heater on. She tried to listen to the radio, but the voices irritated her. She clicked it off. Her one need was to remain focused.

Her phone had been silent from her return home until she left. There were no calls or messages on her cell. The silence seemed ominous. Like a sky pregnant with thunder. She had expected Dan to call with instructions or reassurance. But that would have meant turning on the cell and perhaps hearing his directives for calling the operation off. She had led him this far. Forced him to respond to her ploy. She had to go through with it no matter what.

She averted her eyes as she passed the carnage, glimpsing only the twisted chassis of an SUV as it was being hoisted onto a tow truck past the assembled emergency vehicles. She felt a blane of chill descend her spine at the melded flare of flashing lights. She had been to too many crime scenes. Seen too many similar vehicles.

Ask not for whom the lights flash . . . they flash for thee. . . .

She erased the image from her mind as she eased her foot down on the pedal and accelerated away from the scene, following the long quick upsurge as the lane resumed normal speed.

The HMO was backlit against the darkness by soft spots set in the shrubbery outside and focused on the building. Only a handful of cars were still in the lot. The building would be empty, except for security and the women who worked the crisis line.

Holly parked near the entrance and started inside.

She signed in at the desk, where the second of two security guards was seated, his bored expression already settling into stupefaction. She took the elevator up to the second level, then exited into the long starkly lit hallway that would take her back to where the crisis line was located.

She was late. The others had already gone. She was by herself now.

Open doors faced her on either side. The interiors beyond them were dark, open like empty mouths. The courage it took to walk that long dark corridor was not a factor. Not in Holly's mind. Only to do it, as she had done everything else. To conquer her fear. But that was wrong. She knew fear was never conquered. It was something you learned to deal with as you learned to deal with the prison and your sister and everything else that came your way in life. So she walked the corridor, door by door, office by office, waiting for the hands that would reach out to grab her.

How she reached her station was a mystery. But she found herself inside. Seated in a half-lit cubicle. Alone in the empty building. With a killer stalking her. And a ringing phone at her ear.

The voice at the other end belonged to Dan.

"Why haven't you been answering your phone?" he shouted.

"Sorry," she said, but his voice was her lifeline and she grasped at it.

"We've got us a problem."

"Tell me."

"Someone ratted us out to Pinero."

"Who?"

"I don't know who. Only that I've been suspended."

The words failed to penetrate.

"What do you mean, suspended?"

"Just what I said. Pinero just called and suspended me. I'm no longer running the task force or anything else. He ordered me to call off the back-up. I tried to go around him but I didn't get any support."

Holly was speechless. The walls seemed to swell around her.

"Now listen," he continued, "I want you to get out of there. I'll be over as soon as I can. Call security and have them escort you down to reception. Stay there and wait for me. Do it now."

He hung up and the phone buzzed against her ear.

She sat immobile as the implications of what he said flooded her mind. There had been no task force watching her. All this time, she had been completely and utterly alone.

Through a fog at a deep distance she heard the chimes of her cell phone.

She shook herself awake and reached into her bag. She placed the gleaming chrome rectangle to her ear.

"Yes."

"Holly, it's Beth."

The sound of her sister's voice snapped her alert.

"Beth, are you all right?"

"I'm okay. But I have to see you. Father Terrance sent you a package. It's marked urgent."

"Film?"

"That's right. I had it developed. The prints are being sent up."

"I don't know when I can come for them," Holly said. She felt a slight dizziness.

Beth's voiced dropped to a hushed whisper. "There's something else. Something I found. Something you've got to see."

"Beth. I've got to wait here for Dan. He's coming for me."

"Forget Dan," her sister said. Holly could sense her fear. "Forget everything else. You've got to come now!"

Forty-one

Towers and battlements loomed behind the trees.

It was after midnight and the guard house was unattended. Holly pressed the button on the automatic entry post. It buzzed and the barrier lifted. Holly headed along the curving driveway toward the massive edifice ahead. Amber spotlights illuminated the façade softening the stone and giving it a strange fairy-tale aspect. It gave Holly the feeling of driving backward in time.

The sensation was appealing. She wanted to be somewhere else, somewhere in time before all the killings and the terror she was now feeling.

She'd had a moment of panic on the way over. She had rushed out of the HMO, intending to call Dan as she drove, but her cell would not respond. The battery needed recharging. She would have to call from the institute. She had stopped at the security desk to ask the guard to inform Dan where she had gone, but the desk was empty. The guard was not at his post.

She'd glanced around as she drove looking for a public phone. She'd veered across two lanes toward a gas station with a battery of public phones, but they were located at the remote edge of the property and a surge of fear kept her foot on the pedal and she pulled away quickly. Turning off the highway brought its own spasm of fear. She was alone on the long desolate road. No other cars passed her on either side. The area leading to the institute was heavily forested. There were no houses or buildings of any kind.

She kept her eyes on the rearview, but no lights had followed her.

Driving toward the institute reassured her. The closer she came the safer she began to feel. The spreading wings of the building seemed like welcoming arms that would close protectively around her. By the time she eased her car into one of the spaces in front, she was beginning to feel calm, in spite of the urgent alarm of Beth's call.

The lobby doors were open, but no one was at the desk in front. She took the elevator to the second floor. When the doors opened, Beth was standing outside in the marble-floored lobby waiting for her. Her sister's face was fixed with a look of anxiety. In her hand, she carried a large white manila envelope.

"What's the matter?" Holly said.

"You'll see," Beth responded, turning and leading the way along the dimly lit corridor.

"Did you call, Dan?" Beth said.

"No. I came as quickly as I could. I tried calling from the car but my battery was weak. I'll call him later."

"So he doesn't even know where you are?" Beth asked.

"I told you, I'll call him. Why don't you tell me what's wrong?"

"I can't. I don't know myself," she answered in an anguished tone.

"Beth, stop!" Holly exclaimed. She had seldom seen her sister so agitated. But Beth would not stop; she continued through her office toward the passage beyond.

The room they entered was in darkness except for the single lamp on the desk in the center. They were in Vincent's office. Through the huge bay window the grounds were shrouded in darkness.

"Look at this," Beth said.

She was standing behind the desk, her face deeply etched in shadow.

Holly came around and stood beside her.

The desk was empty except for a large leather-bound volume.

The leather was deeply seamed and cracked with age.

"What is it?" Holly asked.

"I'm not sure."

"Then why . . ." Holly let her voice trail off.

"Because of what you told me last time. About that book. The one with all the names. The punishments."

Holly stared at her sister, suddenly remembering their conversation.

"The Cipher?"

"I think this is it."

Holly stared at her. "It can't be. It's never been found."

"Open it," Beth commanded.

Holly opened the cover and stared down at the cursive writing. It was handwritten like an illuminated medieval manuscript. The paper was extremely old.

"It's in Latin," Beth said.

"Then how could you understand it?"

"Not the text. I couldn't read any of that. It was the names."

"What names?"

"Turn the pages and you'll see."

Holly turned the heavy parchment leaves until she came to the list of names. They were written in bold red lettering. Beneath each name was a series of lines. She was unable to determine what they meant.

"I don't understand."

"Keep turning," Beth said.

Holly turned more pages.

"There."

Holly looked down.

In red was the name of Father McKay. And beneath that Bishop Horan. And then, one beneath the other, the names of each of the other murder victims, including Mary Donnelly.

A chill traversed her entire body. Though it was written in Latin, Holly had enough understanding of the language from her graduate studies in pharmacology to understand that beside each name were inscribed the details of their crimes and the exact nature of their punishment.

"Where did you find this?" Holly said.

"In the cabinet, over there." Beth pointed. Holly turned and saw the open door of the cabinet.

"Found it, how? You mean it was just lying there?"

"No. I had to open it."

"You broke in?"

"I knew where he kept the keys."

Confusion filled Holly's mind. "Beth. You mean, you took Vincent's keys?"

"Of course. How else did you think I got it open?"

She picked up the white manila envelope and offered it to Holly.

"What's this?" Holly said.

"The pictures I had developed."

"Did you look at them."

"Of course. That's why I called you."

"I don't understand."

"Look, then you tell me."

Somewhere distant a series of chimes went off.

"That's my cell," Beth said. "It's in my office. I'll be right back. Look at the last page."

Beth went back into the passage connecting the two offices. Holly watched her go, then sat in the large leather chair behind her. She felt exhausted suddenly. Drained. Her mind refused to think. The logic of what she had been looking at refused to formulate, like knitting needles that would not meet to form the next stitch of the pattern.

As if they were operating on their own, her hands opened the envelope and drew out the sheaf of glossy photographs. They had been enlarged to 8x10's.

She spread them out on the desk beside the leather volume.

They were all of the same subject. Some were in close-up. Others more at a distance but covering each angle of the object. It was a mask. Formed of plaster or some other substance. The eyes were blank. Expressionless. But the features were clear.

Almost familiar.

It was a face she knew.

Her sister's voice echoed in her mind.

Look at the last page.

Almost mechanically, she turned the page of the volume in front of her. Her eyes widened in horror.

On the top of the page was the name of Paul Mastino. And just below it, the name of Brother Dominicus.

And on the last and final line. Another name.

Her own.

Holly stared at the letters. They swirled, going in and out of focus, as the shock rose from deep inside her gut.

She did not feel the blow that rendered her unconscious. Only the strange sensation of falling and the final instant of darkness just before sleep.

Dan felt stymied.

He had arrived at the HMO thirty minutes after he and Holly ended their call. But she was gone. Her car was not in the lot.

She was not at the reception desk where the security guard was stationed. The man had not seen her.

Nor was she upstairs at her work station, or anywhere else on the floor, or in the entire building for that matter. He had made a cursory search aided by the security guard, whose alarm system would have warned him if anyone had entered any of the other sections of the building.

So where was she?

He had tried calling her cell but received no response. He had called her home and left a message on her voice mail. He had tried calling her sister, but there was no answer there either. He woke her friend Clara, who claimed she had not spoken to Holly for several days.

His agitation increased as the moments passed. She knew the danger. She had spoken to the killer and been told that she was marked for death. Then why had she gone off without waiting for him?

He blamed himself for allowing her to draw him into her plan. Trapping the killer by using herself as bait was an insanity he should have prevented. He knew better, but he was desperate. The killer had drawn them into a series of mazes all ending at the same dead end. They had virtually nothing to go on. Their search for Brother Dominicus had ended in a farce. The man had disappeared off the face of the planet, disappeared without a trace. His followers were clamoring for his scalp, claiming police persecution, and two local newspapers had printed it. Fortunately, it had not yet gotten into the mainstream media, but that was not far behind if he were any predictor of the dynamics of the situation.

Then there was the shock of being suspended.

The knowledge that he had been betrayed by one of the members of his own team rankled even worse. He still had not determined who the traitor was.

Did it matter?

Pinero was still trying to sell the public on the idea that the killings were unconnected. Even after the last two. And so far he had buffaloed the media into buying it. But once they knew of the killer's similar MO, how long would it take for them to connect the dots? Especially if someone on the inside helped connect them. Someone like himself, who no longer had anything to lose.

Pinero was angry because Dan had defied him by refusing to get rid of Holly. Now she was missing and he was responsible.

She might have fallen into the killer's hands. She might already be dead. The thought sent a shudder through him along with images of the other victims and the gruesome horror of their deaths. He tried to dismiss the pictures from his mind, but he was too much of a pro for that. The images would stay with him, spurring his anxiety and the quickening urgency in his blood to find her.

Forty-two

She woke suddenly.

It took several moments to accustom her eyes to the light flickering from the oil lamps. They were set out high and out of reach. But they provided enough light for Holly to see her surroundings.

The room was round. The walls were made of stone and covered with tapestries. They were old, she could see that even a distance. The furniture, too, was old. There were round-back chairs and a long wooden table. The bed she was lying on was covered with a canopy. It felt like a stage set and she expected the curtains to part and the orchestra to play. But that was not going to happen. This was a prison.

She sat up and looked down at herself.

She was dressed in a heavy white robe made of some kind of coarse material. Underneath it she was naked. Her feet were bare. The only adornment was the heavy wooden cross around her neck. She had no rings or watch. Even her earrings had been removed.

The room had no mirrors so she could not see the full effect, but she knew enough to realize that she was dressed in the robes of a penitent. Or a victim of the Inquisition.

For an instant, a surge of panic overcame her. But she fought it off. She breathed deep and tried to still the racing of her heart.

She had been rendered unconscious. Rising from it was like rising out of anesthesia. Without dreams or memory. Only a seamless all-enveloping darkness. She assumed she was somewhere inside the institute. In the old cloister that had been imported by the Foresters.

The word struck her suddenly. The Arbori. They were the wealthy and influential family that had protected the abbot and the generations of avengers. Arbori was a derivative of arbor . . . trees, forests.

Forester.

Of course. It all fit now. And with that knowledge came a spiraling sense of loss. What she knew now destroyed all hope. And along with it the comfort of the romantic cocoon she had spun around her self. A dream now splintered beyond recognition. And like the creature in the nursery rhyme, never to be put back together again. A dream that had turned into a nightmare.

She heard a sound and looked up.

The door was opening.

She stiffened and rose. Planting her bare feet on the cold stone floor.

A figure entered carrying a large leather volume. He was dressed in a monk's robe and cowl which shrouded his face. But she knew him instantly.

"Vincent," she said.

He shook his head. "My name is Brother Sebastian."

"You're also the head of this institute and someone I very much believed in."

"That was all a masquerade."

She felt as if a hammer had struck her. "That's all it was, just a masquerade?" Her throat constricted as a wave of emotion pulsed through her like water through a splintering dam. But she held back her tears. She would not give him that.

"You've ordered my death," she said, her eyes fixed on his. His face beneath the cowl was stark. The resemblance to the mask was unmistakable in spite of his beard.

"Nothing is written that cannot be unwritten."

"I think this part of the masquerade is over. The mask of your face. Father Terrance has seen it. He knows who you are."

"Father Terrance will not speak again."

She stared at him.

"You killed him."

"He interfered with the work."

"Is that all that matters?"

"For me, it has to be all."

Holly looked at him and sensed the wall that now existed between them.

"Where is my sister?"

"Somewhere safe," he answered.

"Is she in here?"

He would not answer.

"What will happen to her?"

"That depends on you."

He stepped closer and placed the leather volume on the table.

"These are the words of Fra Alfieri. I would like you to read them."

"I don't understand Latin."

"I have translated it into English so you can follow the text."

"Why?"

"I want you to understand the reasons for what I do."

"Do you think my understanding will exonerate you?"

"I do not need exoneration. I answer only to God."

He was insane, she thought. But she reconsidered. It was

something else. Something the world had always been poisoned with, but that had now blossomed, spreading across the globe like a cancerous growth.

"Why is it that every religious fanatic from the beginning of time has said exactly the same thing to justify their actions."

His eyes were level with hers. They did not flinch at the acidity of her words.

"Read and you may change your mind."

"And if I do, then what? I go to the stake knowing a little more?"

"Perhaps you will not have to go to the stake at all."

"What does that mean?"

"What I said before about everything between us being a masquerade wasn't entirely true. I didn't lie when I said I had deep feelings for you. But I cannot sacrifice my work for my personal feelings, no matter how strong they might be. But should you come to believe as I do . . . and I find that we are united in a sacred trust . . . then you would become my partner in the work."

"You mean, help you kill people," she said incredulously.

"Those who have cheated justice must die."

"I don't believe that." Her voice was empathic. Die if you have to, but die believing in what you are.

"Read. Then we will talk."

"Wait. If when you return I'm not one of the converted, then what?"

He was silent.

"I see. Then you carry out the sentence."

"I am bound by my oath."

"Suppose I told you I agreed. How would you know If I really was converted?"

"I would have to test you, of course."

"You mean, ask me to kill someone?"

"If you truly believe, you will not think of it in that way. You would be carrying out the work of God."

"And if I did believe and passed the test, what guarantee do I have that you'd release my sister?"

"None."

'Then why would I do it?"

"Because you had to. Because you would have believed."

"So my choice is my sister's life in exchange for my becoming an assassin?"

He did not answer. The door closed and he was gone.

Holly took a deep breath. She moved to the table and stared down at the book. She paused, then opened the cover and began to read.

Beth shivered out of sleep and opened her eyes.

It was dark and she was cold.

The blankets she had been covered with had slipped off the bed she was on. Not a bed exactly, she realized as her hands explored in the darkness. More like a cot fixed against the wall.

It took a moment to realize that her hands were in manacles.

Not handcuffs, but heavy antique irons connected to a chain that was fixed to a ring in the stone wall.

Where the hell was she?

She rose with her hands extended. In a moment she contacted the wall. It was made of smooth uneven stone. She began feeling her way around the room. It did not take long. The walls were bare and as cold as the floor. There was a wooden door, bound with iron. She reached up. It had a curving shape, an arch that came to a point. A gothic arch, which meant she was somewhere within the old monastery. A few more shuffling steps and she returned to the cot where she had begun.

She felt down along her body. She was still dressed in her street clothes. She wondered how long she had been unconscious. She remembered the cell phone ringing and leaving

Holly alone in Vincent's office. She went through the connecting passage to her office and picked up her phone when something happened. Exactly what she did not remember.

She slumped back down on the cot and pulled the blankets up around her. She tried to think, but it was all she could do to fight the waves of distress that kept assaulting her. This had to do with Vincent. She knew that for a certainty. Finding the Cipher was proof of that. But what did it prove? The story Holly told her was terrifying enough. If he were somehow part of this avenging angel thing, then he was in it up to his neck with how many killings hanging over his head? She had lost count.

She followed some of the stories in the newspaper only because her sister was involved. Otherwise she would have blocked them from her mind. These last weeks all she had concentrated on was her work, her connection with Vincent, and the waves of feeling that it produced. She had fancied herself in love with him. Which was why his relationship with her sister had so profoundly shocked her. At first, she didn't believe it. Holly was so shut off, so distant from her own emotions. Sure, she had begun a relationship with Dan, but even that didn't seem real. Holly's work was real. The prison was real. The hostage taking had been real. But a relationship with someone like Vincent Pascal, that was as far from reality as the Wizard of Oz.

Yet it was true.

Or was it?

If Pascal was the dark presence behind all the killings, then her poor sister had been as duped as she was. And now she had to believe that he was. No one else could have entered the institute like that without being seen. She would have had to clear them past the security systems as she had done with Holly. Besides, the names in the Cipher only proved it. And by discovering the ancient leather-bound volume, she had condemned both of them to death.

The realization cut like a blade.

She felt a surge of panic. As if she couldn't breathe. She had to get out of there. She struggled against the manacles. But they held her. She was nowhere strong enough to break them. The old iron chaffed her skin.

There had to be a way out.

She searched her mind desperately. She had been given the guided tour on her first day on the job. But much of what she had seen passed in a blur. There was just too much to see. The institute was crammed with art and artifacts. Suits of armor and collections of ancient weapons, manuscripts, and furniture. They had reconstructed the old monastery on the grounds, then connected it to the new buildings. Connected how? She had to think. Somewhere in her memory she had seen plans for some renovations. She had brought them in for Vincent to look at and he'd insisted they go over them together. He'd wanted her input. It was the first time anyone she had worked for had ever said anything like that to her and she'd felt buoyed and impressed. That was the moment she had begun to worship him.

"Think!" she cried aloud.

She remembered that there had been a series of underground passageways connecting all the buildings, even extending to the old section. Passages for plumbing and heating. And she recalled him pointing out the clever way the ancient cloister had similar passages, which they had reconstructed. Yes. She remembered it all now. She had even made a tracing of them to impress him. Memorizing it, so he would think she was some kind of genius. Once she got out, she would know where she was. But first she had to get out.

The question was how.

Her head was clear now. She no longer felt so afraid. First, she had to get out of the manacles. Light was filtering down now from somewhere above. She craned her neck and made out the faint outline of an arched window protected by a thick glass pane.

Light permitted her to examine the manacles. They were

very old. Made of rusting iron, fastened with big ancient locks. They were thick, too thick to think of cutting through, but the locks could be picked.

With what?

She felt along her clothing and found the pin she had put on the day before. It was a small American flag she wore in her lapel. Obviously, he had overlooked it. She quickly unfastened it. Lock picking was something she had learned in one of her past reincarnations when she was in and out of rehab, living with scuzz-balls who foraged the city for drugs and made their living off petty crime. Stealing car radios. Shoplifting. Minor break-ins. Not real burglaries, they were too scatterbrained for that, just little moments of opportunity that required the picking of a padlock or jimmying a car door. She was a master of the art. Often it was she who was sent out to do the heavy lifting while her mate of the moment lay in a drugged stupor. Steal or starve was the law of the street. And she had survived.

She was determined to survive again.

Forty-three

She finally closed the book.

She had no idea of the time. There was no way to measure day or night. But hours had passed and the flames still flickered in the oil lamps.

Holly's mind was in turmoil.

Fra Alfieri was extremely persuasive. But was he right?

To allow the guilty to go unpunished was as great a sin as allowing them to get away with what they had done. To know and do nothing was itself an indictment. Was itself a mortal sin. That was the basis of his belief.

The argument was powerful and persuasive. It could be applied to much of modern life when atrocities were being committed on a daily basis all over the world. Allowing the perpetrators to get away with it was always a cause of anguish for Holly. How many killers went free and unpunished every day? It was a century filled with incredible anguish, impossible for the ordinary human mind to contemplate. A scream out of history. Listen too long and go mad.

Now she was being asked to become an instrument of vengeance. An avenger of the world's wrongs. She would have to kill in order for her sister to live. But her mind rebelled against the idea. She felt trapped. Lost within the walls of his prison.

Despair flooded her being.

She felt the downward spiral sucking her into a numbing depression. Which was when she suddenly rebelled. Something defiantly shook her free.

She would not be his victim.

Somehow there had to be a way out.

She had to find a way to escape before he came back for her.

She rose and her eyes desperately searched the room.

There were no windows other than a series of small semi-circular arches above a ledge set high up on the wall. She went to the door and tried the latch. It turned but the door would not open. The lock was from a bygone era. The keyhole was enormous. There had to be a way to open it. She searched the room but there was nothing she could use. It was bare of implements.

Frustrated, she sat on the bed, her fists clenched, nails painfully digging into her palms.

Like a trapped animal, her eyes darted to every corner ferreting out a way of escape. Her heart was beating wildly. *Help me,* she shouted inside. *Please, God, help me. . . .*

She scanned the walls, the high-domed ceiling, the tapestries, the ledge.

And somehow it connected.

The small arches were lined with boards. She had not seen that before. They must have once been windows. There had to be something behind them.

She quickly rose and went to the wall behind her. The tapestries were hung on antique metal rods, which passed through iron eyelets fixed into the stone wall. Each end of the rod was pointed like a spear. It could be used as a tool or a weapon. If she could reach them . . .

She lifted the coverlet on the bed. It was edged with a thick ribbing of material. With her teeth she tore into the edge managing to pull it separate from the rest of the cover-let. She ripped off a long piece of the edging, then drew up the hem of her gown and using the edging as a belt, tied it securely around her waist, leaving her legs bare.

Now she could climb.

Holly had always been agile. She had excelled in gymnastics. But that had been in high school. The worst that could happen was that she would fall and break her neck on the stone floor below. But did she have a choice?

She stood on the bed and gripped the wooden frame of the canopy. She tested it. The wood was securely set in place. Heavily made as was the style in medieval Europe; it would hold her weight. She reached up and gripped the top strut. It took an enormous effort, but she managed to pull herself to the top of the canopy. She gripped the edge of the tapestry and pulled, testing its strength.

Balancing precariously, both feet securely placed on the strut of the canopy, she rose to her full height holding the tapestry in both hands. She looked up. She had a good ten feet to climb before she reached the ledge.

Shit, she thought. Here goes.

She reached up and grabbed a handful of cloth and slowly began to climb. She swung away from the wall, but by bending her torso she could hold onto the tapestry with both hands as she inched her bare feet up along the icy stone wall. She took a deep breath and let go with one hand and made a stab, gripping the tapestry higher up. Then she pulled herself up using her hands and feet at the same time.

The tapestry was holding. Yard by yard she was gaining.

All of her muscles were on fire. Beads of sweat rolled down her body. She was breathing so hard she thought her heart would come through her chest. She refused to look down. If she did fall, the cloth-topped canopy might break her descent. She hoped.

She was almost to the top when she heard the tear.

She hung for a moment, terrified the tapestry would give

way. It was weaker at the top, where it was fastened to the iron rod by small round hoops of metal. She needed another few moments, then she would be able to reach the ledge.

Her arm went up and her fingers gripped the iron rod.

In another moment, both hands were on the rod. She no longer needed the tapestry to climb. She inched her feet higher and her fingers gripped the edge of the stone ledge. It was narrow but it would support her. She scrambled up, using the rod as leverage, and managed to twist her body onto the narrow ledge.

She lay on her belly. Silent. Allowing herself to rest. Cold stone beneath her bare thighs.

The room below was silent. There was only the sound of her breathing and the flicker of the oil lamps. The leather volume lay on the table where she had left it.

She turned over on her back and looked up. She was within one of the archways. She tested the boards, striking them with her fist. The sound was hollow. There was space behind them. They were securely set. She would need to pry them open.

She spread her legs as wide as she could on the narrow ledge and reached over. She gripped the iron rod and began moving it through the eyelets securing it to the wall. The tapestry was incredibly heavy, making it difficult for her to move the rod.

Little by little she edged it through.

Then it was past the last eyelet. She let go and the tapestry crumpled to the floor below.

She gripped the iron rod and drew it onto the ledge.

She angled it around so that the spear point was facing in. It was difficult to maneuver because of the rod's length, but she managed it. Using all of her strength, she began hammering the point at the place where the boards met. The wood was stubborn and refused to give. She rose on her knees and swung it harder. The rough stone dug into her skin painfully, but she ignored it. Her mind was focused on a single thought. She had to break through.

Then the first board gave way. It flew back exposing the darkness behind it.

She pushed it in and it fell away. She hammered at the next one and it fell. Now that she was through the first two, the others were easier. They were all nailed to a frame that she could pry open with the point of the rod.

She pushed her hand inside.

It was clear. She poked the rod in and down. It struck bottom a few feet below the ledge. Poking further, it struck the wall beyond. There was a passage inside. Holly slid the rod inside and using it as leverage, she eased her legs through. Gingerly, she allowed her toes to touch the floor. She felt grit under her soles. She was on a stone floor, colder than the stone inside. She straightened up and felt around her in the pitch blackness.

She was in some kind of rounded corridor.

More than likely, it curved to follow the small arches in their journey around the chamber. There would have to be an exit. A door to somewhere.

She gripped the rod like a spear and started into the darkness, one hand on the stone wall, blind to what was in front of her.

It took Beth two hours to free herself of the manacles.

They lay on the floor in front of her like two open jaws.

Her wrists were bleeding from the effort of using such a tiny implement as the fastener on the back of her flag pin. She had to constantly twist her wrist to get the right angle. Wearing both manacles made it incredibly difficult. But once she got the first one off, the second went easier. Now that she had mastered the lock, she had some idea of how the ancient mechanism worked.

A lock was an interesting miracle of engineering. There were some mechanisms that would not be defeated. But this was not one of them. The primitive tumblers gave way once she understood how they operated. If she had possessed something larger to work with, it would have gone much faster.

Now she had the door to conquer.

She ignored the pain in her wrists and bent to examine the lock. Inserting the pin revealed that it would have no effect against the large old-fashioned tumbler mechanism. She needed a larger tool.

She knew that the old section had once been a monastery. She was locked in what must have been one of the monk's cells. It was small and bare, except for the cot. Something struck her suddenly. She rose and moved along the walls, her hands attaching themselves to the smooth stone like moving feelers.

If it was a monk's cell, there would have to be a crucifix. If it were still there, she might have something to work with.

Her fingers struck an object. Her hands felt over it. Her instinct was right, it was a crucifix fastened by a wire to a hook set into the wall. The wire was old and rusty. Hurriedly, her fingers fumbled to remove it from the wall. She had to twist it around entirely to get it started. The wire cut her fingers, but she persisted. Finally, it came free in her hands.

She brought it to the cot and knelt on the floor. She lifted the manacles and, using the open edge of one of them, she brought it down on the old wooden cross. The wood was stubborn, but she was more so. After she smashed the manacle down several times, the wood finally gave way, splintering into several pieces. She took the best piece and began working it, using the edge of the manacle, until she had fashioned it to a point.

She went back over to the door and inserted the point into the lock.

"Carefully," she whispered, "we don't want you to break."

But it did. The wood was too soft, too rotten.

She went back to the cot and picked up the crucifix, turning it over in her hands. It was fastened together with a piece of metal that ran almost the length of one of the cross pieces. That might do it. She had to work at the screws. Using the edge of the pin, which she managed to insert into the slot, she carefully twisted the pin.

The screw moved.

She was able to twist with her fingers. In a few minutes she had one off. The second was a little tougher, but the wood was soft. It took a little longer, but she was able to get it going. Now she had something to work with.

Her pulse was hammering as she knelt in front of the door.

She paused, slowing herself down.

Then she inserted the piece of metal into the keyhole.

She had to bend the metal to work it against the tumblers. They were huge and stiff. She felt like a surgeon exploring someone's body. She found the first, lifted it, then lifted the second. One to go. If she slipped she would have to start all over again. Please, she prayed. Make this work.

The third tumbler rose. There was a loud click. The lock was open.

She rose off her knees and turned the latch.

The heavy wooden door opened.

She stepped into the corridor outside. There were no lights. Only the chill emptiness of a cavern.

Carefully, she closed the door behind her. Then she stepped off into the unknown.

Forty-four

The passage went on like a blank piece of film unreeling into darkness.

Holly kept her hand extended and felt along the wall. The stone floor was uneven. Her toes caught in the spaces and caused her to trip. But she kept the iron rod pointed at the ground ahead, sweeping it back and forth like a blind man who has lost his way.

Her heart was pounding. She knew that sooner or later he would return to the room and find her missing. He would look up and it would be obvious where she had gone. She had to find a way out before that happened. She had lost all faith in her ability to reason with him. He was a fanatic who could believe no logic but his own. Confrontation would only lead to one result. To do what he wanted or face death.

She followed the passage as it curved around the room below. The air was still and fetid. It had a musty odor of disuse. There had to be a door, a way out, or she would be doomed to following the passage round and round like a rat caught in a maze. Her fingers felt for a cornice or a molding to indicate a doorway. But there was nothing. Only the smoothness of the stone. Her pulse quickened. She could hear herself breathing in the enclosed space. The panicked breath of a trapped animal.

Then her fingers found it.

She felt the stone indent. Her fingers outlined a low archway. And a wooden door.

There was a latch. She held her breath in panic, praying for it not to be locked, for it to open. And it did.

The hinges squealed like an angry kitten. But the door slid back, grating on the floor.

There was a passage beyond. It smelled of damp. But there was light from a low-wattage bulb in a wire cage. Now, which way?

She held her breath and listened. There was no sound. She had to decide. Her temples were splitting. Left.

She turned and started down the long passageway. There were no doors on either side, only the smooth gray stone. She wondered if it was her fate to wind up in another prison. But that was a fatalism she wouldn't allow herself to succumb to. She was going to get out, she had to tell herself that. Had to believe it or she would go under.

Her feet were freezing. They felt like blocks of granite. She pulled off the makeshift belt and allowed the garment to fall to its full length, but it provided little or no warmth. Her teeth began chattering. The place was like an icebox.

The passageway ended at a transverse. Another long stone corridor loomed ahead, lit by a single bulb. She started down it. The iron rod weighed a ton. But it was her only means of defense. She held it pointed like a spear.

She started to run, as much out of panic as the cold. Her bare soles sounded like slaps on the cold stone floor. She had to find some warmth or she could wind up hypothermic. Freezing and insensible.

The passage ended at a blank wall. Facing her was another door. But this one was newer and made of iron. She stared at it helplessly. God help her if it wouldn't open. She reached for the handle and pulled. It refused to move. She put down the rod, braced herself, and pulled with both hands. It gave a little. Using all her strength, she gripped the handle and drew it back. Little by little it gave way and she just slipped through.

She faced another dimly lit stone passage with a door at its end. But it was warmer on the other side. Thankfully she started forward, then remembered she had left the rod on the floor on the other side of the partly open door. She turned and hurried back. She bent and slipped her arm through, but the rod was just out of reach.

"Shit!' she cursed. She had no more strength. To wrestle with the door was impossible. She would have to do without it. She turned and started down the passageway. The stones were not as cold under her feet. If the area was heated, then it would be used. It must lead to a way out. She hurried to the door. It was made of oak reinforced with iron and set within a stone archway. There were twin handles. She gripped one in each hand and drew them back. Miraculously, they opened.

She stepped through the doorway and felt an updraft of heat.

She was standing in a short passageway. There was an archway ahead, but beyond it she could not see. She reached the archway in several steps, then stepped through it onto a circular stone ledge. A metal railing ran around the circumference.

She was in a large round tower. She looked up and saw a huge wooden hoist. Dangling from it was a thick iron chain. She gripped the railing and looked down, following the plumb of the chain.

Below her was a giant hearth. Flames leapt from it, tonguing the air like hungry wolves.

In the center of the flames was a square iron cage. The bars glowed red from the heat. Holly stared at it for a moment before she understood.

In the center of the cage was a man.

His hands gripped the bars. His head was thrown back. His mouth was open in a silent scream.

Recognition was instant. She was looking into the face of Paul Mastino. He was being roasted alive.

From her throat came a scream of terror and helplessness.

Without willing it, she turned away, trying to run, to flee from the horror she had just seen. But her legs would not take her. They had turned into pillars of stone. She stood with her fist against her mouth, unable to move. Staring at the figure facing her.

In the archway, his face shrouded within his cowl, was Vincent Pascal.

Beth knew she was running out of time.

She had managed to escape the monk's cell she had been imprisoned in, but she had not escaped the institute. She found herself in an intricate geometry of corridors, some of which led nowhere and others that doubled back upon themselves. There must have been exits at one time, but these were all blocked up or had disappeared when the monastery was transported and rebuilt.

How was she going to get out of there?

She was tired, hungry, and cold. She'd had nothing to drink for hours and her throat felt like bark. The place was damp, unheated. And there were no lights anywhere. She had been traveling in the dark. For how long, she had no idea. Her watch had been taken. She wouldn't have been able to see the dial anyway.

What she did possess was her anger.

It was a rage she had been dealing with all her life as the underachieving daughter of two very ambitious people. It had forced her to rebel, then reject everything she thought would bring her parents joy, choosing an outlaw lifestyle that would only bring them grief. It had gone on for years until it dawned on her that her parents were long dead and what she was really doing was punishing herself. So she had stopped poisoning her body with alcohol and drugs and opted for a positive, life-embracing existence that included graduating from college and beginning a career—only to wind up in this shit-hole with a maniacal killer who wanted to end her life.

That was not going to happen.

The anger that had nurtured and sustained her through the three decades of her existence was going to help save her life. She was determined that it be so. She was not going to give up just because she was trapped in an endless maze of tunnels. She was going to fight until she won.

Eyes blazing, she hurried along the passage like a mole on speed, turned the corner, and stopped. Hadn't she been this way already? Maybe yes, maybe no. It was impossible to tell in this darkness. "The hell with it," she said aloud and turned in the opposite direction. She started forward and bumped her nose against a wall.

Only it was not a wall.

It was large metal door.

She felt along the edge until she found the handle. It was thick and industrial.

She gave it a tug and felt movement. She tugged again. More movement. It was doable.

Gripping the handle with both hands, she pulled with all of her diminishing strength.

Incredibly, it opened.

Scalding air belched into her face and she recoiled.

It took a moment to adjust her eyes to the light. It was red and glowing, barely offering any illumination. But from the light it did give off, she was able to make out that she was facing some kind of round windowless chamber. The little light there was came from the huge cauldronlike object in the chamber's center. Some kind of stove, she concluded. But what was it for?

She gave it a wide berth as she moved around the room. The heat seared her skin. The previous moment she had been freezing. Now she was afraid of being scalded. She kept tight to the wall, which circled around the cauldron. Then she saw something that made her heart leap.

A stone staircase.

It rose to a small platform leading to another metal door.

She reached it and began to climb. In a moment, she was facing the door. Gingerly, she reached out to grip the latch.

It turned and the door opened.

She stepped into a small stone-walled room lit by a bulb set into the ceiling. There was a door at the other end.

Strange metal contraptions hung from the walls, none of which she recognized. On a rack against the wall was an assortment of sharp-edged implements. Some were flat and hooked at the end. Others were long and curved.

She felt an involuntary shiver.

She knew what these were. She had seen them in one of the institute's catalogs on one of her first days on the job when she was trying to familiarize herself with the institute's many collections.

They were implements of torture.

Some were used to pierce the skin. Others to disembowel their victims.

She selected a flat tool with an up-curving edge because it seemed less heavy than the others. God knows what use it had been put to. She had no desire to know, only to protect herself.

Gripping it in her hand, she went to the small low arched doorway at the other end. The door opened easily, admitting her into a huge open area. She had to jump back to escape the searing heat that came from the open hearth in the room's center.

She realized that it must be receiving its heat from the huge cauldron in the room below.

She looked up.

She was inside a tower. A huge wooden joist had been fitted into the ceiling. A chain hung down securing something obscured within the up-licking flames.

She had to squint to make it out. It was some kind of cage and something was imprisoned within it.

It took another instant before she realized exactly what she was looking at. Before the horror imprinted itself on her mind.

Forty-five

Holly stared at the robed figure in front of her.

For an instant, she remained rooted to the spot before her legs propelled her away. But his movement caught her before she could retreat. She raised her arms to ward him off, but he swung something at her. The blow caught her on the side of the head. She saw black as she fell.

An instant later, her eyes popped open.

He was twisting something around her wrists. It was the rope he wore around his waist.

She drew away, folding her hand into a fist, and met his jaw with the full force of her arm.

He staggered backward. His eyes widened in surprise at the force of the blow. But he was still on his feet and she was crouched below him, trying to rise.

He leapt toward her as she sidestepped, avoiding the full force of his body as his fingers reached out to grab her. He was stronger than she imagined. His grip felt like a steel claw as it clamped around her arm. She ducked, trying to shove him off balance, but he held on.

She pulled him with her, desperately trying to find something to fight with. The rope lay on the ground in front of her. Attached to it was a large wooden cross.

Holly's fingers closed around the crucifix as his other arm locked itself around her throat. She brought the cross up and back behind her, driving it into his face.

He cried out as the blunt end of the object hammered into the bone of his cheek. His grip loosened for an instant and she ducked under his arm.

She slammed back against the stone wall, trying to side-slip him, but his fingers gripped her hair. She yelped as the pain bit. He pulled and her head snapped back. Her legs slipped from under her.

She went down as he drove his knee into her back.

The pain seared her spine. She cried out as his arm locked around her throat.

She slashed backward with the crucifix, but he was just out of reach.

She felt the pressure against her windpipe and gasped for air. One hand gripped his wrist, as her nails dug into his flesh. But he held on, tightening his arm.

She coughed, struggling to breathe. She dropped the cross and brought her other hand up, trying to plunge her nails into his eyes. She tore his skin above his eyebrow, but he arched his head away.

Her vision was spinning. Colors flashed in front of her eyes. She lost focus and her vision went to black.

She felt a sharp slap on her face and her eyes opened.

She was propped against the stone wall. Her hands were tied behind her.

He was standing in front of her holding the leather volume. She realized that when she had tried to run before, he had struck her with the book.

His cheek was bruised. Blood ran down from the cut in his forehead.

"You didn't read this, did you?"

She stared at him. Once she had felt almost love for him. Now with every fiber of her being she willed his death.

"Answer me!" he commanded.

"Answer you? Do you think you're God?"

He shook his head. "No. Only his implement."

"You just murdered a man!" she cried out. The terrible stench of burning flesh filled her nostrils. She had been unconscious of it before, in the adrenaline rush of trying to get away from him. Now it stung her eyes, like a smoking grill.

"He was judged and punished. He was complicit in covering up the torture of children."

"What do you mean?"

"Child abuse is the torture of children."

"And Brother Dominicus? What was he guilty of?"

"Betraying his vows. Using his position to seduce both women and men, both body and mind."

"So you killed him too?"

"He was judged and found wanting."

"You punished him?"

"Yes."

"Like you're going to punish me?"

He was silent. His eyes were fastened on her like two burning coals.

"I offered you a choice. But you rejected it by trying to escape. You betrayed me once again."

"You betrayed the people who trusted you."

"What people?"

"The institute," she said. She was struggling to think, to find a way out, even as she realized there was none.

He smiled.

"The institute was merely a ruse to accomplish this task. I was groomed to be what I am."

"You're lying. You've done this out of a personal vendetta."

His smile faded. "I was found by the Arbori. Whom the

world knows as the Foresters. Dr. Forester was the last of the Arbori. He had no heirs. Except for me."

"Why you?"

Her heart was beating desperately. She had to keep him talking.

"I was one of the abused. One of the children of abuse. My tormentor was my priest. I was placed in an orphanage in Montreal where I was repeatedly used as a sex object by the rectors. I was a child of an unwed mother. Who would care about me? But Dr. Forester found me. He educated me."

"He used you to further his own ends, don't you realize that?"

"Our goals were the same."

"Revenge."

"No. Justice. For those who had no one to turn to."

Her voice was harsh. Accusatory. "What you've done isn't justice. It's murder. Not justice. You have no mercy."

"Mercy is for God."

"You lied then when you said you'd release my sister. You intended to kill her as well."

His eyes flickered. In them, she read an instant of uncertainty.

"I would have allowed her to go free, if you had joined me."

"Do you think I believe that? You wanted to indoctrinate me the way you were indoctrinated, then you thought I'd agree to killing my own sister so your secret would be protected."

"No. What I told you was true."

She fixed her eyes on his.

"You'd allow her to go free? And if she decided to reveal what this was really all about? What then?"

"She would have promised not to."

"And you would have trusted her?"

"If you did. So would I."

"And you think I believe a word you say. You've killed victim after victim and it's just the beginning, isn't it?"

"Justice must be served. There are perpetrators in every diocese in the country. Many have been protected for years and allowed to continue to commit their crimes. The law has not protected the wronged. That's why I needed your help."

"You could still have it."

"How?"

"By letting me help you. I can relieve some of the agony I know you've been feeling."

"How? With therapy? The way you do in the prison?"

His tone was mocking.

"I work with people very much like you. Men who have been abused the way you were. I know how much pain you're in. And have been in, your entire life."

"Do you think I would give this up just to relieve some pain?" he said in the same sarcastic tone. "Don't you understand? It's pain that drives us, all of us who undertake this task. Our pain is our salvation. To give it up would be to give up our mission. And that we would never do."

"You said we? Then you're not alone?"

"Others perform similar tasks."

"Where?"

He looked at her askance. "That you will never know. Not now."

He turned and carefully placed the book on the stone ledge. Then he strode through the arch. She heard his footsteps on the wooden stairs and imagined that he was climbing toward the hoist. She heard metal groan and the creaking of the cogs and the sound of the handle being turned.

She looked through the archway and saw the chain moving in the tower beyond.

The cage rose into view. Then jerked to a stop.

It was empty.

He must have opened it and allowed the lawyer's body to drop into the fire below.

A shudder passed through her as she realized what he was going to do.

The cage was for her.

She struggled against the ropes binding her, but they were tied too tight. She tried to rise, but he had tied her feet as well. She was helpless, as all of his victims had been helpless. Her heart was trip-hammering. She felt sick, as if she were about to vomit.

She looked up and he was there in front of her.

"It is time," he said.

She struggled to breathe, to think of a way to stop him.

"You killed Father Terrance, didn't you? That's why you went to Rome. To stop him from finding out about you?"

He was silent. He bent and his arms slipped beneath her.

"His blood is on your head," she cried. "He was innocent. By killing him, you condemned yourself to the same punishment as you meted out to others. Stop now. Before it's too late and you damn yourself to eternal hell."

He lifted her in his arms and turned toward the archway ahead, toward the open door of the cage.

She was unable to move. Frozen, she felt the earth slipping away beneath her. She had ceased to hear her heart beat.

Her eyes were fixed on the cage as it swung back and forth on the chain. The iron bars were red hot. The heat licked her skin. Her ears filled with the roar of the fire below, the flames reflected in the smoothly shining stones.

In a moment she would be inside the cage.

Roasted alive.

The scream rose from deep in her gut, a roiling horrified protest torn from the deepest recesses of her being. All of her body fought to live. She struggled like a trapped animal to survive. Her legs kicked. Her arms flexed. Her torso flailed back and forth in his arms. She twisted her head trying to tear at him with her open jaws.

He staggered, thrown off balance by her struggles. His back struck the wall as he righted himself.

Only two steps more and he would be able to unload her

into the open doors of the cage swaying back and forth in front of him. He stepped beyond the archway to the edge of the stone ledge jutting into the tower.

He released her from his arms, allowing her to slide to the floor at his feet. He had only to roll her inside. He stood and took a deep breath before he performed this final task. He knew at all costs that he must not look at her, but he could not help himself. He looked down and for an instant and his eyes met hers. He could read her look. In her eyes he recognized her plea for life.

He hesitated, unable to move. Some spark connected them, some palpable surge of feeling. His hands were extended but they came no closer. He was frozen. Balanced between his need to destroy her and the up-swelling urgency he felt inside that would allow her to live. A plea for mercy echoed inside his skull. But she had betrayed him and there could be no mercy. The Cipher commanded it. And he must obey.

His eyes broke contact. His body lurched forward. His hands reached for her.

Out of the corner of his eye he caught the first blur of motion. Startled, he turned. And his vision filled with the sheen of flame on metal as Beth drove the implement she held in both hands directly into his flesh.

He staggered backward as the razor-sharp point entered his entrails. His eyes widened as he stared at the blade, then up at Beth, whose hands were still positioned on the handle.

Her eyes were enormous. Her jaw was stretched abnormally. She was screaming, but no sound reached his ears.

The blade disappeared into his body until there was only the handle remaining, with Beth's hands still wrapped around it.

His fist struck her on the side of the face. Her head snapped back, but she did not let go. He struck her again. This time she flew backward, off her feet, crumpling against the archway.

He reached down and gripped the handle. But it would not come loose. He knew he must draw it out, but the thought seemed to float lazily in his head. His mind had melted into syrup. The moment elongated as if it were made of latex. His vision broke into pieces.

He turned in a lazy motion. Round and round. And then somehow he was no longer on the ledge. His feet were dancing in air. Somehow he was flying.

Beth's eyes never left his form.

She watched as he turned, trying to draw the implement out of his belly. But his hands would not function. Instead, the cassock flared outward as he spun around. Spun like a dervish as his feet left the ledge. He hung there for an instant, suspended, one hand reaching out to grasp the chain. But he missed and his fingers grabbed for the cage. She read the shock in his eyes as his hand contacted the red-hot bars.

He plummeted.

Into the tower.

Into the fire below.

Consumed within the hungry mouth of flame.

Beth saw only his eyes. The black orbs were connected with hers. She read their fierce hunger to resist. The image lasted only an instant. Then he was gone.

Beth fumbled with the cord that bound her sister's wrists. Holly's eyes were shut. It took a gentle massage against her lids to manage them open.

She could see the film of shock in her sister's eyes. The incoherence as her mind sought to reassemble the world. The grasp of recognition when it finally came.

"He's—"

"Gone," Beth said softly.

"How?"

"One of his implements. Don't ask what it's for. But it was sharp. That I can tell you."

Holly stared at her sister, struggling to understand.

"You killed him?"

"The fire took care of that."

Holly arched her body and looked down. Her hand gripped Beth's shoulder as she stared into the flames. Only the outline of his body was visible.

"My God," Holly gasped.

Beth helped Holly to her feet, massaging her ankles where the cord had bitten into them. "Can you walk?" Beth asked.

"I think so."

Holding onto each other, they moved away from the edge. They stopped in the archway as Holly struggled to stop shaking.

"I thought I was in love with him," she said.

"Me too."

"God, Beth. How did you . . ." Her voice trailed off.

"Good old Lock Picking 101. Comes in handy every time. You learn a lot of shit in rehab."

Holly looked at her sister. "Let's get out of here."

They started back into the passage. Holly allowed her sister to lead her, then abruptly halted.

"Wait."

She turned and went back to the archway. She picked up the leather-covered volume from the ledge where Vincent had placed it.

"That's the Cipher, isn't it?" Beth said.

Holly nodded.

"What are you going to do with it?"

The look in Holly's eyes was clear.

"But it's evidence."

Holly hesitated. Her impulse was to toss the volume from the tier, watch it spiral as it fell, then see it consumed, crumbling finally to ashes. Back to the darkness from whence it came. But something stopped her. Beth was right. It was evidence. It was also a priceless relic, a shard of history, a thing of blood and anguish.

She watched her sister take the volume out of her hands. Beth nodded and Holly turned and stepped back through the stone archway.

Epilogue

When the phone rang, Holly hesitated. It had been two days since the horror of her experience at the institute and she was still exhausted. Her mind reverberated with images too awful to reconcile.

She stood in her kitchen and allowed her answering machine to take the call, but at the clear sound of Clara's voice she stepped over to the phone and scooped it into her hands.

"Hi. I'm here."

"Good. Turn on your TV. Go ahead. Do it now."

"What channel."

"Two. But it's on all of them."

Holly picked up the remote and turned it to Channel Two. The small TV on the counter flickered on.

The screen filled with the image of Art Pinero surrounded by a mass of shouting reporters as the DA struggled to exit the courthouse.

"They got him. The rat," Clara said. "Trying to cover-up all those murders. Imagine. I guess this finishes him."

The image abruptly changed to a close-up of Dan Shepard stepping out of a hearing room with several senior police officers, all of them looking extremely grim.

Holly realized she had failed to turn on the sound.

"What happened?" she blurted.

"Your friend Dan just blew the whistle on him. That's what happened."

"Really?"

"It's an incredible story. The cops say they uncovered some kind of cult that goes back centuries responsible for who knows how many killings. Taking revenge on priests who molested young kids. Anyway, you're not going to believe this. The guy responsible for the killings is Beth's boss. Did you know that?"

"Beth just told me."

"Incredible. And what's more incredible is that you're coming back to work. They just notified us. So congratulations, honey. Starting Monday, you're back on the job. Ted was supposed to call you, but the coward appointed me instead. So what do you say? Isn't it great?"

"Yes. Terrific. Thanks. Can I call you back?"

"Sure. I'll be here until six."

Holly put down the phone. Her eyes were fixed straight ahead. The news resonated through her but she felt as if she were in a state of shock. Unable to grasp what she had just heard. She had given the Cipher to Dan without stating any conditions. So far he had kept both her name and Beth's out of the story. Beth had been asked to remain at her post at the behest of the institute's secretary until a new director could be appointed. Vincent's death was being considered a possible suicide. The belief was that had taken his own life when he realized that the police were closing in. They had found enough evidence in the old monastery to link all the victims' deaths to him. Still Holly wondered if there were others out there, others like him who had pledged their lives to uphold the Cipher.

She heard a car pull up. A moment later the doorbell rang.

Woodenly, Holly went to answer it. Dan stood in the doorway.

"Can I come in?" He said with a smile.

"I just saw you on the news." She stepped aside to allow him to enter. "Clara called me."

"That was this morning. You're a little out of touch."

"More than a little."

"You're still in shock. Do you want some tea?"

She nodded as he went into the kitchen. She was warmed suddenly. His presence somehow reassured her, causing her feelings of confusion to evaporate.

"The good news is that so far I've managed to keep you and your sister out of it. No guarantees. But I'm keeping my fingers crossed.

Dan had been the first person they had called that horrific night after she and Beth had left the institute. Dan had been going crazy trying to locate her. They waited in her car until he drove toward them down the institute's long dark driveway, then Holly had gotten out of her car and handed him the Cipher. Holly waited alone in the car while Beth took him back inside and guided him to the tower. When they returned, Dan was ashen. He instructed Beth to drive Holly home and both of them to remain there. Then he made the necessary calls.

"So. How are you feeling?" he said as he filled the kettle and placed it on the stove, then opened the canister and took out two tea bags.

"I'm supposed to be doing that," she said.

His eyes were warm as they fastened on her. "Every now and then, you need someone to take care of you."

She looked up at him. Their eyes met and she nodded. "You're right. Got anyone in mind?"

"I don't know. What are my chances?"

"Don't you know?"

"Not lately."

A cloud crossed her face, then she shook herself free. Her eyes when they looked back up at him were bright and clear.

"What are you doing the rest of the afternoon?" she asked.

"That depends on you."

She stepped into his arms. Her lips found his and the sudden warmth she felt in his embrace seemed to lift her just slightly off her feet. The kettle was boiling but somehow she never heard it sing.